Journey
to
Welcome

Journey
to
Welcome

by

Jo Christian Babich

ZINKA PRESS

WAYNE, PENNSYLVANIA   SANTA FE, NEW MEXICO

ACKNOWLEDGEMENTS

Page 111: 4 lines from "The Solitary" by Sara Teasdale. Reprinted with permission of Simon & Schuster, Inc. from COLLECTED POEMS OF SARA TEASDALE. Copyright 1926 by Macmillan Publishing Company, renewed 1954 by Marie T. Wheless.

Page 191: 4 lines from "An Irish Airman Foresees His Death" by W.B. Yeats. Reprinted with permission of Simon & Schuster, Inc. from THE POEMS OF W.B. YEATS: A NEW EDITION, edited by Richard J. Finneran (New York: Macmillan, 1983).

ADDITIONAL ACKNOWLEDGEMENTS ON BACK PAGE

Contents

Contents

Journey to Welcome

About the time you hear the grinding of the train's brakes, you'll notice the sign on the depot that identifies this stop as Bienvenidos. That means "Welcome" in Spanish. Perhaps the original settlers pronounced it the Spanish way, but as far back as anyone living can remember, the townsfolk have spelled it "Bienvenidos" and pronounced it "Benbenitas." That's because this town is not located in Spain, or in Mexico, or in South America, but somewhere in the part of Texas that lies west of the Colorado River on the Edwards Plateau, and is known these days as the Hill Country.

But, in fact, this town is located nowhere at all, except between the covers of this book.

Prelude: New York City, Mid-June, 1942

Karrie felt like skipping down the street, and would have, too, if it hadn't been for the heavy knapsack on her back and an armload of groceries. She'd cleaned out her locker at school and it was goodbye and good riddance to seventh grade! The whole glorious summer lay ahead—long days at the beach, band concerts in the park, tramping around the Palisades!

But as soon as she entered the apartment building, she stopped cold. Today of all days, why did nosy Mrs. Arnold have to be standing in front of the elevator? There was absolutely nothing that could blight a fine day like Mrs. Arnold's penetrating gaze and predictable inquiry, "So! How come I don't ever see your father around?"

Karrie made a quick decision and ducked through the entrance to the stairwell. By the time her shoulder pushed open the door to the fifth floor, her arms ached and she was out of breath.

After setting down her burdens, she lifted a thin chain from around her neck to retrieve a key, then opened the door on a quiet apartment. Good! Marty wasn't home yet.

Kicking her knapsack over the threshold, she carried the groceries into the kitchen, quickly cleared a space on the cluttered countertop, and reached for a dog-eared cookbook. It fell open, as if out of habit, to a recipe for Double Chocolate Cake. The words "Marty's favorite" were written in her mother's fine, precise hand in the margin, and Karrie felt a stab of guilt for her own contribution to the page—splatters of milk and vanilla extract. Somehow her cake never turned out like Mom's used to, but it was still Marty's favorite.

1

She was just applying the finishing touches when she heard her brother open the front door and curse mildly as he stumbled over her knapsack. When he appeared in the kitchen doorway she displayed her creation.

"Ta—da-a-a! Happy graduation!"

Marty grinned. "I'm honored—I think. You didn't do anything fatal to it this time, did you? Such as leave out the baking powder?"

"It's guaranteed perfect! Where've you been?"

"Oh—last day of school. Saying goodbye and all."

"Won't you see everybody at graduation?"

"I'm skipping it. No fun this year. Most of the guys will be going right into the service."

"Thank goodness *you* won't be eighteen for six more months! By then maybe the war will be over."

"Not remotely possible, squirt."

"Well—Well, anyway, let's celebrate tonight! It's your evening, so you pick. Movie? Roller skating? How about the concert up at Lewisohn? Oh! And I think there's a string quartet at the Y!"

"Whatever you want to do tonight is fine. But in the morning we clean this dump. Looks like a cyclone hit it."

"I know, but not tomorrow. I'm going to sign up for the free classes at the museum."

"Afraid not, Karrie. Tomorrow we clean. And pack."

"Oh, Marty, no!"

"Karrie, we agreed. It was only till I graduated. Now we have to follow out Dad's instructions."

"Can't we just wait till the end of summer? Please, Marty!"

"Sorry, Karrie. I picked up our train tickets this afternoon. It's time."

Chapter 1
The Young Strangers

1.

They blew into Benbenitas as casually as a summer breeze, without so much as an excuse-me or a by-your-leave.

And they'd come far. Mr. Peevy could see that plainly. He hadn't been depot agent thirty-seven years for nothing!

First off, there were the worn-out old suitcases the baggage man set down on the platform. They were made of real leather, had buckled straps, and there were tattered labels stuck all over them. Those bags had been places, and Mr. Peevy figured they'd have stories to tell if they could talk.

And then, there were the kids themselves. Wherever they'd come from, it was nowhere in Texas!

It was the hottest day yet in that year of 1942, and the girl, who couldn't have been more than thirteen, wore stockings with her saddle shoes and was all swallowed up in a tweed suit. She had dark hair that curled up tight around her pale little face, and big hazel eyes. Foreign-looking child.

The young fellow was a tall one, appeared to be about seventeen. His hair, which could have used a cutting, was a much lighter brown than the girl's, but he had those same eyes. He was all decked out like somebody going to a funeral, in a dark suit and tie, and polished shoes that had known better days.

When the train pulled out of the station, the two of them just stood there on the platform in the broiling sun and looked around them.

Passengers hardly ever got off at Benbenitas. Most times the train only stopped long enough to throw off one mailbag and pick up another. Mr. Peevy's interest was definitely piqued. He made his way toward the young strangers.

"How-do," he greeted them. "Help ya?"

"Please. Any chance of getting a taxi?" asked the boy.

"Well, now, so happens we do have a taxi," the depot agent allowed, with a little pride. "Used to even have another'n but Ole Ben Clinton run him outta business."

"Good deal! How do we summon this enterprising gent?"

"I'll give him a ring." Mr. Peevy was a bit put-off. He didn't cotton to uppity youngsters.

He ambled into the station house, gave the old wall telephone a good crank-up, and, keeping his eyes fixed on the pair outside the window, said a word or two to Mabel Klein, the operator, and a couple of more to Ole Ben. Then he fumbled the receiver into its hook and made his way out again.

"Ole Ben'll be right along," he announced. "I wasn't so sure he'd be able to make it. Has trouble keeping the vee-hickle in running order these days. War on, ya know." He pointed to the bench against the wall that was shaded by the station house eaves. "Just set yourselves down and wait a spell."

They did, thanking him politely, and he sat himself down beside them.

"Staying long in these parts?" he asked.

"Could be," said the young fellow.

"Maybe they'll throw us out," the little girl said, almost under her breath.

"Well, now," said Mr. Peevy. "Well, now." Then he went ahead and asked them straight out, "Say, by the bye, what's your names?"

"Webster," said the boy, putting out his hand to shake. "I'm Martin and my sister is Karen."

4

Mr. Peevy gave a start and stared into the young face, taking no notice of the offered hand. "Now wait just a minute! *Martin Webster*! Ain't no way you're *his* kids! Martin died back in 1918, Battle of Belleau Wood. Been twenty-some years and you ain't that old, no sir!"

The boy let his hand drop. "Martin Webster was our uncle," he said. "Our father was—is *Richard* Webster."

"Oh, by Jupiter," Mr. Peevy whispered. "By the great god Jupiter."

Whatever anybody might have said next was drowned out by Ole Ben Clinton's taxi showing up just then, and making a terrific racket about it. Ole Ben got out, grinning and doffing his dusty old cowboy hat and taking in the young strangers with his sharp little eyes.

Mr. Peevy heaved himself up from the bench and hustled over to him. "Ole Ben, I got a shocker for you! These kids claim their daddy is *Richard Webster*! Don't that beat all?"

"No—you don't say—well I never—ain't that something now?" said Ole Ben Clinton.

The boy got up from the bench.

"Mister—uh—Mr. Clinton?" he said. "Could you take us to a place called Windy Crest—if it's still there?"

"Why, sure!" Ole Ben said. "It's still there, all right! Just help me get these here suitcases into the trunk, young feller. My goodness, you musta packed bricks in this one, little lady! Folks at Windy Crest expecting you kids?"

"I—kind of doubt it. Is Henry Webster still living?"

"Still living? Lordy, yes, boy! Been our mayor for twenty-six years now! Nobody else can afford to take the job. And his sisters—Miss Virginia and Miss Prunella—they're there, too. Well, I swan! Reckon *they're* in for a right surprise!"

"That they are, by Jupiter," Mr. Peevy had to agree.

With two of the suitcases crammed into the trunk and the other two on the back seat, the young people had to squeeze into the front seat next to the driver, and Mr. Peevy was obliged to slam the door shut for them. There was some hesitation and

5

sputtering before the engine turned over, then, just as Ole Ben Clinton was letting out the clutch, Mr. Peevy overheard the little girl sigh and whisper to her brother,

"Guess it won't be long now—by Jupiter."

"By the great god Jupiter," the boy whispered back.

Websters, right enough, Mr. Peevy told himself. Uppity breed if ever there was one.

2.

"Karrie, come *on*!"

Karrie sat, hugging herself, knees pressed together, on a large flat rock near the gate. She was not crying, but her eyes were stark and hollow.

"Marty, please, let's just go back to New York."

"There's nothing to go back to," said Marty. "Come on, get up! We went to the trouble of changing our clothes so we'd look halfway respectable—If we don't get a move on we'll be limp and sweaty again by the time we get to the door."

"I'm limp and sweaty again already."

"Well, Ole Ben Tucker—or whoever he is—wanted to drive right up to the house. Why did you make him put us out here?"

"Did you want to ring the bell and be standing there with a bunch of suitcases—looking pitiful? This way, if they seem mean, we can pretend we stopped by out of curiosity."

"Oh, sure! We happened to be strolling along out here in the middle of nowhere and thought we'd pop in to say 'Hi!' Come on, squirt! Remember what Dad told you the first time you had to take the subway alone? Don't ever show you're afraid. Walk as if you own the city!"

"There's no city to own. There's not even a town. Did you see a town, Marty? Just the train station and some broken-down old farms. And now this—The House of Dracula!"

She allowed him to take her hand and pull her to her feet, and the two of them looked toward the gray clapboard house that waited at the end of the winding gravel driveway. Looming solitary and outsized on the crest of the hill, it seemed a forbidding place. Three stories high, crowned by a widow's walk and a whale-shaped weather vane, it was a house of gables and gingerbread eaves, of long windows and wraparound porches. It had no proper foundation, but rested on piers of rock and cement, and the airspace between the structure and the earth lent the house a precarious, ungrounded appearance, as though it might take off, all of a piece, and fly right off the hill. An ancient live oak tree leaned toward the front of the house, shading the porches on the first and second floors with its twisty branches and dusty foliage, but there was no shrubbery, and no grass. Some hundred yards to the rear stood a barn, and beyond that, a windmill. The property was fenced with barbed wire, and at the entrance to the drive, where Karrie and Marty were standing, a wooden gate hung between two wide gateposts built of stone. On one the words *Windy Crest* were cut, and on the other, *1846*. But it was the house itself that held the attention of the two young people.

"There must be a million rooms in there," said Karrie. "All of them creepy!"

"Never mind the creepy," said Marty firmly. "Let's hope there'll be a couple of rooms in there for us."

He pushed open the wooden gate and, leaving their suitcases concealed behind the gateposts, they started up the drive.

"Hold your shoulders back, Karrie," said the boy. "They could be watching from the window. Walk as if you own—the gravel," he finished lamely.

No one was watching from the window. No one at Windy Crest was expecting company on that lazy afternoon in June. Miss Ginger was sitting at the writing desk in her second-floor bedroom, playing solitaire, while her sister Prune napped in a wicker chaise longue on the adjoining screened-in sleeping porch. The mayor was in his study downstairs, with the door closed. Lulled by the breeze and whir of an electric fan, he dozed in a cane-backed rocking chair, a book lying open across his knees. On the screened porch off the kitchen, Martha and Israel were stretched out on pallets, taking their afternoon rest between the cleaning up after the noonday meal and the preparations for supper. All was quiet, except for the monotonous, rising call of the cicadas, and the occasional moan of the windmill.

Then suddenly, there was the clomp clomp clomp of the heavy doorknocker, causing everyone in the house to sit up with a start. Israel was on his feet in an instant, slipping into his shoes and white cotton jacket, buttoning his collar and smoothing his hair as he hurried toward the front door. By the time his hand was on the knob, Martha was peering out from the kitchen, the mayor was standing in the doorway of the study, and Miss Ginger and Miss Prune were coming down the stairs.

Whatever each may have surmised was on the other side of that door, it is certain that not one of them was near the mark. When it was opened to reveal a short, dark-haired girl and a tall, brown-haired boy, both dressed ridiculously for a June day in Texas, there was a moment of wordless surprise.

Then all the occupants of Windy Crest advanced a step and waited, as if for the other shoe to drop. They didn't have to wait long.

"Good afternoon," said the boy affably. "We're the mayor's grandchildren. May we come in?"

3.

The mayor backed into his study and slammed the door. It was fifteen minutes before he came out again. The girl and the boy were by then seated side by side on the sofa in the parlor, holding glasses of lemonade. Martha and Israel hovered near, one with the pitcher and the other with a tray of graham crackers. Miss Prune was sitting on a footstool in front of the young people, and Miss Ginger was pacing about the room. All eyes turned toward the mayor. He addressed the boy.

"Just who are you?"

Miss Prune rose, rubbing her hands together nervously. "Oh, Henry," she said, before Marty could answer, "they really are your grandchildren! Their names are Karen and—and *Martin*!"

The mayor was silent for a few seconds. Then, again to the boy: "Where are your parents?"

"Oh, Henry," said Miss Prune, "they say their mother died three years ago."

The mayor continued to stare at Marty. "And your father?"

"Oh, Henry—" began Miss Prune.

"Oh, for heaven's sakes, Prune," blurted out Miss Ginger, pausing in her march. "Let them speak for themselves."

Miss Prune sank down on the footstool again, and Marty rose and faced his grandfather. The two were of a height, about six feet, and as they looked squarely at each other the young hazel eyes were as unflinching as the faded blue ones.

"He's away," said Marty.

"Away? In the Army?"

"I—don't think so."

"What do you mean, you 'don't think so'? Don't you know where your father is?"

"He was in Switzerland—he wrote he'd be delayed—"

"*Switzerland*? Who's supposed to be seeing after you?"

"Seeing after us? We're not exactly babies!"

"You're not exactly adults, either. The man just ups and leaves two minors alone while he traipses off to Europe in the middle of a war? Marvelous! Where is it you live?"

"New York City, but—"

"Oh, perfect, perfect! The fool has lost his mind!"

Marty sighed wearily. "He wrote he'd be delayed and—"

"So you said. Just how long has he been delayed?"

Marty hesitated. "Two years."

A murmur went around the room. The blood rose to the mayor's face. "Are you telling me your father has been gone for *two years*? And you've been on your own all that time?"

"That's about it," said Marty.

"Good God!" exploded the mayor. "I don't believe this! Where in hell *is* he? How do you pay rent and buy groceries?"

"That's taken care of. Dad made an arrangement with the bank after our mother died, because he had to travel so much.

9

They pay the bills and keep up our personal allowance account."

"And that's it? No one's asked any questions?"

"Not really. Well, there was one nosy neighbor, but people tend to mind their own business in New York."

"Apparently! Didn't he have an employer or—"

"When he'd been gone about six weeks I called his company. I was told he'd taken an indefinite leave of absence."

"Good God! What is he up to? The people at this company—weren't they in the least bit concerned about you?"

"I didn't say who I was. I guess they assumed his family was with him." Marty reached into the inner pocket of his jacket and withdrew two envelopes. "This is his last letter. The one mailed from Switzerland. And this—this is a letter he wrote a few days after our mother died. He kept it in a drawer in his desk and told us we were to open it if something happened to him. You might as well read that one, too."

The mayor stared at the boy for an instant, then brusquely took the letters, turned and walked out of the parlor. The study door slammed resoundingly.

Miss Prune sat quietly on the stool, and Miss Ginger paced on. Marty and Karrie looked at each other. Marty smiled, but Karrie's face was beginning to sag. Israel bent over her with the tray.

"Here, honey," he said kindly. "You have another cookie."

4.

Alone in his study, the mayor sat down heavily in his rocking chair and gazed at the handwriting on the two envelopes. Then, with fumbling fingers, he opened the one with the Swiss postmark. It was dated June 13, 1940, and was casual and brief.

"Dear Kids: I may be delayed a week or two. Don't worry if you don't hear from me for a while. I might not have much chance to write. Just carry on as usual. I'll be home as soon as possible. Love, Dad."

The mayor drew in his breath, then opened the other letter, dated more than a year earlier.

"My dear children," it began, "Today I spent long, dreary hours at my lawyer's office, making provisions for your future. He urged me to discuss this with you, but I can't bring myself to do that while you're still so upset over losing your mother.

"After the two of you went to bed tonight, I sat by the window in the dark for a while, looking out at the lights of the city your mom loved so much, and I tried to figure out the best way to handle this. I finally decided that for now I would leave this letter in my desk, to be opened in case of an emergency.

"First of all, I've appointed my banker, John Cory, to be executor of my estate. If anything should happen to me, you must contact him right away. He will see to everything, and he has the names of relatives to be notified. There *are* relatives, you know. I've told you very little about them, but—as my lawyer pointed out—that's a mistake I need to correct.

"Your grandfather's name is Henry Webster, and he used to be mayor of Bienvenidos, Texas. He disowned me in 1923, and isn't aware that the two of you exist, but I'm absolutely certain that—no matter how he feels about me—he will give you a home at Windy Crest in the event of my death.

"I don't quite know how to describe Windy Crest. It was once a very happy place, back when my older brother, Martin, and I were growing up, but after the World War came along, things changed. Martin enlisted in the Marines, and was killed in the Battle of Belleau Wood. My mother died during the influenza epidemic, and my father became so bitter and withdrawn that he lost interest in everything, including me. When I graduated from high school, it was a relief to escape to the university in Austin. During my university years I seldom went home. There didn't seem to be any point.

"When I graduated I made up my mind that before I did anything else I was going to visit the battleground where my brother had died. I guess I thought it would please my father. So without telling him my plans, I took off for New York and hopped a freighter to France.

"Your mother used to say that all our happiness began at the

11

saddest spot on earth. Belleau Wood was certainly that—a haunting, tragic place, left practically unchanged since those bloody weeks of June in 1918. I remember wandering around almost in a trance, totally depressed, until I happened to run into a dark-haired girl, who had the prettiest eyes I'd ever seen.

"Your mom couldn't speak English in those days, but my college German was pretty good. We soon discovered we had a lot in common. She had also lost her mother to influenza, and her only brother had died on that battlefield the very same day as mine. Both our brothers happened to be named Martin, and for all we knew, one could have been killed by the other.

"We were so young, the two of us—hardly more than children, it seems to me now—but the tragedy that might have driven us apart drew us together instead. We were married within two weeks, then headed for Germany to break the news to her father.

"That was hard. Poor Opi. His lovely, talented Inge! He'd worked and sacrificed for years to send her to the conservatory in Vienna, only to have her throw it all away to marry a boy of a different religion and sail off to America. It must have broken his heart. But—being Opi—he ended up giving us his blessing.

"Mom may have told you some of that, but I doubt if she ever told you the rest. When we got to New York I wrote to my father. He sent an unsigned telegram. It said, 'Never set foot in my house with your German bride. You are no longer my son.'

"I was furious. I loved Inge so much, and was outraged that he would reject her without even meeting her. She used to say, 'Write to him once more. Perhaps he regrets that telegram.' But I never did, and I never heard from him again.

"I haven't told you this to make you hate your grandfather. Like his father before him, he could be rigid and hardheaded when it came to his own family, but was always straight and fair with everyone else. In Bienvenidos there were quite a few German immigrants, and at the beginning of the war people turned on them and would have driven them out of town if my father hadn't stood by them. That's the way he was, and yet—he couldn't forgive me for marrying a German, because a German had killed my brother.

"I guess I inherited some of his hardheadedness. I never forgave him for that telegram. I hope you kids are more like your mother and can rise above that kind of foolishness. If I die while you're still minors, you'll have to make peace with your grandfather. He and my aunts will be all you have.

"Hard as it is to imagine my two city slickers in the Texas hill country, I know you'll do fine. No matter what lies ahead, you will always be each other's best friend. Mom was so very proud of you, and I am, too.

"And now, this task done, perhaps I can get some sleep at last. I'll tuck this away in my desk and hope you'll never have to read it. I love you both, with all my heart—Dad."

The mayor sat quietly for a while before rising from his chair. By the time he opened the study door and called across the hall, "You! Martin! In here, please!" his hands were as steady, his face was as stern, and his voice was as gruff as ever.

5.

Marty stepped inside the study and, at his grandfather's indication, closed the door behind him. The two stood facing each other as before.

"So he named you Martin," said the mayor.

His grandson met his gaze steadily. "He loved his brother."

"He betrayed his brother!"

"My father never betrayed anyone in his life!"

The mayor turned away and looked out the window for a minute, absently slapping the letters against the palm of his left hand. Finally he turned back to Marty.

"This man Cory—why didn't he contact me?"

"We never got in touch with him."

"You—And just why was that, may I ask?"

"There were reasons."

"Reasons! I would like to hear them, sir!"

"Well, there was school. I wanted to graduate."

"You could have done that anywhere."

"It was a special science high school. Stuyvesant. It's famous."

The mayor slammed the letters hard against his hand. "Famous! And it was so important to graduate from this 'famous' high school that you allowed that little girl to remain in New York City for two years without supervision?"

Marty never dropped his gaze. "I was perfectly capable of looking after Karrie. And we weren't exactly sure of a warm reception in Texas."

"Hrumph! So what finally brought you here?"

Marty hesitated. "Well, for one thing, I've graduated. And now—I have to make certain Karrie is taken care of. I couldn't risk going to Cory. If he contacted you and you refused to have anything to do with us, I was afraid Karrie would end up in an orphanage. I brought her here so we could deal with you face to face. I thought you might place her in a boarding school or something. There must still be plenty of money. You could work it out with Cory."

"I see. You have this all figured out, do you? And what about *your* plans?"

Marty shrugged. "The war's taken care of that. I'm going to enlist in the Navy as soon as I'm sure Karrie's all right."

There was a softening of the mayor's expression. "Enlist, is it? You're not eighteen yet, are you? No, I thought not. You'll need a guardian's consent to enlist. That will have to be me, I suppose. I've signed such papers before. Your uncle chose the Marines. But what's the hurry? The war will wait for you."

"Why postpone it? I'll be eighteen in January. I need to know—will you have Karrie or not? Just till I get back."

The mayor took a couple of turns around the room, again slapping his hand with the letters. "Till *you* get back," he repeated reflectively. "You believe he's dead."

"No!" said Marty quickly. "There's just—some reason he can't contact us. He knew we'd be okay. We—"

"*Okay?* My God, how could a man do such a thing to his

14

own children?"

"You turned your back on one of yours!" Marty flared out, finding anger readily at hand in this place.

"Mind yourself, boy!" said the mayor curtly. He handed the letters back. "Here. Your father was right about one thing. I will not turn you out. I'll write to this banker fellow and explain the situation—insofar as I can. What about your home—your apartment or whatever?"

"We had the furniture stored and moved out. We had all the services discontinued. There aren't any loose ends."

"Very efficient. All right. We might as well tell the others."

"Just a minute." Marty drew a wad of bills from his pocket. "This is what we saved from our personal allowance account. It's about two hundred dollars. It'll help pay for Karrie's keep while you're waiting for the bank to come through. And one other thing. Karrie doesn't know I'm planning to enlist."

The mayor stared at the money that had been thrust into his hand. He seemed baffled and hesitant. Then he made a decision and placed it in his own pocket.

"Very well. Tell the girl in your own time. I'll have myself appointed your guardian and I *will* sign your papers. You carry a proud name, boy."

Marty permitted himself a slight smile. "I was named for *both* my uncles," he said.

6.

When the others were informed of the decision, the tension in the parlor was instantly released, as if with one huge inaudible sigh, followed immediately by a flurry of activity. Israel and Marty were dispatched to retrieve the suitcases, and the mayor's sisters and Martha began discussing sleeping accommodations for the newcomers.

"We'll open the boys' rooms on the third floor," Miss Prune declared.

"Just got through cleaning up there," submitted Martha.

"Now—let's see, they'll need those electric fans—" said Miss

Ginger.

Their planning was interrupted by a stentorian "*No!*" and they all turned to look at the mayor.

"The third floor will *not* be opened up. Those rooms have not been used for over twenty years and they'll remain as they are."

"But Henry—" protested Miss Prune.

"The girl will be put in the guest room. The boy will sleep on the daybed in the sewing room."

"But Henry!" cried Miss Prune again.

"Oh, hush, Prune," Miss Ginger admonished her sister impatiently. "Henry's right, of course. It's hot as Hades on the third floor. Martha, is the bed in the guest room made up? Do we still have those sheets for the daybed?"

The mayor, having settled the matter, left the details to the others and retreated to the comfort of his study—whether to work or to reflect upon the unsettling events of the afternoon, who could say? The only thing certain was that he did not return to the idle dreaminess of his nap.

He was left to himself for about an hour, then there was a tap on his door. It was Martha.

"They're all settled in, Mayor," she reported.

"Oh—all right, Martha," said the mayor, pushing away from his desk. "The girl's in the guest room and the boy's in the sewing room—"

"No sir," said Martha. "Put 'em both on the third floor."

The mayor and the color in his face rose at about the same time. "But I specifically said—"

"I know what you *said*, Mayor, but you didn't think it through," said Martha calmly. "Need the guest room—case you allow Miss Clara and her husband back again—and me and Miss Prune can't have our sewing room messed up."

"But I—"

"Children just fine on the third floor. We got all the windows open and the electric fans going."

"Wha—Wait a minute, damn it! There's not supposed to be

16

electricity up there. When we had it installed, I told them to skip the third floor—"

"Um-m hm-m. But I had 'em go ahead and put the outlets up there, else, where was I going to plug in my new Hoover? Thought we'd kill a chicken for supper if that's all right with you, Mayor. Might manage an apple pie. I don't think those children been eating right."

The mayor, red of face and pulses pounding, slumped back into his chair, vanquished. He waved her off. "Have what you please, Martha. Why ask me? If I said chicken, you'd have roast beef. If I said pie, you'd have devil's food cake. Just—just—go about your business."

"Yes sir." Martha paused in the doorway. "War on, you know, Mayor. Rationing the sugar now. No way atall I could make a devil's food cake."

Then she left him in peace.

7.

Karrie ran her hand across the tattered bindings of the books on the shelves above the desk. She could make out a few titles—*A Tale of Two Cities*, *The Pathfinder*, *Treasure Island*—but most had faded or worn away. She pulled one particularly ragged volume from the shelf and carefully turned the fragile pages. She discovered it was a book of poetry, and a sweet shiver went through her as she recognized poems her father had recited to her when she was a small child.

She hadn't hoped to find anything of comfort in this austere, alien house, and the overwhelming sense of her father's presence in his old room caught her by surprise.

He had carved his name on the desktop—crudely, in wobbly capital letters—RICHARD STONE WEBSTER. But this was not the Richard Stone Webster she remembered; not the tall, soft-spoken man with the long, easy stride; not the prominent consulting engineer who was at home in the major capitals of the world, seven languages at his command.

This was the Richard Martha and Israel had been telling her

about, one she'd never known, and yet, one who was suddenly, poignantly dear to her. This was a scruffy little boy who was hard on furniture and practiced walking on those stilts propped in the corner; who played with those marbles in the cigar box on the desk and read all those books until they were worn out.

This Richard explored caves and fished on the riverbank with his brother, rode his pony bareback, and spent long, dreamy hours sitting in that window seat, gazing across the valley.

Karrie had learned more about her kind, sad-eyed father in the past few minutes than she had in all her years with him.

She sat down on the low, narrow cot. The thin, hard mattress was covered by a threadbare patchwork quilt.

"Miss Sally, your granny, made that quilt," Martha had told her when she'd settled her in, and had pointed out the different triangles of fabric that made up the squares. "That one's from your daddy's baby dress—right there's from his little nightshirt—that piece was from Miss Sally's apron—" The two rag rugs on the plank floor had also been made by her grandmother, as well as the covers on the window seat cushions.

Karrie's hand caressed the quilt as she looked around at the long, narrow attic room. There were three big gable windows overlooking the front, back, and south side of the yard. Under each window was a wide, hinged seat that opened up to reveal storage space. The only modern touches in the room were the electric fan and the floor lamp that Israel had brought upstairs and proudly plugged into the new outlets. He had started to remove the old kerosene lamp from the desk, but Karrie had stopped him. The lamp was useless now, but the young Richard had read all those books by its light.

There was no closet and no chest of drawers. Martha had told her she could put things away under the window seats and hang her dresses in the big wardrobe that stood out in the storage area between the twin attic rooms.

There wasn't much to hang up. Her two suitcases were not really full of bricks, as Ole Ben Clinton had joked, but were crammed with books, photograph albums, and just a few dresses

18

and things that had been her mother's. She and Marty had resorted to pillaging their parents' closets when their own clothes were outgrown. Karrie never let on to Marty how dowdy she felt in her mom's old clothes. Mom must have liked Peter Pan collars, she reflected ruefully.

Karrie sighed. She couldn't really remember. Sometimes it seemed she could hardly remember Mom at all, before she got sick.

She opened one of her suitcases and dug around in it until she came up with a framed photograph, which she set out on the desk. It had been taken—when? She herself must have been about six years old, and Marty about ten. They were dressed up in their best clothes and were sitting, happy and safe, between their smiling parents. Dad looked almost the way Marty did now, young, with no lines of strain in his face. And Mom, with her dark curly hair and laughing eyes, looked healthy and pretty. She wore a dress that Karrie still had. It had been much more becoming to Mom.

There they were, captured forever at a moment when they were a perfect family, with no shadow of what was to come hanging over them.

Karrie sighed again and wandered over to the front gable window. She curled up on the cushioned seat and looked out across the land her father had gazed upon as a boy.

"Real pretty view from up here," Martha had told her.

Pretty! But there was practically nothing *green*! The rolling, rocky landscape was the color of beach sand, and most of the trees were sparse and scrubby, with dull, dusty foliage. In the distance was a small pond and a cluster of larger trees. A few cows stood motionless in the shade and others were lying with their legs tucked under them. They seemed to have found the only friendly spot for miles around.

Where was the town, where were the houses and the people?

At home, their living room window looked out on Central Park, which, when she'd last seen it (was it only three days ago?), had been green, green, *green*! Later on, in the fall, it would turn crimson and gold and brown, and when the leaves were gone, the pathways and giant gray rocks would be visible through the bare branches. Snow would transform it all into a pure, tranquil fairyland, and finally, there would be the limy-green of spring, so miraculous that Karrie's heart would ache and almost burst with the new buds. Oh, there was a view from *that* window!

Now it seemed a million miles away, and she'd arrived here at the very end of the earth, where there was nothing to comfort her but this old-fashioned room that had been her father's.

Her little bedroom back at the apartment—once full of the clutter and reassurance of her own things—no longer existed as *her* room. Someone else would be living there soon.

Marty was right. There was nothing to go back to.

8.

Karrie was about to give into the tears she'd been fighting all day, when Marty appeared at the door.

"What do you think?" he asked her, smiling, as he came in and looked around. "Mine's just like this—Uncle Martin's room, only it's got pictures and awards all over the wall. First in his class, fastest runner, best swimmer, caught the biggest fish! Martin the Magnificent! Poor Dad! How would you like to have *that* for a big brother?"

"I think I do."

"Come on! I never caught a fish in my life. Hm-m. Just think—Dad lived his first sixteen years in this room."

"I can almost *feel* him here."

"I know what you mean. It's the same in Uncle Martin's room. I guess their ghosts are still hanging around."

"I don't want to think of Dad as a ghost!"

"I didn't mean it that way. I was talking about the ghosts of childhood. Hey, *ours* are probably haunting Central Park, even as we speak!"

"I hope so." Karrie couldn't hold the tears back any longer. She sank down on the bed and covered her face with her hands. Marty sat down beside her and patted her shoulder helplessly.

"I wish you'd try not to do that," he said. "It's going to be okay. They're not all that bad, are they?"

Karrie produced a half-laugh, half-sob. "You're kidding! They hate us!"

"They'll get over it! To know us is to love us," said Marty cheerfully, handing his sister a crumpled handkerchief.

"I do like Martha and Israel," Karrie admitted, after mopping her eyes and blowing her nose.

"They're swell, aren't they? Martha's promised a 'proper' supper. We'll both feel better after we've had a square meal."

Karrie sighed, her tears under control. It didn't do to cry around Marty, no matter how hard it was not to sometimes.

"You know what I'd like?" she said bravely. "I'd like to go down to the deli and have hot pastrami on rye with a side order of sauerkraut!"

"Washed down with a bottle of cream soda! It'll all be there when we get back, squirt. For now, let's settle for that proper supper."

Karrie rose and walked over to the back window, hoping it offered a more promising view than the one to the front.

"Martha says you can see all over the—" she began, then suddenly screamed and fell back, her hands covering her face.

"What is it? What is it?" Marty rushed to the window and looked out. There, hopping frenetically around the backyard, was a chicken without a head. "Oh. I guess that's our proper supper. We're in the country now. You didn't think chickens were hatched out headless and plucked, did you?"

"How *awful*! Israel grabbed it by its neck and swung it around—then just let it go! *He twisted its head off!*"

"It was so quick the chicken didn't feel a thing. It's only reflexes that make them hop about like that. You'll learn all that stuff when you dissect frogs in biology in tenth grade—"

"Never! They can't make me!"

"Cheer up! Maybe they don't teach biology here. Maybe they don't have frogs. Maybe they don't have tenth grade!"

The evening meal was served on the large oak table in the airy, commodious dining room. Martha had gone the extra mile in preparing a "meal fit for company"—crispy fried chicken, rice, milk gravy, collard greens, fluffy hot biscuits and apple pie. Miss Prune went the extra mile in her efforts to keep a conversation going, with very little help from Miss Ginger and none at all from the mayor. Marty and Karrie were by then too exhausted to say much of anything. It was an awkward gathering, and everyone was relieved when it was over and the weary young people asked to be excused to retire to their rooms.

Martha, disgruntled that her special dinner had not been received with more enthusiasm, muttered to herself as she helped Israel clear the table, "Child must be getting sick. Didn't eat a *bite* of chicken!"

Chapter 2
Downtown

1.

Benbenitas had been roused from its summer torpor, and the party line hadn't had such a workout since the Methodist preacher's wife ran off with the Fuller Brush salesman.

It had been many years since gossip had touched on the dignified mayor and his family—so many that most younger people were unaware that there had ever been any—but the older folks remembered, all right, and were eager to resurrect it for anybody who cared to listen in.

"...married a German woman and his brother not cold in the grave.." "...said to Eb at the time, how do they know it's Martin they're burying?" "...knew they was foreign first time he set eyes on 'em..." "...coffin got shipped home, but they didn't open it up, so for all we know, he..." "...say they had some kind of funny accent..." "...could be alive to this day..." "...turned German to spite his daddy..." "...weren't even *dressed* like American kids..." "...mayor ain't spoke his name in twenty-two years..." "...now Lollie Beal says, and she's *almost kin*, you know..."

2.

"Oh, Henry, wait!" Miss Prune caught up with the mayor just as he was heading out the front door. "Are you going downtown this morning?"

23

The mayor, dapper in a crisp seersucker suit, striped tie and straw boater, paused with his hand on the knob.

"No, Prune," he said. "I was just going out to work in the garden."

"Henry, don't you think it would be a good idea to take the children with you?"

"I do not. Whatever for?"

"Well, they must be curious about the town, and besides—"

"Oh, Prune, use your head!" Miss Ginger was right behind her. "Henry doesn't want to be bothered with all those questions and explanations today."

"Exactly," agreed her brother, then added sourly, "Not that explanations will be necessary. I haven't the slightest doubt that Ole Ben Clinton called the switchboard and gave Mabel Klein an earful, and by now it's the topic on every party line in the county."

"Well, that's just it, Henry," Miss Prune urged gently, "and you know what happens to news in Benbenitas."

"Yes, Lollie Beal gets hold of it and it takes on a creative life of its own."

"So don't you think it might be better to face people down right away, before all the rumors get started?"

The mayor sighed. "Oh, all right. Let's get it over with. Are they up and dressed?"

"In a manner of speaking," said Miss Ginger grimly. "The girl's clothes are god-awful. She looks like a little old lady. I'm almost ashamed to take her to town!"

"If it bothers you so much, do something about it," growled the mayor.

"Well," said Miss Ginger, "when we write to Clara about—what's happened, I expect she'll be happy to send a few things Ida's girl has outgrown. I think we should *telephone* Clara, don't you, Henry?"

"Oh, do as you please. What's one more long distance call? You're always finding something you have to call Clara about," said the mayor ungraciously. "But kindly do not suggest she send

24

JoBeth's old clothes. I have no desire to see my granddaughter outfitted in Clara's granddaughter's hand-me-downs."

"No need, Henry," said Miss Prune hastily. "Martha and I can make her some things. I'll just come along and pick up a few patterns at the Mercantile."

"All right, all right," grumbled the mayor. "Just hurry up. Israel's already brought the car around. I guess you're coming, too, Ginger, to enjoy the spectacle?"

"Well, if I can take some of the burden off *you*, Henry," said Miss Ginger bravely. "But—what shall we say about—you know—*Richard*?" She whispered the forbidden word.

"Say? Say? We'll say the damned fool went off somewhere and sent his kids to us. What else can we say?"

"Well—" Miss Ginger tried to proceed delicately. "You know, Henry, nobody's dared mention his name to you in years—"

The mayor glared at her. "Well, if they're *smart*, they won't mention it to me *now*!"

Karrie was not happy when told of the plan, but Marty shrugged and unconsciously echoed his grandfather's words, "Let's get it over with."

The two young people rode in the front seat with Israel, and the mayor and his sisters sat in the back.

"Is Bienvenidos—" Karrie began.

"*Benbenitas*," Miss Ginger corrected her stiffly.

"Benbenitas. Is it a *real* town?"

"Of course it's a real town," said the mayor impatiently. "What do you think I'm mayor of—a cabbage patch?"

"It's a nice town, you'll see," said Miss Prune soothingly. "We even have a picture show."

"And a traffic light," added Israel impressively.

"Oh yes," agreed Miss Prune. "We're all electrified!"

"Oh, Prune, really," scolded Miss Ginger. "You make it sound as if we got struck by lightning. You see," she explained to Karrie and Marty, "because of the Rural Electrification Project and the new dams—"

"We've joined the twentieth century," the mayor finished for her. "Up until a few years ago we actually managed to live without electricity, though you may find that incredible."

"It does boggle the mind," said Marty, glancing over his shoulder with that trace of a smile his grandfather was beginning to find irritating.

"Do a lot of people speak Spanish here?" Karrie asked Israel.

"Spanish?" said Miss Ginger.

"Lots of folks spoke German—before the war," said Israel. "That's the first war—World War I, they calling it now."

"No one speaks German here any more," said Miss Ginger firmly. "*Or* Spanish. Why ever do you ask such a thing?"

The mayor stirred impatiently. "Perhaps she has a logical mind, Ginger, and hasn't yet learned that logic is an unknown concept here."

"Now Henry—"

"You're right, Karen," he conceded gruffly, "*Bienvenidos* is a Spanish word, but this town didn't even exist when Texas belonged to Mexico. The first cabin was built here in 1840 by an Irishman named Tolliver. He put up a sign on the trail that said *Bienvenidos! Welcome to Tolliverville!* Pretty soon a small colony of German immigrants came looking for a place to settle—and Tolliver had himself a town. But nobody ever called it Tolliverville. The story goes that a big wind cracked the sign and blew the bottom half away, and all that was left was *Bienvenidos*. So—to conclude—a town founded by an Irishman and settled by Germans ended up with a Spanish name."

"Why, Henry," cried Miss Prune, "I haven't heard that story since Grannie Prudence used to tell it! That's right, children, that's how we came to be called Benbenitas!"

The mayor, disgruntled over his own loquaciousness, looked cross and stared out the window.

Karrie looked out the window, too. She was watching for some sign of a "real town" but saw only a few desolate farmhouses until they reached the railroad station. As they drove by, they all nodded to Mr. Peevy and Ole Ben Clinton, who were standing on the platform. Karrie, glancing back, saw that the two old men had turned their heads and were gazing after the car as it continued down the highway.

"Mabel will be promptly alerted," predicted the mayor with a sigh. "Let the games begin!"

Just past the depot, small houses began to appear. From the car window Karrie stared at sagging front porches, ramshackle chicken coops and unpainted outhouses.

Finally, a high water tank bearing the legend—or greeting— BIENVENIDOS in tall black letters loomed into view; two steepled churches with adjoining graveyards faced each other across the highway; then the mayor's car rolled into the middle of the town square.

The main sights were pointed out to the young people. The two-story house with rocking chairs on the porch and clay flamingos on the lawn was the Bienvenidos Hotel, and it occupied a block all to itself. On the next block, the Bijou Theatre stood next to Mrs. Schulman's Bread and Cakes, which was flanked on the other side by Wilkins Mercantile and a small shop called The Five and Dime. Following around the square, the next block offered the U.S. Post Office in the same building with Miller's Feed and Farm Supplies, Webber's Drugstore, the First National Bank, and Appleby's Shoes For All Ages. The remaining block featured a large store with the startling name of Guns, Coffins & Hardware, then Holt's General Store, and Wirtz's Barber Shop & Opera House. The remainder of that block contained rubble from a fire.

"We lost the new steam cleaning shop and a cute little dress store," lamented Miss Prune. "Firemen didn't make it in time."

"Disgraceful!" said Miss Ginger huffily. "After all those bake sales to raise money for that new fire engine Bill Pruitt was begging for!"

"By the time the firemen shooed them chickens out and got going, half the block done burned," explained Israel.

Marty grinned at Karrie, but said nothing.

"Do they really have operas here?" Karrie inquired, more

interested in the Barber Shop & Opera House sign.

"Oh yes," said her grandfather. "And ballets, symphonies—you name it."

"Henry, hush!" said Miss Prune. "No, dear, the name's left over from olden days. Sam Wirtz's grandfather hoped to bring a bit of culture to these parts—"

"Ha!"

"Well, he *tried*, Henry. I don't recall we ever had a real *opera*, but once in while we did get to see a play, back around the turn of the century. I'm afraid the hall's not used much nowadays, Karen. It's a pity, really."

Right in the center of the square stood two stone buildings side by side. One was the jail and the other was the Town Hall. The car pulled over to the curb and the mayor got out.

"Pick me up at noon," he told Israel, then, as his parting words to his sisters, "Before you unleash these two on the town, you might instruct them in the art of speaking with a civil tongue."

"Have we been uncivil?" Marty inquired with mild surprise after his grandfather had left them.

"Oh, dear," said Miss Prune. "It's really just a matter of different customs—"

"Around here," said Miss Ginger crisply, "children are brought up to address their elders with respect. They say 'yes, ma'am' and 'no, sir.'"

"Got it! All set to grovel, ma'am," said Marty cheerfully.

Miss Ginger glared at him.

"I suppose we might as well begin at the Mercantile, Israel," said Miss Prune. "Children—Oh, well—you'll be fine. Everything will be just fine."

3.

There were already four people standing around in the Mercantile. One was a wizened old gentleman with striking coal-black hair, which was parted, sharp as a knife, on the left and slicked down straight across to the right side of his head.

There were two women of the Webster sisters' generation, one stout and hearty, the other pale and thin as a willow branch. Like Miss Prune and Miss Ginger, they were primly turned out in their downtown clothes, complete with little hats and white cotton gloves. There was another woman, considerably younger, dressed more casually in a blouse and gathered skirt, with sandals on her stockingless feet. She had thick, ash-blond hair, parted in the middle and knotted in a careless bun at the back of her neck. One of her hands was bandaged.

All four looked up and chorused a greeting of "Morning!" as the Websters entered the store.

"Been hurrahing Miss Jane, Prune," said the elderly man, obviously tickled with himself. "You know she tore her hand up tinkering with that old Chevy of hers. Told her she got to get a husband to do that stuff for her."

The lady with the bandaged hand smiled at the old man fondly. "Well, you won't accept my proposal, Mr. Wilkins, so what am I to do?"

"Oh, if I was twenty years younger—"

"Make that forty, Eb," snorted the stout woman impatiently, and turned her attention to the new arrivals. "Well, now, and who are these two young folks, Ginger?"

Miss Ginger, straightening her back and bracing herself for whatever should befall, announced briskly, "This is Martin and this is Karen. Henry's grandchildren. Children—Mrs. Tulla Swenson, Mrs. Louisa Norwood, Miss Jane Llewellyn, and Mr. Eberly Wilkins. Mr. Wilkins is the proprietor here. Miss Jane is the art teacher in our schools."

There was a murmur of how-dya-dos, and a warm smile from Miss Jane Llewellyn. Then Mr. Wilkins, shaking hands with Marty, remarked genially, "Say you kids come from Paris, France, that right? Say you're Martin Webster's kids?"

There was an instant of hushed disbelief, then the exasperated Mrs. Tulla Swenson said, "Eb—*try* not to be a raving lunatic. Martin died in 1918. This is 1942. Just how could they be his children?"

"Oh, well, Tulla," said Mr. Wilkins, injured, "somebody told me it wrong. Said they're from Paris, France."

"No, sir, we aren't," said Marty, amused.

"But you're *foreign*, right?" persisted Mr. Wilkins.

"Well, no, sir. We're from New York City."

"Oh—I see! New York City! Well, no, that ain't exactly foreign. But it's close!" The old man chuckled good-naturedly.

"They're *the other one's* kids," thin Mrs. Louisa Norwood hissed at him.

"Whose? What other one?"

"Richard," said Marty firmly. "Richard Webster is our father."

Miss Ginger directed a warning glare at him, but it went unnoticed.

"Richard?" mused Mr. Wilkins. "Well, I swan, what do you know about that?"

Miss Ginger felt that she had endured quite enough. She turned to her sister. "Prune, you pick out your patterns and meet us at the drugstore. I need a soda."

"At nine o'clock in the morning?" protested Marty, but his great-aunt was hustling them out the door.

Miss Jane Llewellyn left at the same time. Once out on the sidewalk, she put a hand on Karrie's arm. "Did you ever play Party Line?"

Karrie looked puzzled. "Party Line?"

"You know, where one person whispers something in the next person's ear, and it's passed down the line, till the one on the end says it out loud, and it's totally different from the way it started out?"

"Oh! We used to call that Whisper Down the Lane."

"Uh huh. Well, we have a *real* party line in Benbenitas, and that's how news gets around."

"I don't really know what a party line is," admitted Karrie.

"Well, you see, instead of having separate telephone numbers, we're all on the same line, but there's a different ring for each house. To call somebody we have to first contact the operator, then she rings that particular house. The trouble is, there's nothing to stop everyone else from listening in, too. It's the main entertainment around here. It's like Whisper Down the Lane, only *everybody* reports what he *thinks* he heard, and it can get pretty bizarre. Don't be surprised if someone asks if you just landed on a rocket ship from Mars."

She smiled at both young people. "Anyway, welcome to Bienvenidos," she said, giving it the Spanish pronunciation. "You'll get used to us! Nice to see you, Miss Ginger—Bye!"

"Take care of that hand, Jane," Miss Ginger called after her.

"She's so pretty and nice," said Karrie.

Miss Ginger sighed as they began walking toward the drugstore. "Yes, poor thing. Her mother died recently. Jane spent her entire youth taking care of her ailing parents and now they're both gone and she has no one. You see, she was practically engaged to your Uncle Martin, and she never married. She never loved another man." And Miss Ginger sighed again.

"Once one has known perfection—" Marty whispered to Karrie.

4.

Miss Prune, after hastily purchasing patterns and material from Mr. Wilkins, caught up with her sister and their young charges at Webber's Drugstore. The soda jerker, Shirleen Haus, seventeen years old and innocent of olden-day gossip, was busy creating malted milks for them.

"Hope you'll like Benbenitas as much as London," she said cheerfully. "At least we don't get bombed here yet."

Karrie looked baffled, but Marty smiled kindly and explained that they had not come from London. Shirleen was disappointed.

"Gol-lee! *Somebody said*," she complained. "Gol-lee! Hospitality's got *four* and we don't even have *one*!"

"English refugee children," Miss Ginger said thoughtfully, when they'd left the drugstore. "I wish I'd thought of that—"

"Ginger!" remonstrated Miss Prune.

Running the gauntlet, as Marty called it, took most of the

morning. Miss Prune and Miss Ginger stoically steered the two young people around the town square, pausing to introduce them to anyone they happened to run into. Karrie wasn't used to being stared at with such frank curiosity, and she found it harder and harder to obey her brother's whispered reminders to "walk as if you own the town."

One of their stops was at Appleby's Shoes For All Ages, to buy Karrie a pair of sandals. Mr. Appleby was an impatient, plain-spoken man who left the party line to his wife.

"You kids here while your pa's away in the service?" he asked, as he measured Karrie's foot.

Miss Ginger's tense face relaxed into a gratified smile. She aimed a warning thrust of her sharp elbow into Marty's side, and declared blatantly, "And we're so thrilled to have the children with us at last, Mr. Appleby. I was just saying to Henry, it's high time they learned Texas ways!"

"I think that's as good a story as any," she told the rest of her party when they were out on the sidewalk again.

"But Ginger," Miss Prune protested, "we can't out and out *lie*. Henry will be furious."

"Well, I didn't exactly lie," said Miss Ginger. "It's nobody's business anyway. We don't have to say he's in the service, but we don't have to deny it either. I think it's best if you children avoid saying *anything* about your father. If Lollie Beal and her bunch of busybodies get wind of a mystery, they never *will* let go of it."

"But it *is* a mystery," murmured Miss Prune, distressed.

"Haven't we paraded around enough?" asked Karrie wearily.

"One more stop," said Miss Ginger firmly. "Wirtz's Barber Shop. Your grandfather was emphatic about this, Martin. He says you look like a hillbilly with that shaggy hair. Now Sam Wirtz is easy to talk to—so just watch what you say."

The warning turned out to be unnecessary, as Mr. Wirtz, after asking "Where you from?", stuck to the subject of New York City while cutting Marty's hair.

"What's the population there now? My goodness, that right? All kinds, I guess. Say it's a real melting pot. Like to take a trip there someday—just to look around, you know. I'm a country boy, myself, but I sure would like to see them skyscrapers!"

"Sam Wirtz is a gentleman," said Miss Prune fervently, when they had left the barber shop. She signaled to Israel, who was waiting in the parked car across the square.

Karrie had been aware all morning that four teen-aged boys were trailing them at a distance, and it unnerved her to find they were now standing around outside the barber shop. One of them, a burly, unkempt youth with a ruddy, raw complexion, ambled up to her.

"Y'all from New York?"

"Uh—yes."

"That how the girls dress in New York—in their granny's clothes?"

"That's right," Marty intervened. "It's all the rage."

"Yeah? Guess you think you're *something*, huh?"

"Just don't talk to him," Miss Ginger hissed in Marty's ear.

He paid no heed. "I think *you're* something—I just haven't figured out *what* yet."

The boy's face turned redder than ever. "Say what? Say what? I don't take no sass from no damn' yankee—"

His companions crowded near and put restraining hands on his shoulders. "Hold it, Bucko! That's the mayor's grandson—"

"Oh, so ain't *that* scary? I'll show him what kind of something I am!"

But cooler heads prevailed, and it ended with the belligerent Bucko following his friends down the street and shouting back over his shoulder,

"See you around, yankee boy—you and your funny-looking sister—"

Marty smiled at Karrie. "Well, he got *that* right."

"Why did you aggravate him like that?" snapped Miss Ginger. "That boy is just trouble. He'd be in reform school if he wasn't the sheriff's nephew."

"Do try to stay out of his way," urged Miss Prune anxiously.

Mr. Wirtz was standing in the doorway of his shop. "Son,

33

take my advice and don't mess with that trash. Been rotten since the day he was born."

Marty shrugged. "New York is full of clowns like that."

"Maybe so," said Mr. Wirtz. "But you ain't familiar with the Texas variety. It'll be a happy day in this town when Bucko Riddle gets drafted. Let him take his meanness out on Hitler."

"I'm afraid there'll always be a Bucko," sighed Miss Prune. "There's a bad apple in every basket."

By that time, Israel had pulled up in the car, and they were all grateful to call it a morning.

"Well, it was bad enough but it might have been worse," declared Miss Ginger. "At least we didn't run into Lollie Beal!"

5.

Karrie never wanted to set foot downtown again, but the very next morning there was a phone call from the mayor's part-time secretary, Mrs. Morris. She invited Karrie over to her house to meet her daughter, Baby Dodds.

"You're going to like Baby Dodds," Miss Ginger said. "She's a sweet, down-to-earth kind of girl, and she's very popular."

"Is that really her name?" asked Karrie. "Baby Dodds?"

"Well, sweetie, it's a nickname—just the way Martin calls you 'Karrie,'" explained Miss Prune. "Her real name's Dorothy."

"Naturally, nobody around here can leave a perfectly good name alone," grumbled the mayor. "'Baby Dodds!' Ridiculous!"

"Oh, now, Henry, you know it was her big brother who started that," said Miss Prune. "Bubbabill couldn't say Baby Dottie—"

"I rest my case," said the mayor, heading for his study. "Have her ready promptly at a quarter to eight. Israel will bring the car around."

"Do I *have* to go?" Karrie asked.

"Of course you do," said Miss Ginger firmly. "It would be very discourteous to refuse. And you don't have to wear one of those tacky dresses. Your Aunt Prune has a surprise for you."

And right on cue, Miss Prune proudly displayed her

handiwork. It was a short-sleeved white cotton dress with a navy blue sailor collar, set off by a wide red bow. Karrie's heart sank. Surely she had *enough* ugly dresses!

"Stayed up late to finish it last night," Miss Prune said, pleased as punch with herself. "Good thing, since you got this invitation."

"Thank you, Aunt Prune," said Karrie, hoping she sounded sincere. "You sew beautifully."

"She does," agreed Miss Ginger. "Prune got the talent, Clara got the beauty, and I got the brains. Now run up and put it on, honey."

Karrie glanced at Marty. He was smiling. No help there.

The Morris house was two blocks from the town square. It was small and plain and rested two feet off the ground on cedar posts. Karrie thought it looked like a box on little stilts, and found it hard to imagine a whole family living there—a family that presumably consisted of a father, a mother, a Baby Dodds and a Bubbabill. The front yard was shallow and rocky, with occasional clumps of long, unclipped grass, and appeared to be home to several brown hens.

As the mayor's car came to a halt out front, a young girl came flying out the screen door, allowing it to slam behind her. She was pert and pretty, with red hair and freckles, and was dressed in a pair of shorts and a halter top.

"Morning!" she sang out.

"Good morning, Dorothy," said the mayor. "We've brought Karen. Israel will pick her up at noon."

"Yessir!" chirped the girl. "We'll take real good care of her, Mr. Mayor."

The car pulled away and Karrie was left alone with Baby Dodds, who was eyeing her guest's attire.

"Hi!" said Baby Dodds to Karrie.

"Hi," said Karrie to Baby Dodds.

"Aren't you dressed kind of *hot* for this weather?"

At that moment, a cheerful woman who looked like an older

version of the red-haired girl appeared at the screen door. "Hi there," she called out.

"Hi!—ma'am," replied Karrie.

"Well, I expect you girls are going over to Jolene's. My, what a *sweet* frock!"

Karrie groaned inwardly. Only the chickens, it seemed, were uninterested in her dress. "Aunt Prune made it last night, ma'am."

"In one night? I declare! Miss Prune has a *gift*! Well, you girls have a good time, now, hear?"

On their way to the house of someone named Jolene, Baby Dodds kept up a running stream of talk, pointing out different houses and supplying biographical information about the occupants.

"Meanest man in town lives there, say he killed his wife, but nobody could prove it...Lady lives there never leaves her own yard, say her husband walked into the river, only they never found his body, then somebody saw him walking down the street in California, alive as you please...Feller lives there's brother robbed a bank, say the sheriff shot him dead on the sidewalk in El Paso..."

When the girl paused for breath, Karrie felt obliged to fill the gap. "I like your name," she said awkwardly. "*The Wizard of Oz* was my favorite book when I was little."

"Hm-m? Oh, I get it—*Dorothy*! Never read the book but I saw the show. Now Karen's a nice name," Baby Dodds went on. "Never knew anybody with that name. Can't think of any movie stars named Karen, either, can you?"

"My brother calls me Karrie."

"Really? Maid at Jolene's house is called Carrie. Now that's spelled with a C—is yours spelled with a K?"

"Yes. With a K."

"Oh, well, that makes a difference. K is just prettier than C, don't you think? So you wanna be a cheerleader, or what?"

"*What?*"

"You know—a cheerleader for the football team. That's what we're fixing to do today—practice and all. Jolene said I could bring you when I told her my mamma'd gone and asked you over. Jolene's the head cheerleader and drum majorette, and girl, she's *famous*! Everybody says she's the best derned cheerleader Benbenitas ever had! You have any shorts or not?"

"Uh—no," said Karrie, glancing down at her hateful dress. "I had some when I used to go to summer camp, but I outgrew them."

"*Summer* camp? What's that? Some church thing?"

"Church? No. It's—you know—out in the country. You sleep in tents and—"

"*Tents*? Why'd you want to sleep in *tents*?"

"It was fun. Lots of kids who live in the city go to—"

"Hm-m-m! Anyway, later on, if we get back to my house before your ride comes, I'm going to give you something. I got some real nice shorts I grew out of while they were still good as new and I think they'd just about fit you. They're in a box with a bunch of stuff for my cousin Mary Joe in Waco. She's the one gets my hand-me-downs, and lordy, she makes 'em look so-o tacky you'd never recognize 'em! Hate to waste a spiffy pair of almost brand-new shorts on her."

Karrie was too surprised to say anything. Baby Dodds eyed her intently. "You funny about hand-me-downs?"

"Oh, no!" Karrie responded quickly. "I'd love to have a pair of shorts, if your mother wouldn't mind—I mean, since they were meant for your cousin and all."

Baby Dodds shrugged. "Why should *she* care? She can't stand Mary Joe. Okay, if it don't bother you, that's good. Now Jolene Ross would no more wear hand-me downs! I think that girl had rather go *naked* than put on anything somebody else has worn. She's got this cousin in Austin who sends her this real pretty stuff, but it goes right into the Bundles for Britain box. Well, she's spoiled, is all."

"She is?"

"Sure. See, Doc Ross has these two *gruesome* nieces, so he

37

really takes on over Jolene."

"But—what—what's the matter with them—the nieces?"

"Hm-m? Nothing. They're grown up and married now."

"Really? But—they're *gruesome*?"

"Uh huh. Not all that cute."

Karrie, confused and discouraged, fell silent. All she knew for sure was that *not all that cute* didn't even come close to describing her in that sailor dress.

6.

Karrie was surprised when they turned down a pleasant, tree-lined street, unlike any she had seen so far in Benbenitas, and stopped at a rambling, well-kept, two-story house, with a big shaded porch and a grassy lawn. Beside the front door was a sign that said, "Malcolm J. Ross, M.D."

"Hey, y'all!" Baby Dodds called to the collection of young girls lounging around the porch.

"Hi!" they chorused back.

Like Baby Dodds, they all wore shorts and halter tops. Two were sitting side by side in rocking chairs, flipping through a movie magazine together. One was idly swaying back and forth in the porch swing, and another was perched on the banister rail, carefully polishing her toenails. Two others sat on the steps, the girl on the top step brushing and arranging the hair of the girl on the step below.

"What y'all up to?" asked Baby Dodds unnecessarily. She didn't pause before going on with, "Hey, everybody! This is Karrie—spelled with a K—Mayor's granddaughter come to live at Windy Crest."

All the girls sang out another "Hi!" and continued with what they were doing. Baby Dodds steered Karrie up onto the porch and into a rocking chair, then took a place on the rail and began identifying the others.

"Jolene Ross," she said, and the one painting her toenails looked up from her labors to flash a sparkling, straight-toothed smile. She was a long-legged, blue-eyed blonde with a golden tan.

38

"That's Bev Coulter." The one on the swing waved a casual greeting. "Sister Bee and Joycie Wallace—they're twins," Baby Dodds continued, as the pair with the magazine directed identical indifferent glances at Karrie.

The remaining two girls, who were engrossed in hair-grooming and scarcely looked up, were pointed out as Bettie Rae Miller and Snookie Wirtz. One was blond, one had light brown hair, both were pretty.

All were pretty, Karrie thought, acutely conscious of being dark-haired, pale and short. Every girl on that porch looked like a Hollywood starlet. Except for Jolene. Jolene was a full-fledged *star*. Even her feet, gracefully arched and long-toed, were worthy of the attention being lavished on them.

Karrie sat back in the rocking chair and tried to appear at ease. Her great-aunts had sent her forth that morning with anxious reminders not to mention her father or the years she and Marty had spent on their own in New York, and now she braced herself for all the questions she wasn't supposed to answer.

There was a long period of silence.

"Anybody want to go to the show tonight?" said someone at last. "It's Errol Flynn."

"Oh, I don't like those old war pictures."

"Me neither. But I sure do like Errol Flynn! Woo-wee!"

This began a lively discussion about movie stars, a subject in which they were all apparently well-versed and intensely interested. Finally, Jolene held up a hand for quiet.

"Y'all, y'all! We gonna do some work, or what?"

"Well, sure, Jolene, if you're through messing with those toenails! Honestly!" said Baby Dodds in exasperation.

The girls headed out into the yard, and Jolene firmly pushed them into formation.

"Now I want you older girls to set a good example for Sister Bee and Joycie," she warned. She glanced at Karrie, who was still on the porch. "Want to try out?" Karrie shook her head, and Jolene immediately returned to duty.

"All right, now, remember your moves! Here we go! Give me

a *B!* Give me an *I!* Give me an *E! N! V!* Give me an *E!* Give me an *N!* Give me an *I, D, O, S!* What does it spell? What does it mean? *Benbenitas! Benbenitas! Go tee-ee-eam*—FIGHT!"

Karrie watched in glum amazement as all the girls, having executed prances and elaborate hand movements along with the letters, leaped into the air, more or less at the same time. Jolene put her hands on her hips and shook her head sadly.

"Y'all, that was *pitiful!* Now how do you expect our boys to beat Gladhand if we can't cheer 'em on better than that?"

"Oh, Jolene, our boys never *have* beat Gladhand, why should they start now?" grumbled Bev.

"That's a tacky attitude, Bev," said Jolene sternly. "Now listen here: Benbenitas may not have the best football team, and Lordy knows we got the *worst* band—but we are *famous* for having the snappiest cheerleaders in the state, and I, for one, am dedicated to keeping that tradition alive! Now! Look sharp!"

About that time the front door opened and a young black woman wearing an apron emerged from the house with a tray. She set down glasses and a pitcher of lemonade on a small wicker table, and retired as quietly as she had appeared.

Jolene then gave into the pleas for mercy and allowed the girls to return to the shade of the front porch and refresh themselves with lemonade.

"Jolene, this is too much like *work*," said Bettie Rae.

"It *is* work, you bum," responded Jolene. "And next week I expect y'all to bring batons, hear?"

"Who wants to go to the show tonight?" asked Bev.

"Oh, quit talking about the show," said Bettie Rae. "I can't go. This is *our* night. *Preacher's* coming to supper."

There was a large collective groan, followed by exclamations of: "Ghastly!" "Gruesome!" "I *pity* you!"

"Oh, your time'll come around. There's no-o-o escape!"

Baby Dodds turned to Karrie. "You see, our mammas all feel obliged to have Preacher to supper, ever since his wife lit out with the brush salesman. Mercy, you'd think the man would starve to death if they didn't feed him!"

"It's truly a martyrdom, but you don't have to worry, Karrie spelled with a K." Jolene, her more strenuous labors done, had now begun work on her fingernails. "The mayor never goes to church." She held out one of her perfect hands to scrutinize, and continued casually, "Didn't I see you downtown yesterday? That cute, tall guy your brother?"

"My brother Marty," said Karrie.

"Woo-wee, he's handsome! Y'all don't look a bit alike," remarked Jolene without malice.

"I saw him, too," said Bettie Rae. "Cute all right. He still in high school?"

"No," said Karrie, "he just graduated."

"Uh oh! You better make your move quick, Jolene, before the Army gets him!"

There was laughter from everyone but Karrie.

"Oh, y'all!" pouted Jolene.

At this point there was a distraction, and cries of "Hi, Miss Jane!" "Miss Jane, how's your hand?" heralded the approach of an attractive, smiling woman turning in at the walk.

"Why, hello there, Karen! Hi, girls!" Miss Jane waved her bandaged hand. "Let you know after I see Doc."

"Isn't she the sweetest?" remarked Bettie Rae, after Miss Jane had gone inside the house. "But wouldn't I love to get my hands on her hair!" She looked at Karrie. "That a permanent?"

Karrie's hand flew to her head. "Oh! No."

"Just frizzles up on its own, huh? Wouldn't look so kinky if you'd set it on big rollers. You'd probably get soft curls, you know, like Claudette Colbert's."

Jolene patted Karrie's short hair. "Hm-m. That might look real classy."

Joycie, tuning in late, chirped up with, "Want to hear classy, you go over to Mr. Webber's drugstore."

Karrie looked bewildered, and the other girls laughed.

"Joycie, why can't you follow a conversation in simple English?" demanded Sister Bee.

"I'm just telling her!" said her sister defensively. "Mr.

41

Webber's got himself a wind-up Victrola and this whole bunch of one-sided classy records. Bottom side don't even have grooves. Got those old dead singers on them. Like Crusoe."

Baby Dodds snorted. "Yeah, good old Robinson! And his man Friday! They sing a swell duet!"

"Car-*u*-so, Joycie," said Jolene.

"That's what I said. Crusoe," agreed Joycie.

Miss Jane came out of the house, holding up her hand to show that the large bandage had been replaced with a much smaller one. "Almost as good as new!"

"Oh, Miss Jane, you're just lucky you didn't get blood poisoning, my daddy said," scolded Jolene. "Why don't you take that old wreck to Pitcher's garage instead of messing up your hands that way?"

"That old wreck's my best buddy," responded Miss Jane cheerfully. "I like tinkering with it. Besides, just between you and me, I'm a better mechanic than Mr. Pitcher."

"Well, they got women working in shipyards and airplane factories, don't they?" said Bettie Rae. "They do all the same stuff men do."

"Absolutely!" said Miss Jane. "The world's changing, girls. Can't keep those pretty nails for long, Jolene!"

"Then I better enjoy them while I can," said Jolene, regarding her manicure with satisfaction.

Miss Jane laughed. "Got to run. See you again soon, Karen," she added, smiling at the most wretched girl on earth.

7.

Karrie was thankful she wasn't expected to talk during the ride home. The mayor stared out the window and appeared to be absorbed in his own thoughts, and Israel, because of their long years together, knew when to keep the silence.

But the ride had to end, and there were the great-aunts waiting at the door to hear all about her morning.

"Did you have a nice time, honey?"

Karrie looked at the kind, eager faces and heard herself

replying, "Very nice."

"Did you like Baby Dodds? Did you meet any other girls? I think she's friends with Dr. Ross's daughter," said Miss Ginger.

"Yes. Jolene Ross. We went over to her house. I met quite a few girls."

"Oh, that's wonderful, honey, I'm so glad! You're going to just love it here, you'll see!" Miss Prune was delighted.

"Did they ask you many questions?" Miss Ginger wanted to know.

"Not really."

"Oh! Well! What do you have there, dear?"

Karrie showed them the shorts. "Baby Dodds gave them to me. She's outgrown them."

"Well! Wasn't that sweet? Did you happen to tell your grandfather?"

Karrie shook her head, and the aunts exchanged a relieved glance.

"No need to mention it," said Miss Prune. "Men can be funny about things. Oh—your brother's upstairs and he's—uh—he's waiting to have a talk with you, honey."

"Don't be too long," said Miss Ginger briskly. "Dinner's in half an hour."

Karrie found Marty in his room, standing and staring out the window and apparently as lost in thought as his grandfather had been. When he heard her approach he turned around and smiled.

"So! You survived. No shoot-out at the O.K. Corral?"

Karrie shrugged. "What have *you* been doing all morning?" she asked him somewhat resentfully.

"Oh—wandering around. Getting the feel of the place."

Karrie sat down on the bed and allowed her shoulders to slump at last. "That's what I've been doing, too. Getting the *feel* of the place."

"Uh oh! Didn't go too well, huh?"

"It *stank*! The whole place stinks!" Karrie put her hands over her face to hold back the crying.

Marty sighed. "Okay. Cry a little if you have to. But you

don't want to go down to lunch with red eyes."

"Dinner!" corrected Karrie fiercely, drawing her arm across her eyes to dry them. She was *not* going to "cry a little." What was the use?

"Dinner," said Marty humbly. "So—what was it? You didn't like Baby Doe?"

"Baby *Dodds*! She was nice, Marty—I think. It wasn't just her. She has about a million friends, all perfect little golden cheerleaders! I felt like—like—I felt *gruesome*!"

"Gruesome? What are you talking about?"

"You want to know what kind of morning I had? Remember Miss Simms—that housekeeper who tried to explain Purgatory to us? Well, now I understand what Purgatory is. Maybe I should send her a postcard."

"Oh, come on, aren't you over-dramatizing a bit?"

"No, I'm not! You weren't there! Oh—too bad you weren't. You would have been very popular. You're woo—wee good looking!"

Marty smiled. "I know. I've always told you that."

Karrie shot him a hostile look. "Right. *You* got the beauty, as Aunt Ginger would say. What was it *I* got?"

"Karrie, come on! You got Mom's looks and you got her talent. I happen to think that's pretty special. This doesn't sound like you. What did those golden little cheerleaders do to you this morning, anyway?"

"Oh, nothing, nothing! They were all right, I guess. It's just that—I felt like I came from another planet!"

"Really? Which one?"

"Oh, Marty, you just don't understand! You never felt that way in your life!"

"No-o, I always figure it's *my* planet. But now there's Grandfather—I suspect he came from Saturn—"

"Oh, you absolutely drive me crazy!"

"I'm sorry, squirt—really. I *do* understand—I think. The place will take some getting used to. It's going to get better."

"Sure—fine for *you* to say! Everybody leaves *you* alone! You

get to do as you please while I get my mornings planned for me."
Karrie sighed. "And what am I supposed to do about Aunt Prune
and her magic sewing machine? She *means* so well! I can't hurt
her feelings! Oh—it's all just rotten!"

"Now wait a minute, squirt. Use the old noggin. Before she
comes galloping up with more of these abominations, why don't
you head her off at the pass? Ask her to teach *you* to sew. I'm
sure she'll be delighted. Tell her you want to start with
something simple—like that skirt Miss Jane Llewellyn was
wearing yesterday."

Karrie's hostility dissolved into gratitude. "Marty, you're a
genius! You always solve my problems!"

"Well, I can't argue with the first statement, but—hey! Bet
you can solve your own problems. I—You know. It builds
character."

Karrie regarded her brother with interest. "What are you so
jumpy about?"

"Me? Never been jumpy in my life. Oh—you'll be happy to
know that I'm the one who has his morning planned for him
tomorrow. The old man has decreed that I must learn to drive
immediately. Israel is going to give me lessons while His Honor
is at Town Hall doing whatever it is he does there. How much
mayoring do you suppose this town requires, anyway? The whole
downtown area is about the size of Washington Square."

"Driving lessons? I thought everybody was supposed to be
conserving tires and gasoline."

"We won't use that much. I'm a fast study."

Karrie hurled a pillow at his head. "And gorgeous to boot!
Oh, wait a minute—the aunts said you wanted to have a talk
with me. Not about the birds and the bees again, I hope!"

Marty tossed the pillow back at her. "Come on, squirt, let's
go down to lunch—Excuse me! *Dinner!*"

"No, really, Marty, what about this big talk?"

Marty was already out the door.

"It can wait," he said over his shoulder.

8.

In the following days, things settled into a temporary routine at Windy Crest. Marty left early with his grandfather and Israel, and they didn't return until twelve-thirty or one.

Karrie felt a sense of relief when the mayor walked out the door. Even when he was closed up alone in his study, the very fact of his presence in the house lent tension to the atmosphere.

In the morning, it was a relaxed house of women, chatting and laughing as they went about their chores. Karrie was given the job of dusting the numerous rooms, nooks and crannies of the big old house, and while Israel was teaching Marty to drive, she was assigned his task of sweeping the porches. Later, as the noon hour approached, she sat on the kitchen porch and helped Martha shell peas, snap beans, or peel potatoes.

Tension returned when "dinner," as the midday meal was called, was presided over by the mayor in the large dining room. The aunts always tried to keep up a lively conversation, but their valiant effort, Karrie observed, only served to make their brother grumpier than before.

Luckily, dinner was followed by "siesta time" at Windy Crest, and everyone was glad to disappear to a quiet place. Karrie enjoyed that private time in her father's old room. She liked to curl up in one of the window seats to read, as she imagined he must have done. Sometimes, she would lower her book and simply look out the window. Growing up in the city had accustomed her to summer days that were hazy and sticky, and now she marveled that the sky could be so bright a blue.

Little stirred in the midday heat. The electric fan kept up a discreet, methodical drone, and occasionally the windmill joined in with a plaintive creak. The cicadas' song rose and cast a hypnotic spell over the hills and the valley, over the chickens pecking in the yard and the cows kneeling by the distant pond, but most of all over the pale young stranger from New York, to whom it seemed to say that this world, so new to her, had been here forever, would continue forever, under the hot southwestern sun.

Chapter 3
The Websters of Windy Crest

"I like the way the housekeeping's done at Windy Crest," said Karrie with satisfaction. She was shelling the first black-eyed peas of the season from Israel's Victory Garden.

Martha, engaged in peeling potatoes, looked up, amused. "Do you, baby? What you know about housekeeping?"

"Lots," said Karrie emphatically. "I've seen all kinds. After my mother died we had about a million housekeepers."

"A million, huh?"

"Well, let's see—there must have been at least a dozen. Most of them didn't last too long. None of them could keep house without driving you crazy. Here it's all so natural and easy."

"Can't say it's always *easy*. But Miss Prune and Miss Ginger work right along, and normal times it goes pretty well."

"Is it harder now that we're here?"

"Why, no, baby. You're a big help to me, and it's right good to have young folks around the house again."

"We don't want to be any trouble. Marty and I weren't too good at keeping house. We used to let the apartment get pretty bad, then we'd spend a whole day cleaning it inside out."

"Well, we don't do inside-out cleaning except twice a year—spring and fall. It don't get all that dirty around here, us keeping up with things every day."

"That's what I meant. Everything stays clean and pleasant and nobody's fussing about it all the time. We had one housekeeper who was a *fanatic*—always vacuuming and scrubbing and scolding us. Then we had one who read movie magazines all day and never cleaned at all. And there was Miss Simms who made me go to Mass with her every morning, and another one who used to invite her boyfriend over—"

"Goodness sakes, must have been hard on you children, all those different people!"

"It was all right after Dad decided to let us take care of ourselves."

"Well," said Martha kindly, "I know Richard was right proud of you, to put his trust in you like that."

Karrie looked up gratefully. "Thank you, Martha."

"For what, baby?"

"For—saying Dad's name. Nobody ever does, you know, except you and Israel."

Martha shook her head and sighed. "Ain't right. Mayor's a stubborn man, but he got no call to take it out on children."

"He doesn't want us here," said Karrie, her lip quivering a little. "He has to do his duty, but he hates us."

"Oh, baby, he don't hate you. He's just all turned in on himself. Guess he's afraid he can't take no more pain."

"We've had pain, too." Karrie blinked back the tears that wanted to start.

"He knows, honey, he knows. He just can't let himself think about it. Spite of everything, your grandaddy's a *good* man. Always been a friend to colored."

"Really?" said Karrie with interest. "What's he done?"

"Main thing, he gives us our dignity."

"Is that all?"

Martha gave a short laugh. "That's a *lot,* sugar, when it's all you got."

"Maybe you're right. He doesn't give *me* any dignity."

"He does what he can right along, like standing up for us to the sheriff. And he got a colored school started so the children don't have to go all the way to Hospitality to get an education."

"Why don't they go to school with the other kids in town?"

"Ain't the way things is, honey."

"That doesn't make sense."

"Um hum. Lots of things don't make no sense. But a better day's coming. I may not live to see it, but maybe you will. White, black, yellow, and red—going to live like good neighbors, just as the Lord God planned it."

"I hope you're right." Karrie was silent for a moment, then she asked, "You believe there's a God, don't you, Martha?"

"Oh, yes, baby, indeed I do."

"But how do you know it's true?"

"Believing without knowing—that's called faith."

"I guess I don't have faith. I have to ask questions, and so far I haven't heard any real good answers."

"Um-hm. Just like your daddy. Got to find your *own* way."

Karrie concentrated on the peas for a minute. Then she asked quietly, "Do you believe in heaven and stuff like that?"

"Yes, I do, shug."

"So—what do you think it's like?"

"Well, don't know what it *look* like, but what I believe is, in heaven you get to be with all the people you loved on earth. I know I'm gonna be with my mamma and my daddy, and my two little babies that died."

"But then, how *old* would you be? If you live to be older than your mother was, in heaven will you be older than she is, or what?"

"I believe you can be any age, like in your dreams. Don't you ever dream you're bitty again?"

"Oh, yes! I dream Marty and I are little kids in red wool jackets and he's teaching me to skate on Central Park Lake. Once I dreamed Mom was singing to me and I woke up crying. I never dreamed about her again. Mom had such a pretty voice."

Martha nodded. "I dream my mamma's singing to me, too, and I'm hanging onto her apron, following her around in the cotton fields. And I dream I'm down at the river with my daddy and he's teaching me to swim, and laughing at me splashing! And sometimes in my dreams I'm a skinny young woman again, working in this same kitchen, with two little boys playing at my feet—your daddy and your Uncle Martin. And that's what I believe it's like in heaven. You're all ages, like in dreams. And when I go there, I'll be with all those people, just like before."

"Dad's not dead, Martha."

"I know he ain't, baby. I'd know if my Richard was dead!"

"Really, Martha? I—I wish I could—I mean, how would you know?"

"Can't explain it, honey. It's just a feeling inside. Richard was like my own baby. You see, Miss Sally was sick a right long spell after he was born, and it was me took care of the little thing. Mayor was so busy worrying about Miss Sally and little Martin, he didn't hardly pay no attention to that baby. Well, we was all right, me and my Richard."

"What was he like when he was a little boy, Martha?"

"Sweetest child ever lived. Now Martin—he was his papa's joy. Smart, handsome little feller. Could do anything he set his mind to. Took after his grandaddy, Mr. William, and that made the mayor proud. But Richard was *my* boy. Always underfoot when I was working. It was play-like this and play-like that. Him and Abner."

"Who was Abner?"

"Abner was play-like."

"You mean an imaginary friend?"

"Um hm. Could almost see him myself."

"Dad never told me he had an imaginary friend! Oh, Martha, I wish I could see some pictures of my dad when he was little! He didn't have any to show us. There are pictures of Uncle Martin all over this house, but none at all of Dad."

Martha sighed. "Your granddad made your aunties get rid of them—off the walls, out of the albums and everything."

"Oh, that—that makes me so *furious*!" Karrie tossed the peas into the bowl with unnecessary vigor. "They act like he never existed!"

Martha reached out and patted her hand. "Makes me furious, too, honey. For twenty years it's been my grief. But then I saw you standing at that door with Marty, him looking the image of my Richard when I saw him last, and—Well, I got my happiness back."

2.

"It's high time you told her you've enlisted. I'm sick and tired of pussyfooting around the subject."

The mayor was riding in state on the back seat of the Packard, while Marty sat up front with Israel.

"She needs a little more time," Marty said. "I'd feel better if she had a friend or two."

"She's been introduced to the nicest girls in Benbenitas."

"I know, but it's new and strange to her, and—well, it's not all that easy for Karrie to get to know other girls."

"Oh? Not even in the rarefied world of New York City?"

Marty ignored the sarcasm. "We couldn't afford to have close friends. Word might have gotten back to the schools that we were on our own."

"I see! And I suppose you forged your father's signature on your report cards."

"Sure. Anyway, they were good report cards."

"Oh, I have no doubt! Well, young man, you'll soon learn there's more to life than good report cards. You're going to have to hold your own in the world of *men*. How's his driving coming along, Israel?"

"Real fine, Mayor," Israel replied heartily. "He's a fast learner. Just about ready to take the test for his license."

"Good," said the mayor. "I wouldn't want to waste the taxpayers' money by leaving it to the Navy to teach him to drive."

"Don't know why he got to learn to *drive* for the Navy," remarked Israel. "Seems like *swimming's* more to the point."

"Can you swim, boy, or is that a foolish question?"

Marty smiled slightly and passed up the chance to make a

flippant remark. "Yes, I can swim. I have a merit badge to prove it. I was an eagle scout! I learned to canoe, pitch a tent, start a fire with two sticks, and fight off the dead-end kids who tried to steal my hat on the way to troop meetings!"

"Hrumph. I didn't know they did those things in New York City," said the mayor grudgingly. "Where did you camp out—in Central Park?"

"Nope. Mostly in the Ramapo mountains, north of the city. We went by bus, but to get to the bus station we had to take the subway, each of us with a full backpack, of course. There should have been a merit badge for that."

"My, that was a lot of trouble to go camping," remarked Israel admiringly. "Alls *we* had to do was walk down to the river, Henry."

Marty was mildly surprised to hear Israel address his stern employer by his first name. They pulled up in front of Town Hall and the mayor got out of the car.

"Israel," he said, "I'll wind up everything here in about two hours. And you—Martin—be thinking about your talk with Karen. You could be called up any day. The Navy isn't interested in whether or not your little sister has made any friends."

Marty and Israel changed places and Marty headed the car out onto the highway again.

"I find it hard to imagine my grandfather camping out by the river," he remarked.

"Oh, he only did it to please his papa, Mr. William," said Israel. "Your grandaddy never was happy in the out-of-doors. He always druther be home reading a book. Well, he had all those sisters, you know. But Miss Ginger could ride a horse better and climb a tree quicker'n *he* ever could. Made him madder'n a hornet!"

"So you've known each other since you were boys?"

"All our lives. My sister Nona and me growed up right out behind Windy Crest. My daddy had a cabin on the property, but it got burned down."

"Was your father a *slave*, Israel?"

"No, no. He was born a free man. My *granddaddy* was born in slavery, back in Tennessee, but he lived a free man here in Texas, 'count of Matthew Webster—one who built Windy Crest—didn't believe in no slavery. Come from Massachusetts."

"Really? I didn't know that."

"Lord, you don't know much about your family, boy."

"No, I don't. My parents never talked about the past and I guess I didn't give it much thought. The past didn't seem to have much to do with anything in New York City. Here it seems to surround me."

"Lot of Webster history here all right. Now Matthew—he was the mayor's grandpa—he come out from Massachusetts in 1846. Him and my grandaddy built Windy Crest theyselves, put that little porch up on top and all. Only thing like that around here."

"The widow's walk. I wondered about that."

"That's right! Widow's walk. That's what Miss Ginger calls it."

"The houses of the New England sea captains had them, so their wives could watch for their ships coming into port."

"That so? I swan. That's where the mayor's granny and then his mamma after her used to look out for their men coming home from a cattle drive."

"Cattle drive? Was Matthew Webster a rancher? Strange career for someone from Massachusetts."

"Well, he done good at it. So did his son, Mr. William. Mr. William done good at everything, made lots of money. He was the one started the lumber mill, and the mayor still owns that, but he never did run it hisself. Feller named Mr. Ned Welles does that."

"Is that how my grandfather can afford the mayor's job? He told me he doesn't get a salary."

"Salary? For being mayor? Lord, no. Town couldn't pay no salary for *that!* Bad enough to have to pay the sheriff and *he* don't do nothing worth talking about. Just pester folks all the time. Always blowing that mean old siren whether he need to or not."

"Didn't my grandfather ever have a real job?"

"Well, he practiced at the law some, but mayoring's been his main job."

"He didn't take to ranching, I guess?"

"Not him! Sold off all the cattle after Mr. William died. Land was over-grazed by then anyhow. Ain't had no animals on the place for nearly twenty years, 'cept chickens."

"What about horses? You told me my dad and uncle used to ride. Karrie was disappointed there were no horses."

"Horses got old and died. I miss 'em, but don't miss having to take care of 'em. We got our first automobile back in '22. Had to crank up the engine, then jump in right quick! Went fifteen miles an hour." Israel laughed and shook his head, remembering. "Now we got this Packard in '38 and never had a bit of trouble with it. I keep it shining and running smooth!"

"You take it home with you every night, don't you?"

"Sure. Ain't no good to anybody else. I'm the only one drives it. 'Cept for you now."

"My grandfather doesn't ever drive it himself?"

"Lord, boy, *he* never learned to drive. He didn't take no interest in it years ago, and now he's too old to learn. Think it kind of embarrasses him. That's why he been so keen on you learning before going off to the Navy."

Marty laughed. "To save me from embarrassment? A little hard to believe, since he spends every waking hour trying to cut me down to size!"

"Oh, well. Don't take no notice of that. He don't know how to act with you yet. Never knowed he had no grandchildren. Scares him some. He got to get used to being scared that way again."

3.

Karrie's favorite household duty was dusting the framed photographs that hung in the long hallway downstairs. She was fascinated by the old-fashioned clothing, the hair styles, and the handsome, unsmiling faces. One morning she spent such a long time pondering them that Miss Prune came looking for her.

"Here you are! My, those pictures have never been so well dusted!"

"Are all these people kin to us?"

"Yes, my dear, you're kin to every one of them."

"They look so serious, don't they?"

"Well—it wasn't the custom to smile for portraits back then. Pictures weren't just snapped the way they are nowadays. People had to hold still a long time for the old cameras."

"Hm-m. I guess when they got tired their faces relaxed. It makes it easier to imagine what they were really like."

"Why, I never thought about it that way, honey, but perhaps that's why old photographs are more interesting than modern ones. Now this," said Miss Prune proudly, indicating the picture of a lovely young woman with upswept hair, "is my dear mother —your great-grandmother. Her name was Reba Stone before she married. Isn't she beautiful? Your Aunt Clara looks just like her. And right here next to her is my papa, your great-grandfather. His name was William."

"He's very handsome."

"Oh my yes! He was a wonderful man, and a great scholar."

Miss Ginger had come up behind them. "But he could rope a steer and break a horse better than any man in the hill country!"

"Yes, indeed," agreed Miss Prune. "They called him 'the gentleman cowboy' around these parts."

"And he died with his boots on," her sister said. "He was breaking a wild stallion one day and it threw him off and rolled on him. Fifty-nine years old."

Miss Prune mopped away a tear with her handkerchief. "It was exactly how he would have chosen to go."

"Who is this pretty girl?" Karrie asked. The portrait was of a young woman, primly dressed and coiffured in the fashion of her time. Her lips were unsmiling, but the long seconds of holding the pose had not erased the laughter from her eyes.

"Oh! That was your grandmother, dear. Sally Beal before she

married your grandfather."

Karrie looked at the picture with renewed interest. Then this was her father's mother, this vivacious girl who looked as though she longed to let her hair fall free and kick off her shoes and run with the wind. *Why on earth would she marry someone like Grandfather?* Karrie wondered to herself.

"The other Beals are over there—at the end of the hall," remarked Miss Ginger with some distaste.

Karrie walked over and studied them for a minute. She found the Beals to be a collection of people who had every reason to be attractive but somehow weren't. They were neither too stout nor thin, had regular features and were well-dressed for their times, but all seemed to be looking out at her with hostile, suspicious eyes, and she didn't wonder that they'd been consigned to the darkest corner of the hallway.

"The photographers must have told them to say *tut-tut* instead of *cheese*," Karrie murmured.

Her aunts looked at each other and laughed.

"You've caught the essence of the Beals," declared Miss Ginger. "Good for nothing but spying on their neighbors and gossiping over the back fence! And they never change!"

"Now Ginger!" protested Miss Prune.

"Oh, Prune, it's the truth! Karen can't feel any kinship with those people. Besides, the present-day Beals are so distantly connected to her that it doesn't count anyway."

"But my grandmother doesn't look like that," said Karrie.

"No, Sally was different. She was a lively little fox."

"Ginger!" admonished Miss Prune softly.

Karrie walked around and reexamined all the family portraits. She paused before the two that had always intrigued her the most. They were obviously the oldest ones on the wall and had faded to a pale sepia. Only the eyes of the subjects stared out distinctly.

"Your great-great-grandparents, Matthew and Prudence Webster," said Miss Prune. "They were the ones who built this house."

"Did you know them?" asked Karrie.

"We knew our grandmother, Prudence," said Miss Ginger. "Your aunt Prune was named for her."

"Well, actually, dear, for both my grandmothers. My mother's mother was Nell. So Mamma and Papa came up with Prunella. I do think they might have given that a little more thought—"

"Oh, nonsense, Prune!" said Miss Ginger briskly. "It's a perfectly good name. You should feel honored! Both our grandmothers were splendid pioneer women. Especially Grannie Prudence. She was a force to be reckoned with!"

"She was?" Karrie peered at the dim picture intently.

"She certainly was! When she was left all alone to run the ranch and not a man in the hill country would work for her, she thumbed her nose at the bunch of them, rode down to the border and hired a crew of *vaqueros*!"

"But why wouldn't they work for her? Why was she alone?"

"She wasn't really alone," interceded Miss Prune. "Our papa was only a boy then, of course, but her mother and mother-in-law were still living."

"Some help they were!" snorted Miss Ginger. "Ailing and complaining all the time. No, it all fell on Grannie Prudence, and she was a very young woman—"

"But why wouldn't anybody work for her?"

"Why, honey, because she was from Massachusetts! Texas had just seceded from the union, you see, along with the rest of the Southern states, and it was very bad around here for anyone who came from the North."

"She was from Massachusetts?"

"Yes, didn't you know the Websters were originally from Massachusetts, dear?"

"No, I don't know anything about the Websters. Whatever made them come to *Texas*?" Karrie couldn't imagine people doing such a thing of their own free will.

"I've wondered about that myself," admitted Miss Prune.

"Grannie Prudence said it was all Matthew," said Miss

Ginger. "She never wanted to leave New England. Her father had been a ship's captain, and she'd grown up in a lovely old house looking out to sea—"

"Oh, how Grannie used to talk about that house! She was homesick for it till the day she died!"

"But—she wanted to marry Matthew. He'd been a seaman himself, but when *his* father got lost at sea, his mother made him promise he'd take her where she'd never have to look at the ocean again. Well, it was 1846 and Texas was a brand-new state, so he decided to move to Texas and raise cattle. And that's what he did."

"They all came with him—*his* mother, Prudence, *her* mother!"

"And the old ladies going at each other tooth and claw the whole way. Grannie Prudence always said that journey was nothing but a long nightmare!"

"You know that whale weather vane, honey? That belonged to Grannie Prudence's mother. Matthew's mother detested it, because it reminded her of the sea, but when Matthew built this house, the other old lady insisted on the widow's walk and the weather vane. Pretty silly for a ranch."

"Gee, imagine this place a real ranch!" said Karrie. "With horses and cattle and everything!"

"It was still a ranch when we were young, then Papa got killed trying to break that horse and Henry sold off all the livestock."

"It was a very successful ranch in its time," Miss Ginger said. "For someone who'd been a sailor, grandfather Matthew took to ranching as though he'd been born to it."

"How did *he* die?"

"Well—" Miss Ginger and Miss Prune looked at each other. It was Miss Ginger who replied.

"He didn't. Well, of course he *did* die. But how and when, no one ever knew."

There was a brief, dramatic pause. Then Miss Prune added in a hushed voice,

"Disappeared without a trace."

4.

Karrie's startled silence did not go unnoticed by her aunts. Miss Ginger, instantly realizing that their words had pointed up an unfortunate parallel between Matthew and Richard, became flustered and speechless, but Miss Prune was quick to rush into the breach.

"Grannie Prudence always swore he'd been murdered," she explained, then saw that the remark had done nothing to erase the stricken look from the girl's face. "Oh, dear. It was *those times*, you see. Feelings were running high, and a lot of the men who'd voted against the secession had to get out of Texas in a hurry."

"With good reason!" added Miss Ginger, recovering her usual demeanor. "Cabins burned down, cattle run off, men being dragged out of their homes and hanged!"

"Hard to believe it happened here!" lamented Miss Prune. "There were fine men among the frontiersmen, but there were also a good many scalawags, and they used the Civil War as an excuse for terrorizing the whole area. Bushwhackers, they were called. The German settlers had a terrible time, because they tended to be loyal to the Union. Anybody known to be against the secession was fair game. People were running for their lives!"

"What about Matthew?" asked Karrie.

"Well, most of his loyalist friends packed up their families and got together a wagon train for California, but Matthew vowed he would not be driven out of Texas."

"Now, Prune, I don't know where you got that! There you go, being romantic. He didn't vow anything. Grannie said they would have gladly left, but the two old ladies weren't up to it. They would have had to travel through hostile Indian territory!"

"So—then what happened to him?" Karrie persisted.

"Well, one day he rode off to drive his cattle to market and that was the last Grannie ever saw of him. She practically wore a hole in the floor of the widow's walk. She'd go up there and pace and pace, squinting her eyes, trying to catch sight of a cloud of dust on the horizon—"

"Oh, poor Grannie! It was so long before she could accept that he wasn't coming back! She never stopped praying, she never stopped loving him!"

"But Papa didn't feel that way. He was very bitter."

"William?" ventured Karrie, trying to keep the characters straight.

"That's right. He was—oh, twelve or thirteen then—and he took it very hard. To his dying day no one dared mention Matthew's name to him."

The aunts both sighed, lost in their reflections, and this time failing to see the effect of their words on the young girl.

"Why was he so bitter?" she asked at last.

"Why, honey," said Miss Prune, "I expect he felt his father had abandoned him. It was what everybody was saying. That after Matthew had sold off his cattle, he took the money and ran off to join the wagon train."

5.

Later that evening, Marty stuck his head into Karrie's room.

"Guess what I learned from Israel today?" he said. "Our Webster ancestors came from New England! That's why Grandfather reminds me of a cantankerous edition of Oliver Wendell Holmes!"

"I know all about our ancestors."

"Oh, you do, huh?"

"Sure. I dust their pictures every day."

"Hm-m! And the pictures confide in you!"

"Of course they do. If you want to come downstairs with me I'll introduce you to them."

"Well, okay. I suppose it's cleared out down there by now. No doubt the Ogre in Chief is holed up in his study and the aunts have retired to their respective nooks to do whatever mysterious things they do there."

"Aunt Ginger plays solitaire and Aunt Prune sews or knits."

"Figured it was something sneaky like that," said Marty, as he followed his sister down the stairs.

They found the first floor in darkness, except for a ribbon of light showing from under the study door.

"The man never sleeps," whispered Marty.

"Do we switch on the lights?" Karrie whispered back.

"No, no, this is more appropriate for meeting ghosts."

"First ghost." Karrie shone her flashlight on a portrait in the hall. "Matthew Webster, meet your great-great-grandson. Matthew says 'Hi,' Marty."

"Heard it plain as anything. The old boy who built Windy Crest, right?"

"Not such an old boy. He wasn't much older than you are when he came to Texas." Karrie directed her flashlight toward the next picture. "Prudence, his wife. Aunt Ginger says she was 'a force to be reckoned with,' so watch yourself!"

Marty smiled into the wide clear eyes of his great-great-grandmother. "I'll be good, ma'am. Why was she such a force?"

"Tell you all about it later. Here's their son William." Karrie shifted the beam to the next picture.

"I've heard of *him* all right! William the Magnificent, grandfather of Martin the Magnificent."

"The family heroes. I don't think William was so nice. He never forgave his father."

"*Never forgave?* That sounds familiar! Like someone we know but don't exactly love!"

Just then the lights went on. The mayor was standing outside his study door.

"May I ask why you're out here whispering in the dark?" he demanded.

"Karrie was introducing me to my ancestors," Marty explained.

The mayor regarded them suspiciously. "If you want to look at pictures, kindly do it in the daytime instead of skulking around the house like a pair of burglars."

"Right!" said Marty. "Didn't mean to skulk! Sorry if we frightened you." He grabbed Karrie's hand and the two of them bounded up the stairs, holding in their laughter until they reached Karrie's room.

"Do you think we really frightened him?" asked Karrie.

"Not as much as he'd like to think he frightens us," said Marty. "But I got cheated out of the complete tour. There are lots more pictures in the hall."

"Millions! But Matthew and Prudence are my favorites. Prudence is my hero!"

"Ah, yes! 'A force to be reckoned with!' So what was it she did?"

"You want the whole story?"

"Every gory detail."

"The details *are* kind of gory," said Karrie reflectively, then proceeded to recount the history of Matthew and Prudence, as the aunts had told it to her. Marty listened attentively, watching her face as she talked of Matthew's disappearance and his son William's bitterness.

"So he never mentioned his father's name again, huh? And how did Prudence feel about it?"

"Well—she was bitter, too, but not against Matthew. She never believed he deserted her and went off to California. She was convinced the other settlers murdered him. William wouldn't listen to that, but that's what she told her grandchildren."

"And what do *they* think?"

"Aunt Prune thinks Prudence was right, Grandfather thinks William was right, Aunt Ginger is on the fence, and Aunt Clara couldn't care less."

Marty laughed. "How do *you* vote?"

"Oh, I vote with Aunt Prune. She claims that Matthew never would have deserted Prudence, because they were so much in love. When they got married Prudence gave him a beautiful gold watch with a tiny portrait of her in the case, and Matthew always wore it, even when the watch stopped working. He called it his good luck charm. When he had to go out and rope steers and stuff, he'd take it off the chain, put it in a tin snuff box to protect it, and carry it in his vest pocket close to his heart."

Marty grinned, and soulfully played on an imaginary violin.

"All right, all right," said Karrie, smiling, too. "Aunt Ginger says Aunt Prune gets romantic. But even Aunt Ginger admits it's true about the watch. That doesn't sound like a man who'd run off and leave his wife, does it?"

"Maybe not. But I think I'll cast my vote with Aunt Ginger and sit on the fence till I see some evidence. Where do we look for clues, Nancy Drew?"

"Wouldn't it be fun if we could find some? Maybe we could retrace the route he took on the cattle drive!"

"Sure! What's a thousand miles, more or less, to a dauntless detective and her trusty sidekick?"

"Oh! Well—"

"For starters, how about if we climb up to the widow's walk, like Prudence, and watch for a cloud of dust? We might see the spirit of Matthew riding back, since the two of you are on such intimate terms."

"You know what, Marty? Martha told me that Dad and Uncle Martin used to take their pallets and sleep up there on hot nights. Could we do that?"

Marty smiled at his sister's enthusiasm. "Why not? The mosquitoes may eat us alive, but a good boy scout never lets a thing like that deter him."

"Don't tell anyone, though. Aunt Ginger doesn't think the widow walk's safe, but I sneaked up for a minute this morning and it's solid as the Rock of Gibraltar."

"We won't tell a soul. Not a *living* soul, anyway. This is strictly between us and the ghosts."

It was good to see her having fun again, Marty thought. He dreaded having to spoil it. But the mayor was right, of course. She had to be told.

Tonight, he resolved.

6.

Karrie and Marty, each carrying a rolled-up quilt and a pillow, carefully mounted the ladder that led up to the widow's walk.

"Are you *sure* this thing is safe?" asked Marty.

"It's fine," Karrie insisted. Her hand groped for the latch to the trapdoor. "Help me push this open, Marty. I had a hard time with it this morning."

Marty reached a long, strong arm past her shoulder and the trapdoor yielded to their combined efforts. Karrie stuck her head up through the opening and stared.

"*Wow!* The stars look so enormous in Texas!"

"Everything's enormous in Texas," said Marty, still below her on the ladder. "There are cockroaches as big as mice out in the barn. Hey, move along there, lady. I want to get off this ladder."

Karrie scrambled up onto the platform and dropped her quilt and pillow. Marty was right behind her.

"*Wow!*" he echoed.

The two of them stood and gazed at the sky together. It was a moonless night, and there was no man-made light to diminish the brilliance of the stars.

"Have you ever seen anything so spectacular?" asked Karrie.

"A long time ago, in South America. We were on a trip with Dad, before Mom got sick. You were too young to remember."

"But I think I do! It's like remembering a dream. It gives me the shivers! Think of Dad and Uncle Martin up here, looking at that sky. I wonder if Dad's looking at the sky tonight."

"Karrie, we have to try not to wonder too much."

"This morning, the aunts said that Matthew—'disappeared without a trace.' Those were Aunt Prune's exact words, Marty."

"Okay, I know. It started you thinking about Dad."

"Not just Dad. Opi, too. Everybody just—disappears. It's like both sides of our family are under a curse or something."

"Come on, Karrie, don't do this. Opi—Well, we may never know what happened to him. He's probably dead. But I believe Dad's alive. I have this feeling I'd know it if he wasn't."

"Martha said something like that."

"Bless Martha. She'll always stand by you, Karrie."

"If he'd just get word to us—"

"You know he would, if it were possible. I think we have to

accept the fact that we're not going to hear from him till the war's over. We have to go on living our lives, Karrie, the way he would want us to."

"But I have to *talk* about him sometimes. I hate not talking about him. The way they act around here, he never existed—he's just a lie we made up. Well, Martha doesn't act that way."

"Or Israel. You have two good friends there."

Karrie looked at him curiously. "So aren't they your friends, too?"

"Sure they are! But hey, come on! I thought we came up here to concentrate on your buddy, Matthew. So how do we solve this eighty-year-old mystery? Conduct a seance?"

Karrie responded readily to his change of tone. "Well, *I'd* like to, but you wouldn't be serious and you'd spoil it. I think we ought to look for clues."

She walked carefully over to the railing and gripped it firmly before looking up again. "It makes me lightheaded. The sky is so immense! Okay, then, if you had to drive cattle to market, which way do you think you'd go?"

Marty joined her at the railing. "I think I'd go look for another job! What do you have in mind?"

"I don't know! I thought we'd just try to follow his route—just a mile or so—and see if we turn up something."

"What?"

"*I don't know*! Good grief! We'll find *something*—you'll see! You've been touring all over the place with Israel. What's over that way?" Karrie pointed into the darkness.

"Let's see—that's east. The highway, the cedar grove, the lumber mill. And the bustling metropolis of Hospitality, the county seat, is about five miles down the road."

"What about over there?"

"Well, that's west. So we have the dam, which, of course, wasn't there in Matthew's time. Ah! Therein lies a problem. The dam construction could have wiped out all clues."

Karrie was unperturbed. "Okay. He didn't go that way."

Marty laughed. "You're real sure of that?"

"Of course. Now where are the caves Dad and Uncle Martin used to explore?"

"Under Squaw Mountain, about two miles to the southwest." Marty indicated the direction with a sweep of his hand. "They call the hills 'mountains' around here. I wonder what they'd call the Rockies?"

"But the caves are still there?"

"Oh, yes. Israel said the dam changed a lot of scenery, but Dead Man's Caverns are just as they always were."

"Dead Man's Caverns? Really? That's where we'll start! First thing tomorrow morning!"

"Whoa! Dark, spooky caves? Have you forgotten your celebrated claustrophobia? I seem to recall a couple of times when somebody *showed the white feather*!"

"Oh, come on, that's not fair! I was ten years old! You would have bellowed, too, if a mean old witch had shut you up in a closet!"

"But it was worth it, wasn't it? Said mean old witch was our very *last* housekeeper! I never saw Dad so livid."

"That was a really horrible experience, Marty, you don't— Oh, phooey! It's ancient history!"

"Um-m-m. There was a more recent occurrence, in a stalled elevator—"

"Oh, *please*! Caves are different. We'll take a flashlight, and if you don't play any mean tricks on me, I'll be fine."

"Who, me? You must have me confused with my evil twin. No tricks, I promise. If *you* promise not to indulge in an attack of nerves."

"I'll be brave as Natty Bumppo!"

"I see you've been dipping into Dad's old books. Okay. We'll take on Dead Man's Caverns. But we'll have to put it off for a couple of days. I go for my driving test tomorrow morning, and it'll be too hot by afternoon."

"Oh, you and your silly driving! If only they still kept horses here, we could go galloping off to Dead Man's Caverns. Imagine coming to a ranch in Texas and not having horses to ride! Horses would have made a big difference in my attitude, Marty."

"His Honor doesn't care for animals."

"His Honor doesn't care for anything or anybody."

"Um—maybe. But if he's willing to put up with us, we can learn to put up with him. The important thing is to have a good life in spite of him."

Karrie stared at him, but couldn't read his expression in the dark. "You make it sound *permanent*. If I start thinking it's *permanent* I may just lie down and die!"

"Nothing's permanent," said Marty lightly. "Here today, gone tomorrow. Listen, are you serious about sleeping up here?"

"Oh, yes! Let's fix our pallets." She immediately set about shaking out her quilt and folding it to make a bed. "I haven't met any mosquitoes so far, have you?"

"Guess they don't fancy our Yankee blood. Hey, this is kind of swell." Marty was lying on his back on his folded quilt and looking up at the sky.

"We can do this every night," said Karrie happily. "Except that it may be hard to get to sleep. It's so overwhelming! I remember how at camp all us girls would lie and look up at the stars and ask each other things like *what's outside of space?*—until we got scared and dizzy. I feel a little like that now."

"This doesn't seem much like camp to me. I don't hear an owl or a frog or anything. It's so quiet, have you noticed? Not even the windmill's stirring."

"It's hard to believe that battles are being fought all over the world right now while we're lying here. The war seems so much farther away in Texas."

"It does. No officious little men in hard hats banging on the door and ordering us to close the blackout curtains, no rumors of U-boats lurking off Long Island! Around here you wouldn't know there was a war on if it weren't for rationing."

"It scares me to think you could be drafted in January."

"Karrie—"

"Maybe it won't happen. Mr. Appleby was saying to Aunt Prune the other day that the war will be over in less than a year now that we're in it."

"Karrie, Mr. Appleby's still living back in World War I. We've taken a terrible walloping from the Japanese."

"But you said the battle of Midway turned it around."

"Yes, but we've got a long way to go, in the Pacific and in Europe, too."

"Could we talk about Matthew again, Marty? When we talk about the war I wonder about Dad, and you said not to do that. Let's plan how we're going to search for clues." Karrie yawned. "Is that Draco over there, Marty? Or is it the Little Dipper? I never can tell one from the other." She yawned again, then continued lazily, "This smarty-pants at camp used to say, 'Can't you see the dragon's tail, dummy?' Tell me the truth, Marty, do you see a tail?"

"Look, Karrie, we have to talk a little about the war. You don't like to think about me going into the service, but you know it has to happen. I wish you had a friend your own age. Maybe you'll get to know that Baby Whatshername better.

"Of course you'll have Martha and Israel, and I think the aunts are becoming genuinely fond of you. As for Grandfather, well, he's not exactly lovable, but he's going to take care of you—I'm sure of that.

"You have to understand something. If a guy gets drafted he doesn't have much say about where they stick him. I want to be a hospital corpsman in the Navy. It'll be good experience for the future, when I go to medical school, and—Well, it's just what I really want to do. I'd rather patch people up than blow them to pieces. So—try not to be too sore at me—I've already done it. I've enlisted, Karrie."

Marty stared at the stars and waited in the darkness for his sister's response. Her even, shallow breathing was the only perceptible sound in the quietness of the night.

Karrie was asleep.

7.

"Are you going to allow her to go into town tonight dressed

like that?" the mayor demanded of his sisters.

"I don't like it either, Henry," said Miss Prune, "but times do change, and there's no point in the older generation fighting it. Young people don't like to look different, you know."

The mayor regarded his granddaughter dourly. She had just come downstairs wearing Baby Dodds's spiffy pair of almost-brand-new-shorts and a halter top which, with a little help from Martha, she had sewn for herself.

"Hrmmph," commented the mayor. "If this is the uniform of the young woman of the forties, I shudder to think what's in store for us in the fifties."

And with that, he disappeared into his study. Karrie shrugged her shoulders, and Marty laughed.

"You look fine, squirt," he said. "Ever so Texan. Come along now. We'll drop Martha and Israel off at their house, and I'll drive you into town for your rendezvous with the belles of Benbenitas. This is my maiden voyage as a licensed driver."

"Are you nervous?" asked Miss Prune anxiously.

"All a-flutter," Marty assured her.

"What is the picture show you're seeing?" Miss Ginger asked Karrie.

"*Mrs. Miniver*," replied Karrie. "Jolene said it was supposed to be good. And she particularly mentioned that *you'd* like it, Marty."

"Not on your life!" declared Marty. "I've been promising Mr. Wirtz a game of checkers. After the movie, you can come over to the barber shop and we'll drive home."

"Jolene will be crushed," remarked Karrie with satisfaction. "The only reason she asked me was to get to you."

"Now Karen, that's not worthy of you," scolded Miss Ginger. "I'm quite sure Jolene invited you because she likes you. It was very thoughtful of her to include Martin in the invitation."

Karrie rolled her eyes at her brother.

"I saw that!" Miss Ginger said sternly. "That's the same as making a sassy remark!"

"Have a nice time, dear," said Miss Prune in a conciliatory

voice. "And Martin, you drive *carefully*, hear?"

With mumbled goodbyes, the young people went out the door. Miss Prune and Miss Ginger stood at the window and watched the Packard head off down the long driveway. Miss Ginger chuckled.

"The clothes they wear may be different these days," she said, "but some things remain the same. Remember how Sally Beal tried to be your friend just so she could get close to Henry?"

"One thing you can count on," said Miss Prune. "There'll always be a Sally Beal."

Marty kept the conversation lighthearted as they drove into town. Karrie was already grumpy about the prospect of an evening with the cheerleaders, and he didn't feel it was a good time to try again to spring the news of his enlistment on her. If it turned out that she had fun in spite of herself, then he'd tackle the subject on the ride home.

When they pulled up in front of the Bijou he remarked, "There they are, madame—your ladies in waiting! The dazzling Jolene and her coterie!"

There they were indeed. All the girls who had occupied Jolene Ross's front porch on that dreadful morning two weeks earlier were waiting on the sidewalk outside the theater. They were all wearing blouses, gathered skirts, saddle shoes and bobby-socks, and, to Karrie's amazement, they carried sweaters over their arms.

Jolene, seeing Marty, smiled radiantly. "Oh—*hi-i*!" she called.

"Hi!" replied Marty, with a polite smile and a careless wave, then drove away.

Jolene looked devastated. "I thought he was coming," she said to Karrie.

"He has a date to play checkers with Mr. Wirtz," Karrie explained, her pleasure at Jolene's disappointment considerably dampened by the knowledge that she was dressed all wrong again. "I'm supposed to walk over to the barber shop after the movie."

"That's where I live," Snookie Wirtz told her. "My mamma and me moved in with my granddaddy above the barber shop when my daddy went off to work in California." She turned to the crestfallen Jolene and said, "Tell you what, Jolene, y'all can just walk me home tonight!" and that person brightened considerably.

Baby Dodds was eyeing Karrie and the almost-brand-new shorts.

"Girl, you're going to freeze to death," she predicted. "Don't they air-condition the picture shows in New York City?"

The "picture show" in Benbenitas was air-conditioned to a fare-thee-well, Karrie discovered. Even the girls in sweaters were shivering, and Karrie, in her shorts and halter top, felt chilled to the bone. She was sitting between Jolene and Baby Dodds, who each took pity on her and draped an empty sweater sleeve around her shoulders.

Eventually she adjusted to the wintry conditions enough to become absorbed in the story of a family in London during the blitz. She refused to cry, suffering a painful lump in her throat instead, but when the picture ended and the lights went up, she saw that all of her companions had tears running down their cheeks.

Outside again, wrapped in the welcoming dry heat of the evening, the girls laughed sheepishly as they swabbed at their eyes.

"Oh, mercy, I haven't cried like that since I read *Black Beauty*!" said Jolene.

"You didn't tell me it was a *war* movie," moaned Bettie Rae. "They just tear me to pieces."

"Why did they have to kill off so many people?" wailed Joycie.

"It was the blitz, dummy. People got killed," Sister Bee said, then she turned to Karrie. "Weren't you in London during the blitz?"

Startled, Karrie opened her mouth to respond, but Jolene cut in. "Sister Bee, honestly! Who've you been talking to—Shirleen Haus or Mr. Wilkins?"

"Party line," chirped Joycie. "Sister Bee spends as much time listening in as Mamma does."

"I do not!" snapped Sister Bee.

"I've lived in New York all my life," said Karrie quietly. "I don't know where that London stuff came from."

"What I heard was Paris," said Bev. "I swan, they just make these things up!"

"The first thing my mamma taught me was, don't ever believe a word you hear on the party line," said Baby Dodds. "Folks don't have anything to do around here but gossip."

"If we ever get private lines, like they have in Austin, people'll just die of boredom!" said Jolene.

"Well, hel-*lo*, ladies! Don't they look sweet now?" The insinuating voice could only belong to Bucko Riddle. He and three other boys emerged from the shadows of the darkened storefront of Mrs. Schulman's Bread and Cakes.

The girls were momentarily startled, but they kept walking except for Baby Dodds, who turned around, hands on hips, and faced the four boys.

"Bubbabill," she said sternly, "what do you think you're doing, lurking around that store when it's closed?"

"Who's lurking?" grumbled the tallest of the boys. "None of your dadgum business, anyway."

Bucko chortled. "Little sister got to keep an eye out for you, Bubbabill. Gonna run home and tell your mommy on you!"

"Couldn't care less *who* she tells *what*," Bubbabill asserted manfully.

Baby Dodds threw up her hands in disgust, and ran to catch up with her friends.

"Baby Dodds, how come your brother started hanging out with that bunch?" Jolene demanded.

"*I* don't know!" replied Baby Dodds with an exasperated sigh. "You can bet he wouldn't be doing it if my daddy was around. He just won't listen to Mamma. She says if Daddy don't send for us soon she's gonna have to lock that boy in the outhouse to make him behave."

"Her daddy's out in California with mine," Snookie explained to Karrie. "They're working in this airplane factory and making real good money, but they can't send for us till they find places for us to live."

"And there aren't any places," added Baby Dodds, gloomily. "I've about given up on moving to California."

"Not me! I can't wait!" said Snookie. "Oh, Lordy, are they gonna follow us?"

Bucko and the other boys were just a few yards behind them.

"Hey, yankee-girl!" sneered Bucko. "If my legs was that skinny, I'd be right scared of striking out on them!"

Karrie had had enough for one night. She whirled around and snapped, "And if my head were that empty, I'd be *right scared* of opening my mouth!"

"Oh, whoa! Ain't she feisty now?" said Bucko, falling back and putting a hand over his heart. "Hey, Bubbabill, ain't you ashamed to have your little sister hang around with a kid whose daddy's a Nazi spy?"

Karrie stared at him speechlessly. Baby Dodds tugged at one of her arms and Snookie the other. They turned her around and got her walking again. The boys trailed after them, howling like banshees as they passed by the dark, burned-out section of the square, but when they approached the lighted storefront of the barber shop, the tormentors dropped back and headed off in another direction. The girls breathed with relief.

"Lordy, they are so *gruesome*! Why do they always have to ruin the evening for us?" lamented Bettie Rae.

"I'm just glad they weren't at the picture show," said Joycie. "Talking real loud and throwing spitballs. I *hate* that!"

"Where'd he get that about your daddy, Karrie?" asked Bev.

"Out of his own warped mind," declared Baby Dodds.

"Yeah, I mean—what would make him say something like that about your daddy when your brother just enlisted in the Navy, for gosh sakes?" Bev went on.

"Because he likes to talk mean!" said Snookie.

"Just don't you let him get your goat, Karrie with a K," said Jolene soothingly. "Your brother's a hero and Bucko Riddle is *scum*."

At that moment, Marty walked out of the barber shop, smiling his charming, nonchalant smile. Hot as the evening was, Karrie shivered all over as she stood facing him.

"I hate you, Martin Webster!" she blurted out. "I'll never, *ever* forgive you!"

8.

The day Marty was to leave, Karrie sat on the window seat in his room, hugging a cushion while she somberly watched him pack a small knapsack.

"Is that all you're taking?" she asked.

"The Navy's promised me a swell new wardrobe, from skivvies out," he explained cheerfully, "and Dad's old clothes are on their way to Bundles for Britain."

Karrie was silent for a moment, then she mumbled, "It's just not fair!"

"Karrie, listen! War's not fair. I'm not going off on some madcap adventure. We all have to do what we can. Including you, ma'am. *They also serve who only*...and all that stuff."

"If I have to *stand and wait*, why does it have to be here? Why not in New York? I would've been all right!"

"Hey, hang it up now, squirt! Time to pull yourself up by your little Yankee bootstraps and make the best of it. What's done is done—even if you *do* hate me!"

"I told you I didn't mean that!"

"Well, it was in keeping with the family tradition. *I'll Never Forgive You* is probably emblazoned on the Webster coat of arms."

Karrie covered her face with the cushion. "I was just—so furious! Everybody in town knew you'd enlisted, except me."

"That's the mystery! Nobody was in on it outside of the people in this house, and they're not what you'd call a bunch of blabbermouths. Do you suppose the ubiquitous Lollie Beal was lurking about the recruiting station in Hospitality? Grandfather warned me, but I put off telling you and really botched things up. Behaved like a craven coward. Not my usual style at all."

"No, it wasn't! You've always told me the truth. That's why I—but I *do* forgive you, I guess."

"Good! I'm back in the will! For a while there, I was afraid I'd be cut off with a shilling."

"Marty—you jerk—you haven't even left yet and I'm homesick for you."

"I've got a touch of that myself. But I know it's easier to be the one going than the one who has to stay. Look, I'll write every day and you promise to do the same. I'll expect plenty of adjectives and direct quotes—the full flavor of Benbenitas, okay?"

"The full flavor of Benbenitas! That's about the last thing in the world—! Oh, golly, what am I going to do in this awful place on my own? I was counting on you! When Dad didn't come back, you said—you *promised*—you'd take care of me!"

"I know, squirt—but the usual rules have to be suspended for the duration. There *is* somebody you can count on, though."

"Please! Don't say *Grandfather*!"

"No, no. *You*. Squirty old Karrie Webster." He poked a finger at her. "You're a tough little kid and don't you forget it. You can make it through anything and come up aces."

Karrie shook her head. Her throat felt tight and dry. Even if she could have found words to express all of the scared, lonely things that were in her heart, there was no time. The mayor was bellowing from downstairs: "The train won't wait!"

As it turned out, they arrived at the station with only minutes to spare. There were two other boys waiting on the platform—two well-scrubbed, gangly youths who didn't look old enough to shave, much less go to war, but it was obvious from the stoic cheerfulness of the families seeing them off that that was indeed where they were headed.

The train came clanging in on schedule. Marty quickly hugged his great-aunts, shook hands with his grandfather and

Israel, then turned to his little sister. He grinned at her and roughly tousled her hair.

"Keep a lamp in the window, squirt," he said. Then, on the heels of the other boys, he swung on board the train, which promptly began to rattle away down the tracks.

The depot agent and the families left behind stood together and watched till it was out of sight. Mr. Peevy broke the silence.

"They're going off every day now," he observed wistfully. "Pretty soon there ain't going to be any young fellers left in town."

Twenty-five years earlier Mrs. Tulla Swenson had watched her son depart on that very same train, and just now she'd bid her oldest grandson goodbye. She patted Miss Prune on the shoulder and sighed.

"Oh Prune, who would have thought we'd have to go through this twice in a lifetime?"

At that, the stricken expression on the mayor's face caused a chill to run down Karrie's spine. She didn't want to guess—oh, she didn't even want to guess what he was thinking!

It was a subdued group that drove back to Windy Crest that afternoon. When they entered the house, Karrie went directly up to her room. The mayor retired to his study and closed the door. His sisters attempted conversation, but soon gave it up, and each went her separate way. Israel found Martha, who had said good-bye to Marty at home, crying over the dinner dishes in the kitchen.

The remainder of the afternoon had to be gotten through, and eventually there was supper. No one had much appetite, and soon they all dispersed again.

As evening darkened, Karrie lay on her cot and stared dry-eyed at the ceiling. Finally she rolled over, buried her face in the pillow, and began to sob raggedly. When she heard the sound of someone entering the room, she didn't move, but tried to check her tears. A broad, warm hand gently rubbed her back.

"It's all right, baby," said Martha. "*I'm* here."

Chapter 4
Alone

For one pleasant second Karrie forgot she was not in her own
bed. She stretched and opened her eyes, then, fully awake, turned
over and buried her face in the pillow. This wasn't New York—it
was Texas—and she was trapped in a house of elderly people who
didn't know what to do with her.

Why bother to get up?

She knew exactly what awaited her downstairs: grouchy old
man, cheerful aunts, same old suggestion, "Why not ride downtown with your grandfather today?" No, *thank you*! She *hated*
riding in that car. And what on earth was there to do downtown? "You might call up Baby Dodds."

Just great! Baby Dodds was a nice enough girl in her way,
but the two of them had absolutely nothing in common.

Karrie sighed heavily. Marty had really scolded her in his last
letter.

"What do you think great-great-grandmother Prudence would
say to all this 'poor little me' stuff? Bet she'd pop back from the
grave and spank your bottom. That lady was left alone in a far
hairier situation, and she became A Force To Be Reckoned With.
That, my squirt, is exactly what I expect of you!

"For starters, how about giving the belles of Bienvenidos half

77

a chance? You might actually discover a kindred spirit among them. And what's happened to the old zest for adventure? For a change, I'd like to hear what you're *doing*, not what you're *feeling*. Unless you're feeling fine.

"Hey—Uncle Sam expects you to cheer me up—remember?"

As if Marty ever needed cheering up! Boot camp was supposed to be a tough experience, but he found it as entertaining as he found everything else in life. She wished she could be that way, too, but she wasn't, and she just couldn't help it.

All right, she thought wearily, as she got out of bed at last. In her next letter she'd write about something she'd *done*. But what? *Not* going downtown to the movies with Baby Dodds! What she needed was a real adventure.

Well, she couldn't hitch up a wagon and ride to the border like great-great-grandmother Prudence. There weren't even any horses! It seemed to Karrie that all the likely adventures to be had in Benbenitas disappeared when Packards were invented.

2.

After breakfast, Karrie quickly did her household chores, then slipped out the kitchen door and headed toward the hills.

The morning air was fresh and sparkling. Birds called to one another from mesquite trees, and soft, warm breezes set off the lonely grind of windmills across the valley. But after a while, as the sun began to climb, the breeze died down and the bird calls became infrequent.

Karrie, following an ill-defined trail through high dusty weeds, took little notice of anything. She trudged on glumly, chanting under her breath,

> "Tell me not in mournful numbers,
>   Life is but an empty dream!"

Longfellow was good for setting a pace, she reflected, wiping the perspiration from her brow with the back of her hand.

ALONE

"Life is real! Life is earnest!
And the grave is not its goal;
Dust thou art, to dust returneth
Was not spoken of the soul..."

The day was becoming hotter and the trail rougher. She glanced at her watch. *Ten o'clock!* She'd left the house around half past eight. Hadn't Marty said that Dead Man's Caverns were two miles southwest of Windy Crest? She must have walked twice that in an hour and a half.

Marty usually got things right, but it was hard to gauge distance in this open country. In New York it was easy: one mile equaled twenty city blocks—a pleasant stroll from Central Park South to the Metropolitan Museum.

"This was a really dumb idea," she muttered, wheeling around and heading back the way she'd come. She'd make it home just in time to help Martha prepare the vegetables for dinner, and no one would be the wiser. Next time, she'd make sure she knew exactly where she was going, and would certainly bring a canteen of water.

Thank goodness she'd at least had enough sense to filch Aunt Prune's wide-brimmed gardening hat from its hook on the kitchen porch, she thought, as her foot pushed aside something on the trail. She stopped short and stared at the object. A skull!

Karrie had never before seen a real skull, except under glass in the Museum of Natural History. She looked at it closely. It was too big, probably, to have belonged to a squirrel or a rat. A jack rabbit? Israel had told her all about the long-eared, long-legged jack rabbits of Texas, but she had yet to see one. Maybe this was a jack rabbit's skull—but why hadn't she noticed it there before?

She hesitated, hardly daring to wonder if she could somehow have drifted onto a different trail. All at once it seemed urgent to get home as soon as possible. If she walked swiftly, perhaps it wouldn't take another hour and a half. Oh, for a tall glass of ice water, she thought, or a *whole pitcher* of Martha's lemonade!

Martha always apologized for scrimping on sugar, but that was the way Karrie liked it best—slightly tart and thirst-quenching.

She tramped onward, trying to remember poems she knew and muttering snatches of them.

> "Stand straight, step firmly, throw your weight.
> The heavens are high above your head,
> The good gray road is faithful to your tread..."

How lovely that sounded! Oh, she longed for a good gray road lined with big shade trees—somewhere in upstate New York, perhaps, where she used to go to summer camp before her mom died and her dad went away.

This ragged, overgrown path was not faithful to her tread. No one would write a poem about *this* place!

After a while, she stopped again and looked around her. The landscape was unfamiliar, and the uncertain trail she'd been following had finally died in the weeds. The sun beat down through Aunt Prune's straw hat and she could feel her scalp burning. She looked at her arms and legs and saw that they had turned quite red.

"I must have already been lost when I saw the rabbit skull," she reflected. "Now I'm twice as lost. But if I retrace my steps to where I was lost the *first* time, then I won't be as lost as I am right now."

This suspect logic was making her head whirl, but she knew she had to keep moving. "Back to the skull!" she urged herself, and began to sing bravely,

> "A hundred bottles of beer on the wall,
> A hundred bottles of beer—
> Take one down, pass it around—
> Ninety-nine bottles of beer on the wall..."

She thought about the day she'd learned that silly song. It didn't seem so long ago, yet at the same time it seemed *forever* ago—in another life. She'd been a little kid, at camp. The counselors—two high school girls who seesawed between hilarity and hysteria—had taken the group of eight-year-olds on a hike. On the return trek, when they were still a long way from camp, the children became tired and cranky, and some of them cried (but not Karrie, she recalled with a little pride). The frantic, giggling counselors kept their weary charges going by teaching them that song.

Karrie felt as exhausted now as she had then. Only that had been in a *green* place, and they'd all had canteens of water—and she hadn't been alone.

"Keep up the pace, keep up the pace," the counselors had urged. "The faster you walk, the sooner you'll get back."

"Forty-nine bottles of beer on the wall,
Forty-nine bottles of beer..."

But now she was keeping up the pace and going nowhere. This was not the path with the skull. This was not a path at all. She was lost. Really lost.

The sun was directly overhead. She looked at her watch. Twelve o'clock! She had been walking for three and a half hours. The table would be set at Windy Crest. The aunts would be cross, would complain that it was inconsiderate of her to be late. Halfway through dinner they'd start to worry. Israel would set out to find her. Only he wouldn't know where to look.

With some surprise, Karrie realized that she could die out there. There was not a single tree to shade her, no water, and little chance of rescue.

Dust thou art, to dust returneth... The words went through her mind again and sent a chill down her spine. Suddenly they spoke of something very real and possible. By the time anyone found her, she might be nothing but clean, dry bones like that jack rabbit.

She had to get out of that sun. Whether she lived or died, she had to get out of that sun. There was a craggy hill some distance ahead. If she could make it that far, there might at least be a rock big enough to crawl under.

Beyond exhaustion now, she trudged on, tripping on stones and occasionally falling, scratching and bloodying her sunburned legs. Brilliant colors flashed across her eyes. One foot in front of the other—nothing else mattered.

Finally she reached the hill, and, scrambling almost blindly over the rocks, she searched for *something*—anything she could crawl under—but there was nothing—nothing. Dropping to her knees, she surrendered herself to searing heat, pounding head, mouth of cotton. Her throbbing eyes closed and her face came to rest on the burning surface of a rock. She lifted her head quickly and opened her eyes halfway—then all the way, wide. She was looking down—down into a shallow canyon, down into clear, sparkling water.

Whether she climbed or slid down the almost smooth canyon wall, she was never able to remember afterwards. Whatever way she managed to get there, she was soon in the water, drinking it, splashing it all over her burning body, and then drinking it again. After a minute or two, her swimming eyes discerned a shaded spot, and she stumbled to it, sank down, and began to shudder violently.

Good, she thought. She was not going to die after all.

3.

Karrie slept. Crouched beneath the sheltering rock, she slept the blazing afternoon away, and when she awoke, rather suddenly, she found herself staring at an incongruous sight. Neatly arranged on a jutting rock that formed a natural shelf was a child's china tea set—plates, cups and saucers, and a fat little teapot.

She shifted position and reached out to take a cup, but as her sunbaked fingers tried to grasp the small object, it fell to the rocks and shattered.

A sense of shock and regret caused her to sit back and remain motionless for a moment. Then she held out her hands and stared at them, hardly recognizing the fat, red things as her own. Her arms and legs were in the same condition, and she was aware of a steady, dull ache in her head.

Her watch showed the time to be 1:47, but a faint rosy streak on the horizon told her that it was much, much later. It was nearly twilight. She had been away from home all day, it would soon be growing dark, and where on earth was she?

"Somewhere in Texas," she said out loud. Her voice sounded startling and obtrusive in the silence, and she felt vaguely apologetic. But no—this place had to be accustomed to human voices—*children's* voices, she thought, as she gazed at the dainty dishes. And if this was a place where children came, then it couldn't be too far from *somewhere*.

Bending down, she cupped her hands and took a drink of the fresh, cold water. How abundantly good it was! It had to be the most delicious water in the entire world!

Then, in the fading light, she looked around at the haven that had sheltered her all afternoon. She was sitting beneath an overhanging rock, not far from the entrance to a cave. Her first thought was that she had accidentally found Dead Man's Caverns after all, but when she got up to explore, she discovered that the cave was only a few feet deep, hardly more than a recess in side of the canyon, cooled by the spring water that seeped from a crevice in its back wall. The water gently rippled over the rocks and dallied in the sparkling pool that had given Karrie drink, then it continued onward in a thinner stream.

Standing transfixed at the mouth of the little cave, Karrie was suddenly filled with a curious sense of peace and home-coming, yet she knew she had to leave, and without delay. If she waited till morning she would have to face that relentless sun.

She paused to gently touch the little teapot and to admire its delicate floral decoration. Whose dishes could they be? They were clean, not dusty, so they must have been used recently, and yet they seemed like something out of the past, too fragile for modern-day children. She looked remorsefully at the shattered teacup lying among the rocks. Then she knelt, and with stiff, clumsy fingers, she carefully picked up the pieces one by one, and laid them next to the other dishes on the rock shelf. It was the only way she could think of to leave the message: "I'm sorry."

Then she stood up and looked toward the hills where the sun had almost completely set. It would be dark in no time at all. The fear that had gripped her earlier in the day was stealing back. She was no stranger to being alone and afraid. She could remember long, dark city blocks, derelicts slumped in doorways, stirring as she hurried by; she could remember subway cars almost empty except for her, and someone down at the very end, looking at her—

But this was different, this kind of being alone—being *really* alone. It wasn't likely there was any *person* to fear out there, only the big, empty land, and the night coming on.

Which way to go? "If you get lost, follow the path of the water," was what her camp counselors used to say.

She set forth again, following the stream, and in spite of her aching head and painful sunburn, she soon forgot to be afraid. Something of what she'd experienced in the little cave remained with her. Never in her life had she felt so whole, and free, and exhilarated.

The words *Dust thou art, to dust returneth* came into her mind again, and she thought about the rabbit skull and was interested to find that she could think of herself as being like that rabbit with no sense of horror. Out there on her own, she was a part of the dust, the meandering stream, and the vastness of the twilight.

Darkness was lowering when the trail of water trickled to its final destination, a pond beneath a lonely stand of trees. Karrie halted there, too, wondering what to do next. Should she spend the night by the pond, follow the stream back to the cave, or keep going? The evening star was out, and soon it would be impossible to see the outlines of the hills against the sky.

She sat down and thought it over. Sailors navigated by the

stars, but even if she were able to do that, it wouldn't help her much. North, south, east, west—she would have no idea which direction to choose.

But—something about the pond and group of trees—

Suddenly she was on her feet, scanning the darkening horizon. She could make out a windmill, and there, on the crest of a hill, looking for all the world as though it were about to take off and fly away, was the dark shape of a tall house topped by a widow's walk. And, as Karrie began running, she saw, one by one, the lights go on in every window.

4.

"Well, you got off easy this time, little lady," Dr. Ross said, as he snapped his satchel closed.

"Boy-highty, are you going to *peel*," Jolene remarked. She had insisted upon accompanying her father when he was summoned to Windy Crest that evening.

"But that's about all," said Dr. Ross reassuringly. "Your sunburn's going to hurt for two or three days, then you'll be fine. Could have been a lot worse—in fact, I don't know why it wasn't. Miss Prune tells me you were gone all day."

Karrie was stretched out on the cot in her room, rigid with pain and humiliation. She had no desire to discuss the day's misadventures, especially in the unwarranted presence of Jolene, but some explanation to Dr. Ross seemed to be called for.

"I—I wasn't in the sun all that time," she said. "I—found shelter in a cave."

"A cave?" said Jolene. "Gol-lee, girl—don't you know we have rattlesnakes out here?"

Rattlesnakes? Karrie looked up with definite interest. Not once during the entire day had she considered the possibility of snakes.

"All's well that ends well," concluded Dr. Ross. "I'll just look in on the mayor again before I go."

Jolene started to follow her father out the door, then paused on the threshold and stood pensively twisting a golden lock around a well-manicured finger.

"Hey, there, Karrie spelled with a K, hear from your brother much or not?" she finally asked.

Karrie sighed. She was in no mood to deal with Jolene Ross and her ridiculous crush on Marty. "He writes every day," she replied.

"Really? He must be *lonely*! They say the boys really look forward to mail call. Think I should write to him, or what?"

Just go away, Karrie thought. "Sure, Jolene," she said. "See if there's an envelope with his address on it there on desk."

Jolene all but fell upon the desk and seized the envelope eagerly. "Here it is!" she cried, then flashed her brilliant smile at the suffering girl on the bed. "Oh, well, I'm going to go on and write to him, then. You know, tell him all the news, maybe some funny things to cheer him up. Think he'd like a snapshot— to tack up, you know, the way they do?"

"Uh—*Sure*, Jolene," said Karrie.

"Well, Daddy just took some real good pictures of me. Okay then, you get better soon, hear? We'll go to the show or something next week."

With a wave of her graceful hand she was gone at last, but Karrie was not left alone for long. Miss Prune and Miss Ginger, both looking surprisingly grim, came into the room together.

"It seems you'll live," said Miss Ginger curtly.

Karrie was bewildered. When she had appeared at the door that evening, she'd been met with nothing but enormous relief and solicitude. They had helped her up to her room, gently rubbed her flaming limbs with a soothing ointment, and given her periodic sips of ice water. Then she'd been left to doze until Dr. Ross showed up. Now that he'd declared her all right, it seemed they were going to be angry with her after all.

"I—I'm really sorry I worried you," she said. "I thought I'd be home before noon, but I got lost. I didn't know it was so easy to get lost around here."

"If you had informed someone where you were going, we would have known where to search," said Miss Ginger flatly. "As it was, we were flying off in all directions. We didn't know *what* had become of you."

"I won't do it again," Karrie promised humbly.

"Indeed you won't," declared Miss Ginger. "We're going to have some rules around here and they're going to be obeyed, young lady!"

And she turned on her heel and left the room. Miss Prune remained, but her demeanor was so uncharacteristically stern that Karrie found it difficult to meet her eyes.

"Aunt Prune, I don't know what else I can say."

Miss Prune pulled the desk chair over next to the bed and sat down. "Honey, you've got to understand that we're just a family of old people here. We don't have the stamina for these adventures."

"Aunt Prune, I know! And I'm truly, truly sorry! It's just that I'm used to coming and going as I please. I—"

"Well, you can't come and go as you please here, Karen. You may be chafing at the bit, but you have to learn to show a little consideration. We have adjustments to make, too, you know, and that's even more difficult, at our age."

"I'm sorry!" cried Karrie again. "I've said it and said it, and I don't know what you want from me. I'm sorry I worried you, I'm sorry I'm such a burden, I'm sorry I ever came to this place and I'm sorry I was ever born! If that isn't enough being sorry, then I just can't satisfy you!"

There was a brief, tense silence; then Miss Prune shook her head and rose from the chair with a sigh.

"We won't discuss it any more tonight," she said. "Dr. Ross said you're to rest for a couple of days in case you suffered a mild sunstroke."

"You didn't have to get the doctor out here," said Karrie through clenched teeth. "I told you that I was all right."

"Karen, we didn't call the doctor for you. We called him for your grandfather. We thought he was having a heart attack."

Karrie sat up in bed. "*What*? Was he? Is he all right?"

"He's apparently all right. It wasn't a heart attack, Dr. Ross said. Just exhaustion and stress. He's too old for what you put him through today."

"But—"

"He was like a wild man. First, Israel went out looking for you in the car, while Ginger and I were calling all over town to find out if anyone had seen you. Your grandfather even climbed up to the widow's walk with the binoculars. Then, when it was getting late in the afternoon, he and Israel both struck out on foot. They didn't get back till after sundown, and when Henry found us sitting around in the kitchen just wringing our hands, he started screaming at us—why didn't we have all the lights on? 'I want every light in this house turned on,' he said. 'She's out there somewhere in the dark.' So we all ran around the house switching on lights. Well, you came staggering in pretty soon after that. After we got you upstairs and tended to, we came down and found that your grandfather had collapsed. Israel got him to the couch in his study and we rang Dr. Ross."

Karrie sat trembling on the bed. As dreadful as it had been out there under the blazing sun, this homecoming was more dreadful yet. *What had she done?* She had invaded the quiet world of these elderly people and turned it upside down. If her grandfather *had* had a heart attack and died, it would have been all her fault.

Without another word, Miss Prune switched out the light and left the room, and for a long while Karrie sat there in the dark, her thoughts going around in circles. The day that had begun with soft breezes and bird song had turned into a nightmare, and one of her own creation. She couldn't see beyond it, or imagine how she could go on living in this place after what she had done.

"Oh Marty," she whispered. "Where are you when I need you? How am I going to get through this?"

She knew what Marty would tell her: she could get through anything. But *he* had always been there before. Now she was alone. One by one, everything she'd counted on had slipped away from her—mother, father, home, and finally, her brother.

Marty said she could count on *herself*, but he was *wrong*. She could only be counted on to mess things up.

Around and around went Karrie's anguished thoughts; but even as she concluded that hers was a hopeless case, a new resolve was forming and a plan was being shaped in her mind. Despair yielded to practical determination, for she was, after all, the "tough little kid" her brother had called her.

Though every movement caused her to wince, she managed to get up from the bed and ease her way down the two flights of stairs. The house was dark now, but she found the door to the study open, and moonlight flooding the room. The mayor was lying on the long couch in front of the bookcase. His breathing was even, but Karrie could see that his eyes were open. She slipped into the room and halted a safe distance from the couch.

"I'm sorry I did such a stupid thing, Grandfather," she said quietly. "I really didn't mean to, but, you see, I just don't belong here. You didn't ask to have me dumped on you, but I didn't ask for it either. I know Marty thought he was doing the right thing, but if he'd just *told* me he was going to enlist, I would have made him let me stay in New York. Anyway, now it's too late. I know I can't go back. But—I've thought it over carefully. It would be best for everybody if I went away to boarding school. And—well, that's all I wanted to say. Except that I'm glad you didn't have a heart attack."

There was a deep sigh from the supine figure on the couch.

"Quite finished?" growled the mayor. "That was a very long speech. Now if you don't mind, I've had just about enough of this particular day. Do you think we can agree to declare it at an end? *Goodnight*, Karen."

5.

The mayor suffered no lingering effects from his spell, and the aunts soon returned to their usual cheerfulness. The only reminder of that unfortunate day was Karrie's peeling skin and the unaccustomed tan beneath it.

Karrie needed no reminder. Though the pain of the sunburn

was gone, her sense of guilt and humiliation remained. She tried to be especially courteous and accommodating to make up for the distress she had caused, but at the same time, when she thought of how she'd been scolded like a naughty child, she felt a deep, gnawing resentment. After all, she and Marty had functioned very well as grown-ups for over two years. What right did these people have to treat her this way?

She was more restless and unhappy than before, and was convinced that every drop of the affection she had started to feel for the aunts had been squashed forever. As for her grandfather, she tried to keep out of his way and to speak only when spoken to. All she lived for was to leave, leave, *leave!*

Her hopes centered on boarding school. The mayor gave no indication that he was considering that plan, but—"After all, this is his opportunity to get rid of me," she wrote to Marty.

She daydreamed about it constantly. She didn't expect it to be *easy*. There were bound to be lots of rules, but if she broke one she wouldn't have to worry about giving anyone a heart attack.

The head mistress, now, would most likely be strict. In books, head mistresses always were, but that was all right, too. She could write Marty funny letters about her trials and tribulations at boarding school, just as he wrote her about boot camp.

Marty's letters and her dreams of escaping Windy Crest helped ease the tedium of the long summer days. But after two weeks of waiting for some word from her grandfather, Karrie began to grow anxious and discouraged. Then one day, as she flipped through the mail on the hall table in search of a letter from Marty, her heart made a sudden leap. There was a thick envelope addressed to the mayor, and the return address was Saint Monica's School for Girls in San Antonio. The very next day there was another such envelope, this one from Mrs. Wakefield's School for Girls in Dallas.

"It's going to happen!" she wrote to Marty. "But not one word has been said to me! Oh, if I could only see those brochures! There'll be uniforms, don't you think? I don't care how ugly they are. For once in my life I'll be dressed just like everybody else!

"I wonder which school Grandfather will choose? Of course he wouldn't dream of letting me have any say about it! He'll simply announce his decision after he's let me cool my heels for a while. Stubborn old coot! I'm sure he's just *dying* for me to ask, but I won't give him the satisfaction. I can wait him out! Now that I know I'm getting out of here, I can take anything!"

6.

"Not a word, Marty, not a word from anyone!" Karrie wrote after another week had passed. "How long can they keep this up? I'm trying not to rock the boat, but the aunts have me right where they want me. They drag me to all sorts of old-lady things like Aunt Ginger's Ladies Auxiliary meeting, where all they do is yak about organizing their *war work*, and Aunt Prune's sewing circle, where they sit around and gossip and knit long, khaki-colored scarves for *the boys over there*. I'm certainly being exposed to that 'full flavor' of Bienvenidos you were so eager for me to write you about.

"There is a funny mixture of women at these meetings. The aunts are the most refined and educated by far. Mrs. Tulla Swenson and Mrs. Louisa Norwood dress nicely and speak well. Most of the others are farm wives, and look tired and weather-beaten, like they've worked themselves to a frazzle all their lives. Some take a break to sit out back and dip snuff, and bring little paper sacks to spit in. I have to say that Aunt Prune and Aunt Ginger treat everybody alike, and don't act a bit stuck-up.

"On our way downtown, we stop and pick up a woman named Maybelle, who lives way out in the sticks with her grandmother. Grannie Opal—that's what everybody calls her—is very old (Aunt Ginger said she was 'born when Texas was a Republic') and can't be left alone, so we leave off Martha to stay with her. Maybelle is a very cheerful person, who has a very tight permanent wave. She always wears a string of pearls, white gloves, and a little straw hat with purple flowers on it.

"Oh, and guess what! I finally met the infamous Lollie Beal! I was beginning to think they'd just made her up so they'd have someone to blame the gossip on. She's only a Beal by marriage, but she looks exactly like the Beals in the pictures in the hall—handsome and mean. She gave me the fish-eye and said: 'We're *kin*, you know.' I said, 'That's nice!' You see what a liar I've become.

"The worst thing I have to go through is being dragged to church. Grandfather gets a little sneer on his face when we walk out the door, all gussied up in our Sunday best (in my case, that awful sailor dress Aunt Prune made me).

"Well, I *do* like singing the hymns. They have these hymnals with the words and music. And it's kind of a kick to watch all those seriously dressed-up people sit and fan away the flies with cardboard fans that have 'Hospitality Funeral Home' printed on them. It's not a bit like going to Mass with Miss Simms!

"Preacher (I don't think he has any other name!) drones on and on forever. He does a lot of lamenting about 'miserable sinners.' I guess he's still thinking about his wife and the brush salesman.

"After the service, he plants himself at the front door so that everybody filing out has to shake his hand and mumble 'how lovely' the sermon was. That first Sunday, Aunt Ginger shoved me in front of him and introduced me as 'Henry's grand-daughter.' He put his big hairy paw on my head and groaned something about 'the sins of the fathers.'

"I don't know what he meant by that, but it made me *fume*. As far as I'm concerned, the man is boring, mean and stupid, and I hate him! And I hate being an object of curiosity to the whole congregation. Lots of people make a pretense of chatting with the aunts just so they can take a close look at 'the little foreign child' from New York. So I concentrate on looking as totally *foreign* as I can! My new sun tan helps, though I'd gladly trade it for my old subway pallor.

"Oh, Marty, I can hardly wait to escape! If I knew who Saint

Monica was, I'd certainly pray to her! I guess they make you attend chapel in a Catholic school, but that's okay. A Catholic girl I knew at camp told me nobody preaches in chapel—you just kneel and recite prayers. Maybe you say them in Latin. I would like that. And I like the idea of living in a tiny cell and taking cold showers and leading a very disciplined life. *Not* Aunt Ginger's idea of a disciplined life, but sort of a *basic* life—do you know what I mean? Kind of like boot camp."

In her next letter Karrie wrote:

"Martha's been telling me all about Aunt Clara (the one who got the beauty). She has a daughter named Ida and *she* has a daughter named JoBeth, and guess what? JoBeth *just so happens* to be a student at Mrs. Wakefield's in Dallas! Maybe that's what the aunts have been whispering about on the phone!!!!! (They're forever calling Aunt Clara, much to Grandfather's disgust!)

"Do I dare get my hopes up? To tell the truth, I was kind of leaning toward Saint Monica's, but Mrs. Wakefield's might be okay, too. The uniforms are probably better looking.

"By the way, Martha also told me that Grandfather can't abide Aunt Clara's husband, whose name is 'Hoot'—believe it or not. The last time they were here Grandfather blew his top and threw them out, and refuses to let the aunts ask them back! Seems this character Hoot made some remark to Israel that infuriated Grandfather—Martha wouldn't tell me what. She'd only say that 'Miss Clara's Hoot' is 'lewd and crude and filthy rich' and he never heard the news that Lincoln freed the slaves!

"Well, anyway, it's looking more and more like Grandfather really intends to send me to boarding school, don't you think? Cross your fingers! I should know soon!"

7.

But days went by, and Karrie still did not know. Time was growing short. The calendar revealed that summer, though it seemed hotter than ever, was officially on the wane, and the *Bienvenidos Bugle* was featuring advertisements for school clothes.

Karrie knew that she was partly to blame for creating an

atmosphere wherein she asked nothing and was told nothing. It had become a stand-off game between her and her grandfather. She also knew that she could end the game by asking straight out, "Well, what is it, Grandfather? Am I to go to boarding school, and if so, which one?" But somehow she held back and waited a little longer.

"He's an impossible old man," Marty wrote to her, "but you're as pig-headed as he is! You're not behaving honestly, squirt. I don't approve of your Miss Goodie-Two-Shoes act. Don't think for a minute that His Honor isn't on to you."

In fact, Karrie was convinced that he was, and she was weary of waiting him out, but the longer it went on, the harder it was to change anything. Everyone had come to expect her to be passive and pliable, and the aunts were quite happy to organize her life for her. She was beginning to feel that she had no will of her own.

Just as she was becoming totally disheartened, another letter from the Catholic school appeared on the hall table, and her spirits rose again.

It was not to be for long.

That same evening she came in from her walk earlier than usual. Her grandfather and her great-aunts were sitting in the parlor talking, and Karrie stood unnoticed in the doorway, waiting for a moment to politely make her presence known. Then she became aware that *she* was the topic of conversation.

"Of course Mrs. Wakefield runs an excellent school, Henry," Miss Ginger was saying, "and she does stress the social graces."

"Pah!" said the mayor, dismissing Mrs. Wakefield and her ilk with one gesture. "Would you like to see the child turned into a little snot like JoBeth?"

"Henry!"

"Actually, Ginger," said Miss Prune, "Karen would feel very much out of place at Mrs. Wakefield's. I know *I* would. But I'm not sure about a Catholic school. She's at an impressionable age, and we *are* trying to make a Methodist of her."

"I don't see why she has to go away at all," said Miss Ginger.

"She's fine here. I feel we're beginning to make real progress with her. There was just that one incident, but she learned her lesson, and frankly, Henry, I believe the child ought to be with family. Her life has been disrupted so much already."

"Well, then, I think we're agreed," said the mayor gruffly. "We'll enroll her here. She'll ride in every morning along with me, and Israel will pick her up after school. It will be an extra trip for him afternoons, but he won't mind that."

"Prune, we ought to take her into town tomorrow and let her buy school supplies," Miss Ginger was saying to her sister, just as Karrie, who had been listening speechlessly, suddenly burst into the room.

"No, no, no, *no!*" she cried. "Grandfather, you *can't* mean it! I don't *care* about my life being disrupted! I *have* to go to boarding school! What's the matter with the Catholic school? I'm not a bit impressionable! I'll be a Methodist or anything you like, only please, please, please, don't make me stay here and go to school in that awful town. I'd rather *die!*"

"Karen!" gasped Miss Prune.

"Shame on you!" said Miss Ginger huffily. "With your brother away in the service—what a thing to say!"

"Grandfather—"

"The matter is settled, Karen, and the subject is closed," said the mayor, rising from his chair. He stalked out of the parlor and a few seconds later there was the sound of his study door closing.

Karrie stared at the aunts for an instant, her eyes as wild and desperate as those of a cornered animal. Then she turned and fled the parlor.

8.

The mayor looked up with a start. Karrie was standing in the doorway to his study, but such a Karrie he'd never seen before! Her thin little legs were braced apart, her hands were on her hips, and there was fire in her eyes.

Before her grandfather could open his mouth, she declared sternly, "I can't *make* you send me to boarding school. So be it!

I may not be in control of that, but I *am* in control of myself, and if I have to stay here in the middle of nowhere and go to your dinky little school, then I'll do it on my own terms."

The mayor stared at her. "*Your* terms? What—?"

"I'm about to tell you what they are," interrupted Karrie, "if you'll keep quiet and listen."

"See here, young lady!" thundered the mayor.

"No, *you* see here," Karrie thundered back, and, having achieved a very satisfactory stunned silence, continued, "Number one: I will no longer abide by arbitrary rules."

"*Arbitrary*—?"

"That's right. I'm willing to listen to anything reasonable, but I won't do something or *not* do something just because it's decreed from—from *on high*!"

"Just what—"

"I'm not finished! Number two: I'll go to school because the law says I have to, but I will not be delivered there and picked up in that—*darned* car! I'll walk."

"It happens to be four miles."

"I don't care if it's a million. I always managed to get to school on my own in New York and I'll do it here."

"And is that *all*?"

"No! Number three: The people in this house can just stop behaving as though they found me under a cabbage leaf. I *will not* pretend my parents never existed. I will talk about them whenever I please, and if that offends you—well—well, *good*! Just remember: you *could* have sent me to boarding school."

Karrie turned and walked away, but before the mayor could recover from the unfamiliar experience of having been on the receiving end of flat pronouncements, she was back in the doorway.

"One other thing," she said. "No more church."

Karrie expected to be called on the carpet for the scene and she steeled herself for combat. However, when two days went by and it didn't happen, she had the uncomfortable suspicion that she and her grandfather were again engaged in some sort of game.

The showdown with the aunts came on Sunday morning. When Karrie was summoned, she came downstairs in her shorts.

"Karen, why aren't you dressed?" Miss Ginger demanded.

"I won't be going to church any more," Karrie replied calmly.

"But, dear—" Miss Prune urged gently.

"My father," said Karrie deliberately, "was of the opinion that people can live moral and ethical lives without benefit of organized religion. I've been exposed to quite a bit of church-going in my time, and I must say that I agree with him absolutely."

The mayor, sitting at the breakfast table, rattled his newspaper and took a sip of coffee.

"Karen," said Miss Ginger, "as long as you are living in this house, we are in charge of your upbringing—physical, educational, and spiritual. Get yourself dressed and be quick about it!"

"I'm sorry, Aunt Ginger, but my parents—*Inge and Richard*—were in charge of my spiritual upbringing when I was little, and I'll take over from here. It's really no one else's concern."

"Karen!" cried Miss Prune in dismay.

"Now you listen to me, young lady," Miss Ginger began, but she was interrupted by a gruff "Let her be!" from behind the newspaper.

"Henry—?"

"Why do you insist on subjecting the child to this weekly martyrdom?"

"*Henry*—"

"Listening to that fool preacher carry on couldn't possibly improve her in any way. The man's a moron."

"Henry, really! I'd be the first to admit that Preacher is—no Rhodes scholar. He's a bit rough around the edges, but he does know his Bible and he's a man of God—"

"Pah!"

"Henry, you've never even heard him preach—"

"He *preaches* every time I meet him on the street."

"Well—Well—that's beside the point, Henry. The Websters have *always* gone to the Methodist church—"

"Well, not actually, Ginger," Miss Prune put in. "Back East they went to the Unitarian church, only there wasn't one in these parts. Preacher's not our cup of tea, either, Henry, but we're lucky to have any minister at all. So many are serving with the military—"

"And that's not the point, either," declared Miss Ginger firmly. "The point is, we expect Karen to accompany us to church. The child needs some sort of spiritual training—"

"Pah! Spiritual training! Let her be!"

"And that," Karrie wrote to Marty, "was the final word! The aunts departed without me, Grandfather stalked off to his study— slam!—and I came upstairs to write you all about it. I didn't expect to win that battle so easily, because I certainly hadn't counted on Grandfather's support. He's always sneered at church-going, but I figured he enjoyed seeing *me* suffer.

"The aunts are upset, and I guess I feel a little bit sorry about that. But the alternative is to let them lead me around like a poodle on a leash, Marty.

"Am I wrong? Don't answer. And don't lecture me or give me advice. I'm on my own now and I'm determined to stand my ground. It's the only way I can survive. Call it my war effort."

Chapter 5
Clouds and Rainbows

1.

The day before school was to start, Karrie decided to walk to the Five and Dime to buy supplies. She was halfway to town before she was overtaken by the Packard. The mayor, on the back seat, stared straight ahead. Israel slowed down, but Karrie waved him on and kept walking.

"The hike in wasn't all that bad," she reported in her letter to Marty that evening. "Going home was another story, but I'll get to that. The first thing I did when I got into town was stop at the drugstore for a soda to cool me off. Shirleen Haus asked about you and when I told her you were in boot camp, she said, 'Gol-lee, I didn't even know sailors *wore* boots!' That girl is a *brain*!

"Mr. Webber was sitting in a chair behind the pharmacy counter winding up his Victrola. 'Hey, girlie,' he called to me, 'you like music?' I said I did and he invited me behind the counter to admire his record collection. It really is impressive— and *ancient*. He said he had an old-maid aunt in Dallas who died and left him all her stuff. He asked me to pick a record to play, so I chose the sextet from *Lucia*, with Galli-Curci, Chaliapin and all. Mom had that one, remember?

"When it was over Mr. Webber said, 'Now you listen to one of *my* favorites,' and he put on something called 'What a Friend

We Have in Jesus.' Then we took turns choosing—opera, hymn, opera, hymn! Definitely weird, but kind of fun!

"I liked being downtown alone. I stopped by to see Mr. Wirtz, and he asked for your address and said he might drop you a line every now and then. He is probably the nicest person I've met in town next to Miss Jane Llewellyn. I don't think I've ever heard him say anything nasty about anyone—except Hitler and Bucko Riddle.

"After I picked up my school supplies at the Five and Dime, I went by Mrs. Schulman's Bread and Cakes to get a doughnut to eat on the way home. Mrs. Schulman is a sweet lady, but very sad, and I had a hard time getting out of there because she wanted to talk. She thinks Grandfather put up the moon and tied it with a bow, because he stood by the German folks in town during the first World War. She said it was real scary around here in those days.

"She has a grandson overseas in Europe, in the Army Air Corps. She had another grandson but he got killed in the Battle of the Coral Sea. He was on the *Lexington*. His name was Doug. Mrs. Schulman said he was 'like your papa Richard, always reading poetry.' When I told her I like poetry, too, she insisted on giving me Doug's favorite book of poems. 'Better it should be passed on to someone who will love it as he did, than it should sit on my shelf and make me sad,' she said.

"It's a lovely book, Marty, full of Doug's notes and scribblings in the margins. He must have been a really nice boy. I promised Mrs. Schulman I'd come back to see her real soon. Maybe she'll tell me things about Dad when he was young. She's the only one in town who's ever said his name to me.

"I knew it would be hot on the walk home, and I've had quite enough sunburn, so I stopped by the Mercantile to buy a big hat from Mr. Wilkins. He said he bet it didn't get this hot in Paris, France, and I said I bet it didn't either!

"So, anyway, here comes the bad part. I started walking up the highway, and everything was fine until Bucko Riddle and his pals passed me in a pickup truck, then stopped up ahead and just waited. I *had* to keep on walking—what else could I do? They followed me at a crawl all the way to the gates of Windy Crest. Four of the longest miles I ever hope to walk!

"I got home before noon, and nobody made any comment, but I had a feeling they were all relieved to see me come through the door. Not as relieved as I was, I can tell you!

"It's not that I'm *afraid* of that creep, but life here is miserable enough without having him give me a hard time. I really dread the walk to school tomorrow. But I can't back down, not after the stand I took with Grandfather. I have my pride, Marty, and that's about all I have."

2.

As Karrie was leaving for her first day of school, she found Israel waiting by the gate. He handed her a small paper sack.

"Martha fixed you a sandwich," he explained.

"Oh! I was going to buy lunch in the cafeteria."

Israel chuckled. "Honey, there ain't no cafeteria. Children either go home for dinner or pack a sandwich." He patted her shoulder. "Now listen, honey, I'll drive the mayor into town and come right back for you. Be *our* secret."

"Thanks, Israel, but no. I told him I was going to get to school under my own steam and I have to do it."

Israel shook his head. "Well, you got the Webster hard-headedness, that's for sure! Now baby, I was watching from the window yesterday, and I saw Bucko Riddle driving alongside you in his pickup. I don't like that a bit."

"I don't like it either," admitted Karrie uneasily. "He wouldn't dare really *hurt* me, would he?"

"There ain't no telling what that boy will do. Some young fellers like to tease, but Bucko—he just mean. Always been. Mean to colored, especially. I hate that white boy."

Karrie was surprised to hear such harsh words from someone as kind as Israel. "Did he ever do anything to you, Israel?"

"Not to me. Used to devil my niece's boy, Jimmy. Tied him to the stirrup of a ole horse once, then swatted the horse. Jimmy

101

was near dragged to death."

"That's horrible! Why wasn't Bucko arrested?"

"Mayor tried to get him arrested. Never saw your grandaddy so mad. Went straight to the county judge. But the judge don't take serious nothing that's done to colored boys, and Bucko's Sheriff Hoss Bateson's nephew. Sheriff say Bucko's mischief-loving. Sheriff say folks got to make allowances count of Bucko's pa is dead, but his pa weren't no good either." Israel shook his head ruefully. "*He* was the one used to be after me all the time. They just alike. Not happy 'less they picking on somebody."

"Well, I guess I'm the one Bucko's decided to pick on now. I've got to figure out how to handle him."

"Ain't no way to handle him. He near drove Jimmy crazy. Jimmy was older than Bucko, but he was a little feller, and Bucko always got a gang with him. Think that's why Jimmy joined up with the Navy—so's he could get clear away from here."

Karrie sighed. "I wish *I* could join the Navy."

"Honey, you'll be all right mornings. Bucko lives on the other side of town. But I'll pick you up after school, hear?"

"No, Israel, I can't. I have to deal with it."

"Lord, you and your grandaddy! Two peas in a pod. All right, all right. I got something for you. Hope it helps some."

Israel went behind one of the wide stone gates and rolled out a boy's bicycle. It was old, but sturdily built, and had been painted sky blue. Bedraggled feathers of red and blue hung from the rim of a straw basket attached to the handlebars.

"Brought it from home this morning," said Israel. "Jimmy left it in my shed when he went off to the Navy. Boy was always picking up pretty bird feathers. Said they made him feel like he was flying when he coasted down the highway."

"It's a great bike," said Karrie admiringly.

"Get you there quicker. But coming home, it's all uphill."

"That's okay. Marty and I used to walk our bikes across the George Washington Bridge and ride up and down the hills in New Jersey. I'm pretty strong on hills."

Israel looked at the small, thin girl doubtfully. "Well, you be careful, hear?"

"I will! And oh, thank you, Israel! I'll take real good care of Jimmy's bike till he comes home."

Israel paused. "That's okay, honey. It's *your* bike now. Jimmy ain't coming home. His ship went down at Pearl Harbor."

Karrie was pierced with a sudden, personal grief. She watched in silence as Israel began fumbling with the strings that secured the feathers.

"You ain't going to want these," he said. "All tattered anyways."

Karrie put her hand over his. "Leave them, Israel. I'll add some fresh ones."

"Honey—Bucko see these feathers, he know right away this is Jimmy's bike—"

"Oh—to—to *heck* with Bucko Riddle!"

Karrie put her notebooks and lunch bag in the basket and mounted the bicycle. As she rode off down the highway, the morning breeze was warm against her stricken face, and the red and blue feathers fluttered lightly against her hands.

3.

Karrie sat at the desk in her attic room, frowning at the wall. Presently, she bent over her tablet and began writing in a savage scrawl:

"Do you want to know why you haven't had a letter from me all week? Because you fuss at me when I complain, that's why! Well, if you think I'm going to *lie* and tell you everything's terrific, forget it! Everything *stinks*!

"I don't even know where to start. Do you remember that dreary brick building you said looked like a jailhouse? It *is* a jailhouse, brother dear—it's the elementary school, grades one through eight. I don't think it's been painted since *Grandfather* was a schoolboy. And guess what? No indoor bathroom! There are two long, low buildings out in the schoolyard, one for boys, the other for girls, ten-seaters each! When somebody's using the girls' outhouse, another girl has to stand watch outside because the roof is partly off and the boys think it's a great joke to climb up and look in. That should give you a pretty good notion of what my classmates are like!

"The seventh and eighth grades are stuffed into one room and one teacher teaches all the subjects. I have to sit at the same cramped little desk in the same dingy room and look at the same ugly face all day long!

"Oh, but wait! We *do* get to escape for twenty minutes every morning, when we line up like little storm troopers and march into a big gloomy room for assembly, which begins with the singing of an idiotic song called 'Welcome to Bienvenidos'— *the friendliest town in the friendliest state...*! Right! I never felt more *un*-welcome anywhere in my life!

"After that inspiring beginning, we sit our little behinds down on folding chairs and listen to the principal instruct us in the art of being good little Texans—in other words, how to heroically refrain from tossing spitballs and sticking gum under the desks. Then we line up like storm troopers again and it's back to dear Miss Buzzard—that's our teacher's name, believe it or not! Incredibly appropriate! She pronounces it Buzz*ard*, but nobody else does, except to her face. The old witch hates me. I think she hates all kids, but especially me.

"There are ten of us in my eighth-grade class (the only ones I know are the Wallace twins), and nine in the seventh grade. There are two tall boys in the seventh grade who must be at least sixteen years old. I think they are stealing my lunch. We are supposed to put our lunches on a shelf in the back of the room, and mine is never there at lunch time. But those boys are always splitting a sandwich and I'm pretty sure it's mine.

"The first day it happened, I took off and went to the drugstore. I got a grilled cheese, a soda and a prophecy from Shirleen Haus—'Gol-lee! You're going to be in bi-ig trouble!'

"She was right. When I got back Miss Buzzard took great

pleasure in informing me that students are not allowed to leave the school grounds at lunch time unless they have permission to go home to eat, and then she reminded me that this is *not* New York City (her absolute favorite remark). I had to sit in a chair next to her desk, facing the class, for the rest of the day, like a bad little kid in kindergarten! You should have seen all the smug little smiles I had to look at!

"So now I skip lunch. Joycie Wallace says those tall boys are real poor and they ride into town to school on one old plowhorse with a saggy back, so maybe I don't begrudge them my sandwich, though they certainly look like they get plenty to eat. I'm too tied in knots to be very hungry, anyway, but my stomach growls all afternoon, and a boy with greasy hair who sits next to me sniggers every time it happens.

"I asked the Wallace girls why the teacher has it in for me (she really *does*, Marty), and Joycie said Old Buzzard is still fighting the Civil War and hates Yankees. Then Sister Bee got *her* two cents in. She said maybe it's because I *put on airs*! 'You use all those big words and walk around with your nose in the air like you *own the town*!' Great! Thanks a bunch for all that super advice, Marty!

"Well, at least now I know what they really think of me. Not that I could care less!

"But it would all be bearable, Marty, if it wasn't for the deadly *boredom*. We go *over* and *over* and *over* the same old stuff! *Sheer torture*! The seventh-graders don't even know their times tables, and the eighth-graders aren't much better.

"The only good thing I can tell you is that Bucko Riddle goes to the new high school down the street, which lets out a half hour later, so at least I can bike home without getting run off the road.

"Just do me a favor, okay? Don't write me one of those Hip Hip Hooray! Onward and Upward! Excelsior! letters. It might drive me right over the edge."

105

4.

Karrie spent less than two weeks in eighth grade. One morning when she arrived in the classroom and slipped quietly behind her desk, Miss Buzzard glanced at her indifferently and said, "As you've apparently covered this curriculum, it's been decided that you will skip eighth grade and go directly into high school. You are to report to Mr. Mitchum over there. He's expecting you, so you'd better hurry along or you'll be late and disrupt the class."

Karrie's heart leaped up. She quickly gathered up her notebooks again. For one instant her eyes met Miss Buzzard's, which were openly hostile.

"You may find that high school is not such a breeze, missy. You'll be expected to *toe the mark*."

Karrie fairly flew out the door, in her haste leaving her lunch behind on the shelf in the back of the room. It didn't matter. It was one last sandwich for the tall boys in seventh grade to split, and she hoped they enjoyed it. She was getting out of there, and whatever awaited her couldn't be as awful as what she was escaping.

She grabbed her bicycle, threw her notebooks into the basket, and quickly pedaled down the street to the new two-story high school building. She was just propping her bicycle beside the others in the rack, when she was approached by an elderly black man in overalls.

"That your bike, little lady?"

"Yessir," said Karrie, wondering what she'd done wrong now.

"I know that bike. That's Jimmy's."

"I—Yes. Israel gave it to me. I'm from Windy Crest."

"Uh huh," said the old man. He took the bicycle by the handlebars. "I'm gonna put this bike in my room and keep it for you till after school. I'm the janitor. From now on you don't park it out here. You bring it 'round the side door and leave it with me. That way, nobody mess with it."

"Uh—yessir. Thank you," said Karrie, somewhat dismayed.

"I'm supposed to go to Mr. Mitchum."

"Second floor, room 201. He's a gentleman, **Mr. Mitchum.** You gonna have a fine teacher. Now you run on. **You tell** Israel, Rollie Johnson looking out for you."

Karrie entered the building, noted with pleasure the clean, light hallways, and ran up the stairs, two at a time, to the second floor. The door to 201 was closed, and she carefully turned the knob and tried to push it open as noiselessly as possible.

All eyes were on her as she came into the classroom. The teacher, a brown-haired young man of medium height, gave her a welcoming smile and walked toward her with a slight limp.

"You must be Karen," he said, offering his hand to shake. "I'm Mr. Mitchum, your homeroom teacher. Class, this is Karen Webster from New York City. We're looking forward to hearing about your school back there, Karen."

Karrie looked out over the classroom and spotted Baby Dodds, Snookie, and Bev. Baby Dodds gestured toward the empty desk next to hers, and Karrie slid into it with a grateful sigh.

"Whoopee!" she wrote to Marty that evening. "I've been let out of jail! Without any discussion or anything—boom! I'm in high school! No more Miss Buzzard, no more lunchless days, no more all the rest of that stuff I want to forget! Isn't it amazing?!!!!!

"Guess what? I'm taking Latin! My teacher is Miss Pringle, and the first thing she said to me was, 'Your father was the best student I ever had.' My English teacher is Miss Duvall, and I'm afraid she's going to be the kind who has you read something, then tells you what you're supposed to think of it. I *hate* that! Algebra looks like fun. We have a nice, new textbook, and a weird old teacher named Mr. Mayhew, who has a big Adam's apple and wears a bow tie.

"I have Miss Jane Llewellyn for art, of course, and she's neat. Baby Dodds says it's a pity she's an old maid, but she seems happy. Maybe that eternal torch she carries for Martin the Magnificent, our illustrious uncle, keeps her warm.

"My World History teacher is Mr. Mitchum, and he's *super*! Baby Dodds told me he's 4-F because he had infantile paralysis when he was a kid. He tried to enlist anyway, but they wouldn't take him, lucky for Bienvenidos High. He teaches music, too, and is in charge of the band, poor guy.

"Yes, we actually have a band! There are five kids in it, one of them borrowed from the elementary school, and nobody has any money to buy instruments, so they use whatever's survived the years. There's a tuba, a bugle, a saxophone, a drum and cymbals. Think about it! *Ouch!* They play at the football games, and Baby Dodds says they're just a little bit worse than the team! The team has exactly eleven players, two of *them* borrowed from the elementary school—those tall boys in seventh grade who stole my lunch! Miss Buzzard was right— 'This is *not* New York City!'

"So—to sum up, high school is a million times better than eighth grade! The only drawback is that now I'm going to the same school as Bucko Riddle. He's a junior, for the second or third time, I hear. I saw him in the hall, but he was too busy slamming a locker door on some poor guy's hand to notice me.

"Riding home this afternoon, I kept looking over my shoulder to make sure that truck wasn't following me. It wasn't, but there was one other person biking up the highway. She started out behind me, but she passed me when the hill slowed me down. She went right by and never said 'boo.'

"I know who she is. She's in my class. Her name is January Welles and her father runs the lumber mill for Grandfather. She's tall, has blond hair and blue eyes, and if that sounds like Jolene, believe me, those two are *nothing* alike! This girl came to school in a faded old dress that was miles too big for her. Compared to her, I was a regular fashion-plate in my sailor dress! She's really skinny and her hair is absolutely straight and hangs halfway to her waist. Bev told me that she doesn't care a fig how she looks or what people think of her.

Baby Dodds says her father's 'crazy as a hoot owl' and so is she.

"All I know is that she never smiles and never opens her mouth, except to answer the teachers' questions, but she always knows the right answers.

"When I got home I was surprised to find out that the aunts knew about my being transferred. They were anxious to hear how I liked high school. I said, 'Fine,' and they looked a little disappointed. I guess they thought I'd be jumping with joy, but I'd *still* rather be going to boarding school!

"I told Israel about the janitor keeping Jimmy's bike safe for me. He was very pleased. 'Mr. Johnson going to keep an eye on you at school,' he said.

"Well! What a day it's been, Marty! Looks like I might survive! Love—K."

5.

After four months in Texas, Karrie had come to the conclusion that no significant rainfall ever occurred there. Then, one Friday evening, the skies opened up. All night long rain pounded the roof. Thunder boomed, receded into the distance, then returned to explode directly overhead. Lightning lit the attic room, and Karrie was almost paralyzed with terror.

She tried to remind herself of how brave she'd been during thunderstorms when she was a little girl at summer camp, huddled in a tent in the woods with her bunkmates and counting the seconds between lightning flashes and thunder claps.

"The more seconds in between, the farther away the lightning really is," they would reassure one another, then shriek in unison when thunder and lightning seemed to occur simultaneously.

It had certainly been scary, but she'd always felt protected by the woods. And at home—in New York—no matter how fiercely a storm raged, Marty had been there to tell her that the Empire State Building was standing guard over the assaulted city like a gigantic lightning rod.

But now, in the top room of a tall house perched alone on a hill, in the middle of a tempest that was surely sent to herald the end of the world, Karrie's skin prickled and her heart pounded. Just as she made the decision to grab up her quilt and sneak downstairs to sleep, the door to her room opened softly and Miss Prune appeared, holding a lighted candle.

"Are you all right up here, honey?" she inquired anxiously. "The electricity's gone out. There's no danger, you know. The lightning rods on the widow's walk protect the house. But if you're scared, why don't you come down and sleep in my room?"

Scared? With Karrie, pride outweighed everything, even stark terror. She released her grip on the quilt.

"I'm fine, Aunt Prune," she said evenly. "It's really quite exciting."

Miss Prune and her candle disappeared. Then lightning illuminated the room once more and there was an enormous crash of thunder. Karrie grabbed the quilt again and scooted under her cot. And there she remained for the rest of the night.

By the next morning, the fury of the storm had abated, with only occasional rumbling reminders in the distance, but the rain continued to fall steadily.

"We need the rain," Miss Ginger declared, as though graciously granting it permission.

Israel shook his head. "Dry summer like we had, ground's hard as concrete. Gonna have us some gully washers for sure."

Karrie spent a pleasant Saturday morning in her little attic room, listening to the rain's heavy tattoo on the roof and doing her homework at a leisurely pace. Occasionally she left her desk to sit in one of the window seats and watch the valley being drenched in even, vertical streams from the sky.

Texas sure doesn't do anything halfway, she thought.

She wondered if everyone was sitting around talking downstairs. It had been her custom, ever since her showdown with her grandfather and the aunts, to treat them to her polite presence only at mealtime. Otherwise, she stayed in the kitchen with Martha or kept to her room.

The truth was, after the dramatic improvement in the school situation, her attitude toward her elderly relatives had begun to soften, though she stubbornly fought against it. She was still convinced that her survival in this place depended on her being strong enough to go it alone.

She found a poem, "The Solitary" by Sara Teasdale, in the book Mrs. Schulman had given her, and the last verse expressed her feelings exactly:

> Let them think I love them more than I do,
>   Let them think I care, though I go alone,
> If it lifts their pride, what is it to me,
>   Who am self-complete as a flower or a stone?

But as the morning wore on, and the muted sound of cheerful voices wafted up to the little attic room from downstairs, Karrie sighed. It could get pretty lonely, being as self-complete as a flower or a stone.

6.

Sunday morning the rain was still heavy, and after a telephone consultation with Mabel Klein, the aunts made the unusual decision to forego church.

"Mabel says everybody's staying home," Miss Prune reported. "Water's standing in the streets, right up to the store fronts."

"Coming down so fast, ground can't absorb it," said Israel. He and Martha had stayed at Windy Crest the night before, choosing to sleep on pallets in the kitchen rather than risk the drive home to lower ground.

"At least the phones are working," said the mayor. "I talked to Bill Pruitt about using the fire truck to move people to high ground, but he wants to wait a little, see how it goes."

"Town's never had to be evacuated before, and we've had worse storms than this," said Miss Ginger.

"Oh, but Ginger," said Miss Prune, "remember what happened to Hospitality twenty years back? That was just awful."

Karrie wanted to know what had happened to Hospitality, but she kept quiet, as she usually did. She was feeling restless and anxious. There was an atmosphere of foreboding in the house, and it all had to do with the weather. In New York, weather had never seemed important to her. It was pleasant, or it was bad, but it was never a *threat*.

"Well," said the mayor. "Bill's a sensible man, but I don't want to wait too long if there's any danger. Be prepared for a large number of guests, just in case."

"But, Henry," said Miss Prune nervously. "How can we be? I can't think how we'll feed droves of people, or where they'll sleep, if it comes to that."

"Oh, nonsense, Prune, we'll manage," declared Miss Ginger. "We can always shake out a bunch of pallets, and we'll feed them cereal, if we have to."

Martha and Miss Prune exchanged a worried glance.

Karrie was up and down the stairs that morning. She tried to stay in her room, but kept coming back down to hear about the latest developments.

Around noontime the rain began to slacken, and in another hour it had stopped, though the skies remained heavily overcast. The electricity came back on. Miss Prune called Mabel Klein and was told that the water in the streets was receding and people were beginning to go about their business.

By evening a light drizzle recommenced, but Israel and Martha felt confident enough to drive home as usual. Everyone appeared to be reassured except for Karrie. The violent weather had unnerved her, and when she went to bed that night she found it hard to fall asleep, dreading the thought of trying to get to school the next day. She was prepared, she finally decided, to let her grandfather insist that she be driven in the car.

The following morning, Karrie awoke once more to dismal skies. She dressed and went downstairs to the breakfast table. Her aunts and her grandfather were already in their places. Israel set a glass of orange juice in front of her.

"Now Honey," he said predictably, "you gonna let me take you in today, aren't you?"

"Oh no, Israel," said Karrie, just as predictably. "I'll be okay." She'd give in to the *third* plea, she thought nervously. Well, maybe even the *second*.

"All right then," said Israel with a sigh. "I'll see if Martha got some oilcloth to wrap around your books so's they don't get ruined."

Miss Prune looked unhappy, but continued to drink her coffee, as did Miss Ginger and the mayor. Karrie saw that she had finally outsmarted herself, just as Marty had been warning her she would.

There was nothing to do but carry it off. But what if the storm got really bad again? What if she got halfway down the highway and got caught in thunder and lightning?

After breakfast Karrie went back upstairs and rummaged through the wardrobe in the hall. She pulled out a raincape that had been her mother's and draped it over her shoulders. It reached nearly to the floor. It had looked very elegant on her mother when she went to the opera on rainy nights.

Karrie sighed heavily, feeling sorry for herself. This was all she had for rainwear. Her father's old umbrella had always seen her through in New York. For a moment she was sorely tempted to beg a ride to town.

Of course she did no such thing. Instead, she gathered up her books and wrapped them carefully in the oilcloth tablecloth Martha had provided for their protection. Then she hurried downstairs, called a brisk goodbye into the breakfast room and went out the door.

It was a dark, foggy, drizzly day—an *ominous* day, she told herself gloomily. She positioned her oilcloth bundle in the basket of her bike, and carefully tucked the long skirts of the cape under her to keep them from being caught in the spokes. Then, there was nothing to do but *go*. Four long wet miles to town.

Grimly she began her journey—down the winding driveway of Windy Crest, then out onto the highway. Just as she started to coast downhill, another bicycle overtook and passed her, without a word from the rider. It was January Welles, on her way to school.

7.

It was after school on that same miserable day that Bucko Riddle first noticed Karrie wheeling Jimmy's bike out of the janitor's room, and by the time she reached the highway, he was trailing her in his pickup truck.

The drizzle had turned back into serious rain, and as it pelted Karrie's face, she found it hard to keep the bicycle on the road and out of the flooded ditch. It was slow work pumping up the hill, and the muscles in her legs cramped with tension. The pickup kept immediately behind her.

Karrie was furious, but more than that, she was afraid, now that she knew what Bucko Riddle had done to Jimmy. All she could do was keep going, and hope that Israel, when he saw the weather had worsened, would set out in the car to rescue her. Tears of frustration streamed down her cheeks with the rain. The cape dangled from her shoulders, and she was wet through and through.

All at once Bucko pulled out ahead of her and turned off the highway onto a farm road. Karrie was perplexed by his change of tactics. Then she became aware that she was not alone on that highway. She glanced over her shoulder and there was January Welles, enveloped in a bulky raincoat, pumping steadily and facing the rain without expression. Karrie kept expecting to be passed, but January held her place.

Presently, Bucko's truck came up from behind, hesitated an instant, then sped away. The two bicycles continued their dogged journey uphill, and twice more the truck reappeared and drove away in the same manner. It wasn't until Karrie had gained the entrance to the Windy Crest driveway that January Welles bore down hard with her strong legs and shot past her up the highway.

Not a word had been spoken. Karrie paused for a moment to watch her silent companion ride away, then she shrugged, hopped back on her bicycle, and headed up the driveway to the house. The rain had abruptly ceased. A streak of afternoon light was edging its way under the clouds in the west, and there was a faint rainbow on the horizon.

The mayor and his sisters were in the parlor listening to President Roosevelt on the radio when they heard the front door open. They all looked up at once, and there in the hallway stood Karrie, clutching her oilcloth bundle of books and looking as if she had just been washed up on a riverbank. Her dark hair framed her wet face in thin, drooping corkscrews. The front of her dress was soaked, as were her shoes and socks, and the opera cape hung from her shoulders to the floor like bedraggled wings.

Both the aunts gasped and stared at this pitiful apparition.

"Ah! Icarus plucked from the sea," remarked the mayor. "Nice flight?"

It was precisely the comment needed to make Karrie stiffen her back and square her shoulders.

"The usual," she replied, and, with all the dignity she could muster, she draped the skirts of the cape across her arm like a bridal train, and sailed up the stairs.

8.

"You don't have to say it—I brought it on myself," Karrie wrote to Marty. "But *one* nice thing came out of it. Aunt Prune knocked on my door last evening and asked me to come

115

down to her sewing room. Aunt Ginger was waiting there, and there was this big box on the table.

"'Now, Karen,' Aunt Ginger said, ever so firm and prim, 'I certainly hope that you will take this in the spirit in which it's offered.'

"'And that you won't mention it to your grandfather,' Aunt Prune said, anxious as always. 'Of course—you wouldn't be likely to, would you?'

"No, not likely, I thought, since I hardly speak to the man.

"And then they started taking all these *beautiful* clothes out of the box—skirts, sweaters, blouses—and a nifty raincoat. It must have been the sight of me in Mom's opera cape that made them decide it was time to act. It seems that Aunt Clara sent these things a few weeks ago, and the aunts were afraid I'd get in a snit about being offered JoBeth's hand-me-downs. Ha! After Mom's Peter Pan collars and Aunt Prune's sailor dress?

"Okay, maybe there was one teeny second when my pride almost made me say, 'Tut, tut, ladies, I much prefer my own tacky togs.' But I *didn't*. My pride had taken enough of a beating in the rain, and I wasn't about to let it do me out of the first pretty clothes I've had since Mom died. I accepted—*graciously*!

"You know what? It hardly hurt at all."

9.

"Some of these things, I'll *never* grow into," said Karrie with a sigh. She was standing on a footstool in the sewing room, wearing one of JoBeth's cast-off skirts, while Miss Prune was on her knees, pinning up the hem. "JoBeth must be nice and tall, like you and Aunt Ginger—and *all* the Websters, except for me."

Miss Prune took a pin out of her mouth and carefully maneuvered it into the fold of a pleat. She, too, sighed.

"Nice and tall!" she said ruefully. "I wish someone had said that to me when I was your age! I think girls must have come shorter back in those days. Ginger and I felt like a pair of giraffes!"

"Really? But you're both so straight and graceful," said Karrie sincerely.

"Oh well, Papa insisted on good posture—and it *was* said that no one could sit a horse like the Webster girls. Girls rode side-saddle then, you know. Not as easy as it looks. 'Posture!' Papa would shout as we rode off. 'Heads high—watch your elbows!' *That* was something we could be vain about—that and basketball. I was good, but Ginger was the star. So—that was fine. I suppose we had respect, if not friendship."

"Didn't you have friends?"

"Oh, well, of course, we had *some* friends. Tulla Swenson always stood by me—Tulla *Hobbel* it was then—and Ginger was close to Leticia Adams. Leticia's gone now. She was Jane Llewellyn's mother, you know. Jane is her living image!"

Miss Prune continued her pinning, lost in thought.

"But," prodded Karrie gently, "it seems to me you would have been—*popular*."

"No, honey, no one could have described Ginger and me as *popular*. Well, we were bookish, you know. Papa made us read the classics. Bookish girls were thought to be odd, back then. Girls were supposed to be pretty and know how to flirt."

"*That* hasn't changed! Not in Benbenitas! If you use a two-syllable word they say you're putting on airs!"

"Um. They used to say the Websters were stuck-up."

That had not changed either, Karrie reflected.

"And—well, we were what we were," Miss Prune continued. "Papa never let us forget we were the descendants of New England abolitionists, and that didn't sit too well with our classmates. They'd been exposed to totally different attitudes at home. Sometimes they said things that we simply couldn't suffer, and we were always getting into arguments. You know, about slavery and the Civil War. The more righteous and outraged we were, the more the other children made fun of us. I suppose we should have learned to—dissemble a little. No, Henry and Ginger and I didn't have a very happy time at school."

"What about Aunt Clara?"

"Oh, Clara!" Miss Prune laughed, and shook her head. "Clara

117

never had a hard day in her life. She was raised the same way we were and read all the same books, but she just batted her eyelashes and looked beautiful and everybody forgot she was a Webster! Clara was always the belle of the ball!"

"And she married that Hoot character."

"Well—yes." Miss Prune shifted position, frowning.

"I'd rather never have a boyfriend at all."

"Now, Karen!" But it was a mild remonstrance, and Miss Prune went on talking in an intimate vein. "You know, dear, Ginger and I understand some of your feelings better than you realize. We remember what it's like to be young and to feel trapped in a small town with people who seem small-minded. Of course we've learned to be less judgmental."

Karrie sighed. "But you were *born* here."

"And, believe me, it's not easy to be regarded as outsiders in your own hometown. We used to plan how we were going to run away."

"*Really*? Golly—where to?"

"Oh—New York, or Chicago. The same places young folks still dream about, I guess. Austin was as far as we ever got."

"You ran away to Austin?"

Miss Prune laughed. "Goodness, no! We were grown women when we went to Austin. It was after Papa died. We didn't want to be a pair of old maids living under our brother's roof, so we just up and moved to Austin." There was a trace of defiance in Miss Prune's tone that made Karrie think there had been more to it than that.

"How old were you then?"

"Well, let's see. I was twenty-three and Ginger was twenty-four."

"Gee, you weren't exactly *old maids*!"

"That's what they called us! Neither one of us had ever had a beau. We were too busy taking care of Papa after Mamma died. Clara married young, and so did Henry. He and Sally Beal—your grandmother—lived here with us, and the babies came along, so it was a crowded house. Then after Papa died, Windy Crest came

118

to Henry, so that made Sally lady of the house. Time for Ginger and me to move on."

"You mean you didn't get along with my grandmother?"

"Oh! Sally was—really very nice, and she was certainly the best of the *Beals*, but—there were too many women under one roof. That never works out well."

"So you went to Austin?"

"Yes. Dear me, we expected to find everything there! Adventure and romance!"

"And—?"

"Well, I suppose we did." Miss Prune smiled and blushed faintly. "We were very happy in Austin. We rented the sweetest little bungalow, walking distance from downtown. We enrolled in business college and after we graduated, we both got jobs at the Capitol. Ginger was an expert stenographer. I didn't take to the typewriter too well, but I did bookkeeping. Oh, we were *very* happy! We had friends. We went to the picture show and we were asked to parties. There was this huge swimming hole called Barton Springs on the south side of the river, and our crowd used to go there for all-day picnics, and at night there'd be singing in the moonlight. Sometimes there was a band and Chinese lanterns, and oh, how we danced! Those were wonderful times!"

"Did you have boyfriends?"

"Well, there was this young engineer with the Highway Department who was sweet on Ginger, and I used to step out with one of the bookkeepers. My, he was a *gentleman!* They both were. They knew how to *court* a lady. Nowadays young men just—"

"Make passes," said Karrie with a wise nod. "I doubt if anyone would ever make passes at *me*!"

"Well, I think they will, dear, when you're older," said Miss Prune, looking worried, "and somehow Ginger and I are going to have to prepare you for that. But goodness knows how."

"Aunt Prune, why didn't you and Aunt Ginger stay in Austin, if you liked it so much there?"

"Well, honey, we *did* stay—for nearly eleven years. Then the war came along and it seemed like the whole world came crashing down on us. Martin was killed in action, and then your grandmother died of the influenza. It was a terrible time! We had to come back to take care of Henry."

"I don't think it's fair that he asked you to give up your own lives."

"Honey, he didn't *ask* it. It was our duty. It was what Papa would have expected of us."

Karrie frowned and mentally did some arithmetic. "But Grandfather must have been pretty young then."

"He was only forty. Everybody said he would marry again, but I don't think the thought ever crossed his mind. He *adored* Sally, and Martin's death devastated him. He was in an awful state."

"But *your* lives counted, too!"

"Oh, honey, we don't have any regrets. Our lives have been good. We love this old house, and we even love Benbenitas now!"

"But in Austin—"

"We have our memories." Miss Prune straightened up. "There! I believe that hem's about as even as I can get it. Those pleats were a challenge! All right, dear, take it off and I'll get it basted and pressed."

Karrie carefully stepped out of the skirt and Miss Prune immediately took it from her, and settled into her sewing rocker.

Karrie pulled on her shorts, then hesitated, reluctant for the conversation to end.

"Run on, dear," said Miss Prune, not looking up from her work. She sat by the window in the afternoon light that was filtering through the leaves of the live oak tree outside. For an instant—one instant only—her grandniece had a glimpse of a young woman with the promise of life still before her.

Then Karrie slipped out and softly closed the door, leaving Miss Prune to her memories.

10.

"Marty, you wouldn't recognize me!" Karrie wrote. "Aunt

Prune did a great job of fixing JoBeth's things for me, and after the way I've been freezing her and Aunt Ginger out (albeit politely), I feel a little guilty. They really are good souls, and they look so pleased when they see me dressed in these nice clothes.

"Baby Dodds wishes *she* had a rich second cousin who sent her such stuff! I like Baby Dodds, even if she's not what you'd call a 'kindred spirit,' and Snookie and Bev are okay, too. I mean, at least they *speak* to me, which is more than the other kids in my class do. Not that I'm missing much!

"By the way, guess who I ran into in the hall today? None other than—Ta-da-a!—Jolene Ross, the best derned cheerleader this town's ever had! And guess what she said to me, flashing that famous Pepsodent smile: 'Oh, isn't it just *wonderful* about Marty being sent to Oakland for hospital corpsman training?'

"Well! *That* didn't come from Lollie Beal! Why didn't you tell me you're writing to her? Incredible! My own brother has fallen for a pea-brained glamour girl who spends every Friday night jumping up and down in tasseled boots in front of the football team! Honestly, Marty! Think you know a person—!"

11.

When Karrie brought home her report card she was obliged to hand it over to her grandfather to be signed. Her two great-aunts peered over his shoulder. Both ladies drew in their breath with relief when they saw the A's after every subject. Then the mayor turned the card over to read the teacher comments. There were two.

"Karen has an unusually fine singing voice," Mr. Mitchum had written. "Karen's English compositions are excellent, but she has an unfortunate tendency to argue in class," was the report of Miss Duvall.

"Singing voice?" said Miss Prune eagerly.

"Argue?" said Miss Ginger with a frown.

The mayor signed the card without a word and handed it back to Karrie.

Later on, at the supper table, he suddenly remarked gruffly, "No one in this family could ever carry a tune."

Karrie looked up from her plate and said calmly, "My mother was studying to be an opera singer at a conservatory in Vienna when she married Dad." Not on any account would she be drawn into their conspiracy of silence about her parents, and when there was an opportunity to bring their names into the conversation, she did, with grim satisfaction.

There was a brief, tense silence. Karrie resumed eating.

"Hrumph!" the mayor finally responded. "And is that your aim—to sing opera?"

"No, I just like to sing," replied Karrie.

The moment was still in her thoughts the next morning as she rode down the highway, singing happily. Then January Welles went flying by.

January passed her every morning on the way to school, but every afternoon she rode silently in the rear until Karrie safely arrived at the gates of Windy Crest. Bucko nearly always appeared in his truck, slowed down, then sped away.

At lunch that day, Karrie told Baby Dodds about this curious situation.

"Isn't that something?" marvelled Baby Dodds. "That girl's actually protecting you! Bucko's scared of her, you know."

"He is? But why?" asked Karrie, astonished.

"Shoot! Everybody's scared of crazy people. You just never know what they're gonna do. But it's really her daddy got him worried. See—about a year ago, Bucko took it into his head to devil January like he does you now. She'd strike off after school on that old bike of hers, and Bucko'd be right after her in his truck, cat-calling, the way he does. Then one day he got so close he forced her off the road into the ditch and she got pretty scratched up. Well, before you know it, crazy old Ned Welles is banging on the door of the Riddle house, yelling for Bucko to come out. Big bad Bucko's hanging back behind his mamma. Mrs. Riddle peeps out through the curtains, and old Ned bellows so loud half the town can hear, 'Mrs. Riddle, I don't care to cause you grief, but if that no-good boy of yours ever comes around my girl again, I can guarantee he'll never give you another day's worry—not if I have to go to the penitentiary for it!' Bucko hasn't gone within fifty feet of January since. Crosses to the other side of the street when he sees her!"

"Bucko hiding behind his mother! I love it!" Karrie said. "I wish I could thank January for scaring him away from me. Do you think I should try?"

Baby Dodds shook her head. "If you thank her, she might just stop doing it. That girl is too weird for words."

When Karrie was riding home from school that afternoon, Bucko Riddle's truck showed up as usual, but disappeared in less than a minute. Karrie glanced back, and sure enough, following a few yards behind her was her strange guardian angel, staring straight ahead.

Chapter 6
Kindred Spirits

1.

Karrie woke early one Saturday in November and stretched pleasurably in the mild morning air that was sifting through the open windows. If she hadn't known better, she would have sworn it was spring.

She kicked back her quilt and went to sit at the window. Resting her chin on her folded arms on the sill, she gazed out on the far-off windmills, the gently stirring mesquites, and the cows standing beneath the stand of trees by the pond. Suddenly she had to be out there; she had to feel the roughness of the earth under her feet and the warmth of the sunshine stealing through the clouds.

It was exactly the day to make a return trip to the little cave.

"I'm going for a walk," she announced at breakfast.

Cautious looks were exchanged around the table.

"It's all right," she explained. "I know exactly where I'm going, but I won't be back for lunch. I'm going to take a sandwich and a canteen."

"Karen—" Miss Ginger began, but the mayor rattled his newspaper and silenced his sister with a glance.

"Well," said Miss Prune uneasily, "I hope you'll carry a sweater, dear. I know it seems like springtime, but you never

124

know when a blue norther's going to blow in, this time of year."

Soon Karrie was on her way, heading toward the cow pond with a light stride.

"I think I *love* November in Texas," she admitted to a mockingbird on the branch of a mesquite tree. He promptly took to the sky and Karrie's spirits soared after him.

When she reached the pond, the cows turned their heads and looked at her with their uncomprehending eyes. "Moo—oo!" one of them offered.

"Moo yourself," responded Karrie cheerfully.

She picked up the trail of the stream and began climbing the low, rocky hills, singing softly to herself and relishing the sensation of being alone and free under the huge, ever-changing autumn sky. Why, she could sing at the top of her lungs and no one could hear her!

She was doing just that when she finally came up upon the cave, then she stopped cold. For she was not alone after all. There, sitting on a rock and staring at her, was January Welles.

2.

Karrie was embarrassed, and a little unnerved. What was the polite thing to say, she wondered, when meeting a possibly crazy person one saw every day but had never actually spoken to? January continued to stare at her, and Karrie noticed that she was holding one of the little china teacups.

"Oh—hi," Karrie murmured at last, after too many seconds had elapsed for the words to have an easy air. "I—uh—Hey, are those your dishes? I wondered who they belonged to."

January shrugged and glanced away. "They're not really mine. I found them here."

"Oh." Karrie approached slowly, wondering if the girl was going to suddenly leap to her feet and sprint away. "They look old-timey, don't they?"

January nodded, and cleared her throat. "They were real dirty when I found them, like nobody had touched them for years and years. I brought some soap and washed them up real good."

"Last summer I broke one of the teacups by accident," Karrie confessed.

"I know. I found the pieces. I knew somebody nice had done it, because they were picked up so carefully."

"I felt really bad. I thought maybe the tea set belonged to little children."

"I guess it used to. Seems funny, though, to think of little children playing way out here. But then—*I* did."

"I'll bet your folks didn't know."

"Well—my mamma died when I was three."

"Oh! Mine died when I was ten."

"Then at least you can remember her real well."

"Yes, but she was sick a long time. What I remember best, before then, was how she liked to sing."

"You were singing when you came up. You have a nice voice."

"Well, thanks. I like to sing, but I don't have a *real* voice like my mother had. She studied at a conservatory and everything."

By now, Karrie had joined January at the entrance of the cave and had found a rock to sit upon. She took her knapsack off her shoulders and opened it.

"I brought sandwiches. Are you hungry? It's not lunch time, but I could eat a bear. Let's split one now and the other one later. Peanut butter or chicken salad?"

"Peanut butter," decided January. She reached up and took two tiny saucers and cups off the rock shelf. "We'll have a tea party." She smiled shyly. "Peanut butter sandwiches and spring water."

"Lemonade, should you prefer it, madam," said Karrie, unscrewing the cap on her canteen.

"Golly, I haven't had lemonade since I left Austin!"

"Oh! Are you from there?"

"Well, I was *born* here. But my grandmother took me and my sister when our mamma died. Then *she* died, and we had to come back here. I was just nine, but April was fifteen and she had a lot of friends in Austin. It was real hard on her."

"It must have been just as hard on you. When you're a little kid you think things will always stay the same. Changes are scary." Karrie downed the contents of the her teacup in one gulp. "My great-aunts lived in Austin once. They were real happy there. They had this nice little bungalow."

"April and I were happy there, too. Austin is a *green* place. Nana had a big backyard, full of big trees and flower beds. There was a special tree I climbed, and the yardman fixed me a tire swing. We had tea parties in the gazebo. It was like fairyland."

"After that you must have *hated* Benbenitas!"

"I still do. And it hates me!"

"I know *that* feeling!"

January regarded her curiously. "But you hang out with that cheerleader bunch. They don't even talk to *me*!"

"January—they say you don't talk to *them*!"

January set her jaw stubbornly. "Well—why should I? They treat me like I crawled out from under a rock. If you don't dress like them and talk like them, they think you're crazy."

"Or stuck-up. They say I put on airs."

"Oh—they say that about all the Websters."

Karrie laughed, then January laughed, too.

"Let's eat the chicken salad!" proposed Karrie, and the two girls split the remaining sandwich and devoured it hungrily.

"Next time, I'm bringing a *dozen* sandwiches," declared Karrie, licking her fingers.

"Next time I'll bring some, too," said January, and they glanced at each other happily. "So how come you found this place anyway? I never see anybody here."

"Well, it was by accident. I was searching for Dead Man's Caverns so I could write my brother I'd had an adventure. But I had more of an adventure than I bargained for. I got lost."

"No, you didn't. This is part of Squaw Mountain. Dead Man's Caverns is on the other side of the hill."

"Really? I was that close all along?"

"Sure. I'll take you some time. Once in a while, Bucko

127

Riddle lurks around over there, but he pretty much steers clear of me. He's got a notion my pop'll blow his head off if he looks at me cross-eyed."

"You're lucky! By the way, I've been wanting to thank you."

"What for? Oh! That's okay. The only problem is, I like to stay downtown Wednesdays. That's the day they get the Sunday *New York Times* at the library. Maybe you'd like to come, too."

"The Benbenitas library gets the Sunday *Times*?"

"Uh huh, it's the mayor's gift. The *Chicago Tribune* and the *Dallas Morning News*, too. Maybe he thinks all those newspapers will smarten people up, but I doubt if anybody ever looks at them but me and Miss Jane. She comes on Wednesday, too. She reads the art news and I read about the theater. We talk about how we're going to go to New York someday, and she'll study art and I'll—"

"You'll what?"

January flushed. "Go to drama school."

"Really? You want to be an actress?"

"Well, not a *movie star*," said January with contempt. "A stage actress. I want to do Shakespeare and the Greek plays and stuff like that."

"Did you ever see a real play?"

January shook her head. "I've never seen a real play and Miss Jane's never seen any real art. Where *would* we, around here?"

"I know. This seems like the ends of the earth."

"*Seems, madam! Nay, it is; I know not 'seems'*," quoted January bitterly. "Shakespeare."

"What's it from?"

"*Hamlet*. Act I, Scene II. He was miserable, like me."

"January, I bet you *will* get to New York, and you know what? You and Miss Jane can stay with me. I'd *love* to show you New York! Our apartment looks out on Central Park and—and—Oh."

"What?"

"I keep forgetting. It's not our apartment any more. One of those changes we were talking about."

"That must have been some change—from New York to *this*! Like a different planet!"

"I'll say! I felt like a little green creature from Mars."

"They make you feel that way around here! Anybody who comes from further away than Hospitality or Gladhand is too strange for words!"

"You know, Miss Jane and Mr. Mitchum are the only ones who ever ask me a thing about New York. I don't think anybody else believes there *is* a New York—I just made up the whole thing to show off."

"Did you and your brother really live there alone for two years?"

"How'd you know that? That's supposed to be a big, dark secret!"

"Then you did? Neat!"

"It was great, only we were worried about our dad. I'm not supposed to talk about him, either, or my mother. Officially, I was hatched out of a train at the age of thirteen. No parents, no past, no *nothing*!"

"Well, you can tell me anything, because I never talk to anybody, except Miss Jane. I've been dying to ask you about New York!"

"Well—why haven't you?"

"Because you're always with those girls I can't stand!"

"They're not so bad. As a matter of fact, they're the only kids at school who speak to me."

"Yeah—well, you're not missing a thing. Did you have lots of friends in New York?"

"Not really. My brother was my best friend."

"I have a brother," said January. "But I hardly know him."

"I thought it was just you and your sister."

"No. See—when my little brother was born was when my mamma died. Our aunt in San Antonio adopted him. She used to bring him over to Austin to see us when Nana was living. I haven't seen him in nearly five years, but April goes over to visit sometimes. His name's Danny. Aunt Fay named him. Otherwise

129

I guess he'd have a dumb name like November."

"Oh! You and April were named after the months you were born in?"

"Isn't that awful! I hate my name! April calls me Jano."

"I'll call you that if you like, but I think January's a neat name. *January Welles*—I can see it up in lights!"

January laughed and shook her head. "Right! Broadway, here I come! April says that's a pipe dream."

"I don't believe I've ever seen April."

"She's married to an Austin boy. He's overseas, so she and her baby live with his mother. She drives over once in a while to check up on me and Pop, but not so much lately, with gasoline rationing and her job and all."

Karrie did some quick arithmetic. "If April was fifteen and you were nine when you moved back, she must be just nineteen."

"Uh huh. She ran off and got married when she was sixteen. Pop was sure mad. I think he counted on her taking care of *me*."

January, frowning, concentrated for a minute on washing out the little teacups in the spring water. Karrie watched her in silence, then said, quietly,

"I guess I'm not the only person who's been left high and dry. Marty's always telling me that. He says I shouldn't sit around feeling sorry for myself."

"But he didn't have to stay here!"

"That's what I tell him! I'd much rather be in the Navy!"

"He sure is handsome." January flushed slightly.

"I've certainly heard *that* all my life. Well, I think he is, too. You can meet him when he comes home for Christmas. He's hoping to get a leave."

"That should make Jolene Ross very happy."

"*What?*"

"They're supposed to be sweet on each other. Overheard it on the party line, so it *must* be true!" January grinned at Karrie's dismayed expression.

"He's spoken exactly *one* word to her—'Hi.' She started writing to him and sending him pin-up pictures, that's all."

130

January shook her head with mock seriousness. "Nope. Party line says they're engaged!"

"*Oh-h*! This place is *too* weird!"

The girls looked at each other and burst out laughing.

"I tell you what: let's form a club," suggested Karrie. "We'll call it something like the Secret Society of Little Green Creatures from Mars—Benbenitas Chapter."

"Excellent! And the cave will be our clubhouse." January paused. "This cave has a secret that no one knows except me."

"Really?"

"Uh huh. I have to get on home and see about my pop now, so I'll save the secret till we have lots of time. Okay?"

"Fine. I love mysteries. Give me just one clue!"

"No clues! I'm going to keep it for a day when no one expects us home too early. I really have to go." And January stood up, nimbly scaled the canyon wall, waved briefly from the top, and was soon out of sight.

Karrie collected her knapsack, then paused to remark to the little cave: "Hey, what do you know? January Welles is a kindred spirit!"

3.

Anyone who has ever been lucky enough to make an *instant* best friend knows what an exciting and special thing that is. Both Karrie and January would have chosen to be somewhere far from Benbenitas, but they were very happy to be together, anywhere at all.

Karrie expected her aunts to object to her choosing such an odd companion as January, but they seemed quite pleased.

"Her grandmother, March Maclaine, was one of our dearest friends in Austin," Miss Prune explained. "January comes from good people, but she's had a very difficult life."

"She's like a wild Scottish thistle," said Miss Ginger, with an uncharacteristic poetic touch. "I'm glad you girls have found each other. Poor little thing needs a friend."

Karrie had to smile at hearing her new pal described as a

"poor little thing." January was many things—fierce, untamed, obstinate, dramatic, sensitive, funny—but she was *not* pathetic.

The aunts may have been pleased, but Baby Dodds, Snookie and Bev were dismayed.

"I think Baby Dodds is really upset," Karrie wrote to Marty. "She was sort of the best friend I had at school, and I guess her 'nose is out of joint.' (That means jealous.) It's all a little uncomfortable. The girls ignore January and she ignores them, and I'm caught in the middle.

"But I don't care. It makes such a difference, having a *real* friend! Jano and me against the world! I haven't felt so invincible since you went away!"

4.

Thanksgiving came along, and, though the traditional turkey appeared on the table, it was a quiet occasion at the mayor's house.

Soon it was time for Christmas, a holiday that had been ignored at Windy Crest for twenty-four years. To the mayor it was the same as any other day, except that it made him feel grouchier than usual. His one concession to the season was to present Martha and Israel with their annual cash bonus. Miss Ginger and Miss Prune also gave them something, and discreetly exchanged small gifts with each other. Neither would have dared offer a present to their brother, or so much as hum a carol while he was on the premises.

But this year they had the children to think of, they told each other staunchly. Martin was coming home on leave, and he and Karen deserved a proper, festive holiday.

The decision made, their courage wavered when it came to informing the mayor.

"I'll take care of it," Martha volunteered calmly, and the next morning, as she was serving breakfast to her stern employer, she remarked, "Israel and Karrie going over to Beals' to pick out a tree, Mayor. Want to go along?"

The mayor did not look up from his paper.

"I'm sure they can handle it, Martha," he said gruffly.

His sisters breathed a sigh of relief in unison.

Going over to Beals' to pick out a tree had become a tradition for most Benbenitas families. Every year the field behind Beals' farm was, like magic, transformed into a green forest of East Texas pines and locally cut cedars.

Karrie thought that at least half the town must have shown up on that particular Saturday morning.

"Christmas gift!" folks greeted one another genially.

"What does that mean?" Karrie asked January, who had been invited along on the expedition.

"Heck, Karrie," said January, "don't expect things to make sense around here."

The two girls selected a pretty little pine, but Israel insisted that Windy Crest had to have a cedar, and the tallest one in the field.

His eye estimated the size of the tree perfectly. When they got it home they found that it reached exactly to the parlor ceiling, and it took all hands (except the mayor's) to set it up right. Two boxes of decorations were brought down from the attic, and, amid considerable excitement, the adorning of the Christmas tree began. Miss Ginger and Miss Prune were as thrilled as children, as they recognized the ornaments they hadn't seen in nearly a quarter of a century.

"Prune, wasn't this your favorite—the silver bell?"

"Oh, no, Ginger, it was Clara's! She always had to hang it herself, way up high. Papa would hold her on his shoulders, don't you know? Oh, my! Here's one of the wise men! Henry broke the one carrying myrrh—"

"No, no! Here's the one with the myrrh. Henry broke the one carrying *gold*."

"Remember the little trees we used to have at our bungalow in Austin, Ginger?"

"Oh, yes. And we used to bake gingermen for decorations, do you remember, Prune? I wonder if we still have that recipe?"

"Got no sugar to waste on decorations," Martha reminded

them.

"We didn't *waste* them, Martha. We'd have friends over, and they'd eat them, right off the tree!"

"Did that when we was children, too," said Israel. "Cookies, gingermen, popcorn. Always had the tree right here, too, front of the parlor windows."

"Only we didn't buy it from Beals' in those days, did we, Israel," said Miss Prune. "Our papas used to take us children out to the cedar brakes and let us select the tree, then they'd chop it down with an axe."

"Nobody chops their own cedars no more," said Israel. "Not since ole Mr. Woody Beal got the idea to fill up that field of his with cut trees. Pretty soon folks got lazy, and now everybody goes to Beals'. Had some fine trees there today, but going out to the cedar brakes was *tradition* when we was bitty. Wouldn't have seemed like Christmas no other ways."

"That's right," agreed Miss Ginger. "And then we'd hunt through the corn for those rare red ears, remember? And tie them to cedar branches with wide satin ribbon and hang them on the front door."

"Corn at Christmastime?" asked Karrie incredulously.

"Why, honey, we had it stored, to feed the pigs. We kept a few pigs back in those days. Cured our own hams."

"But it was always wild turkey for Christmas dinner," Miss Prune said. "Christmas Eve, our papa and Israel's papa would go out hunting before sun-up, and they'd come home with the biggest turkey you could imagine. Usually about forty pounds, wouldn't you say, Israel?"

"Um hm," agreed Israel. "My papa had to cook it outside in a washtub over hot coals. That was a job! Had to watch every minute, see it didn't get too hot or too cold. Took near 'bout all day."

"And we children would hang around and Israel's papa would tell us stories," Miss Prune recalled.

"And just when we was getting a little cold, here'd come Mamma with the hot chocolate and popcorn," Israel added.

"You just trying to get me to go make hot chocolate," Martha grumbled good-naturedly. "And I don't know as I can spare the sugar, what with Christmas baking to do when that boy comes home."

"Oh, look, Ginger, remember this angel?" cried Miss Prune. "Sally liked to put it at the top, but Henry used to fuss because *our* mamma always liked the star up there."

"Sally usually won, but here's Mamma's star. Which do you think, Prune?"

"Well—" Miss Prune looked undecided. "Henry was fond of the star. Maybe he'd like to see it there, Ginger."

"If he'll even come into the parlor while the tree's up," Miss Ginger said with a sigh.

Miss Prune glanced at Karrie and January, who were quietly and happily hanging tarnished colored balls and bells on the branches.

"Why don't we let the girls decide?" she suggested. "Angel or star, girls? It's up to you. Goodness me, Ginger, I think I could use a cup of tea. Let's take a recess and leave a little work for these two energetic young ladies."

When the older people had retired to the kitchen, Karrie smiled at January and remarked, "They're cute, aren't they? But it really must have been more fun back in those days, don't you think?"

"I guess so," said January. "Hard to imagine Benbenitas ever being much fun. Did you have big Christmas trees like this in New York?"

"No, this is my first Christmas tree."

"It *is*?"

"Uh huh. We used to spend the holidays at a ski lodge in the mountains—before my mother got sick."

"What about when it was just you and Marty?"

"Well, our first Christmas alone we stayed home and ate cereal because we'd used up our month's allowance, but last Christmas we had fun. We saved up and got tickets to the ice show. Do you usually have a tree at your house?"

"Well, a *tiny* one. April drives up Christmas Eve and brings a little tree in a pot, already decorated, and fruit cake and candy. She makes a nice dinner, and she and I sing carols while we wash the dishes. Then she drives back to Austin. That's it. At Nana's we used to hang our stockings from the mantle and the next morning they'd be full of surprises, and there'd be all these toys under the tree. That's what I think of when I think of Christmas."

"I think of the smell of roasting chestnuts, and people bustling around Fifth Avenue in the cold, and store windows that look like fairyland."

"Neat! I'm going to have that kind of Christmas someday! I'll bet your brother will be surprised when he sees this tree."

"Just two more days! Jano, I'm so excited I could *burst*!"

"Am I going to meet him?"

"Of course you are! I wrote him all about you."

"I thought maybe when he was home would be a good time to show you my secret about the cave. But—"

"But what?"

January shrugged. "If he's only got a week, maybe he'll want to spend a lot of time with Jolene."

"Ha! Doesn't she *wish*! You know, she calls every minute or so to make sure she has the day right. I'd be *ashamed* to act that silly over a boy. Anyway, if I know Marty, he'd rather learn the secret of the cave."

The grown-ups, having stayed away as long as they could bear to, were soon back to help finish up the decorating. Martha began to sing "Silent Night," and soon everyone joined in. Karrie didn't know all the words, but she hummed along happily.

"What sweet voices you girls have!" commented Miss Prune.

"Karrie can *really* sing," January volunteered like a proud parent. "She's going to be an opera singer someday."

Karrie flushed. "Honestly, Jano! I *told* you I don't have that kind of voice. My mother—"

She caught a warning look on Miss Prune's face, and turned her head to see her grandfather standing, stiff and unsmiling, in the doorway of the parlor.

"Karen," he said, his voice strained but not unkind. "I'm afraid I have some bad news for you."

The room which had been filled with singing and laughter was suddenly hushed.

"The knock at the door—apparently none of you heard it. It was a telegram—from Martin. His leave has been canceled. He won't be coming home. I'm afraid it means—he's being shipped out."

There were murmurs of disappointment and sympathy. Karrie remained motionless, holding Sally's angel and staring at the tree. Her first Christmas tree. How happy she'd been, hanging the old-fashioned decorations and singing carols; how happy, imagining Marty doing a double-take when he walked through that door. "Wow!" he would say.

It had been a wonderful tree, just a moment ago. Now it seemed a silly, dreary thing, decked out in the tired relics of Christmases long-past—which might better have been left in the darkness of the attic, safely packed away from the hard light of the present, where there was little to celebrate.

5.

Marty shipped out on his eighteenth birthday. Now his only address was a Fleet Post Office number.

"I'm sending this letter out into the unknown," Karrie wrote forlornly. "Grandfather tells me that you won't be allowed to say where you are or even where you've been. I'm not going to be able to picture you somewhere, just as I can't picture Dad somewhere. At least I'll be getting letters from *you*. Lots of letters, please, Marty, as often as possible.

"We had a Christmas tree all ready for you. It was un-decorated and dragged out behind the barn today. It looks the way I feel.

"Jolene wanders the halls at school with a tragic expression on her face. When she stops to talk to anyone, the words that waft through the corridors are: 'leave canceled—shipped out—no mail in days—' A person would think she'd been left at the altar! But it doesn't keep her from going over to Hospitality with Bettie Rae on Saturday nights to dance with the soldier boys at the canteen.

"I hope this letter doesn't ruin your morale! Take care of yourself!!!!!! Love—K."

6.

"It's just not fair," said Karrie, for the five hundredth time. "Mr. Wirtz said they *always* get leaves before shipping out."

She was sitting with January on the rocks outside the little cave, chucking small stones into the pool of spring water.

"Well—maybe they needed his group in a hurry," said January. "He's a hospital corpsman, isn't he? They may be desperate for them some place."

"That's what Grandfather said. It doesn't sound good. That means he's going where it's dangerous—"

"Karrie!" January was sympathetic, but her patience was beginning to wear thin. "It's a war! Of course it's dangerous! Be glad he's not a pilot like Howie Schulman. Hospital corpsmen are probably—behind the lines or something."

"He's on a ship in the middle of the Pacific Ocean—which is full of submarines and torpedoes—"

"All right, all right! But you can't sit and think about it, day in and day out. Come on—how about if I show you the secret?"

"Jano, I'm just not in the mood. Save it for another day."

"No—now!" said January firmly. "I'm going to cheer you up or die trying!"

She grabbed Karrie's hand, pulled her to her feet, and propelled her into the shadows of the small cave.

"Okay—what?" said Karrie, watching January's hands explore the back wall in the dim light.

"See?" said January. "Up here behind this ledge where I keep my flashlight—it's the entrance to a hidden tunnel!"

"It *is?*"

"Neat, huh? Nobody knows about it but me! And now you! It's only big enough for a skinny person to slip through. The best way is to lie on your back and scrooch yourself along till it starts to get wider. Then it's easy—you can turn over and crawl till it gets narrow again at the other end. It goes right through!"

"Right through to what?" asked Karrie dubiously.

"All the way to Dead Man's Caverns!" said January triumphantly. "You wanted me to take you there."

"Uh—yeah, I did. How far is it? I mean, how long do you have to—scrooch yourself along?"

"I do the whole thing in about fifteen minutes. Come on!"

Karrie held back. "Jano—I can't do that."

"Sure you can. You're littler than I am."

"I know, but—but I think maybe I have claustrophobia. I don't even like elevators."

"Good grief! You *had* to ride elevators in New York!"

"Of course I did. We lived on the fifth floor. But that doesn't mean I like them. They make me feel trapped."

"Dadgum it, Karrie, I didn't think you were afraid of *anything*! Look! I've been through this tunnel a dozen times. The important thing is not to lose your nerve."

"Jano, I can *make* myself do it, and someday I will, okay? I'd just rather not *today*."

January looked disappointed, but she shrugged and said, "All right, then. I'll take you the long way around."

Karrie sighed. All she really felt like doing was staring at the water and brooding about Marty, but she couldn't say no to *everything* January proposed.

"Okay, okay, let's go," she agreed drearily.

January retrieved her flashlight from behind the ledge, and they struck out in silence across the rocky hill. Though they were walking in bright sunshine, Karrie's thoughts were on that dark passageway far beneath them. Her relief that Jano hadn't insisted was mingled with shame for having begged off. *Showing the white feather* was what Marty would call it.

"Someday I *will* do it," she promised herself. But hadn't

139

Jolene said something about *snakes*?

The girls finally came to a halt in front of a large cave in the side of the hill. Karrie looked at it, then shrugged.

"Gee, you're determined not to like anything today!" said January in exasperation. "It's not Carlsbad Caverns—what did you expect? You'll be surprised though. There're lots of twisty tunnels in there. It's easy to get lost if you don't know what you're doing."

"How come it's called Dead Man's Caverns, anyway?"

"The early settlers found the dead body of an old Indian in here. The Indians had pretty well left these parts by then, but this one old fellow must have stayed behind for some reason. There were signs that he'd been living in the caves. You know—blankets and jugs and firewood."

"Did they kill him? The settlers?"

"No, I said they found him. He was already dead."

"Aunt Ginger says the early settlers were a rough bunch. They murdered my great-great-grandfather."

"Who? You don't mean Matthew Webster? He ran off to California because of the Civil War and left his wife holding the bag. That's a *legend* around here."

"I know, but that's not what my great-great-grandmother Prudence told Aunt Prune and Aunt Ginger. She said the settlers killed him because he voted against secession."

"Well, anyway—they didn't kill the Indian. Let's go in. You're not afraid, are you?"

"Of course I'm not afraid! *Go on—I'll follow thee.* Act I, Scene—whatever. You're not the only one who's read *Hamlet*."

7.

As the girls progressed deeper into the caverns, Karrie grew more and more uneasy, and when they lost the outside light entirely and had to rely on January's flashlight, she found it hard to keep a grip on herself.

"What would happen if there was an earthquake while you were down here?"

"Karrie, we don't have earthquakes around here. What's the matter with you?"

"Nothing. I just wondered. What about bats?"

"Sure, there're bats. They come flying out like a swarm of bees in the evening. It's neat!"

"Yeah, I'd like to see that." Karrie hoped she sounded more adventuresome then she felt. "Hey, this is pretty impressive!"

"Just wait! It's really something when you get further down. But watch your step. It gets a little steep and we're going to have to crawl—just for a bit."

A huge overhanging boulder blocked their way. January dropped to her knees and started crawling under it and downward along a narrow ledge. Karrie followed her, liking the whole experience less and less.

"If we got lost in here, nobody would ever find us," she said, and found nothing reassuring in her echoing voice.

"We're not going to get lost. I know this place like the back of my hand."

"Um-m. My dad and uncle used to explore these caves."

"My dad, too. Now—take a look." January stood upright on the ledge and flashed her light around the cavern.

Karrie rose up, too, then caught her breath and hastily crouched down again, feeling lightheaded. "My gosh! It's—it's a *gnome-kingdom*!" she cried in astonishment.

"It's a what?"

"An underground world where gnomes live! I've got this old book of fairy tales my mother brought from Germany—Wait!— hold the flashlight on one spot, will you? Golly, look at all the stalagmites!"

"The hanging-down ones are *stalactites*. Stalagmites point up. So—what do you think about Dead Man's Cavern *now*?"

"I think—it's—Golly! Let me have the flashlight, please. You're making me dizzy."

January, squatting down beside her, handed it over. Karrie slowly directed its beam around the chamber's various levels, her sudden curiosity outweighing her fear for the moment.

What she saw was an eerie underworld, so like a familiar illustration in her mother's storybook that it stirred afresh forgotten childhood imaginings. It was a place of startling shapes and shadows, dark crannies, hideaways. Ghostly stalactites hung from the ceiling like chandeliers; mysterious paths snaked through labyrinths of boulders and stalagmites; fantastical rock formations glittered in the flashlight's beam.

"See? That's their treasure," Karrie whispered, as if afraid of being overheard.

"Whose treasure?"

"The gnomes', of course."

"I see! Just what do your gnomes look like?"

"You know! They're little! Very little, and they have pointy beards. And pointy ears. They mine for precious jewels and stuff."

"Um-m. So how come they're not down there mining?"

"Why, they're hiding, of course! At the first sound of human intruders, they escape into secret passageways."

"Can't say that I blame them."

"Oh, Jano, this is really something!"

"It *is* neat, isn't it? Told you. Excuse me for not believing in your gnomes, but when I was a little kid, I decided that an invisible giant lived down here, and the stalactites were leaking ice cream cones he'd bitten the bottoms off."

The echo of Karrie's laughter sounded maniacal to her ears. "Did you really come down here alone when you were *little*?"

"When I was nine or ten, yes."

"Didn't you scare yourself silly with your invisible giant?"

"Yeah, sort of. But I liked being scared. The giant was my friend. I liked him better than the people in Benbenitas."

"Do you think he'll mind if my gnomes move in with him?"

"Well—not if they try not to get on his nerves. Shine the light straight down."

Karrie did. And saw nothing but hungry blackness below the ledge that supported them. She gasped, then tried to gulp back her panic.

142

"Bottomless pit," said Jano proudly.

Karrie's mouth felt totally dry, but she attempted to speak casually. "It's got to have a bottom."

"Well, they've gone down real deep on ropes and nobody's ever reached it. Maybe if there was a rope ladder long enough, you could climb down to China. Of course halfway down you'd have to turn upside down and start climbing up instead. Did you ever wonder how gravity works in the center of the earth?"

"Yes, of course, it's constantly on my mind! Jano, you really *are* crazy!"

"What about your tiny miners? You're balmier than I am!"

"Not even close! So how far do these caves go on?"

"Nobody knows. They're always discovering another chamber. This is as far as I usually come."

Karrie let out a grateful sigh. She'd had quite enough of trying to act nonchalant while perching on a narrow, clammy shelf over a bottomless pit. Then January added, "But we can go further if you want to. Feel like exploring?"

"Not today," said Karrie quickly. "Some other time. Let's get out of here, all right?"

She began to crawl back beneath the overhanging rock, following the shaky beam of the flashlight she clutched in her fist.

"I'm right behind you," reported January cheerfully. "Someday we ought to bring canteens and sandwiches and see how far we can go. It's a good idea to have extra batteries along, just in case. It would be pretty dangerous to get stuck down here without light. One false step and whoosh! Over you'd go!"

When they reached safer ground and could again stand up, Karrie tried to hand the flashlight back to January, but she shook her head.

"Hang on to it. Think you can make it back alone from here? Just follow the wall around till you see daylight, then you can find the way out."

"Why? What are you going to do?"

"I'll show you. Shine the light up here. That's fine."

January hoisted herself up onto a ledge halfway up the wall. "Go on back to our cave. I'll meet you there."

"Jano, let's not do this today."

"There's nothing to it. Now go on. I'm getting started."

Then suddenly and adroitly January thrust her head and shoulders into what appeared to be only a cranny, and quickly wriggled out of sight. Karrie shone the light in and saw nothing but the soles of her friend's shoes.

"Go on," said Jano's muffled voice.

"I hate this!" Karrie grumbled to herself. "Follow the wall—follow the darned wall—follow—Daylight! Oh, thank goodness!"

When she emerged into the blinding sunshine, she had to shield her eyes with her hands. Scrambling back over the hill at breakneck speed, she made the return trip in half the time, and hurried breathlessly into the little cave just as a head was emerging, face up, from the narrow passage.

"Nothing to it," cried January, as she slid out and jumped down.

"Jano," said Karrie, "next time you want to cheer me up, do you suppose we could just go to the movies or something?"

Chapter 7
January Welles

1.

Karrie cheered up. She had to. One thing she'd learned over and over in her fourteen years was: life goes on. And now that Marty was overseas, she decided that henceforth she would write only chatty, cheerful letters, and complain about nothing more personal than the Fleet Post Office.

"I wish the FPO would get its act together! Not one letter since you shipped out! I hope at least you're *receiving* mail, because I've been faithful as can be about writing, and *someone else* has, too. Every day at school your little pin-up girl approaches me in the hall, and I have to tell her, 'No, Jolene, I haven't heard from him yet.' 'Well, now, don't you worry, Karrie with a K,' she says bravely. 'I just know we'll hear *real* soon!'

"Things are okay here—that is, no stranger than usual. I saw our favorite relative, Lollie Beal, downtown yesterday, and I've come to the conclusion that she's what Mr. Wirtz calls 'one brick shy of a full load.' Every time I run into her (and believe me, it's only when I can't avoid it!) she gives me a suspicious look and says, *Been to Bastrop lately?* Is that insane, or what? There *is* a town called Bastrop, but why would she think I go there?

"Jano and I have been stopping by to see Mr. Wirtz now and

145

then, because Aunt Prune says he must be lonely since Snookie and her mother moved out to California after Christmas. Mr. Wirtz doesn't seem all that lonely, but he's always glad of the visit and wants news of you. Wish I had some to give him! He says I can't expect letters regularly any more, but I'll probably get a bunch all at once.

"Mr. Wirtz didn't know Jano very well till I started bringing her around, but they hit it off right away. I think he says things to us he wouldn't say to other people. When I told him about the school janitor keeping my bike out of Bucko's reach, he told us that he and Rollie Johnson have been friends since they were boys. They play checkers together, and he gives Mr. Johnson haircuts after hours, with the shades pulled. 'If folks knew I was cutting a colored man's hair, I'd lose every customer I got,' he said, chuckling. 'Now ain't that the silliest dadgum thing you ever heard of?' I really like Mr. Wirtz.

"Good news! The war's as good as won! Bev's little sister heard President Roosevelt on the radio asking every American to make sacrifices, so she donated her tricycle to the scrap metal drive. Then bawled her head off for a week. Yes, Bienvenidos is doing its all. Beat-up cars and tractors, even rusty old wash tubs, are scooped up and sent somewhere to be turned into battleships. At the Bijou they have a big barrel for tinfoil from cigarette and chewing gum packages. If they build battleships with *that* stuff, you're in big trouble!

"The housewives save bacon fat in coffee cans, but I can't imagine where it ends up. I sure hope the Navy isn't feeding it to you!

"Besides the Draft Board and the Ration Board, we now have the Tire Rationing Board, and I've heard they're a *mean* bunch. Only people who travel on business can buy tires. Mr. Wirtz says the Board should confiscate the tires on Bucko Riddle's truck and bring peace to the streets of Bienvenidos.

"Well, that's it for the local news. Exciting, huh? Everybody sends best wishes. Israel claims that Grandfather is proud of you. I am, too! Love—K.

146

"P.S. Did you notice the date of this letter? *Ta—da-a-a!* Today I am fourteen! So is January. We were born an hour apart! I'm older! She skipped a grade, like me, so we're the youngest kids in our class. Martha has been saving up sugar to make us an extra-special cake. Aunt Prune called up Mr. Welles and invited him to come to supper tonight, but he made some excuse to get out of it. Nobody was surprised. I've still never met him, and I can't help wondering if he's as peculiar as people say.

"P.P.S. Do you remember my birthday last year, when we blew all our allowance on the show at Radio City and dinner at the Deli, and then had to live on cereal for the rest of the month? That was the greatest birthday ever! Love—K."

2.

If being friends with January changed Karrie's life, it changed January's even more. Though she continued to hold herself aloof from her classmates, there was a visible relaxing of her stony attitude, and she began to express herself in class, beyond simply answering the teacher's questions.

This was a mixed blessing, Karrie discovered, when the English teacher, Miss Duvall, announced that the new semester would be devoted to the study of Shakespeare's plays.

"Jano thinks she *owns* Shakespeare," Karrie explained to Marty, "and Miss Duvall always expects us to write endless papers that echo her own opinions. I can see trouble brewing."

A day or two later, she reported: "It's even worse than I thought it would be. Jano's threatening to drop out of school. Here is a typical exchange in the classroom: Miss D., smiling toothily and trying to quote *Hamlet* from her meager memory: 'There are more things between heaven and earth than you ever dreamed of in your philosophy, Horatio.' Jano, between gritted teeth: '*In.*' Miss Duvall: 'What?' Jano: 'In. There are more things *in* heaven and earth, Horatio, than are dreamt of in your philosophy.' Miss Duvall, haughtily: 'It's not the words themselves that matter, it's the *spirit* of the words.' Jano: 'It's *Shakespeare's* words that matter.' I don't know who's harder to take—Miss Duvall or January."

Karrie was thankful for Wednesday afternoons, because January forgot to be grouchy about Miss Duvall when they were at the library with Miss Jane, poring over the *New York Times* together, whispering and giggling.

"I'll bet Miss Jane is the only high school teacher who ever gets shushed by the librarian," Karrie wrote to Marty. "Miss Weeks must think sound is damaging to books, because she shushes us even if we're the only ones in the library—and we usually are. Miss Jane is just like another girl. How I'd love to walk through the Metropolitan Museum with her! She'd be in 'hog's heaven,' as they say around here.

"She dreams of being a starving artist in Greenwich Village, and Jano, of course, yearns to be a great actress. I get pretty homesick, looking at the *Times*, and I guess my only burning ambition is for you and me to go home to New York again. I'd like to take Jano and Miss Jane along. Okay with you?"

3.

As Mr. Wirtz had predicted, Karrie received several letters in one day, and she immediately ran upstairs to her room to feast upon them. But she was soon interrupted by Aunt Prune.

"Phone call, Karen! It's Jolene!"

"*Inevitably*," Karrie grumbled on the way downstairs.

"Did you get letters?" cried Jolene's voice on the line. "I got *three*! Isn't it wonderful? Listen, Karrie with a K, it's amateur night at the Bijou and the Wallace twins are in the jitterbug contest. We're all fixing to go root for them. Why don't you come?"

"I never go downtown at night. Israel takes the car home."

"Well, I tell you what. If he'll drop you off at my house on his way, I'll drive you home after the show."

Karrie found herself fresh out of excuses.

"You know," Jolene continued, "we need to cheer up Baby Dodds. That child has had her chin in her socks ever since Snookie went off to California. Tell you what. Bring January

148

Welles. I'll drive you both home. Come on, Karrie with a K! We can compare letters!"

Karrie reluctantly agreed, and after they hung up she called January to pass along Jolene's proposal.

"No," said January flatly.

"Oh, come on," Karrie begged. "I can't get out of it—"

"No backbone," said January.

"Jano, if you'll do this tonight, I'll do something *you* want to do, whether *I* want to or not."

"Hm-m-m." January took her time considering this foolhardy offer. Finally she said, "Will you help me build a raft?"

"A raft?" repeated Karrie, relieved. "Sure! Uh—why?"

"I've always wanted to go down the river on a raft, like Huckleberry Finn."

"Swell! We'll build a raft! And we'll manage to have fun tonight, okay?"

Later that evening, Israel drove both girls to the Ross home. Bettie Rae, Bev, and a somewhat somber Baby Dodds were already there, waiting on the front porch with Jolene.

It was a mild evening, more like May than February, but Karrie had brought a sweater at Miss Prune's insistence.

"Oh, leave it in the car with Israel," Jolene advised. "The theater will be hot as Hades. They don't air-condition in the winter, even if it's eighty degrees out."

After Israel drove away, the girls set out on foot for the Bijou.

"It's the biggest night in town, now that football season's over," Bev said. "If you don't get there early you can't get a seat, then you end up standing in the back of the theater."

"And Bucko Riddle and his gang are usually hanging around back there, acting ugly and heckling the performers," added Bettie Rae. "The manager always has to call Uncle Sheriff to come remove his pride and joy!"

The girls arrived early and found good seats. The theater quickly filled up and quite a few people had to stand up in the back, but everyone was happy to note that Bucko Riddle was not among them.

"Probably out torturing a cat or something," Baby Dodds theorized gloomily.

Though everyone had come for the talent show, they had to sit through a rather poor movie first.

"They always show their 'B' pictures on amateur night," whispered Bev, "because they know they'll get a good turn-out anyway. Oh, I sure hope the Wallace girls win tonight!"

"What do they get if they win?" asked Karrie.

"The *big* winner gets a twenty-five dollar War Bond. Second prize is free passes for a month."

"*Sh-h-h!*" someone behind them hissed.

Finally the movie ended and it was time for the main event. It started off with a dog act, featuring Mr. Pitcher, who ran the town's only garage and filling station, and his two lean mongrels. The dogs leaped through the old tire rim Mr. Pitcher grandly held out for them, barked four times in unison when asked to add two and two, and attempted to walk across the stage on their hind legs. They earned a warm round of applause and a few whistles.

Karrie glanced over at January to share a laugh with her, but saw that she was staring impassively at the stage. Karrie sighed. Jano was obviously bent on being a pain in the neck.

The next performers were a gangly boy named Gene Bob Jessup and his two little sisters. Gene Bob played the accordion while the girls, who managed to scratch their heads without missing a beat, tap-danced with energetic abandon.

"Why, those children got *head lice*," Baby Dodds declared, scandalized.

Next, a plump, pretty girl named Angie Beal—grimly accompanied on the piano by her mother, Lollie—sang "Lover, Come Back To Me." The piano was dreadfully out of tune, reflected Karrie, and so was Angie Beal.

"Can't stand that girl," Bettie Rae remarked. "She's so boy-crazy."

Baby Dodds elbowed Karrie and whispered in her ear, "Talk

about people living in glass houses! Guess who steals her father's car Saturday nights to go dancing at the Hospitality canteen?"

"I heard that," said Bettie Rae without resentment. "I'm just being patriotic, that's all."

"Angie Beal sure can sing," said Bev.

The finale was the dance contest, with four couples and the Wallace twins jitterbugging to a Glen Miller record, and Karrie, who looked on the evening chiefly as amusing material for her letters to Marty, had to admit to herself that they were really quite good.

The Wallace twins won the dance competition and the second prize of free passes, but the big winner of the night was Angie Beal, who graciously blushed and curtsied and blew kisses when she was presented with her War Bond.

After the show was over, Jolene suggested they all go to Webber's for a soda. It was there that January made her one remark of the evening.

"Karrie can sing much better than Angie Beal."

There was a startled hush, then, after the girls recovered from the shock of hearing January Welles voluntarily speak, they immediately started in on Karrie. "Why don't you try out next month?" "Oh, *do*, girl, it'll be such a *kick*!" "Now, you *have* to, doesn't she, y'all?" "We'll get Gene Bob to play the accordion for you!"

"I'd rather jump through Mr. Pitcher's tire rims," said Karrie grimly. "I'll *never* sing in public in Benbenitas."

"Oh, you will, too! Mark my words!" prophesied Bev.

"Forget it! You're a real pal, Jano."

But January had spoken her piece and never uttered another word until later on, when Jolene dropped her off at home.

"Thanks," she said, slamming the car door, and headed toward the house without a backward look.

Jolene let out the clutch and drove on. "Well! Nobody could ever accuse her of being a magpie, could they?" she said lightly. "It's wonderful you've befriended her, Karrie with a K, but I declare I can't figure out what makes that girl tick!"

"Umm," said Karrie noncommittally.

"Wasn't it a thrill getting all that mail today?" Jolene said, moving on to the subject that truly interested her. "Marty writes the most hilarious letters, doesn't he? But he never talks about what he's *feeling*, you know? Or maybe he does to you."

"Nope," said Karrie.

"Does he—like—ever write anything about *me*?"

Karrie smiled into the darkness. "No, Jolene, he writes mostly about his buddies and stuff."

"Oh. Well, that's what he writes to me, too. I wish he'd send me a picture. Do you have any pictures of him?"

"No recent ones. Sorry."

"Well, anyway, I'm just so relieved the letters have started coming, and he's all right. Of course we don't have any idea what he's going through, since he can't tell us anything, but there's something just—*real brave*—about the way he writes those funny letters when he must be scared to death."

"Marty's never scared!"

Jolene was silent for a moment, then said in a voice suddenly grave and grown-up, "*Everybody* gets scared, Karrie with a K. It's part of the human condition."

They pulled up in the Windy Crest driveway and Karrie got out of the car. "Thanks a lot, Jolene. Goodnight."

"Night-night," cried Jolene gaily, quite like herself again.

During the last half hour, the false, mild May had been routed by February, and the temperature had dipped dramatically. Karrie hugged her bare arms and shivered as she stood watching the car drive away.

"Jolene, you're much harder to figure out than January," she muttered to the evening in general, then she ran inside.

4.

Karrie had already gone to bed when she heard the sound of a truck below in the driveway. She quickly slipped into her robe and ran down the attic stairs. She met Miss Prune and Miss Ginger, also in their robes, on the second-floor landing. They had

152

switched on the lights, and were murmuring, "Who can it be at this hour?" Then came two hesitant thuds of the door knocker. The mayor, emerging from his study, was the first to reach the door.

He opened it to reveal a shivering, embarrassed January. She wore no coat or sweater, only the same thin dress she had been wearing earlier in the evening, and a gusty, cold wind was whipping her long straight hair about her face.

"Why, January!" said the mayor.

By then Karrie and her great-aunts were also at the door.

"Oh, honey, come in," cried Miss Prune, pulling her inside. "You're freezing to death!"

"Is something wrong, January?" the mayor asked her.

January shook her head and tried to laugh. "I—just need a favor. Do you think I could sleep here tonight? See—Pop must have dozed off. He has all the doors locked and—Well, a blue norther blew in—"

"Oh, my!" exclaimed Miss Prune. "Do you suppose he's ill? Shall we phone Israel to come drive us over and—"

"Oh, no thank you!" January said hastily. "I'm sure he's okay. He's a real hard sleeper. I just thought maybe I could spend the night—"

"You are welcome here any time, January," said the mayor so kindly that Karrie looked at him in surprise.

"Are you hungry, dear?" Miss Ginger asked.

"Oh, that's okay. I had something before we went to the picture show—" replied January, but Miss Prune and Miss Ginger soon had her sitting in the kitchen sipping soup, with a blanket around her shoulders. When she had finished they insisted she have a hot bath and change into a pair of Karrie's pajamas.

Karrie turned down the bed in Marty's room for her friend, and tried to joke with her about how funny she looked in the borrowed pajamas, which were at least a size too small for her. But January seemed too tired to talk, and Karrie left her alone to get some sleep.

The next morning January was up and dressed early, but was

just as uncommunicative. Miss Prune and Miss Ginger invited her to have Sunday breakfast with the family, but she declined. She accepted a glass of orange juice, thanked everybody, and started out the door.

"But January," said the mayor, "what if you still can't get in? Don't you want—"

"Oh, it'll be all right, Mr. Mayor," she said. "It's easier to wake Pop in the morning. He'll hear me banging."

And with that she was out the door. She climbed into her father's old truck and drove off down the driveway.

"I never even knew she could drive!" Karrie said.

"Sometimes she *has* to," said Miss Prune. "Even the sheriff looks the other way. She's been driving since she was eleven."

"*Eleven?*"

"She's fourteen now, isn't she?" said the mayor. "I believe she can get a license. I'll look into it."

"But I don't understand!" protested Karrie. "What do you mean, sometimes she *has* to drive? She's never said anything about it and she—she tells me *everything*!"

"Oh, honey, she wouldn't tell you that. It's her pride," said Miss Prune. "Her father—well, he simply can't be relied upon. She's always having to drive him to the doctor—"

"Ned Welles never had any business raising that child," declared Miss Ginger. "I can't understand why the aunt didn't take those girls when their grandmother died."

"I haven't met her father," said Karrie, troubled. "I've never even been to her house."

"I doubt if she'll ever invite you there, dear. She never knows what condition he'll be in," said Miss Prune.

"But—then is he really *crazy* like they say at school?"

The mayor and his sisters exchanged a look, then the mayor walked off to his study. Miss Prune put her arm around Karrie's shoulders and said,

"Come eat your breakfast and I'll tell you about it."

5.

When they were seated at the breakfast table, Miss Prune poured Karrie a glass of orange juice, and sighed. "He's not exactly crazy, honey. He's just very *sad*, and—he drinks."

"The man's a hopeless drunk!" Miss Ginger declared brusquely.

"Now, Ginger," murmured Miss Prune.

"Well, it's true. Why pussyfoot around the subject? Poor January! Lord knows how many times she's been locked out and couldn't rouse him by banging on the door. I expect she usually sleeps out in that old truck when it happens, but last night it turned off so cold she couldn't stay out there."

"Ned Welles used to be such a fine, good-looking boy," recalled Miss Prune. "He was in your Uncle Martin's class. He was a brilliant debater and elocutionist."

"What happened to him?" Karrie asked.

"Well, his wife died so tragically—"

"Oh, Prune, it wasn't that one thing!" said Miss Ginger. "He's weak—always has been."

"Well—he does have his mother's sensitive nature."

"*Too* sensitive, entirely. He could have had a brilliant career. I can remember him sitting at this very table with Martin and—with our boys—planning their futures. So many dreams they had! Ned wanted to become a Shakespearean actor, or an English professor at some fine university, but his father thought it was all nonsense."

"But he did let Ned go to the University, Ginger."

"For all the good it did. It was about the same time your Uncle Martin went into the service, Karen. They wouldn't let Ned sign up because he'd lost two fingers helping his father in the mill. Oh, he hated that mill!"

"What happened to him at the University?" Karrie asked.

"Got sidetracked by love," said Miss Ginger grimly. "Met June Maclaine and nothing would do but he had to marry her, and his father said, fine, then quit school and support her! So—that was that! No more career!"

"I always felt a little responsible, since he met June at our house in Austin," said Miss Prune. "March Maclaine—June's mother—was our good friend, you know."

"Why should we feel responsible?" scoffed Miss Ginger. "We didn't tell them to fall in love."

"So what happened?" prompted Karrie.

"Well, they moved in with her mother in Austin. He kept losing jobs and June kept losing babies. It was terrible! He wasn't built for working and she wasn't built for childbearing. Finally she did have April, and January, a few years after that."

"By that time, they were back here," explained Miss Prune. "Ned took over running the mill when his father died, and the funny thing is, he's done a fine job, even though he always hated it. So did June. She couldn't stand Benbenitas!"

"Weren't they ever happy?" asked Karrie.

"Oh, who knows?" said Miss Ginger. "They were crazy about each other, at any rate, wouldn't you say, Prune?"

"Oh, yes! Poor Ned! The light went out of his life when June died!"

"It never should have happened. We thought June was through trying to have babies, but then there she was, in the family way again. With the little boy—"

"Danny," supplied Karrie.

"Yes, Danny. *He* was all right, but June died right after he was born. Ned was hopeless. Well, I suppose he was in shock. He let March Maclaine take the little girls to live with her in Austin and the baby was adopted by the sister."

"What was her name again, Ginger?"

"Something ridiculous—like October. I could never imagine why refined people like the Maclaines chose to name their children after months!"

"No, no, it was *February*. She changed it to Fay."

"That's a long way from February. Not that I blame her. But I do blame her for not taking in those girls. April ended up eloping when she was sixteen, and poor little January's grown up like a weed."

156

"She—she's all right," said Karrie. "And she really loves her father. I don't think he's mean to her or anything."

"No, there's nothing mean in poor Ned," agreed Miss Prune.

"But isn't working at the mill *dangerous* if he drinks?"

"He doesn't start drinking until after closing time," said Miss Ginger. "J.J. Beal dropped by one evening and found Ned sitting at the kitchen table reciting poetry at the top of his lungs, drunk as a hoot owl. January was trying to get him to eat some supper. Poor child tries her best to take care of him, when he should be taking care of *her*."

"I suppose she'll end up like Jane Llewellyn—looking after a helpless parent till her youth is gone." said Miss Prune with a sigh.

"But Jano *hates* it here! And she has such dreams!" protested Karrie.

"So did Jane. People do what they have to do. But it's a terrible pity."

The aunts wandered off onto the subject of Jane Llewellyn and her plight. They were beginning to rehash her undying love for the lost Martin, when Karrie decided it was time to excuse herself and leave them to their reminiscing.

She went up to her room and wrote a letter to Marty. But the tone was all wrong—just not cheerful enough—so she tore it up and decided to try again later.

She remained at her desk for a little while, staring out the window across the valley. Finally she rose, went downstairs to the telephone, rang up Mabel Klein and asked for the Welles house.

January's answering voice sounded subdued.

"Hey," said Karrie brightly, "when do we start on the raft?"

Chapter 8
Whisper Down The Lane

1.

Her first winter without snow left Karrie feeling cheated, but when spring arrived in the hill country, it astonished the young stranger from New York.

"I never thought I'd describe this place as 'beautiful,'" she wrote to Marty, "but I wish you could see the wildflowers. They have great names, like Indian blanket, Indian paintbrush, Mexican hat. Beals' field is one mass of bluebonnets. They're called that because each flower is a like a cone made up of tiny, perfect little blue *bonnets*. It's the state flower.

"Down by the river, the redbud trees are blooming, and they look just like their name, too. I spend all my Saturdays down by the river because of The Raft! By the way, this is Top Secret, so not a word to Jolene. Remember: Loose Lips Wreck Rafts!

"You asked how work's progressing. It's not! We spend all our time searching for the right logs and then lugging them back to our secret clearing in the woods. January is very particular about every log we choose. I'll bet Noah didn't take this long building the ark. He probably knew what he was doing, which we certainly don't! If you have any tips on how to lash logs together, we'd like to hear them. After all, you *are* a sea-going man!

"At least this keeps Jano from dragging me off to explore the

158

bottomless pit in Dead Man's Caverns, and it sure solves the problem of What To Do On Saturday!"

But about the one Saturday they did not work on the raft, Karrie wrote nothing, because she was determined to stick to her resolve not to worry Marty with her troubles.

2.

January was busy at home that Saturday, as her sister had driven up from Austin for the day. Karrie felt at loose ends at first, then decided to take the opportunity to square things with her conscience. She'd been feeling guilty about neglecting Baby Dodds, who, after all, had been her first friend in Benbenitas.

Baby Dodds sounded pleased when Karrie telephoned and suggested they meet for the matinee at the Bijou. "Only thing is, I promised Mamma I'd do some chores for my Great-Grannie Morris this morning. Want to meet me out there around noon? She lives down the way a piece from Grannie Opal. Only other house on that old road, so you can't miss it. We can bike into town together, grab a sandwich at my house and still make the one o'clock show."

Grannie Opal's little house, where Karrie's family often stopped to pick up Maybelle, was out on a lonely, unpaved farm road, which made for rough going on a bicycle. Karrie passed the familiar house, and continued on for a long, bumpy distance before she came in sight of what had to be Great-Grannie Morris's place. As she drew nearer, she stared in astonishment.

Baby Dodds and her family lived in a spanking clean little house that smelled of cut flowers, and Karrie could hardly believe this was the home of a relative of theirs. In fact, it was hard to believe it was the home of *anyone*. The house seemed on the verge of falling in on itself, and the yard was cluttered with abandoned furniture, rusted-out wash tubs, and all kinds of trash. Tattered sheets, towels, faded housedresses and underwear hung from a sagging clothesline strung between the branch of a dead tree and a cedar post. Chickens were everywhere—even in the house, Karrie soon discovered.

Baby Dodds met her at the door and seemed eager to leave, but was elbowed out of the way by an alarming old woman, who insisted, crossly, that Karrie step inside. Baby Dodds groaned, then allowed her friend to enter.

Great-Grannie Morris looked just like a witch in a fairy tale. Her eyes were glinty slits in her gnarled face, her hair was a wild, yellowing nest, and her body was crouched, as if poised to spring. The hem of her dirty, shapeless dress dragged on the floor, and there was a sour, unpleasant odor about her and about the house itself.

From the front door, all three rooms were visible. In the bedroom, the bed had been neatly made, and in the kitchen, stacks of recently washed dishes had been left to dry on the sinkboard. The grease-stained living room floor, newly swept, was already being soiled by a pair of promenading hens, and a large number of eggs were spread out on a round oak table in the center of the room. Ladder-backed chairs with collapsed rush seats, a small lamp table piled high with old magazines, and a filthy-looking easy chair with the stuffing half out of it completed the furnishings.

"Set yourself," the old woman croaked hospitably.

"Better not," Baby Dodds advised calmly. "You might sit on an egg or something worse."

"Watch that fresh mouth, missy!" squawked her ancient relative.

To Karrie's relief, Baby Dodds announced that it was time to leave.

"What's your hurry?" demanded Great-Grannie Morris. "Set. Visit. Have a bite!"

"Can't, Great-Grannie," said Baby Dodds firmly. "We're going to the show, and we have to hustle or we'll miss the beginning. Now you remember to bring in the wash. I don't want to see it still hanging there next week, hear? And you be sure and eat that food Mamma sent. I'll be real mad if I come back and find it rotting on the sinkboard. That's our good ration stamps gone down the drain. You look and try to find your ration book, hear?"

"Chickens ate it."

"I'm sure they did," muttered Baby Dodds grimly, as she and Karrie went out the door and down the rotted wooden steps. "She made Mamma let her keep her own ration book. Now we have to stretch *our* stamps to keep her fed, and half the time she don't eat what we bring her! Lordy, we *never* have enough meat on the table! And Bubbabill's got the appetite of a grizzly bear!"

The old woman watched from the doorway as the girls righted their bicycles. Suddenly she squalled:

"*Now* I know who you are, girlie! You're the one whose daddy's a German spy! Don't you come 'round here no more! Ain't gonna learn none of *my* secrets! Don't you tell her nothing, Baby Dodds!"

Karrie stood still for an instant, but Baby Dodds was already riding away, so she jumped on her bicycle and pedaled hard to catch up.

"Crazy as a hoot owl," said Baby Dodds, looking straight ahead. "Don't you go and tell Mamma I let you see this place. She'd read me the riot act. I have to come out once a week to try to clean that pigsty! It's enough to make you sick! Don't know why Bubbabill can't do it now and then. It's not fair! He gives Mamma nothing but sass, but she waits on him hand and foot and I have to do all the dirty work! He wants to send Grannie to the asylum in Austin, but Mamma says no point in burdening *them* with her. She's perfectly happy, just her and her chickens."

Karrie said nothing. Presently Baby Dodds glanced at her.

"You didn't let the old harpy get your goat, did you? Shoot, she spends all day listening in on the party line, and gets it all mixed up and—and—Good grief, girl, that dumb spy story was just something Bucko Riddle started. Nobody pays any never mind to what *he* says!"

They rode on in silence after that, but by and by, Karrie became aware that her companion was as edgy and unhappy as she was.

"All that stuff Bucko's spreading around about *my* daddy,"

Baby Dodds suddenly blurted out. "I guess you've heard it. I guess *everybody* has. How my daddy's got this lady in California and don't plan on ever sending for us?"

The corners of her mouth pulled down and her pert face collapsed. She scrubbed furiously at her eyes with one hand while she steered her bike shakily with the other.

"That's just *trash*!" she said. "Pure-dee *garbage*! My daddy would *never* do that to us!"

Then she had to stop her bike and stand down as she began crying hard, dragging her arm across her eyes.

Karrie stopped, too, and looked at her friend helplessly. She had never thought she would see Baby Dodds cry. She knew she should say something comforting, insist it was all a lot of nonsense, but the words stuck in her throat.

For the rumors had not come from Bucko Riddle. Karrie knew that. She had overheard her aunts talking and tut-tutting. It was all over the party line. Snookie Wirtz's mother had written from California to her friend Pauline Miller; Mrs. Miller had let something slip to Leticia Hoffman, who lived next door to Lollie Beal—

Karrie, letting her bike drop to the ground, awkwardly put her arm around the crying girl's shoulders, as she felt the tears begin to roll down her own cheeks.

3.

Karrie and Baby Dodds went on to the movie that afternoon, and stopped at Webber's for a soda afterwards, just as if nothing had happened.

But something *had* happened. Karrie had been shaken to the core, and all her perceptions about her life in Benbenitas had been turned upside down. She knew that if Great-Grannie Morris had picked up that Nazi spy story on the party line, it was bound to be all over town.

And that was the reason some people passed her on the street with barely a nod, and why most of the kids at school shunned her. It wasn't because she talked like a Yankee and "put on airs."

It was because they believed that horrible rumor!

In that light, the kindness of people like Mrs. Schulman, Mr. Johnson and Mr. Wirtz seemed incredibly generous, and the loyalty of Baby Dodds and the other cheerleaders positively heroic.

After their sodas, the two girls parted casually, and Karrie pedaled home alone. She gave no sign to anyone at Windy Crest that her day had been other than ordinary, but at the supper table, she caught herself searching the faces of her grandfather and her aunts for some clue that they were aware of the stories being circulated through town. But of course they were. They always had been. She'd been the only one in the dark.

As the days went by, Karrie tried to go on exactly as before; but whether she was laughing with her friends, reading the *Times* in the library with January and Miss Jane, or shelling peas with Martha on the back porch, she felt all alone, with something terrible and cold locked inside her.

Bravely, she kept her letters to Marty bright and chatty, but she hadn't counted on how well he knew her.

"Dear little squirt," he wrote at last, "I just received another letter from my favorite cheerleader. No, *not* Jolene! *You!* I think I liked it better when you were complaining. Okay, out with it, lady! You won't be compromising your admirable patriotism if you tell me what's wrong. I promise I'll *still* win the war!"

Karrie laughed and cried a little when she read the letter. Then she read it over and over again, and for a time, missed her brother so fiercely that she despaired of going on without him.

After a while, she sat down and carefully wrote him a long letter, and the cold, tight place inside her almost disappeared. Things didn't seem so unbearable when she could share them with Marty.

When the school term ended at last, Karrie was thankful not to have to go into town every day.

"I know it's tough," Marty wrote. "In many ways your war is tougher than mine. At least everybody knows who the bad guys are, and nobody thinks I'm one of them.

"You can't bury your head in the sand, though, and you mustn't shut out the people who've been standing by you. Go to the movies, sit on the porch with Jolene and her pack; stop in and chat with Mr. Wirtz."

But it was so much easier to pass the summer days down at the river with January. It was their safe, secret world, and Benbenitas seemed a million miles away. They brought sandwiches and canteens of ice water, and kept at their work far into the afternoon, cooling off once in a while with a dip in the river, clothes and all. But around four o'clock, vanquished by the heat, they reluctantly headed their separate ways home, dirty, exhausted, and ravenously hungry.

And in the hot summer nights, Karrie's sleep was the deep, dreamless sleep of escape.

4.

One day January insisted they bicycle into town to buy some rope from the General Store, and by the time they started home, the storm clouds had turned mid-afternoon into twilight. They pedaled as fast as they could, not relishing the thought of being on the highway with a cloudburst in the offing.

They were halfway to Windy Crest when something happening in a nearby field caught Karrie's eye. Two boys appeared to be tying a big rope around something small. Karrie couldn't make out what it was, but she was certain that it was alive.

"Jano—look!" she said.

"Keep going," January advised. "It's Bucko and that moron Warren Rumford."

"Jano, I think they're going to hang an animal!"

January pulled up short to take a better look. "They're up to no good, that's for sure!"

The girls turned off the road, laid their bikes down on the grass and struck off across the field at a run. As they got nearer, they could see that the boys had a noose around the neck of a scrawny, quivering puppy.

164

Warren looked up and poked his companion. "Hey, Bucko, we got company!"

Bucko was visibly startled. "Whaddaya coming around here for? We ain't bothering you."

"What do you think you're doing with that dog?" January demanded, fire in her eyes.

"What's it to you?" Bucko growled. "I ain't come near you, hear? Don't you go telling your daddy I come anywheres near you. This mutt ain't none of your beezwax. Ole Mr. Reuben give him to me."

"He done give Bucko a dollar to drown his pups," explained Warren.

"Just shut your trap, Warren," Bucko told him. He shuffled his feet around. "Y'all just beat it, hear? I don't want no trouble with you two."

"Drown his *puppies*?" Karrie was aghast. "*Why?*"

"Why?" Bucko mimicked her. "I'll tell you why, city girl. Because the mamma dog done weaned them and he can't afford to buy them no food. They too blamed ugly to give away, so he give me a buck to get rid of them."

"Where are the others?"

Bucko raised one arm in a mock Nazi salute, and replied sneeringly, "Gone to doggie heaven, oh *Fräulein*."

Karrie winced and Bucko grinned. Then he started to walk away with the trembling puppy under his arm.

Karrie was right at his heels. "You *drowned* them?"

"Drowned 'em in a big old washtub," Warren brayed. "But Bucko say—what'd you say, Bucko? I know! Say we gonna get *creative* with this one!"

"If you don't keep your yammering trap shut, I'm gonna get creative with *you*," Bucko muttered.

January stepped in front of Bucko. "Give me that dog," she said flatly.

"Get outta here," Bucko responded uneasily.

"I want that puppy, Bucko," January said.

"What you want this mutt for? Ugliest one I ever seen," said

Warren, baffled.

"If you don't hand over the dog, I'm telling my pop," said January. "And I might get creative, too."

"Oh, take the mangy cur," Bucko said suddenly, and almost threw the puppy at January. He took off in a hurry, with Warren lumbering after him, still protesting, "Don't know what they want that ugly dog for, do you Bucko?"

January handed the puppy to Karrie. He smelled terrible and was crawling with fleas. When Karrie took him he stopped trembling and set about licking her chin with his little rough tongue.

She laughed and looked at January, "So—want a dog?"

"*I* can't take him!" said January. "Every dog I ever had got run over. We live right on the highway, you know. But Windy Crest is set back aways, with that long driveway and all."

"But my grandfather hates animals!"

"Well, we sure can't leave him here. We'd better get moving before the skies fall in."

With the little animal cuddled in Karrie's arms, the girls hurried back across the field to their bicycles. Karrie tucked the puppy into the basket on her handlebars, crooning to him soothingly.

"What if he jumps out?" January asked.

"He seems okay. You'll be good, won't you, pup?"

They reached Windy Crest without incident, and rode around to the back of the house. Karrie was wondering how to best spring her surprise on the family, when she saw Israel standing ready to open the kitchen door for them.

"Oh, my," he murmured. "That's a mighty pitiful varmint."

"I'm going to call him Abner," Karrie said, smiling at Martha, as she and January brought their trophy inside.

Martha shook her head and laughed ruefully. "So I got *Abner* back in my kitchen! Only this one's real and mighty ugly!"

She immediately set about warming milk for him, and ordered Israel to find a washtub and some old towels. "This thing needs a bath—bad!" she said grimly, and no one disagreed.

Israel quickly provided a washtub and filled it halfway. The puppy was gently eased into the tepid water, but it took both January and Israel to hold him there while Karrie scrubbed at him with a wash cloth and soap. The exclamations, laughter, and squeals soon brought the mayor and his sisters into the kitchen to find out what was going on.

"What's *that*, may I ask?" demanded the mayor.

"Dear me, it looks like a baby warthog!" cried Miss Prune. "Why on earth are you giving it a bath?"

Karrie and January looked at each other and laughed. Wet, wild-eyed, and struggling to escape from the tub, Abner was not a pretty sight, and his soapy head appeared much too large for his emaciated little body.

"Bucko Riddle was trying to hang him, Grandfather," Karrie explained.

The mayor peered at the frantic creature in the tub. "What is it? A puppy? Bucko Riddle was hanging a puppy? When will that evil little rotter be old enough for the draft?"

"He's old enough now," said Miss Ginger. "They're letting him finish high school."

"Ha! That's a joke," said the mayor.

It was Miss Prune who came up with the pertinent question. "When you finish bathing the little dog, what do you plan to do with him?"

Karrie, January, Israel and Martha all looked at the mayor.

"He's kind of ugly, Grandfather," Karrie pointed out unnecessarily. "I don't think I could get anybody to take him."

"January—?" suggested the mayor.

"Oh, I can't, Mr. Mayor," protested Jano. "My dogs get run over. He wouldn't last a week at our place."

"I never could have a dog when I lived in an apartment," Karrie mentioned wistfully. She took Abner out of the tub and wrapped him in a ragged towel. He began licking her chin again, while vigorously wagging his little tail under the towel.

"Oh, dear me," Miss Prune said faintly.

"Now Karen," Miss Ginger began.

"All right—All right!" the mayor said suddenly. "But no animals in the house! There's a perfectly good barn out back."

Karrie looked at the tiny, wiggling thing in her arms and thought about him being all alone in that great big barn. She was just opening her mouth to protest when Martha spoke up.

"Barn'll be fine, Mayor. But tonight I'll fix him a box in Karrie's room."

"But—" said the mayor.

"Just had a bath, you know. And they saying a norther gonna blow in tonight."

"Martha," said the mayor patiently, "just who is it that's predicting a norther in the month of June?"

Martha smiled faintly. "Gonna *rain* for sure. Little dog die of pneumonia in that damp ole barn. Then Bucko'd get his way, after all."

"Oh, well, then," said the mayor, with a sigh, "we certainly can't let Bucko get his way. Now, Karen. You make sure that animal stays away from me."

"I will, Grandfather, I promise! He won't be a bit of trouble, will you, Abner?"

"Tomorrow, we gonna take him to the vet and get him wormed," said Israel, scratching the pup's head fondly. "He got the rickets now, but we feed him good and he gonna grow up right handsome, you'll see, Henry."

"I'm sure he'll be a real beauty, Israel," replied the mayor drily. "Just—keep him away from *me*!" And the mayor departed the scene with his usual dignity.

"I got to get going before the rain starts," said January. "Not that it matters—I'm already wringing wet!"

Karrie, holding Abner close, walked her outside to her bike. "Jano—you were terrific!"

"I was? All I said was I couldn't take the dog—"

"No, no. I mean before—with Bucko. You whipped him again!"

"Hm-m. One of these days he'll figure out that my pop is harmless, and—Bucko doesn't like getting whipped."

168

Later that evening, with the rain beating down on the attic roof, Karrie sat at her desk and wrote all about the afternoon's adventure to Marty, while Abner dozed contentedly on her bed.

"Martha fixed him a box to sleep in, with a piece of old blanket to make it cozy, but he seems to like my pillow best. I hope we washed all the fleas off him!

"Marty, I think I'll never get used to this town! Drowning unwanted puppies and kittens is common practice, Jano told me. Maybe most people don't do it for *fun*, like Bucko and Warren do, but it's still horrible!

"Aunt Ginger says I should worry more about the human beings who are suffering all over the world right now. Sure I do, but that doesn't stop me from getting mad when I see an animal getting hurt.

"Well, nobody's ever going to hurt Abner again. He may be the ugliest dog in the world, but he's *my* dog—now and forever. If you really behave yourself, I might share him with you when you come home. Love—K."

5.

The coffee table in the parlor was set with lace doilies and Grandmother Reba's china tea set.

"A real English tea!" said Miss Jane. "Windy Crest must be the only house in Texas where hot tea is served on a July afternoon, with little sandwiches and cakes! I feel deliciously Victorian!"

Miss Ginger and Miss Prune smiled at each other with satisfaction.

"Jane, my dear, you're the only person in town we would *dare* serve hot tea on a summer day," declared Miss Ginger. "Henry thinks we're totally mad, but this is a small indulgence Prune and I allow ourselves now and then. When we lived in Austin, we had our tea parties every Sunday afternoon."

"I'm sorry the cakes aren't iced," apologized Miss Prune. "We let Karen and January make fudge the other day, and our sugar is running low."

"Where *is* Karrie?" asked Miss Jane. "And the cakes are great! I love them this way."

"I hope she didn't forget you were coming," said Miss Prune anxiously.

"Oh, she's down at the river with January," said Miss Ginger. "They're hatching some scheme and it's a big secret. Those two!"

"They're terrific kids," said Miss Jane warmly. "I'm so happy they discovered each other. I saw such a difference in January last semester. Karrie's good sense and good manners have rubbed off on her. She actually started saying 'hi' to some of the other kids, and she survived a *very* rough semester with Miss Duvall."

At that moment, Karrie came flying in.

"Sorry!" she cried. "I lost track of time and I ran all the way. I'm afraid I'm kind of sweaty—"

"Karen, really!" said Miss Ginger huffily, feeling the spirit of her English tea party was being compromised.

"Just wash your hands and join us, dear," suggested Miss Prune.

Karrie dashed off to the kitchen, shouting back over her shoulder, "Did you hear about the Allies invading Sicily? Jano said it was on the radio this morning—"

"That *is* good news!" exclaimed Miss Ginger.

"Sicily," repeated Miss Prune. "That's at the toe of the boot, isn't it?"

"It's a big island between Italy and North Africa," said Miss Jane, "right off the toe of the boot."

"Then we're not on the mainland of Italy yet?"

"We will be soon! This is the beginning!"

"We won't see the light at the end of the tunnel till we invade France," said Miss Ginger with a sigh. "And heaven knows when *that* will be."

"But it will happen, Ginger," said her sister. "It's just a matter of time. Oh, dear, do you suppose there'll be anything left of Europe, when this war is finally over? All the treasures of Western civilization may be destroyed!"

"Surely, Prune, we should regret the loss of human lives

more," Miss Ginger reproached her.

"Of course we do!" agreed Miss Jane. "But that doesn't mean we can't feel bad about the old cathedrals and the priceless art. You know, my life-long dream was to visit all the fine museums of Europe. But now—as you say, Miss Prune—who knows what will be left after this is over?"

"Well, Paris has never been bombed. I suppose the Louvre is still intact."

"Maybe not. It's probably been looted. The Louvre was what I always wanted to see above everything else—"

"I've been there," said Karrie, arriving back in the parlor with clean face and hands, but still looking rather scruffy to her aunts' eyes.

"You *have?*" cried Miss Jane.

"Uh huh. I have a picture of us all standing in front of it. But I don't remember anything about it. I was only about four."

Karrie, sitting down at the coffee table and helping herself to a sandwich, noticed that her aunts looked displeased. Okay, she thought resentfully, so she'd had the bad manners to hint that she'd actually had a life before stepping off the train in Benbenitas.

"Could I see it?" Miss Jane asked eagerly. "The picture?"

Karrie glanced at her aunts, who were primly sipping their tea. After all, Miss Jane had *asked*.

"I'll run upstairs and see if I can find the album," she said, pushing the last of her sandwich into her mouth as she rose and flew off again.

"Well," said Miss Ginger. "I'm afraid it works both ways. A lot of January has been rubbing off on Karen lately. She's getting to be a terrible tomboy!"

"Oh, Ginger, you were the biggest tomboy of them all!" Miss Prune reminded her, laughing. "Always climbing trees and tearing your dress. Belching at the table!"

"Prune, really!" But Miss Ginger laughed, too, and both sisters were hoping the album would go unfound.

However, Karrie returned with it promptly. Moving the tea

things to one side, she placed it on the coffee table in front of Miss Jane, thumbed through it quickly, and opened it to a page labeled "Paris, June 1933."

"Why, there you are!" cried Miss Jane. "In front of the Louvre! Imagine! Same little face! You haven't changed, Karrie. And Marty! What a cocky young gentleman! Is this your mother? You look exactly like her! Wasn't she pretty?"

She turned the pages eagerly, commenting on the pictures, asking questions, and reading out loud the inscriptions Karrie's mother had written under each one. Miss Ginger and Miss Prune didn't seem to know which way to look or what to say. They continued sipping their tea, but couldn't resist occasionally craning their necks to take a peek.

"And where were you here? Where is 'Stilldorf'?" Miss Jane asked, when she turned to a page with that heading.

"In Germany. We were visiting my mother's hometown in the Black Forest," Karrie explained deliberately, looking at her aunts.

"Let's see—there you are! What a cutie! And here's Marty. Who are you with? 'Opi, Meyer, Paul, Frieda—' Who's the nice-looking man holding you by the hand?"

"That's my grandfather," Karrie told her. "We called him Opi. I think we're standing outside his tailor shop. I don't really remember him, but he used to write letters to Marty and me, and my mother translated them for us. This man—that's Meyer, one of Mom's uncles—he lived in Stilldorf, too. He was a doctor. Yes! And the kids are his grandchildren. Frieda was my age and Paul was Marty's."

Miss Prune and Miss Ginger craned at the same time.

"Hrumph," said Miss Ginger, now frankly staring at the picture with distaste. "If that boy's Martin's age I suppose he's now a German soldier!"

Karrie thought about that for an instant, then, "Oh, no," she said, "I don't think so."

Miss Jane was absorbed in studying the photographs. "Here's your grandfather—and his brother Meyer—and who are these other men? 'Julian, Nathan, Frederic'—"

"They're Mom's other uncles. They lived in Munich or some place, but they all came to see us when we were there. Okay, let's see: Julian was the youngest. He was a musician. Nathan, the guy with the beard and the hat, was the oldest. He was a rabbi. And Frederic, he was—I can't remember what he did. It's all written down somewhere. Mom wrote everything down."

Karrie was frowning thoughtfully at the photograph, trying to call up something in her mind about the day it had been taken. Gradually she realized that everyone had become silent. Looking up, she saw the mayor standing just inside the parlor.

"Rabbi," he said without expression. "Your mother was Jewish."

Before Karrie could say anything he breathed, "Thank God!" and left the room.

6.

The tea party broke up soon after that, as Miss Jane had to get back to town to give a painting lesson. She thanked the Webster sisters for a pleasant visit, and told Karrie she'd love to see more photographs the next time she came by. After she left, the aunts bustled off to wash the tea things, and Karrie picked up the album and went up to her room.

She plopped down on her cot and considered the curious turn the day had taken. She was mildly surprised that the fact of her mother being Jewish had come as a revelation to the family. Well, they might have learned it sooner, if they'd ever stood still long enough to hear anything at all about her mother. But what a strange reaction from her grandfather! *Thank God?*

Karrie stirred restlessly. He wasn't easy to figure out. Though she couldn't forgive him for the way he'd treated her parents, there were things about him she grudgingly admired—his dignity, his fairness (with everyone *outside his family*), his concern for what was going on in the world.

She felt she would never, ever really know the man, but she was conscious that the two of them shared certain deep feelings, and that made it impossible for her to really hate him.

Whenever the family gathered around the radio in the parlor to hear the war news, she found herself watching him. The aunts responded to everything, with gasps, sighs, cheers, or tut-tuts, and were often silenced by a sharp "Sh-h-h!" from their brother. He always listened without comment or expression, but he was Karrie's barometer, and she experienced mounting anxiety or leaps of optimism according to what she sensed of his reactions.

There had been that one evening back in March when she'd had no need of a barometer. The newscaster had reported Hitler's latest promise: *This struggle will end with the extinction of Jewry in Europe.* Her mouth had gone dry and she'd felt her stomach twist into knots, while the aunts voiced their indignant opinions of "that maniac!" But her grandfather, his face drained white, had risen and walked out of the parlor without a word.

Karrie picked up the album again and idly leafed through it. She recalled almost nothing about that family trip to Europe, except for the big ship they'd sailed on. Little things came back to her now, flashback scenes of throwing bread crumbs to pigeons, an old man handing her a flower in the park. What park, in what country, she had no idea. And there was a dollhouse—

She sat up abruptly, and, though she stared straight out the window, she didn't see the cows kneeling by the distant pond, or hear the lazy echoes of summer from the valley.

There was a dollhouse. She closed her eyes against the Texas sunshine and saw it standing on a veranda shaded by big friendly trees and bordered by gentle flowers. An enchanting three-story dollhouse with perfect miniature furnishings. The staircase and the sofas—the chifforobes with tiny drawers that really opened! Two little girls—she could see them both—herself and Frieda.

Frieda. An importantly busy, fuzzy little presence in that sudden recollection, but in the photograph, her four-year-old face was vivid. A thin child, like Karrie, with huge dark eyes, dark hair hanging in two short braids, the corners of her mouth turned up in a sweet clown's smile.

174

There had been a pony. Yes! A gypsy came by with a pony, and led him around while she and Frieda sat on his back and laughed.

Karrie began to slowly pace the room, as fragmentary flashes of that long ago morning teased her mind. A fairy tale morning, with a dollhouse, a pony, a nice playmate. Something made her resist remembering, just as something always made her resist remembering her mother's long illness. But that memory was there, too, and for an instant she was nine years old again, hunched up on her bed, holding a pillow over her ears to shut out the sound of her parents' voices through the wall. She hadn't known what they were talking about, only that somehow it was terrible—terrible! "What have they done with them?" her mother was wailing. *"Richard, what has become of my family?"*

Karrie shivered, and closed the album. She got up and gently put it back in its place under the window seat.

Now she looked out on the valley and saw the cows by the pond. Now she listened to the whir of the electric fan, the creak of the windmill and the rising song of the cicadas. But through it all she seemed to hear Aunt Prune's hushed voice saying, *Disappeared without a trace.*

7.

Miss Ginger and Miss Prune tried to keep a casual conversation going at the supper table, but the mayor and his granddaughter were both quiet. Afterwards, instead of joining the others in the parlor for the evening newscast, Karrie excused herself and went up to her room to write her nightly letter to Marty.

She was sitting at her desk, thoughtfully tapping her pen on the tablet, when her grandfather appeared in the doorway.

Karrie rose hastily. "Come on in, Grandfather."

He took a couple of steps inside, and hesitated. It occurred to Karrie that it was probably the first time he'd seen that room in twenty-five years.

"Karen," he began, then cleared his throat crossly. "Karen,

that—letter. The one your father left in his desk. Do you think I might have another look at it?"

Karrie took the well-worn envelope from her desk drawer and silently handed it to him.

Now he seated himself stiffly in the chair she had offered him, and slipped the letter out of the envelope with hands that seemed to have lost their customary steadiness.

Karrie, who knew the letter by heart, guessed what he was rereading so carefully. It was where her father wrote of going to Germany with her mother to tell Opi about their marriage.

...That was hard. Poor Opi. His lovely, talented Inge! He'd worked and sacrificed for years to send her to the conservatory in Vienna, only to have her throw it all away to marry a boy of a different religion and sail off to America. It must have broken his heart. But—being Opi—he ended up giving us his blessing.

The mayor carefully folded the pages and returned them to the envelope. Handing it to Karrie, he asked quietly,

"His name was Opi? Your German grandfather?"

"His name was Herman. Opi means grandfather—I guess."

"Of course. Opa. I forgot. He's dead?"

"I don't know." Karrie hesitated. "He—he disappeared."

That word seemed to hang in the air between them. The mayor stared out the window—at nothing, because it was now dark outside. Finally he turned his eyes back to Karrie and asked,

"When did—when was he last heard from?"

"I don't know exactly. It must have been in 1938 or '39. My mother was already sick. She used to get really upset. I think his letters just stopped coming, and hers came back unopened. Yes, I remember! They were stamped *Address Unknown.*"

"Surely some attempt was made to trace him?"

"Oh, yes. Dad had his business friends in Europe try to find out what had happened to Opi and the other relatives, but he couldn't leave Mom to go to Germany himself. He did go later on, after she died."

"And—?"

"Well, he went to the town where Opi lived, and his shop was boarded up and Dad couldn't get anybody to talk to him. Then the Gestapo found out he was asking questions, and they hauled him in and—I don't know—gave him a hard time. I think they canceled his visa, or something, and told him he could never come back to Germany. I may not have the story straight. Marty would be able to tell you."

Her grandfather stood up and walked around the room, staring out one window and then another, into the darkness. He paused in front of the desk, picked up the framed photograph of Karrie and Marty sitting between their smiling parents. He studied it for a few seconds before putting it down.

For a moment his eyes met his granddaughter's. Reaching out his hand, he gently, briefly stroked her dark curly hair. "All right, Karen. I'll leave you to write your letter. Give Martin my—best."

Karrie listened to his footsteps going down the stairs. Then she sat down at her desk and took up her pen. Again, she found it hard to make a start.

What a strange day it had turned out to be! It had begun in an ordinary way, but it had taken that curious turn mid-afternoon and just now—

It was the first time her grandfather had ever touched her.

8.

"It's perfectly clear why your grandfather reacted that way," said January.

"Not to me," said Karrie. They were standing in the Windy Crest driveway waiting for Jolene to come by and drive them into town for a matinee at the Bijou.

"Well, if your mother was Jewish, then that stuff about your dad being a Nazi sounds pretty dumb, doesn't it?"

"*You* heard that?"

"Everybody hears everything in Benbenitas. Including your grandfather. It must have really upset him."

"Why? He hates my dad."

"Oh, come on! You don't think it bothered him to have people say his own son was a Nazi?"

"Oh, God, what a stupid, vicious lie!"

"Well, that's the way people are around here. Stupid and vicious. But anyway, now your granddad knows it's all a bunch of hooey. That's why he said 'Thank God.'"

"Well, he should have known it was a bunch of hooey in the first place."

"Yeah, that story made *my* pop furious. He really liked your dad and your uncle. But Karrie, how come you never told anybody about being Jewish?"

Karrie sighed. "Golly, Jano, I really wasn't brought up to think of myself as Jewish or Christian or anything else. I wasn't deliberately *not* telling it. I guess I thought everybody knew. Especially the family. I figured that was why my aunts were so determined to turn me into a Methodist. But they said they never would have insisted I go to church if they'd known."

"Well, *I* sure didn't know, up to five minutes ago. And I thought I knew *everything* about you! Are you going to tell the others?"

"Gee—I'm certainly not going to make some dramatic *announcement!*"

At about that time, Jolene arrived in her father's car. Bev was sitting in the back seat and Baby Dodds up front. Karrie and Jano climbed in beside Bev.

"This is supposed to be a real good picture this afternoon, y'all," Jolene told them. "It's *The Pied Piper.*"

"Oh, no, is this one of those kiddie pictures?" wailed Bev. "The theater's gonna be swarming with sticky, noisy brats!"

Jolene laughed. "Honestly, girl, don't you ever read the reviews or anything? It's about an old man trying to get some kids out of the war zone. My cousin saw it in Austin a year ago. She said it was wonderful."

"A *year* ago? If we ever got to see a picture when it first came out—! By the time they get here, they're such old news I've forgotten all about them. I didn't know it was gonna be another war movie. They always make me cry."

"I like to cry in picture shows," said Baby Dodds. "I plan to bawl my head off. You don't have to come, you know."

"Oh, good grief," grumbled Bev.

It turned out that they all cried. Even Jano had to hastily draw an arm across her eyes before the theater lights went up, and afterwards, when the girls were walking over to Webber's for their after-show sodas, she appeared to be more relaxed with the group than she'd ever been before. *Nothing like a sad movie to break the ice!* Karrie thought with satisfaction.

Karrie also noticed that people along the way seemed to be looking them over, and she had the distinct impression that it had more to do with *her* than with the others. By the time they reached Webber's, she was certain of it. Shirleen Haus could hardly get the sodas made for staring at her.

"So did I sprout an extra head while we were in the theater, or what?" Karrie asked, when they left the drugstore.

"Oh, you know how folks are around here," Jolene said.

"Not really," said Karrie. "They're still a mystery to me."

"Oh, you're a bigger mystery to them," said Bev. "They never saw a Jew before."

Karrie and January exchanged an astonished glance.

"Oh!" said Karrie.

Later, around the supper table, Miss Prune and Miss Ginger were both poking distractedly at their food, and it was obvious they had something on their minds that neither quite knew how to come out with. The mayor, on the other hand, was more serene than usual and attacked the fried chicken as though it were to be his last meal on earth. Both women kept glancing at Karrie. Finally, Miss Ginger delicately cleared her throat and said,

"Prune and I were in town today, Henry—"

"I suspected as much, Ginger," said the mayor. "As you rode in with me this morning, and then rode home with me at noon, I said to myself, 'By golly, my sisters were in town today!'"

"Now, Henry," said Miss Prune firmly, "Ginger is trying to tell you about something that—came to our attention. Something that puzzles us."

"Well?"

After that brave beginning, Miss Prune was silent, and Karrie was almost certain she gave Miss Ginger a kick under the table.

"All right, all right, out with it!" the mayor said briskly.

"Henry, now listen, please," urged Miss Prune. "It's about— Karen."

Karrie looked up mid-chew. Miss Prune continued:

"Some people said—I mean, references were made— Well, Henry, everyone seems to know that—that her mother was Jewish."

"Um-m-m," grunted the mayor, helping himself to another drumstick. "So—? Is that it?"

"Well, Henry," Miss Ginger said, "*we* didn't realize that ourselves until day before yesterday. Certainly you know we don't talk family business in town. And we haven't phoned Clara since then, so we can't even suspect Mabel Klein of listening in—"

"Actually, Mabel is quite discreet, Ginger," put in Miss Prune.

"Well, that's not the point," Miss Ginger said. "The point is, it *couldn't* have been Mabel, and Jane Llewellyn would never— Well, there's no reason for it being a *secret*, of course, but we simply can't imagine how it got all over town so quickly. Karen, did you—?"

Karrie shook her head. Her mouth was full.

"Oh, well," said the mayor, wiping his chin on a napkin and getting up from the table. "That's the charm of Benbenitas, its eternal mystery. I've heard there are primitive tribes in Africa who transmit information over hundreds of miles without benefit of telephone or telegraph. No one can figure out how they do it."

"Oh, come now, Henry," protested Miss Prune. "We're not some primitive tribe in Africa. Things do have a way of getting around Benbenitas, but it has to start *somewhere*."

Her brother paused at the door, and appeared to be thinking it through.

"Well," he said at last, "I might have mentioned something or other to Lollie Beal."

In a few seconds, *wham* went the study door, signifying that the mayor would be incommunicado for the rest of the evening.

9.

And so, thanks to the tireless tongue of Lollie Beal, which had started all the trouble in the first place, Karrie's summer took a sudden turn for the better.

"I get stared at more than ever," she wrote to Marty, "but it sure beats being shunned. Now my friends are beginning to tell me about some of the crazy stories that were going around. Remember Lollie Beal and that 'been to Bastrop lately' stuff? Well, it seems that German POW's are kept at Camp Swift near Bastrop and one of the stories was that Dad was locked up there and I'd moved to Texas to be close to him! Lollie Beal still doesn't like me. I think it irks her to know she's kin to a real live Jew!"

There were some people who couldn't figure out why the revelation about Karrie's mother had changed everything. Nevertheless, when they heard others declare, "Richard Webster married a Jewess, you know, so he derned sure ain't no Nazi," they simply nodded wisely and repeated it to the next person.

Thus, that ugliest of rumors died overnight, and was soon wiped out of the town's collective memory, in the mysterious way that sometimes happens in Benbenitas.

Chapter 9
The End Of Summer

1.

Karrie never thought she'd live to see the day that January would be sitting on Jolene's front porch. She wasn't saying a word, of course, but still, she was there, drifting back and forth on the swing.

It was one of those timeless, lazy summer days, meant for porches, lemonade and girl-talk. The current subject was the weekly dance at the Hospitality canteen.

"But I don't go any more," said Jolene, throwing a glance Karrie's way. "Why'd you tell Marty I was going? He teased me!"

"Marty teases about everything," said Karrie comfortably.

"So are you still going to marry him, or what?" asked Bev, chomping down on a piece of ice from her glass.

"*Marry* him?" Jolene laughed delightedly. "You are *too* much!"

"Guess your folks wouldn't want you to marry out of your own religion," said Bev thoughtfully.

"Child, *what* are you talking about?" demanded Jolene, irritated. "My parents are *not* prejudiced people, and where did all this marrying stuff come from, anyway? I never even had a *date* with Marty!"

"So how come you don't go to the dances any more?" asked Baby Dodds. "I thought you always went with Bettie Rae."

Bettie Rae wasn't among those present. She seldom was in recent weeks.

"Oh, Bettie Rae's daddy was raising Cain about it. *My* daddy knows I wouldn't do anything to make him ashamed, but you know how Mr. Miller is! So I just stopped going—"

"Well, Bettie Rae didn't stop," remarked Bev. "Her daddy hides the car keys, but she still finds somebody to take her, like Angie Beal."

"I thought she didn't like Angie Beal," said Karrie.

"So what?" said Bev. "If Hitler offered her a ride to Hospitality on Saturday night, she'd jump right in."

"Hitchhiked last week," said Baby Dodds. "Walked right out on the highway and stuck out her thumb. Boy, my mamma would tan my hide if I did a thing like that! Why is she so fixed on going to those dances, Jolene?"

"She likes to dance," said Jolene.

"Oh, come *on!*" the others chorused.

"Is she sweet on some soldier or what?" demanded Bev.

Jolene smiled and held out a freshly manicured hand to admire. "I don't gossip."

"Oh, sure, since when?"

"Jolene, I never saw anybody fuss with their nails so much," said Baby Dodds. "Sure can tell your mamma don't make *you* wash dishes."

"She does, too," said Jolene. "Ever since Carrie—that was our maid, Karrie with a K—ever since Carrie got that job with the Army in San Antonio, Mamma and me have to do *all* the housework. Y'all don't know any good cleaning women, do you?"

Baby Dodds snorted. "Yeah, sure, Jolene. Just who else do you think ever *had* a cleaning woman? Except the mayor!"

"We all pitch in at Windy Crest," said Karrie, a little defensively. "Well, everybody but my grandfather."

"Martha and Israel are too old for war jobs, so you're lucky," said Jolene.

"Speaking of jobs, Shirleen Haus is gonna make a WAC, did

you hear?" said Bev. "I wonder who'll take her place?"

"Hm-m-m. Maybe Mr. Webber would hire *me* part-time," mused Baby Dodds. "Sure could use the money."

"Oh, I'd hate that job!" said Jolene. "Waiting on people and your hands always in dishwater!"

"But Jolene, it'd be such good practice for when you get married to you-know-who!" teased Bev.

Karrie looked annoyed, but Jolene was unperturbed.

"Well, maybe I'll marry and maybe I won't," she remarked serenely, studying her other hand. "That's certainly not *all* I plan to do!"

"I know! You're gonna be a movie star!" said Baby Dodds. "*Everybody's* gonna be a movie star."

"I wouldn't mind," said Bev. "But my mamma'd rather me go to business school in Austin when I graduate. You can get a real good job at the Capitol if you can learn shorthand."

"That's what I'm gonna do," said Baby Dodds. She no longer talked of going to California. "What about you, Karrie?"

"What *about* me?" Karrie said, somewhat crossly.

"You know, after you graduate. What're you gonna do?"

"Gee, that's three years away. Who knows?"

"Come on! Don't you have any plans?"

"I don't know. When Marty comes home we'll go back to New York. Maybe I'll get a job or go to college."

"Well, Marty may not want to go back to New York," said Bev, with a meaningful look at Jolene. "Anyway, why would you want to leave good old Texas? Come to Austin with us. We could all get an apartment together, couldn't we, Baby Dodds?"

"Suits me," said Baby Dodds. "But Jolene, you graduate next year. So what are *you* gonna do, really?"

"Going to the University. Premed."

"Premed? What's that?"

"It's what you take when you want to be a doctor," said Karrie, amazed.

"Jolene, honestly? But you mean a *nurse*, don't you?"

"No, Karrie got it right. I'm gonna go to medical school and be a doctor like my daddy. He thinks I'll be real good."

"Well, heck, you've never said a *word*! When did you get this big idea?"

"When I was a little girl. You remember—I was always the one to stick band-aids on your scrapes. Hey, y'all, I'll deliver your babies!"

"No, thank you," said Baby Dodds firmly. "Band-aids are fine, but I think I'll let your daddy do the baby-birthing."

Jolene laughed. "But he'll charge you money. I'll do it for free!"

"Oh, Jolene, you can't be a doctor," said Bev solemnly.

"Why can't I?"

"It'd just *ruin* your manicure!"

2.

"Well, so now you've been officially initiated into what Marty calls the 'porch pack,'" Karrie remarked to January, as they pedaled up the highway that evening.

"Hm-m. Big deal," said January.

"It wasn't so bad, was it?"

"The lemonade was good. But I can't take all that girl talk."

"Hey, they're *girls*! So are you, ma'am, if you'll pardon my mentioning it."

"Well, they don't have to make a *career* of it."

"What do you want them to talk about? The latest Broadway play? Great Books?"

"Yeah—or the war, or *something*. Great Books! That's a laugh! Do you think any of them ever read a book, except when they have to for homework?"

"I'll bet Jolene does."

"Yeah, but she wouldn't admit it! I wonder what her letters to your brother are like?"

"Witty and intelligent, Marty says."

"Amazing. She's a weird one. But that Bev ought to have her mouth sewn shut."

"She doesn't mean anything. You mind it more than I do.

185

They're okay, Jano. You know, they always make a point of telling me to bring you along."

"Sure they do. It keeps Bucko Riddle out of their hair."

"I never thought of that! But I know he was lurking around the Bijou today, watching us."

"I didn't see him."

"I didn't *see* him, but I always know when he's nearby. I can *feel* it. Really."

"Hm-m. *By the pricking of my thumbs, something wicked this way comes!*"

"*That's* not from *Hamlet!*"

"*Macbeth*. Act IV, Scene I. Second witch."

"Swell! Thanks a lot! But he *was* there—I don't care if you *do* think I'm crazy."

"Well, I may think you're crazy, but I believe he was there. He's always watching us. I've lost my magic, Karrie. He's not afraid of me any more. He's going to get even with us for the dog, I'm sure of it. It's just a matter of time. I hope he doesn't try to do something to Abner!"

"He'd better not! But I don't know how he could. When Abner's not with us, he's in the house."

"In the house? What about your grandfather?"

"Well, as a matter of fact, Abner spends most of the afternoon asleep at his feet. Abner dearly loves the study—and Grandfather!"

"Wow, that's practically a miracle!"

"Yep. Like you on Jolene's front porch."

"Yeah, right. Well, at least Bucko can't get to Abner in the mayor's study. But he'll do *something* to get even—mark my words. Bucko never lets anybody get the better of him for long."

3.

Miss Prune was unusually quiet when she sat down at the breakfast table.

"All right, Prune, what is it?" demanded her sister crossly.

"You'll just make fun of me, Ginger. Besides, I won't say a

word until I've had my breakfast."

"Ha!" Miss Ginger slammed her hand down on the table. "Do you know what this means, Karen? Your Aunt Prune has had one of her prophetic dreams and she won't tell it before breakfast for fear it will come true! Did you ever hear of anything so nonsensical—for a grown woman?"

Miss Prune held her peace and sipped her coffee with dignity.

"I didn't know you were superstitious, Aunt Prune," said Karrie.

"Honey, I'm no more superstitious than anyone else. Everybody's got something they're superstitious about, don't you think?"

"Not everybody," growled the mayor, rattling his newspaper impatiently.

"Hm-m-m. Like the mayor throwing spilt salt over his left shoulder," suggested Martha wickedly, as she poured that gentleman another cup of coffee.

"Harmless habit," said the mayor, unperturbed.

"And Ginger has her little ways, too," added Miss Prune. "She once let me go downtown wearing my sweater inside out because Mamma used to say it was bad luck to change it if you'd accidentally put it on that way."

"Oh, pooh!" said Ginger. "I was twenty years old then, Prune. A little more excusable, I would say. But a woman pushing sixty who thinks if she dreams something it'll come true—!"

"Now, Ginger, you know I don't think that. But some dreams have a special feeling about them. This one was eerie."

"All right, all right. Eat your toast and let's hear it."

"Well," said Miss Prune, swallowing a bite hastily, "I dreamed about Howie Schulman. Now that's strange enough in itself. Why should I dream about Howie Schulman? But the strangest thing of all was—he was behind bars!"

"It would make more sense if you dreamed Bucko Riddle was behind bars," said the mayor.

"No—no. It was Howie Schulman. And it was dark and sad

and I woke up feeling very disturbed."

"The last time you felt that way, you dreamed that Lollie Beal left Woody and eloped with Clark Gable," her sister reminded her.

"Oh, now, Ginger, I didn't expect *that* to happen! Dreams often have a hidden meaning, and you have to figure it all out. Now what did happen after that, if you remember, was that Lollie got mad at Preacher and went over to the Baptists—"

The mayor almost choked on his coffee. He mopped his mouth with his napkin, stood up and headed for the door with his newspaper. Abner, who had been lying under the table, promptly got up and trotted after him. The mayor paused on the threshold long enough to remark, "Sometimes I have to remind myself, Prune, that you were once considered a scholar!" With Abner at his heels, he stalked off, and *wham* went the study door.

Miss Prune sighed. "If we don't find a minister soon, we'll *all* have to join the Baptists."

"What?" said Karrie.

"We've lost our minister, dear. Didn't you know? Ginger and I are on the committee to find a new one."

"Preacher? No kidding! What happened to him?"

"What, indeed!" said Miss Ginger grimly.

"Now, Ginger," said Miss Prune, with a meaningful glance toward Karrie.

"Oh, Prune, it's all over town. I'm surprised you haven't heard, Karen. Except you spend all your time down at the river—"

"Let's not forget that the poor man's wife ran off and left him."

"And that makes it perfectly all right for him to take off with a widow from Gladhand?"

"Really?" said Karrie, delighted.

"Oh, dear," said Miss Prune with a sigh. "You see, Karen, he was keeping company with this widow. Nothing wrong with that. And they decided to go out to California together and find war jobs. More money, you know."

"More *everything*," muttered Miss Ginger.

"Now, Ginger. Karen, please let's not discuss this in your grandfather's presence. He never says anything very helpful about such matters, and we *are* left with a problem."

"We're left holding the bag! Henry was absolutely right about Preacher, but a church *must* have a pastor, even if he's a blithering idiot—"

"So many ministers have gone to chaplains in the service, you know, Karen. We can't be as particular as we'd like."

"If only we could have kept Mr. Eagleton! I'll never forgive the congregation for firing him. He was too intelligent for them—*that* was the trouble!"

"Mr. Eagleton? Who was he?" asked Karrie.

"He was before Preacher, about five years ago. He—"

"Mighty fine man," Martha interjected. "Friend to colored. Come and preached at our church, as our guest. 'Spect that's why they throwed him out."

"No, Martha, it was more what he preached at *our* church," said Miss Ginger grimly. "He had the nerve to ask people to behave like Christians."

"You know, dear, to abide by the Golden Rule," Miss Prune explained to Karrie. "Do unto others as you would have them do unto you. People took offense with him for—making such a point of it. They just weren't ready to examine their old attitudes. I guess they need time—"

"Yes, after all, it's been only about eighty years since the Civil War!" said Miss Ginger bitterly. "Anyway, Karen, they fired him! Your Aunt Prune and I fought for him like tigers—"

"So did Jane Llewellyn, Ginger, and don't forget dear old Sam Wirtz—"

"Four of us against the rest of the congregation! We almost quit the church ourselves, but Mr. Eagleton told us it was our duty to stay and keep up the good fight, as he called it. 'They're blind, but someday they'll see,' he said, but I wonder!"

"So what happens if you don't find a new minister?" asked

Karrie.

Miss Prune sighed. "Well, right now we have volunteers who stand up and read the Scriptures—"

"Maddening!" said Miss Ginger in disgust. "It's just like being back in school! People stumbling over words—! Worse yet, Karen, they get up and give these sermons—"

"Not sermons, Ginger," her sister corrected her. "Little talks, sharing their insights—"

Miss Ginger put her face in her hands and moaned. "Heaven deliver us from their insights! Last Sunday Mr. Wilkins stood up and rambled on and on and we thought he'd never stop! Then finally Tulla Swenson said, 'Eb, shut up so we can all go home to dinner.'"

"We really should try to organize the speakers more carefully—" Miss Prune began, but was interrupted by the ringing of the telephone in the hall.

"That's our ring," said Karrie. "It's probably January. I'll get it."

The Webster sisters were still discussing their church situation when she returned to the breakfast room a few minutes later with a serious expression on her face.

"Why, who was it, Karen? What's wrong?"

It was Miss Ginger who asked, but it was at Miss Prune Karrie looked when she replied quietly, "It was Mabel Klein. She wanted you to know. The Schulmans got word this morning that Howie is missing in action."

4.

Karrie excused herself and ran upstairs, not caring to witness Miss Prune's distress, or hear talk of prophetic dreams.

"But at least there's *hope* this time," she heard Miss Ginger say as she left. "He's only *missing*."

Missing! That terrible word! As Karrie entered her room, she paused to gaze at her father's smiling face in the photograph on her desk, and felt sick inside for the anguish of the Schulman family. She picked up Doug's book and sat down in the window seat, thinking with dread of seeing Mrs. Schulman the next time she was downtown. What was a person supposed to say?

Doug, killed in action, and now Howie missing! She was filled with grief for those two boys she had never known. Only—she *did* know Doug. He was just a country boy, like the ones at school, but—*different*. For her, he was a "kindred spirit," and this secondhand book, with someone else's name scratched out above Doug's on the flyleaf, was a secret, sacred connection between the two of them.

She flipped the pages idly and read at random,

> My soul to-day
> Is far away
> Sailing The Vesuvian Bay;
> . . . .

Someday! was printed in a childish hand beside that poem. Doug had been a margin-scrawler, and she could almost follow his growing up by the subtle firming of his handwriting and the poetry he came to appreciate as an older boy. *Howie* was written next to a poem by Yeats called "An Irish Airman Foresees His Death."

> . . . .
> Nor law, nor duty bade me fight,
> Nor public men, nor cheering crowds,
> A lonely impulse of delight
> Drove to this tumult in the clouds;
> . . . .

Howie had enlisted first, in the Army Air Corps, then Doug had followed, but he had chosen the Navy, like Marty. Of course Doug chose the Navy. He'd always dreamed of going to sea, she knew that about him. But about Howie, she knew nothing at all, except that once, perhaps, he'd known *a lonely impulse of delight*—and he was missing in action.

191

5.

Karrie and January met the porch pack in town for a movie, and all the girls agreed that they should first go by the Bread and Cakes and offer a few words of solace to Mrs. Schulman.

The others were better at it than she was, Karrie concluded unhappily. With hugs and murmured expressions of sympathy, tempered by assurances that Howie was bound to come back safe, Jolene, Baby Dodds, Bev, and the Wallace twins seemed to offer positive comfort, while Karrie, feeling gauche and inadequate, found she could do no more than squeeze Mrs. Schulman's hand. As for January, she hung back until they were leaving the shop, then briefly touched the grieving woman's arm before following the others.

"Oh, that shook me up," Baby Dodds confessed, when they were outside again. "I'm glad we're not seeing a war picture today. This one's supposed to be a comedy, isn't it?"

But as things turned out, they never got to the movie at all. There were several people standing on the sidewalk in front of the theater, watching something going on in the street. An angry, red-faced little boy was jumping up and down, bawling, "That's mine! Bring it back! You bring that right back, you old Bucko Riddle!" Shopkeepers came out of their stores. Somebody called out, "Now you cut that out, Bucko!" and someone else yelled, "You gonna hurt her, you damn fool!" Others simply stared.

The girls immediately saw what was attracting so much attention. Bucko Riddle had appropriated a bicycle much too small for him, and was riding in reckless circles around an elderly woman, who was standing on unsteady legs, clutching a bag of groceries.

Karrie recognized Charlotte Johnson, the wife of the high school janitor. Bucko was jeering and hooting, egged on by the raucous cheers of Warren Rumford, who waited nearby in the pickup truck. Bucko's circles became increasingly smaller and more haphazard, and as he careened closer and closer to the frightened woman, she teetered and seemed in danger of falling.

"Stop it! Stop it!" screamed Karrie, pushing her way to the

192

front of the spectators.

With that, Bucko gave another hoot, bore down on the pedals, seemed to lose control of the bike, and plowed into the woman's right side. She, her bag of groceries, Bucko and the bicycle went down in a heap together. Bucko picked himself up, still laughing, and galloped across the street to his truck. He jumped in beside Warren, gunned the motor and sped away.

Mrs. Johnson lay in the middle of the street among scattered groceries and broken glass.

"Look! She's bleeding bad!" someone said.

For one instant Karrie was frozen in her tracks, then she raced into the street. But Jolene was already there, had deftly whipped off her own blouse, wadded it up and was pressing it hard against Mrs. Johnson's arm, all at the same time talking soothingly to the stunned woman and shouting orders to the bystanders.

"It's okay, Charlotte, hear? I'm just gonna hold this real tight while you lie quiet—*Somebody call my daddy—fast!* Now don't you try to move, Charlotte—*Call the ambulance from Hospitality!* Now my daddy'll be here in just a minute, Charlotte, don't you worry. We're just gonna stop this bleeding, okay? *Can't somebody put something under her head? We need a blanket here—Mr. Wilkins?*"

And in rapid response to the instructions from the half-dressed girl kneeling in the street, Mrs. Schulman was off to the telephone, Mr. Wirtz's barber smock had been rolled up and eased under Mrs. Johnson's head, and Mr. Wilkins had managed with uncharacteristic speed to secure a blanket from the Mercantile, as well as a plaid flannel shirt. With the one the old man carefully covered Charlotte, and with the other he attempted to hide Jolene's bare shoulders.

Dr. Ross arrived on the scene to find his daughter, her upper body clad only in a bra, an old flannel shirt hanging off one shoulder, calmly in command of the situation. He squatted down beside her as he opened his medical bag, never taking his eyes off the woman who lay open-eyed and dazed in the middle of the street.

"Hey there, Charlotte, you're gonna be fine," he said. Then, to Jolene, "Anything broken?"

"Can't tell, Daddy, but this bleeding's real bad. I've kept a steady pressure on it."

"That's my girl! Now hold firm while I get it wrapped up tight—All right there, Charlotte, how's that? She's pretty banged up and she's in shock. We need to get her to the hospital."

"Ambulance on the way," reported Mrs. Schulman.

"It'll be all right, Charlotte, you hear?" said Jolene, as she slipped her arms into the sleeves of Mr. Wilkins's flannel shirt. "My daddy's gonna take real good care of you!"

"Did anyone call Rollie?" asked Dr. Ross.

"I will," said Mr. Wirtz.

"Better yet, go pick him up, Sam, and meet us at the hospital. Tell him she's going to be okay."

Soon the ambulance arrived, collected Mrs. Johnson and Dr. Ross, and hurried off again to Hospitality. To Karrie, shaken and humbled by a sense of her own inadequacy for the second time that day, it seemed that the whole thing had taken hours, but when she looked at her watch, she saw that less than twenty minutes had passed since she and her friends had left Mrs. Schulman's shop.

People continued to mill around, talking about the incident. A few of them tried to sort through the groceries to see what could be salvaged, but found it was too much of a mess, because of the broken jars and bottles. The little boy who owned the ill-fated bicycle sat unnoticed on the curb, crying over his bent wheels.

As Jolene stood buttoning the old shirt and laughing at her own appearance, somebody started a round of applause, and many came up and patted her shoulder warmly.

"You were flat-out wonderful, sweetheart!" "What a nurse you'll make, honey!" "You do your daddy proud, girl!" "Jolene, you're as smart as you are pretty, and that's saying *a lot*!"

"Oh, y'all," said Jolene blushing becomingly. "That's just real sweet. Thank you much!"

January looked at Karrie and shook her head in amazement.

But it was Baby Dodds who expressed the sentiments of the porch pack. "Jolene, I've changed my mind. You can deliver all my babies!"

Later that evening, Karrie wrote all about it to Marty.

"She was the hero of the hour, and cool as a cucumber. Maybe I'll let you marry Jolene after all. I'll think it over and let you know.

"Mrs. Johnson is badly bruised and had to have surgery to stop the bleeding, but Dr. Ross won't charge her anything, Jolene says. Mrs. Schulman took up a collection on the street to pay the hospital bill. I think everybody who was there chipped in something. Maybe the most generous thing was, people donated precious ration stamps so the groceries Mrs. Johnson lost could be replaced. I guess even folks in Bienvenidos have their finer moments!

"But meanwhile, Marty, Bucko Riddle goes scot-free! When Grandfather heard about it, he was furious and he called up the sheriff and really gave him a blast. But of course, the sheriff said Bucko didn't mean any harm, just hurrahing *the colored lady* a bit, no crime in that, wasn't his fault Charlotte fell down, *she must have been drinking*, etc., etc. Grandfather was so livid his hands were shaking, and the aunts kept saying, 'Now calm down, Henry, some things you can't do anything about,' and 'Henry, you'll have a heart attack!'

"Aunt Ginger says that Bucko is out of control. Israel says he always *has* been, and Lord knows what he'll do next."

6.

The mayor was not the only one to lodge a strong complaint with the sheriff. Mr. Appleby and Mrs. Schulman also gave him a piece of their minds, and Mr. Wirtz threatened to use his last drop of gasoline touring the county and telling everybody he met that if Hoss Bateson couldn't control one teen-age hooligan, he

195

sure didn't deserve to be reelected sheriff in '44.

Whatever the reason, Bucko Riddle wasn't much in evidence for the rest of the summer, and though stories drifted through town about how he and his cohort Warren Rumford were raising Cain over in Gladhand, Benbenitas was content to let that be Gladhand's problem.

Karrie, enjoying the tail end of summer, almost forgot how unhappily that season had begun. The townsfolk, their first curiosity spent, hardly bothered to stare any more, letters from Marty were arriving regularly, and her relationship with her grandfather, though it still couldn't be described as free and easy, had subtly improved. And, last but not least, she had the dog she'd longed for all her life.

Abner was thriving. He was not turning out "right handsome" as Israel had promised, but he was funny and appealing. He spent his mornings frolicking by the river with Karrie and January, teasing them by running away with their tools and rope, plunging into the water for a quick cool-off, then leaping out to shake himself vigorously. He was, they agreed, a most satisfactory companion.

But a few hours out in the heat were all little Abner could take, so at noon the girls delivered him back to Windy Crest, for his siesta in the study.

"Grandfather never says a word about it," Karrie reported to Marty. "Abner dozes under the table throughout dinner (read lunch!), and when Grandfather gets up to go to his study, Abner's right at his heels. And that's all that's seen of either of them for the next few hours. 'Next thing, we gonna have snow in August!' says Martha, and the aunts just shake their heads in wonderment.

"Guess what! The Raft is practically completed! I know I've made a joke of it, but we've really worked very hard. We took her apart and started all over several times before we got her right, but now she's a beauty. Just a few finishing touches and we'll take her on her maiden voyage down the river. I'm as excited as January. We've decided to name her *Mars* after our native planet. At first January said we should pick a female name, since we refer to the raft as 'she,' but I pointed out that battleships are *always* called 'she' even when their names are things like *Admiral Peary*.

"We haven't told a soul (except for *you*, old soul) about the raft, not even Miss Jane. I hope it doesn't come as too much of a shock to Grandfather and the aunts, especially when I spring our Big Plan on them. What we're hoping to do is pack some food and a couple of blankets and camp out a night or two farther on down the river. Doesn't that sound great? Jano says her father will let her do anything, but I have no idea what kind of reaction I'll get. I think I have some persuasive arguments—experienced camper, good swimmer, all that stuff.

"I'm afraid Grandfather may be a problem, as he's never been the outdoor type, but I may be able to get Aunt Ginger on my side. She used to do all sorts of wild things when she was a girl. Aunt Prune and Israel have told me some rare stories!

"Anyway, I think my best bet is to work on the aunts first. They're pretty mellow right now, because they've just managed to hire a new minister. Actually it's their *old* minister, Mr. Eagleton. He spent a couple of years as a chaplain in the Navy, but his health isn't good, so he's out now, and the aunts convinced him to have another go at it here. The rest of the congregation didn't object, maybe because he got decorated for keeping a bunch of wounded men afloat after his ship was torpedoed. Bienvenidos likes a hero. Also, I imagine they're sick of listening to each other's 'insights.'"

And so, as the summer of '43 drew to a close, Karrie and January plotted their great adventure, their last fling before the start of the school year. Bucko Riddle was the farthest thing from Karrie's mind. She had long since stopped waiting for the other shoe to drop.

7.

The plan was not received at Windy Crest with any more enthusiasm than Karrie had expected.

"Two girls alone on the river—it's just too dangerous," declared Miss Prune.

"January's very tough," Karrie argued. "And so am I!"

"It's the camping out part that bothers me," said Miss Ginger. "Far from everything—if you got into trouble, there'd be no way you could call for help."

"But—"

"The *real* problem here is," said Israel, "y'all can go *down* the river all right, but just how you gonna get back up it, against the flow?"

Karrie was prepared. "Poles!" she replied triumphantly. "We have these neat long poles, and the river is really low right now, and there's not much current at all. It's more like a creek."

The mayor had said nothing so far.

"You girls have been working on this thing all summer?" he finally asked.

"Yes, Grandfather, and it's *beautiful*! It's a wonderful raft!"

"It wouldn't—leak or anything? Have you tested it?"

"Yes, it's sound as can be! Grandfather—"

"Takes a lot of strength to handle them poles," said Israel.

"Israel, I'm strong as a horse," Karrie declared, displaying her calloused hands. "We've spent months hauling huge logs for *miles*."

Israel grinned and shook his head admiringly, as he felt the biceps Karrie flexed for him. "Well, now. That's some muscle there. I 'spect you girls can handle it, then. Henry, you recall how Mr. William and my papa used to brag on that ole raft they had when they was boys? We say we gonna do the same thing, but we never done it—"

"Hm-m-m! Too late now," said the mayor. "Well, I think we should take a look at this creation before we agree to any wild schemes."

"You mean—walk down to the river, Henry? *Yourself*?" asked Miss Prune in disbelief.

"Unless you wish to save me the trouble by hauling the thing up the hill, Prune," replied her brother. "I *have* done it before, you know, and my legs are still functioning, thank you."

"We can drive part way on the trace road," said Israel. "Just have to walk a mile—mile and a half, maybe."

"I'll call Jano to meet us there!" cried Karrie, and ran off to do that before her grandfather could change his mind.

The mile and a half at the pace of the elderly people seemed more like ten to Karrie, who was accustomed to covering that, plus the other mile on the trace road, in no time at all, but she patiently accommodated her steps to theirs, and was uncomfortably aware of the sweat pouring off her grandfather's stoic face. Miss Prune and Miss Ginger fanned themselves vigorously as they walked, but there wasn't a lot of conversation.

When they neared the clearing, they saw that January had arrived ahead of them. She stood facing the river, with her back to them.

"Jano! We're here!" cried Karrie excitedly. She galloped forward, then stopped abruptly, realizing that something was amiss as soon as January turned around. Her face was pinched and drawn.

"Jano, what—"

January said nothing, just stepped aside and gestured at the wreckage that had been their raft. It had been hacked to pieces, its parts scattered along the river bank.

Karrie gasped, then gave a low moan and turned her stricken face to her grandfather. "It was Bucko, Grandfather, it had to be Bucko! Oh, Grandfather, you don't know—it was the most wonderful raft—!"

The mayor's face was frozen in an expression of outrage and frustration.

"Nothing we can do, Henry," said Israel. "Can't prove it, and if we could, guess it ain't no crime. Knowed he'd do *something*. Thought it was the dog he'd come after—"

"This was a secret!" Karrie wailed. "*Nobody* knew—nobody! He must have followed us down here and spied on us. Oh, I hate him! I hate him!"

"Oh, honey, you mustn't *say* that!" cried Miss Prune.

"Why not?" snapped Miss Ginger. "I hate him, too!"

Karrie couldn't keep from crying, but January continued to stand and stare, dry-eyed, at the ruins of their raft.

"Mr. Mayor," she said quietly, "I'd appreciate it if you didn't mention this to my father when you talk to him. No point in getting him all riled up. In fact, I'd rather we didn't say anything about this at all. Nobody knows we made the raft and nobody needs to know it's been wrecked."

"But Bucko—" began Karrie.

"Just go on like nothing's happened," said Jano. "As Israel said, we can't prove Bucko did it, and we're not going to give him the satisfaction of having us accuse him, okay?"

"Probably the best way to handle it," admitted the mayor. "But I hope I live long enough to see that hoodlum get his come-uppance!"

"January," said Karrie, "we'll build it again. We'll pick a better hiding place and start all over. It won't take so long this time because now we know how. We'll just have Saturdays, but I'll bet we can get it finished by the end of October."

"Just in time for Bucko's Halloween high jinks," observed January. "No. Forget it. We won't build it again. I—I don't have the heart any more."

Chapter 10
Grannie Opal

"We have all the same teachers we had last year, but still, it's different," Karrie wrote to Marty.

It was different. Something besides the secret raft had disappeared with summer vacation.

Most of the boys who had graduated in May were gone. It seemed to Karrie that one day they were raucous, pimply-faced pests, and the next they were coming home on brief furloughs, subdued, self-conscious and somehow vulnerable in their well-cut uniforms and short haircuts. Boys who had so recently been banished from the Bijou for throwing wads of gum and making too much noise, were now admitted free, with a smile and a handshake from the manager.

Bettie Rae Miller, who would have been in Jolene's senior class, had stunned her friends by eloping with a soldier from New Jersey she'd met at the canteen in Hospitality. Her absence was a disquieting reminder for the porch pack that the days of childhood were fading fast.

In fact, the porch pack itself was becoming a thing of the past. Most of the girls now had after-school jobs, and the main diversion was no longer picture shows at the Bijou, but dances at Mr. Wirtz's opera house.

After Bettie Rae's elopement, some alarmed mothers had

201

persuaded Mr. Wirtz to provide a place where the servicemen who passed through town could stop to enjoy a cup of coffee, doughnuts and dancing. It was not only the patriotic thing to do, they pointed out, it would keep the young girls from gadding off to Hospitality.

"The Baptists raised a howl, of course," Karrie wrote to Marty, "but their hearts weren't in it. I think they've given up trying to convince their daughters that dancing is sinful, and just hope to keep them out of Hospitality. (Angie Beal is a regular at the canteen!) There'll be lots of chaperons at the Opera House, and Mrs. Schulman is providing the doughnuts. Mr. Webber donated his old wind-up Victrola and his weird record collection, but as nobody was keen on dancing to things like 'Che Gelida Manina' or 'Nearer My God To Thee,' the girls bring their own records from home.

"You have to be fifteen to go. That leaves out the Wallace twins, who are *devastated*, and Jano and me, who couldn't care less."

A short time later, she wrote to Marty, "All the kids are so busy these days. It sounds silly, but I really miss going to the movies and having a soda with them, and even hanging around on Jolene's front porch. I was just getting used to everything, and now it's changing."

One thing that had changed, and then returned to the way it used to be, was the soda fountain at Webber's. Shirleen Haus was back, rejected by the WACS because of her asthma, she said, though the rumor was that she'd failed the intelligence test. For whatever reason, Mr. Webber and his customers were grateful, as her replacement, Baby Dodds, couldn't get the hang of concocting a decent ice cream soda.

"But she was awfully disappointed to lose the job," Karrie wrote, "so Mr. Wirtz said she could sweep up his barber shop after school and tidy up his kitchen. Mr. Wirtz is very neat and I doubt if he really needs the help, but he knows that Baby Dodds needs the money. Her father stopped sending any home. On the days Mrs. Morris isn't working in Grandfather's office, she does cleaning for Jolene's mother, which must be very strange for her, because they're good friends. Of course that punk Bubbabill isn't working. He just loafs around town showing off his bad attitude. Poor Mrs. Morris!

"Joycie and Sister Bee's father has been called up. For now the family is staying in Bienvenidos, but they may follow him when he gets assigned after basic training. The girls have jobs cleaning the beauty parlor where their mother works.

"Bev is working at Mr. Miller's feed store, because his helper got drafted. Bettie Rae was supposed to do that. I hear she's waiting tables at a restaurant in Killeen (her husband's stationed at Camp Hood). Weird, weird, weird! I'm actually writing about the *husband* of one of my friends!

"I don't suppose it's necessary to bring you up to date on our head cheerleader. I guess she wrote you that she and her mother are volunteers at the Hospitality Hospital on weekends. Mrs. Ross may go back to nursing full time, as there's a big shortage of nurses. I still find it hard to imagine Jolene giving sponge baths and emptying bedpans! But she does. She has her nails cut almost to the quick, because she says she wouldn't want to accidentally scratch a patient she's bathing. Funny thing is, Jolene's nails cut to the quick still look glamorous!

"Well, that leaves me. I feel like a ne'er-do-well. So I've decided I'm going to get a job, too!"

"But you don't *need* one, dear," said Miss Prune, when Karrie brought up the subject with her family.

"I'm the only one not doing anything," Karrie explained. "Jano can't get a job because she has to keep house for her father, but what's *my* excuse?"

"You'd only be taking work away from somebody who needs the money," said Miss Ginger firmly.

"But—"

"You know, dear, Benbenitas is a *poor* town, and it's not fair for people of privilege to—"

"Oh, please!" said Karrie. "Excuse me if I have a real hard

time thinking of myself as 'people of privilege.' Marty and I spent two years wearing our parents' old clothes and watching every penny!"

"But the pennies were there, the first of every month," Miss Ginger reminded her. "You were provided for. The rent and utilities were paid and you had enough to eat on."

"You have no notion of what it's like to be as poor as most of your friends are," added Miss Prune. "Now you can say that we don't either," she continued, seeing Karrie's expression. "But our papa brought us up to be thankful for our privileges and aware that we don't deserve them any more than the next person. That's why we do our volunteer work."

"Oh," said Karrie, deflated and frustrated. "But Aunt Prune, I don't want to knit scarves and roll bandages or—"

"Well, now, Jolene and her mother—"

"—or empty bedpans and stuff. I know that sounds selfish, but I—I don't think I could stand being around sick people."

Miss Ginger started to retort, but Miss Prune laid a warning hand on her sister's arm. "Your mother was ill for a long time, wasn't she, dear?"

Karrie nodded, not trusting her voice.

"Well, I think I have a brilliant idea," announced Miss Prune. "Ginger, Maybelle says that Ludy Steel—that sweet girl who helps out sometimes with Grannie Opal—she's going to marry the Banks boy and follow him to Oklahoma where he's stationed. Now that will leave Maybelle without anyone to stay with Grannie Opal Sundays, and you know how Maybelle loves her Sunday school and church. Poor soul, it's the only time she gets out except for Thursday when we leave off Martha and drive her to the beauty parlor."

"You want me to stay with Grannie Opal on Sundays?" asked Karrie in dismay. "But I wanted a *job*!"

"It's not exactly a job, but it's *service*, dear. Doing something for someone else. Now you just try it. You may be surprised at how rewarding you find it."

2.

"Trapped!" Karrie lamented in her letter to Marty. "All I wanted was to have a job, like my friends, and earn a little spending money—because Grandfather isn't all that generous, believe me! I hate giving up my lazy Sundays poking around the hills with Jano and Abner! The aunts know I'm not a bit happy about this, but I've agreed to try it, starting next week.

"This may be my last free Sunday, and you'll never guess what I'm planning to do. I'm going to church! Mr. Eagleton is back, and I want to take a look at him. I tried to talk Jano into coming. She says she's curious, too, but not enough to make her spend a morning with all those people in hats and gloves."

So Karrie went alone, on her bicycle, and sat unnoticed in a shadowy corner of the back pew.

Mr. Eagleton turned out to be a thin, gray-haired man with the soft, easy drawl of a Southern gentleman. He didn't look much like a hero, and didn't speak like the fiery crusader she'd been led to expect. Yet Karrie knew at once that she liked him.

He talked mostly of the war, recalling acts of courage and sacrifice he had witnessed under fire, which he said had reinforced his belief in man's innate nobility. He spoke, too, of Christian brotherhood, and gently urged those present to practice it in their daily lives.

When services were over, Karrie waited until the other people had filed out, then gave them time to finish their milling and chatting before she quietly emerged from the church. As she was starting down the steps, Mr. Eagleton was just coming back up them, having said his goodbyes to his congregation. He smiled at Karrie in passing, then suddenly halted and turned around on the top step.

"You're Karen Webster, aren't you? I noticed you sitting in the back."

Karrie turned, too, and nodded shyly. "I enjoyed your sermon, Mr. Eagleton. I know everybody says that, but *I* really mean it!" She stopped, flustered. That hadn't come out right!

Mr. Eagleton chuckled. "Well, *thanks*, I guess!" He sounded like Marty.

Karrie grinned. "What I was trying to say was that I don't usually like sermons, and I *did* like yours."

"Good! Heard a lot of sermons, have you?"

"Well, I've certainly heard enough—" Karrie stopped herself again. *Better just shut up*, she decided.

But Mr. Eagleton laughed and didn't seem at all offended. "Does that mean I will or won't be seeing you here every Sunday?"

"No—I mean won't! I can't come any more because—"

"It would be bad for your image?"

"—because I'm going to be staying with Grannie Opal on Sundays so Maybelle can come. I really don't go to church."

"I know. I was teasing you a little. Your aunts told me you're Jewish."

"Well—sort of. I wasn't raised that way. When I started school my mother told me to say I was 'unaffiliated with any formal religion.'"

"Hm-m! I doubt if *that* fell 'trippingly off the tongue'!"

"I got pretty good at it. Once a kid asked me if we had nice hymns in Unaffiliated, and I told her yes, we sang all the time."

Mr. Eagleton laughed. "So what brought you here today, Miss Unaffiliated? Curiosity?"

"I guess so. My aunts told me a lot about you."

"Then I'm afraid I disappointed you. But give me a chance. This is my first day back. If I'm a little bit careful, maybe I'll keep this job for two or three weeks. As you know, I'm not real popular!"

"You are with my aunts!"

"Unusual women, your aunts."

"I know." Karrie responded automatically, then realized, all at once, that she *did* know. "*They* understood what you were saying, anyway."

"But you don't think anyone else did, is that it?"

"Everybody liked the war stories. I doubt if they heard anything else, but as long as they've been to church, they think

206

they're *good*."

"What's the matter with being good once a week?"

"Nothing, only I don't think they really are! Their idea of 'Christian brotherhood' is being nice to other white people who go to the same church and aren't too foreign-looking. They don't even allow black people in the movie theater except for one night a week, and then they have to sit in the balcony! I don't think that's what you meant by 'Christian brotherhood' somehow."

"No, it's not, but I keep hoping a little of its real meaning will seep in through their pores. Whatever else you are or aren't, Miss Unaffiliated, you're a Webster! All fire and backbone!"

"My aunts tell me I shouldn't shoot off my mouth. But they did, too, when they were kids. It made them unpopular."

"I was raised in a little town like this, back in East Texas, so I know what that's like! They used to call me a bolshevik!"

"I've been called—all sorts of things."

"Karen, I may not sound like the firebrand you were expecting, but I don't want you to think I've thrown in the towel. If the congregation doesn't turn around and fire me again, I still hope I can make some kind of a difference. One miraculous Sunday, somebody might be listening."

"Martha believes a time will come when everybody will live together like good neighbors, even in Benbenitas."

"I believe that, too. If I didn't, I'd take up some other profession."

"Like what?"

Mr. Eagleton sighed, and for an instant his pleasant, worn face looked infinitely weary and discouraged. Then he replied, in his previous bantering tone of voice, "Oh, shepherding, or light-house keeping. Something that would limit my exposure to my fellowman. But say! You'd better get home to dinner, and I had, too. I don't dare keep my wife waiting. She's already mad at me for bringing her back to Benbenitas!" He grinned at Karrie. "Know something? I have a feeling that you and I aren't too far apart in the way we think."

"You think I'm a Methodist?"

"No, ma'am! I don't think you're an anything with an *ist* at the end of it, and I respect that!"

They said goodbye and went their separate ways, Mr. Eagleton in a rattling, ancient automobile, Karrie on her bicycle. No, he wasn't a bit what she'd expected, she mused, as she pedaled up the highway, but she was ready to believe he was a hero.

3.

The memory of her encounter with Great-Grannie Morris still fresh in her mind, Karrie felt nervous about her first Sunday with Grannie Opal, who was said to be senile.

"I don't know about *senile*," said Martha. "She's deaf. Hard to make sense when you can't tell what folks are saying. But don't you worry. She's right sweet and won't give you a bit of trouble. Just take your homework along and the time'll go fast."

"How old *is* she?" Karrie asked her aunts on the way to Grannie Opal's house.

"Nobody knows," said Miss Prune. "Not even Maybelle. They didn't keep very good records here back then. But she was born when Texas was a Republic."

"I know, but when was that, exactly?"

"Between 1836 and 1845," Miss Ginger answered. "I would guess she was born about 1840. It's always been said she was one of the first babies born in Benbenitas. Oh, she's had quite a life! Buried two husbands, raised two families! Poor thing outlived most of her children, but she has dozens of grandchildren and great-grandchildren."

"All scattered," said Miss Prune sadly. "Only Maybelle is left to take care of her."

Israel and the aunts waited in the car when Karrie went up to the house. She was met at the door by a beaming Maybelle, dressed up for Sunday school and church in her best print dress and white felt gloves, a little veiled hat with flowers propped on her perfect curls.

"You'll find everything you need," said Maybelle cheerfully, waving her in. "Lunch is in the ice box, cookies in the cookie jar.

Outhouse just out back. You won't need to take her more than once."

Outhouse? thought Karrie with a sinking feeling.

Grannie Opal was sitting in a rocking chair, dressed in a crisply ironed housedress, a pink bow in her sparse white hair. Though it was a warm day, a crocheted cotton shawl was draped around her hunched shoulders. Her round, faded blue eyes gazed out the open door, and her skeletal, milk-white face wore a faraway smile.

Maybelle leaned over and bellowed in her ear, "This is Karen Webster, Grannie, mayor's granddaughter. Come to sit with you while I go to church, all right? Bye bye!"

And with a happy wave, Maybelle was out the door, leaving Karrie alone with the old woman, who appeared to be serene and unconcerned with her presence.

She sat down in a chair beside Grannie, and, after a few futile attempts at conversation, she decided she might as well get out her books and start on her history assignment. Whenever she glanced up, she found Grannie still gazing contentedly out the door. Karrie began to relax somewhat.

There was a pleasant atmosphere about the little house. Though it was identical in plan to Great-Grannie Morris's shack, there was all the difference in the world between the two. Maybelle kept both Grannie and the house clean and fresh. There were starched calico curtains at the windows, faded hooked rugs on the scrubbed floors, and cut marigolds in mason jars where Grannie could see them.

The hours passed easily. Maybelle had left a good, cold lunch and iced tea, along with freshly-baked cookies, which Karrie suspected had been made just for her. There was little for her to do, other than feed Grannie and wipe her chin, until the old woman finally touched her arm, looked into her face and uttered the one word, "Outhouse."

That was the task Karrie had been dreading. She managed to get Grannie to her feet, then very carefully walked her out the back door. Grannie, leaning heavily into the girl's supporting arms and placing one slippered foot in front of the other, seemed to enjoy the excursion. The outhouse turned out to be as clean as the house itself. Afterwards, it was back to the chair again, and as Karrie settled her in, Grannie turned her head ever so slightly, smiled a tiny bit more, and nodded, as if to say, "We did that very well, didn't we, dear?"

Grannie said little that first day, but the next Sunday she was talkative. Holding Karrie's hand in a remarkably strong grip, she seemed eager to entertain her guest with stories. Karrie could catch a little of it—Ern dunked Prissy in the horse trough—Buddy fell off his stilts and broke his collarbone—Hester got the typhoid and lost all her hair—and Grannie chuckled as she shared these recollections. About all Karrie could do was chuckle with her, and nod as if she understood.

Karrie soon found herself looking forward to Sundays. Her aunts were pleased with her attitude, but it was not selfless, as they thought. She was fascinated with Grannie Opal. She'd never seen anyone so very old, so old that she was a grown woman during the Civil War, and it was intriguing to think of all the other stories she had to tell, if only she could hear the questions Karrie longed to ask.

Sometimes Grannie spoke hardly at all, but seemed happy and comfortable just looking out the window. Karrie, watching her, often wondered how was it that, at the end of a long life lived through such hard times, the frail, bent, little old lady could gaze out at the Texas hills with that contented smile on her face.

4.

The busy days of that autumn seemed to pass quickly, and before Karrie knew it, Christmas rolled around again.

"My second one in Texas!" she wrote to Marty. "So much has happened since last year, when we had the tree all ready for you and your leave got canceled and you shipped out.

"There was a discreet buzzing among Martha and the aunts—to get a tree this year or not? I knew they really wanted one, but were afraid of offending my Jewish sensibilities. Of course, my sensibilities are no different from what they were last year. So I came right out and voted for a tree. They were quite relieved. Jano and I went to Beals' with Israel, and our splendid choice now stands in front of the parlor windows, looking like a huge, bejeweled dowager.

"I love the old tarnished ornaments, and I like to think of the generations of Websters who've handled them. Some of them even date back to Massachusetts days. Again the aunts debated—their mother Reba's star, or my grandmother Sally's angel on top? I believe they feel that, one way or the other, there's some sort of disloyalty involved. This time Reba won, and that upstart Sally was put in her place.

"Grandfather makes no comment, but I have this curious feeling that he likes to see the tree there but is too stubborn to admit it. It must bring back memories of when he was a boy, and later on, when he had two little boys of his own all excited about Christmas. Jano said she thought he looks wistful. Strange adjective to describe Grandfather!

"I hope your package has arrived, wherever you are. I have my own idea of where that is, but if I write it here, the censors will block it out. Mail has been very slow. I had a letter yesterday but it was written before the last two.

"You've been overseas almost a year now, and in a couple of weeks you'll be nineteen. That sounds so old! And then, I'll be fifteen! That doesn't sound quite as grown-up as it used to. When *you* were fifteen, I thought you were the very *epitome* of maturity. You *were* pretty mature. That was when we started living on our own, after Dad left, and you did a good job of taking care of me. We got along fine, didn't we, Marty? In my dreams, we're always little kids again, playing in Central Park, taking the subway to Coney Island or to the Bronx Zoo, just the two of us. When we *were* little, Dad and Mom were doing those things with us, but somehow they're never there in my dreams. Only you and me.

"Well, 1943 is old and tired and about to vanish into history. Some history! Stalingrad, Guadalcanal, Tunis, the Solomons! All

211

those places I and a lot of people never heard of before, but nobody will ever forget them now. Here's hoping that 1944 brings the *best* day in history—the end of the war!"

5.

"She ever talk to you?" Maybelle asked, before leaving for Sunday school one mild morning in January.

"Oh, yes," said Karrie. "I can't always understand it all."

"Uh huh. She don't make much sense 'less you know who all those folks are she goes on about, and can kind of read her mind, like I do," said Maybelle cheerfully. "But she's happy, God bless her, and if she talks to you, means she likes you, honey. Thinks she's telling you stories of the long-ago."

Karrie nodded, wishing she had a little of that ability to read Grannie's mind and piece together those garbled tales.

Karrie's birthday fell on Sunday that year, and her aunts suggested she might like to beg off her duties this once, but she insisted on going to Grannie Opal's as usual.

"This is my birthday, Grannie," she told the old woman, as she sat down next to her. "I'm fifteen today. I wonder if you can remember being fifteen?"

Grannie looked into Karrie's face curiously, but she seemed to be having one of her silent days. Karrie knew it was useless to try to get her talking, so she picked up her science book and began to read. After a while, Grannie made a little groan. Karrie looked up and saw a troubled look on the frail face. She was wondering if perhaps Grannie needed a trip to the outhouse, when suddenly the old woman whispered, "Oh, poor Prudence. Poor, poor Prudence."

That was all. Karrie's promptings were in vain. Grannie watched the girl talking to her for a while, then her eyes shifted to the open window. She was through saying anything for that day.

But she had given Karrie an unexpected birthday present, the possibility of a glimpse into the lives of her own ancestors. It hadn't really occurred to her before, but of course Grannie would have known Prudence and Matthew.

The following Sunday morning the Webster sisters discovered their grandniece lifting several of the old portraits from the wall in the hallway.

"I'll bring them back this afternoon," Karrie promised. "I just want to show them to Grannie Opal."

"Why, honey, whatever do you have in mind?" asked Miss Prune.

"She talks to me a little," explained Karrie. "I thought I'd prod her memory with these."

"Well, I doubt that," declared Miss Ginger. "Her memory went long ago."

"I don't think so," said Karrie. "She sits and remembers all the time. She's always trying to tell me things."

"Well, I guess there's no harm," admitted Miss Ginger. "But be careful with them. They're irreplaceable."

Later that morning, Karrie showed the pictures to Grannie, one by one. Grannie's faded old eyes shone with interest as she regarded faces from her far-off past.

"William!" she exclaimed. "Oh, he were a handsome boy! Reba Stone! Reba Stone! She done captured William Webster!" She prodded Karrie's arm with a shaky finger, then chuckled as though the wedding had been the week before.

Karrie let her ramble on a bit more about William and Reba, then showed her the picture of Prudence. The light in the old eyes seemed to dim. Grannie looked away.

Karrie then held Matthew's portrait in front of her face. Grannie's hand traveled uncertainly up to her mouth, and she said nothing. Disappointed, Karrie put the pictures away, not wanting to distress her.

It was almost an hour later when Grannie suddenly spoke up again.

"Oh, they was fine horses!" she said with a sigh. Karrie put down her book and moved closer. "Papa'd uv kilt him," Grannie whispered to her in confidence. "Woulda tooken a horse whip to him. Papa were so strict with us girls. But oh! His hair was

213

brown and curly, and oh! The devil was in them eyes!"

Karrie leaned in, interested. She knew that Grannie had switched subjects and was not now describing her father.

"Papa'd uv kilt him," Grannie repeated faintly, her voice trailing off. Karrie was afraid she'd heard all she was going to hear of that tantalizing story, when the old voice started up again.

"Brung a horse for me and a horse for him. I got right on and rode a-straddle like a man. Papa'd uv kilt me. Took him to the little cave where the spring run." Grannie turned her eyes to Karrie. "Played there—when I were bitty," she explained and touched Karrie's arm with her cold, bent hand.

Karrie nodded. She hardly dared breathe for fear of disrupting the unexpected flow of words, but she had a sudden thought. "The china tea set—was it yours?"

Grannie turned her face toward the window again. There was a long period of silence, then she resumed:

"Devil in them eyes, but talked like a angel and oh!—kissed sweeter'n molasses. Papa'd uv kilt him." Grannie chuckled, then after a while she sighed. "We heard 'em. Heard 'em in the tunnel talking. They didn't know nobody could hear. 'Cover him,' one say, 'get that dirt in here.' 'Shouldn't gone and kilt him,' t'other say. 'Law be after us for sure.' 'We be long-gone over the border before the law find out,' mean one say. 'Cover him, cover him, cover him.'" Grannie turned clouded eyes to Karrie. "Papa'd uv kilt me."

Karrie, holding her breath, reached for Matthew's picture and again held it in front of Grannie's face. "Who do you think they killed? Could it have been Matthew?"

Grannie didn't seem to focus on the picture, but continued in a troubled voice, "'Man's dead,' he say. 'Telling won't help him none.' He say, 'don't you tell—you get me kilt for sure.'"

"You never told a soul?" Karrie asked tremulously, thinking of poor Prudence and her lifetime of uncertainty.

"Kissed sweeter'n molasses," Grannie said, looking far away into a lost, stolen moment in time.

214

Chapter 11
Home From The Hill

1.

"Ka-ren! Tele-phone!"

Karrie hesitated and looked back at the house. She was already late getting started. It was probably Jolene calling, anxious to know if there'd been a letter from Marty. And that girl *never* knew when to get off the phone!

Karrie resolutely resumed walking, and allowed the cry of "Telephone!" to recede into the distance. She was well-prepared for this expedition. Her knapsack contained the biggest flashlight Windy Crest had to offer, along with extra batteries, two of Israel's garden trowels, a thermos of lemonade and a supply of sandwiches.

She had left a reproachful Abner tied up in the barn. A clumsy, accident-prone dog was not a suitable companion for a skeleton hunt in Dead Man's Caverns.

January had expressed doubts.

"There's no telling *when* Grannie heard that stuff in the cave, and those bad guys could have been burying a horse, for all she knew! It probably had nothing to do with Matthew Webster. You just don't want to believe that your ancestor left his family and ran off to California."

"He didn't," Karrie had retorted. "Prudence knew he didn't, Aunt Prune knows, and *I* know!"

January had shrugged and grinned. "Okay! Count me in! I'll be there with my shovel! I've always wanted to hold up a skull and say, *Alas! Poor Yorick!*"

And knowing January, she was probably already there, impatient to begin the adventure.

Karrie hurried along, absently singing under her breath a sentimental, old-fashioned song.

> "Tell me the tales that to me were so dear
> Long, long ago—long, long ago..."

She was thinking of Prudence—imagining her proud and strong, but forever homesick for the sea—living out her life, lonely and friendless in this rough land, without ever learning the truth about Matthew.

When Karrie approached Dead Man's Caverns, she paused, cupped her hands on either side of her mouth, and sang out, "Ho! Jano!" But there was no answering call. She readjusted her knapsack on her back and galloped towards the caverns. "Jano! Hey, Jano!" she called. "Sorry I'm late!"

But January was not waiting at the entrance to the cave. Karrie pulled out her flashlight and snapped it on as she entered into the darkness. "January? Jano?"

She proceeded farther inside, shining the light in front of her. It wasn't like January to be late. Karrie was about to turn and go back outside to wait when she heard a faint noise, and paused to listen.

There it was again. A soft moan. Could January have hurt herself? Karrie stepped deeper into the cave, then tentatively rounded a curve where no comforting hint of daylight could follow.

"Jano? You all right? Say something!"

Another low groan. But this time it was coming from behind her. Karrie whirled around and shone her light full on the grinning face of Bucko Riddle.

216

2.

"Ja-no, Ja-no, where are you?" Bucko mocked her in falsetto. "Down here!" he answered himself in a high-pitched wail. "Save me, Karen, save me! I'm dy-y-ing...!"

"Just get out of my way," said Karrie gruffly, keeping the flashlight aimed at his face.

"Yeh, or *what*?"

"Let's not hang around here, Bucko," said a voice in the darkness behind him.

Karrie briefly shifted the beam of her flashlight and glimpsed the ghost-like faces of Warren and Bubbabill.

"Scared of the dark, Bubbabill?" inquired Bucko sneeringly. "I kind of like it here." He leered at Karrie. "Good place for a picnic, ain't it, tootsie? What you got in the knapsack? Something good to eat?"

"None of your business," said Karrie. "I'm leaving."

"What's your hurry? That ain't friendly. Let's see what's in the bag. Dear me, I hope it's kosher!"

Bucko took a step toward her. Karrie stepped back and he laughed with satisfaction.

"Hey, the way out's *this* way, sugar cakes—you going wrong! Oh, I know! You're looking for your little playmate. Oh, Ja-no!"

"Bet she's fallen down the bottomless pit," Warren's voice brayed.

"Did you do something to January?" demanded Karrie.

"Well, she didn't have no picnic lunch for us. We got all upset," said Bucko soothingly.

"Aw, Bucko, let's get out of here," said Bubbabill. "We ain't even seen January," he told Karrie.

"Bubbabill, you getting so you ain't no fun at all," complained Bucko, with a menacing note in his voice. "If I wanted a ole lady to follow me around and say 'don't do this,' 'now doncha do that,' I'd bring my mamma along. Suppose you just scram outta here if you're gonna get on my nerves like that."

"Let *her* leave," said Bubbabill nervously. "Don't mess with her. She's the mayor's granddaughter."

"The mayor's granddaughter!" Bucko mimicked him. "Well, now, I tell you, Bubbabill, that really fills this faint heart of mine with terror!" He turned to Karrie again. "Come on, cow-eyes, let's see what's in the pack!"

"Oh, *take* the pack!" cried Karrie, and hurled it at him with all her might. It struck him hard in the stomach. She made a lunge to get past him, but was intercepted by Warren.

"Let her go," said Bubbabill to Warren.

"Well, I've sure had a bellyful of you," muttered Bucko. "Hold her, Warren." He headed after the retreating Bubbabill.

Karrie tried to fight, but Warren gripped her wrists so tightly that the pain caused her to drop her flashlight. He laughed foolishly in her face and she was repulsed by his rank breath. All she could do was twist and attempt to kick at him.

There was a sharp cry of pain from somewhere, and soon a flashlight beam was on Karrie's face, blinding her.

"Whatcha do to him?" asked Warren.

"He'll live," growled Bucko. "Damn' sissy-boy. Getting tired holding our little wildcat? You ain't her type, Warren. New York gals need a man of the world like yours truly."

Bucko came up behind Karrie, put his flashlight down on the ground and grabbed her by both her arms. As Warren relinquished his hold on her wrists, Karrie seized the split-second opportunity to twist suddenly and deliver a vicious stomp to Bucko's instep. He yelped in pain and his grip slackened just enough for her to wrench herself free.

The only way she could go was deeper into the cave, and she no longer had a flashlight. Frantically she hurried, feeling her way along the walls. Echoing voices followed her.

"Can't get out that way, sweet cakes. Gonna fall down the bottomless pit—"

"Hold it, Bucko."

"Ain't you had enough? Get him, Warren!"

Scuffling and grunting noises echoed through the chambers. Karrie didn't pause. Her hands searched the walls of the cave. Nothing. Had she gone too far or not far enough?

Then suddenly there it was—the ledge, halfway up the wall, and the opening above it. A flash of light came from around the curve. With one concentrated effort, Karrie hoisted herself up, making it on the first try. She hastily lay down on her back and began to wriggle and work her way into the opening. She was not a second too soon.

"Little hellcat's in the hole," she heard Bucko Riddle say.

Light washed over her.

"Hey, Jew-girl, that's a dumb place to hide. Bet there's an ole bobcat in there. Come on out. I ain't gonna hurt you. We'll all sit down and have a nice picnic—come on!"

His hand attempted to close on Karrie's foot. Savagely she shook it off, and wriggled out of its reach.

She dug her heels in and pushed, her hands clawing at the rocky surface above her, dislodging dirt and stones which fell onto her face.

"Hey, where'd she get to? There she is! Wow! She's way in there. You gonna get stuck, gal. Nobody gonna be able to get you outta there!" His flashlight played about the narrow passage.

Karrie kept going, inch by inch. She felt her heart would stop when she heard Bucko say to Warren,

"Get on in there and pull her out. You're skinny."

"*I* ain't going in that dadburned little hole!" responded Warren. "Bucko, she ain't coming out as long as we're here. We better scram. Heckfire, she could die or something in there."

"Hear that?" Bucko shouted into the tunnel. "Gonna die in there! Come on, we ain't gonna hurt you. Give you a ride home! Mayor'll gimme a medal."

Karrie grimly continued onward. After a few minutes, the muttering of Bucko and Warren grew further away, and the beam from the flashlight disappeared, leaving her in the blackest darkness she had ever experienced.

Then abruptly her head slipped downward, and she realized that she must now be where the narrow part of the tunnel fell off into wider space. Here it was supposed to be possible to crawl. But she attempted to turn over too soon, and became painfully wedged on her right side, her head dangling.

"The important thing is not to lose your nerve," January had said.

Karrie tried to ease onto her back again, but she was stuck. With her right hand she reached around and clawed at the ceiling above her, hoping to gain a little room in which to maneuver. The surface was hard and rocky.

The soil beneath her seemed less so, and with her left hand she tried to dig out under her right shoulder. The dirt there was surprisingly free of large rocks and was beginning to yield a little to her efforts, when her nails struck something solid and metallic. She managed to work it free and her hand closed around it. It seemed to be a little square box. Using it as a tool, she soon chopped away enough dirt to enable her to slip onto her back again.

That position made her entry into the wider space bumpy and bruising, her head and shoulders taking the brunt of the punishment. For a moment she lay still, grateful for the sudden sense of space, and allowed tears to wash her gritty eyes. Then she turned over and began to crawl on her hands and knees, the small metal box still clutched in one hand.

She crawled for a considerable distance, much longer, she felt sure, than the fifteen minutes Jano had claimed it took. Finally, her head bumped against a hard surface, and she knew this had to be where the tunnel narrowed again. Groping with her hands, she determined the size of the entrance, then she lay down on her back and worked her way into the narrow wet space. Again she had to wriggle and claw her way along, this time with water dripping down on her face.

Soon the darkness appeared less black; then she could see her hands above her. At last her head emerged into the familiar shadowy light of the little cave.

With a sob rising to her throat, she pulled herself out and dropped to the ground.

"Karrie—"

She wheeled about and stifled a scream. Standing in the

entrance to the cave was a tall, bloody apparition.

3.

"Karrie, come on, let's get out of here before Bucko shows up."

Bubbabill's freckled face was washed in blood. It was coming from his scalp and his nose. His curly red hair was flattened and matted with it. His hands, arms and clothes were soaked in it. He would have looked like a walking dead man, had it not been for the clear blue eyes that looked out at Karrie with such intensity.

"Come on—hurry!"

Karrie let him grab her hand and pull her along. The two ran and stumbled down the hill and didn't pause for breath until they reached the cow pond.

"Wait—wait!" cried Karrie, falling to her knees. "I've got to—stop a second."

Bubbabill's eyes anxiously scanned the hill behind them before he dropped down beside her.

"Just a few seconds. Geez, I'm in for it now," the boy said with a sigh. "Bucko won't stop till he breaks every bone in my body."

Karrie glanced shyly at her bloody companion. "Thanks—thanks for helping me."

"That's okay." Bubbabill rose and pulled her up by her arm. "Let's not stick around. He don't know about the tunnel, how it goes all the way through, but he's sure as shooting going to figure it out. Hey, that's Windy Crest way over there, ain't it? Let's go!"

"How—did you know about it?" asked Karrie breathlessly as they hurried along. "The tunnel?"

"Heck, I helped dig it! Me and the Schulman boys. I used to tag along after them when I was little. We never told nobody about it, but when I heard Bucko say 'she's in the hole,' I figured you must know, too. January, right?"

"She thought it was her secret!"

"Might have known *she'd* find it. Doug and Howie and me—

we swore an oath in blood not to tell."

"Thank God you never told Bucko!"

"Yeah—I'll say!"

Karrie's legs ached with the effort of trying to keep up with Bubbabill's long strides.

"Wait, please, I've got to stop again," she gasped.

"Oh—okay," said Bubbabill, nervously looking back. "No sign of them yet."

"Maybe they think I'm still stuck in that hole," said Karrie.

"I *hope*. Let's go. What I *really* hope," he added, as they resumed running, "is that the whole derned cave fell in on them!"

"Wait! Could you just slow down a little? My legs aren't as long as yours."

"Oh—excuse me. This better?"

He shortened his gait to better accommodate hers, but kept looking over his shoulder.

"You dug out that whole tunnel?"

"Huh? Naw—naw—not the whole thing, geez!"

"Well, how—"

"We used to play these games in the caverns, see. We each had a flashlight. One of us would hide something for the others to look for. Howie buried this baseball in a hole in the wall. Turned out the dirt was softer there. Seemed kinda queer, so we started digging. Doug was always looking for buried treasure."

"Did you find anything?"

"You kidding? Naw. We must have spent two or three months digging that ole hole—and finally we broke through to that place where you can almost stand up. If you're a little kid, that is! Then we found out it led into that wet part and it come out in the little cave on the other side of the hill. Our own secret passage! Almost better'n finding buried treasure!"

Karrie's hand tightened around the little metal box.

"Did you keep things in the hole?"

"Yeh. Sometimes. We had a candy stash in there one summer."

"This yours?" She showed him what she was holding.

Bubbabill halted briefly and examined the object.

"What's this thing—some old snuff box? It rattles. Something in there, but I can't get the top off. Naw, we didn't have nothing like that." He handed it back to her. "Come on—we're nearly there. Lord knows what your folks gonna say! You'll tell 'em I didn't do nothing, won't you?"

4.

When a dirty and bedraggled Karrie pushed open the kitchen door and staggered in with the blood-covered boy beside her, Martha looked up from the dishes and screamed. That brought the entire household into the kitchen.

"Tell them I didn't do nothing," Bubbabill said nervously, with a poke to Karrie's arm.

Karrie's nerve had not failed her throughout her ordeal, but as she faced her shocked family she suddenly went to pieces.

"It was Bucko Riddle, Grandfather," she blurted out, then collapsed into the mayor's outstretched arms.

"My God!" he cried, clutching her close. "What—what's happened—?" He stared savagely at Bubbabill.

"Bucko got her trapped in Dead Man's Caverns and scared the tar outta her," explained Bubbabill. "Tell them I didn't do nothing, Karrie."

By that time Karrie was sobbing.

"Bubbabill helped me," she blubbered. "It was Bucko— Bucko and Warren Rumford."

"How did they hurt you?" the mayor demanded, holding her out from him and staring into her face.

Karrie shook her head vigorously.

"They just scared her good," said Bubbabill again.

"I want to know what they did to you!" said the mayor.

Miss Prune interceded. "Henry, Henry, let me—"

But it was Martha's gentle hands that pried the girl from her grandfather's grasp.

"Let me look at you, baby," she said softly, peering into Karrie's scratched and dirty, tear-stained face. "She's all right, mayor," Martha reported. "You all right, ain't you, baby?"

Karrie nodded.

"I'm sorry!" she spluttered. "I'm sorry! I don't know what's the matter with me—"

And her teeth began to chatter uncontrollably.

"Let's get her into a warm tub," said Miss Ginger.

"It's Bubbabill who's hurt," Karrie managed to say, as Martha and the two aunts were leading her away.

"Israel gonna see to him," Martha assured her.

Bubbabill was left alone with the two men.

"What's your part in this?" demanded the mayor. "Aren't you one of Bucko Riddle's cronies?"

Bubbabill shifted his weight from one foot to the other.

"Yessir, Mr. Mayor," he admitted uncomfortably. "Guess so. Bucko went too far this time. Tried to stop him. He beat me up pretty good. Think he broke my nose," he added ruefully, tentatively touching it. "And now I guess he'll be out to get me good."

"He won't get you or anybody else," said the mayor, shaking with fury. "I'm going to find him and strangle him with my bare hands."

"No, you ain't, Henry," said Israel. "I feel the same ways. But what I'm gonna do is clean this boy's face up. And what you gonna do is get on the phone and call the sheriff!"

5.

Even the sheriff admitted that Bucko had gone too far this time. He stood in the hallway at Windy Crest and shifted his weight from foot to foot, much as Bubbabill had done.

"Always been rambunctious," he mumbled. "Had to grow up without a daddy, you know."

"A lot of people grow up without a daddy," said the mayor bluntly, "and manage not to become hooligans."

"Oh, you're right, Mr. Mayor, you're right," agreed Sheriff Bateson. "I ain't excusing him. My poor sister done her best, but the boy's always been full of mischief. This'll break her heart,

224

this'll surely break her poor heart!"

"Bucko's done too much damage in this town for me to worry about your sister's heart, Sheriff," said the mayor. "I want to know what you propose to do."

"Now, Mr. Mayor," said the sheriff. "I ain't gonna let this go by. You can count on that, yessir. Bucko's gonna answer to me for this, you can bet your bottom dollar on it. Of course, he didn't really hurt your little girl. Hurrahed her, you know, and she got scared. But he didn't rightly *hurt* her."

The mayor was losing his patience.

"Dr. Ross just drove off to take Bubbabill Morris to the hospital in Hospitality. The boy has a broken nose, probably a concussion, and we don't know what else yet. Call me a fool, Sheriff, but I'd say that boy's been hurt!"

"Oh, yes indeed," agreed the sheriff. "But boys fight, you know. Sometimes they get hurt. That's the way of things. The important thing is, your little girl's all right, ain't she?"

"The important thing is, you lock that ruffian up or I'll have you both run out of town on a rail. And you can be sure the whole town will stand behind me! Now you go out and arrest him!"

"Mr. Mayor, you can't ask me to arrest my sister's boy! That ain't right! I can't do that to her!"

"Then hand in your resignation and I'll find someone who will."

"Oh, now wait. I'm sheriff of the whole county here, not just Benbenitas. You can't—Wait, wait, Mr. Mayor—!"

For the mayor, with surprising strength, had grabbed the sheriff by his upper arm and was literally dragging him to the door.

"I'll get him out of town!" cried the sheriff. "He'll enlist! I hoped he'd finish high school first, but we'll let that go, all right? The Army'll straighten him out, Mr. Mayor. Ain't that fair? 'Cause there's nothing criminal here, don'tcha see? Even if I arrested the boy, the judge would just bawl him out and let him go. Let the Army deal with him, that's all I ask, Mr. Mayor."

The mayor stared at the sheriff with frank loathing. Finally he released his grip on the man's arm and said,

"Go pick him up. That idiot Rumford boy, too. Throw them in jail. I'll talk to Mrs. Morris and hear what she wants done. If she decides to press charges, so be it. If not, I'll agree to let the Army deal with your worthless nephew. I predict he'll spend his entire career in the stockade. Now get the hell out of my house."

The mayor slammed the door after the sheriff, then turned to see Karrie standing on the stairs.

"Is that it?" she said. "He's getting away with it again?"

"He'll leave town, Karen," said the mayor. "He won't bother you or anybody else around here any more."

"No, he'll just bother other people in other places."

The mayor sighed. "Unfortunately, that fool sheriff was right. The judge would bawl him out and let him go, then he'd be up to his old tricks. The best place for him is in the Army."

"I see. Okay. I guess I just have a hard time understanding how you decide to forgive some people and not others."

With that, she turned and ran up the stairs, leaving her grandfather to stare disconsolately after her.

6.

January sat in the chair in the attic room, fiddling with things on Karrie's desk. Karrie sat cross-legged on her cot beside Abner, who rested his head on her knee and gazed up at her with sorrowful eyes.

"I tried to call, but you'd already left," explained January. "Pop chopped off the tip of his finger and—"

"Oo-ooh!" cried Karrie, shuddering.

"Well, he's okay. Doc Ross had me drive him *and* the tip of his finger to his office. Doc sewed it back on."

"I didn't know that could be done."

"Me neither. But Doc did it. I called Windy Crest from his office and they said you'd gone."

"Dr. Ross had a busy day, I guess. He also had to take Bubbabill to the Hospitality Hospital."

"I know. He's going to be all right. I called Baby Dodds. She says his nose sure looks funny."

"That's too bad! I should call, too. I just—I don't know. I'm kind of rubbery still, isn't that silly? I haven't wanted to talk to anybody, except you. Everybody's been calling here. Word sure gets around! The aunts keep making the excuse that I'm sleeping, but I guess I'll have to start going to the phone pretty soon. People will think I really got hurt or something."

"Must have been mighty grisly. I just wish I'd been there with you! But maybe it's a good thing I wasn't. Pop might have done something drastic—then *he'd* be the one in trouble. Hey! Look on the bright side! Because of you, Bucko Riddle has left town! Benbenitas may build you a monument!"

"Has he really gone?"

"Absolutely. The sheriff picked up him and Warren Rumford and skedaddled with them to San Antonio or some place. Came back alone. Says they've both enlisted. Heaven help the Army!"

"They should be in jail."

January nodded. "Have faith, little one. I have a feeling they soon will be. Bucko can't stay out of trouble for more than five minutes at a time. The Army has jails, too."

"He shouldn't have gotten away with it. He gets away with everything. I told you about Israel's nephew Jimmy. He wouldn't have joined the Navy if Bucko hadn't deviled him so. He would never have been on that ship at Pearl Harbor—"

"I know, Karrie. You don't have to tell *me* that Bucko Riddle is vermin. But now he's gone. Hallelujah! Let's rejoice and forget he ever existed."

Karrie was silent, wondering if it were possible to ever forget those desperate moments in Dead Man's Caverns.

"Do you want to go to the picture show or something, Karrie?" suggested January. "Take your mind off it."

"No—I don't know what I want, January. Maybe just to go to sleep for a couple of months and wake up and have it all in the distant past."

"Hey, what's this thing?" January picked up an object from

Karrie's desk. "Looks like an old snuffbox!"

Karrie took it from her and examined it for the hundredth time.

"That's what Bubbabill said." She rattled it gently. "There's something in it, but the lid's stuck. I found it in the tunnel—at that spot right before it gets wider."

"Hm-m." January took it back from her and looked at it carefully. "That's real strange."

"Jano, the dirt is *different* in that narrow part. Have you ever noticed that? It's not as hard and rocky as it is where it's wider. Bubbabill told me that he and the Schulman boys were the ones who dug that section out."

"They did? You mean there was no hole there before?"

"Just a little one. They started digging and were able to tunnel through to the wide section."

"No kidding!"

"Jano, what if it used to be a bigger tunnel, a long time ago, but somebody filled it in?"

"Whoa—hold it! Grannie Opal's bushwhackers?"

Karrie nodded gravely. January sat back and stared out the window.

"You mean all this time I've maybe been crawling over somebody's bones? Wow! And I thought you were crazy, listening to all those ravings!"

Suddenly she jumped up. "Karrie, come on! Let's get a couple of shovels and get over there!"

"Wait a minute, wait a minute! About the last place I want to go is Dead Man's Caverns right now."

"Oh, don't act like a sissy. It'll snap you right out of it. Like getting back on a horse when you've been thrown. Come on! This is fantastic!"

"January, slow down! You're impossible!" And Karrie laughed for the first time since her ordeal. "First of all, let's get the top off this box and see what's inside."

January rattled the box next to her ear. "Can't tell what it sounds like. We need a tool."

"I've tried everything short of a can opener."

"Well—?"

Karrie shook her head. "I hate to do that. This box is really old, and I've sort of disturbed its burial place. I don't like to go crashing in with a can opener."

"Well, we *must* open it," declared January impatiently. "Doesn't your Aunt Prune have knitting needles and crochet hooks and stuff like that?" She leaped up again and ran halfway down the attic stairs, shouting, "Miss Prune! Miss Prune! Would you do us a favor, please?"

Soon the two girls were kneeling on the floor in Miss Prune's sewing room, watching with suppressed excitement as first Miss Prune and then Miss Ginger tried to gently pry the lid from the little square can. Then Karrie tried again, then January—but she tackled it with such energy that the others quickly rescued it from her. In the end, the victory went to the patient, skillful fingers of Miss Prune.

A few minutes later, with Miss Ginger close behind her, Miss Prune knocked on the door to the mayor's study.

"Henry," she said quietly, trying to keep her voice from shaking. "There's something here I want you to see."

She held out her closed hand and unfolded it slowly. She was holding a gold pocket watch. The mayor took it and examined it for a few seconds, then carefully opened its case. There on the one side was exactly what he'd expected to see, an old-fashioned watch face, but what he saw on the other side caused him to catch his breath. It was an exquisite tinted miniature of a young woman, very old, but so well-preserved that the mayor had no trouble at all recognizing the proud head and clear level gaze of his grandmother, Prudence.

7.

It was not January who dug up the bones of Matthew Webster, much to her disappointment. She and Karrie had to wait outside Dead Man's Caverns with the mayor and his sisters while that task was painstakingly undertaken by two workmen from the lumber mill. Dr. Ross also stood by, with Mr. Spikes, the undertaker from Hospitality, who wore such a solemn and dignified countenance that one might never have guessed that the remains he awaited had already been buried for over eighty years.

When at last the workmen emerged from the cave, carrying their burden in a blanket, Miss Prune and Miss Ginger turned their faces away, but the others stepped forward to have a look.

Dr. Ross picked up the skull and put his finger through a hole in the left temple.

"He was shot all right," he said. He put the skull back with the rest of the skeleton, stepped back and dusted his hands. "And I think we can conclude from Grannie Opal's account and from the miniature of Prudence in the watchcase that these are definitely the remains of Matthew Webster. Probably robbed and murdered on his way back from the cattle drive, perhaps by a couple of the men who rode out with him."

"Or by his neighbors," said Miss Ginger stubbornly.

"Not too likely, Miss Ginger," said Dr. Ross gently. "Grannie Opal told Karen she heard the killers say they were going over the border. Doesn't sound like the settlers, or even the bushwhackers. No, I'd say Matthew had had a successful journey, and was on his way home to Prudence with a substantial profit in his money belt, when a couple of scalawags who knew what he had on him seized their opportunity. They found the perfect place to dispose of the body, too."

"All those years!" cried Miss Prune. "Oh, Ginger, our poor, poor grandmother! It breaks my heart!"

Along with the bones, Matthew's spurs were retrieved, and his large silver belt buckle. The mayor expressed a wish to keep the spurs, but he presented the buckle to Karrie.

"Martin's to have the gold watch," he said. "Perhaps a jeweler can replace the works."

"And Karen's to have the miniature," Miss Prune said, then glanced at her sister, who looked a little put-out. "When you graduate, honey."

But it was Mr. Spikes who got custody of the bones, placing

230

them carefully in a simple pine coffin, and following sedately behind as the workmen carried it away to the hearse that waited by the side of the highway.

8.

Matthew was to be buried between his faithful wife Prudence and his unforgiving son William. The mayor was in favor of a simple and private interment, but Miss Prune and Miss Ginger wanted a real funeral. As a compromise, they agreed upon a quiet, graveside service, with Mr. Eagleton officiating.

Miss Ginger and Miss Prune insisted on inviting their sister Clara and her family to attend, but (to the mayor's relief) they declined. Clara's Hoot got on the phone himself to declare:

"Silliest damned thing I ever did hear of! Digging a man up where he's been lying peaceful for eighty-some years and then sticking him in the ground again!"

It may be that plenty of the people in Benbenitas were of a similar opinion, yet such a number turned out for the occasion, either to show respect for the mayor's family or out of frank curiosity, that the little graveyard beside the Methodist church couldn't contain them all, and many had to stand out in the street.

"This is turning into a damned circus," muttered the mayor.

But there was respectful silence when the Reverend Mr. Eagleton stepped to the head of the open grave, softly cleared his throat, and opened his Bible.

"Psalm 40," he announced, and proceeded to read: "*I waited patiently for the Lord; and he inclined unto me, and heard my cry. He brought me up also out of an horrible pit, out of the miry clay, and set my foot upon a rock, and established my goings. And he hath put a new song in my mouth, even praise unto our God: many shall see it, and fear, and shall trust in the Lord.*"

Mr. Eagleton closed his Bible and cleared his throat again.

"And now—Karen has asked me to say these lines. Hr-uum! This is from Robert Louis Stevenson."

The mayor and his sisters glanced quickly at Karrie, who

calmly concentrated on the minister, as he took a piece of paper from his pocket, unfolded it and read:

> "Under the wide and starry sky
>   Dig the grave and let me lie:
>   Glad did I live, and gladly die,
>   And I laid me down with a will.

> "This be the verse you 'grave for me:
>   *Here he lies, where he long'd to be.*
>   *Home is the sailor, home from the sea,*
>   *And the hunter, home from the hill.*"

"Let us pray," said Mr. Eagleton, and he led the gathering in reciting the Lord's Prayer.

As the dirt was being sprinkled over the casket and the crowd began to edge away, Karrie plucked at the mayor's sleeve.

"I would like to sing something, Grandfather," she whispered. "It's not a hymn. It's really for Prudence."

"Oh, very well, do as you please," said the mayor with a sigh. "You seem to be in charge of this show." His sisters looked alarmed. "You wanted a public funeral," he reminded them. "Enjoy it."

Karrie took a step nearer to the open grave, and, as she stood alone and lifted her voice in song, those who were in the act of leaving paused to listen.

> "Tell me the tales that to me were so dear
>   Long long ago, long long ago.
>   Sing me the songs I delighted to hear,
>   Long long ago, long ago.

> "Now you are come, all my grief is removed.
>   Let me forget that so long you have roved.
>   Let me believe that you love as you loved
>   Long long ago, long ago."

And so Karrie did, after all, sing in public in Benbenitas, as Bev had once prophesied she would.

When the clear young voice subsided, no one moved for a little while. Then, slowly, people once more began to make their way out of the churchyard, as the gravediggers heaped dirt on the brand-new grave in the old, old cemetery.

Thus was Matthew Webster properly laid to rest at last, and with him the oldest rumor in Benbenitas.

Chapter 12
The Home Front

Benbenitas was quick to forgive bad boys who redeemed themselves by enlisting, even Bucko Riddle. The sheriff went around
telling anyone who would listen how Bucko was straightening
himself out in the Army, and poor Mrs. Riddle was as proud as
any other "Blue Star mother." Still, it was an all around relief to
have him gone, nor was Warren Rumford missed.

Bubbabill also left town. People called him a hero for
standing up for Karrie, but he decided to stay with his aunt in
Waco for the remainder of his senior year.

"Baby Dodds says it's for the best," Karrie wrote to Marty.
"He's given his mother a very hard time ever since his father left,
but he's not a bad kid underneath. I found that out!

"It's a different town without Bucko, and a much safer
highway. Just in time, too! Grandfather wants Israel to teach me
to drive now that I'm fifteen. Bev is very envious. Her folks
won't let her learn because they're trying to baby their old Ford
along till the war's over.

"I'm not that keen on driving, myself. I think I'd rather stick
to Jimmy's bike. Except that when I'm riding up the highway
and I hear a truck behind me, I still nearly jump out of my skin.
Jano is the same way. I asked her if she was ready to start on

another raft, but she said she'd rather wait a little while longer—just in case!"

Bucko Riddle was gone, but not easily forgotten.

2.

Jolene Ross was valedictorian of the Class of '44.

"Not exactly a surprise!" Karrie wrote to Marty. "You'll no doubt soon be receiving a few million pictures of her, looking radiant in her cap and gown. Dr. Ross's trusty camera never stopped clicking."

Graduation day was not what it once was at Bienvenidos High, as most of the boys were due to go right into the service. Except for a sad-sweet dance at the Opera House, there was none of the revelry of prewar days.

A few days after graduation, Jolene left for Austin to begin summer classes at the university.

"Hospitality Hospital will miss her, especially when they meet her reluctant replacement. *Guess who?* How do I get myself into these things? Well, Mrs. Ross begged and I couldn't say no. I really dread it, but then, as Aunt Ginger pointed out—she's so good at pointing things out!—I dreaded my duties with Grannie Opal, too, and that worked out fine.

"So—I mean to see this through, Marty. I think you know I have a kind of phobia about being around sick people, but I've decided that I'll no longer put up with having phobias. My 'celebrated claustrophobia,' as you used to call it, got cured in about fifteen minutes in a tunnel under Squaw Mountain. This may take a little longer, but here goes!"

3.

Karrie was setting up a lunch tray for an elderly patient, when suddenly a loud cheer went up from the nurses' station.

"Go see what's happening," ordered the woman. Karrie rushed out into hall, where she found a gathering of nurses, doctors, and patients, everyone talking at once, every face beaming.

"D-Day!" someone trumpeted, and "D-Day!" echoed down the corridors, as more people ventured out of their rooms to find out what the commotion was about.

Karrie hurried back to repeat the news to her waiting patient, who immediately reached out an amazingly strong old arm to draw the girl's face down for a kiss.

It was June 6, 1944, and far away from Hospitality Hospital and the Texas hill country, Allied Forces were storming the beaches of Normandy. The invasion of Europe had begun at last.

In Benbenitas, there was other good news. The Schulmans had been notified by the Red Cross that Howie was a prisoner of war.

"I think they'd almost given up," Karrie wrote to Marty that night. "It's hard to go on hoping when there's no word at all. Some folks in town are saying the war in Europe will soon be over. Grandfather doesn't agree, but I know he's wondering, the way I am, if we're going to have news of Dad one of these days. He must be somewhere in Europe, if he's still alive."

It was the first time Karrie had ever written the words *if he's still alive*. She hesitated, sighed, then resumed writing.

"I feel very sad tonight, in spite of all the good news. I keep thinking about Israel's nephew, Jimmy, who tied bird feathers to his bike so he'd feel like he was flying, and Doug Schulman, who was always looking for buried treasure.

"Sorry! You have to face enough depressing things every day without me going on like this. I can't even begin to guess what it's like for you, wherever you are, but I know if I were wounded, you would be exactly the person I'd want there to patch me up. I can imagine you telling the guys, 'You'll be all right, you're going to make it,' and convincing them of it, too.

"Sometimes people ask me why you became a hospital corpsman, but if they knew you, they wouldn't need to ask. When we used to talk about what we were going to be when we grew up, you always said doctor. That was the same as saying butcher, baker, or candlestick maker to me. But you were *born* to be a healer, just as Dr. Ross and Jolene were, because you always go straight ahead and do what has to be done. I wish I could be like that!

"Can you stand all this mush? Blame it on D-Day and the news about Howie Schulman. I promise not to make a habit of it. I don't want to make you throw up or anything.

"Only, Marty, while you're taking care of all those other guys, please, please, please, take care of my brother, and come home safe—come home *soon*. Love—K."

4.

At Windy Crest, the summer of '44 was filled with ongoing worry and quiet hope, as dramatic events in both theaters of war unfolded. The Japanese were badly beaten in the Battle of the Philippine Sea, the Allies invaded southern France, and, on August 25th, Paris was liberated from the Germans. The unspoken thought that Richard might surface at last was always present, and letters from Marty, less frequent now, were more anxiously awaited than ever.

The busy life of the Home Front went on, one day at a time. Karrie was very involved with her work at the hospital. She was a favorite with the older patients, and the staff declared her "indispensable" because of her willingness to sit at a bedside and softly sing a troubled old soul to sleep.

"I'm acquiring an interesting repertoire," she reported to Marty. "They want to hear things like 'Amazing Grace,' and 'The Old Rugged Cross.' Mrs. Ross brought me a hymnal, but it's really the time I put in listening to Mr. Webber's curious record collection that stands me in good stead when a patient asks the nurse to 'send in the little Jewess.' Yes, that used to make me wince, but I don't mind any more. Most of these poor old people have never been away from these parts. They're good-hearted, really. The cranky ones don't ask me to sing."

When school started again, Karrie could only work at the hospital on Saturdays, but she put in a full day, and, with her Sundays still reserved for Grannie Opal, she found herself with little free time.

"Jano's getting real cross with me," she reported to Marty. "It's gotten so we only see each other biking to and from school and during classes. I invited her to come over and help with the canning (the aunts and Martha are putting up vegetables from Israel's victory garden), but she said she does enough domestic stuff as it is.

"I think that's why she's so moody. It must be hard on her to watch everybody else bustling about doing their bit, and she's stuck with cooking and keeping house for her father. She never complains, but it has to be tough—especially when he's drunk.

"Oh—and as if I didn't have enough to do, the principal decided I had to stay after school two afternoons a week with Mr. Mitchum, to make up a seventh-grade course I skipped. The school board, in its infinite wisdom, has decreed that Texas History is a requirement for graduation. I tried to convince the principal that I'll be safely home in New York by the time I graduate, but he didn't buy it.

"Actually—I hate to admit it—I'm really enjoying it! Mr. Mitchum tells a rollicking story, and it all seems so recent and real. I was never able to picture Peter Stuyvesant stomping around Manhattan on his peg leg, but it's easy to imagine Sam Houston galloping around these parts.

"One day I persuaded Jano to sit in. I think she only agreed because it was an opportunity to act like a pain in the neck. She plopped herself down in a seat at the back of the room and declared that she'd had Texas History with Miss Buzzard and she *hated*, *loathed* and *despised* it, just as she did everything else about Texas, and it would have been all the same to her if they'd lost their stupid War for Independence!

"Mr. Mitchum just smiled at her in his tolerant way, and began telling about the siege of San Antonio in 1835. Mexican forces had been holed up in San Antonio for weeks, with the Texans camped outside, and nothing much was happening. Then a couple of Americans escaped from town and reported that the Mexicans were in sorry condition. It was a good time to attack, but the Texas general kept dragging his feet. His men were growing more and more restless and discouraged, until finally an old frontiersman got fed up waiting and shouted, 'Boys, who will come with old Ben Milam into San Antonio?'

"At that point in Mr. Mitchum's story, this clarion voice rang out from the back of the room—'I WILL!' Mr. Mitchum and I burst out laughing, Jano blushed, then she started laughing, too. Now she sits in on the class regularly. I believe she *will* be an actress someday. She has *drama* in her bones!

"Joycie and Sister Bee's father was home on furlough last week. He looks so young in his uniform! Bettie Rae's father finally forgave her for eloping and let her come home when her husband got shipped overseas. Guess what? She's *expecting*, and she's the size of a barn! Imagine! One of *my friends* is going to be a mother! She's made us all promise to babysit. I managed to get out to a movie one night with her and the other girls, but it was a war movie, and Bettie Rae sat there and cried and cried.

"Jolene calls me from Austin about once a week! When she doesn't hear from you she frets her little heart out! She's taking a heavy load of classes at the university, and turned down the sororities that wanted to 'rush' her because she said she didn't have time for all that stuff. 'The best derned cheerleader Benbenitas ever had' has certainly changed!"

5.

The presidential election that year was regarded as an unnecessary distraction by the people of Benbenitas, and when Roosevelt was elected for a fourth term, that unique occurrence in American history was taken in stride.

There was a war to be won, and Benbenitas was satisfied that the same leader who had brought electricity to the impoverished hill country would continue at the helm, steering the nation to victory.

"The poor man looks so *tired*," Miss Prune lamented.

But he seemed immortal.

239

6.

On a mild afternoon in late November, Karrie sat under the overhanging rock in front of the little cave doing her Latin homework, with only Abner for company.

Suddenly the dog began to growl back in his throat, then he jumped to his feet, bristling and wagging at the same time, and gave two or three threatening barks. Karrie stood up, too. There was a figure approaching, a couple of hundred yards away. Her heart began to pound. It was a tall young man, in a sailor's uniform. *Marty!*

Almost immediately, her heart settled down again. That gangly, loose-jointed gait did not belong to her brother.

"Hey, Karrie!" the sailor called out.

Karrie waited; could it be—? "Why, Bubbabill—Hi!—"

He shuffled up to her, grinning shyly. The last time she'd seen him his head had been covered with blood. Now his short-cropped hair gleamed golden red in the sunshine as he doffed his sailor's cap, and his freckles blended almost gracefully into his tanned face.

"They told me at Windy Crest you were probably up here," he said. "Gee—I'd think you'd never want to see this place again."

Karrie shook her head. "This is my special place. I wasn't about to let Bucko ruin it for me."

"Yeh—Bucko," muttered Bubbabill, kicking the dirt with the toe of his shoe. "He made sergeant, did you hear?"

"Oh, yes, I heard. The sheriff did everything but take out an ad in the paper."

"Yeh. Warren got kicked out, though. He was in the brig a while, then got a dishonorable discharge. Say he's staying in Mississippi where he was stationed. Got a sweetie there. Imagine somebody taking up with goofy old Warren!"

"Heard that, too."

"Yeh. Hear everything in Benbenitas, right?"

"Well, I didn't hear that you were home."

"Oh, well, got a leave at the last minute. Think we're

shipping out pretty soon. I'm just gonna be here a couple of days, then I'm heading back to California. Want to see my dad before I go. Ain't seen him since—He don't come home no more."

"I know. I'm sorry. But Baby Dodds and your mother are doing okay, and you look just great, Bubbabill!"

The young man brightened, and flushed. "Thanks. Uh—my buddies call me Bill. I've got me buddies from all over—Indiana, Washington State, North Dakota, even! Hey, my best friend's from up your way—Brooklyn! Whatcha thinka that? Nobody's heard that Bubbabill stuff, thank the Lord. They'd rib the tar outta me."

"You've really changed, Bu—Bill. You might not want to come back to Benbenitas after the war."

"Nah, I don't think I will. Heck, I never knew there was choices before. I thought Benbenitas was the world. Now I know it ain't—isn't. I can go anywhere and do anything. I'm in the Seabees—did you know that? Our motto's 'Can Do!' We build all kinds of stuff, and we build good and we build fast. Think maybe after the war I'm gonna go to college and make an engineer."

"That's wonderful! Your mother will be so proud!"

"Yeah. Say, speaking of mothers, Bettie Rae's got a kid now, right?"

"Uh huh. Bobby. Her father's really crazy about him."

"Can you beat that? Funny how things change, ain't it? Karrie, I gotta go. Gotta hitch a ride back to town. My mamma's having a bunch of relatives over to gawk at me. Gonna hear a lot of 'Bubbabilling' today! Guess I won't have a chance to see you again."

"I'm glad you came by, Bill. It's really good to see you."

"Uh—think you might write to me? I'll send you my FPO. I'd be right proud to get some letters from you."

"Sure! Of course I'll write. You take care of yourself. All the luck in the world, okay?"

Bubbabill hesitated, as if he had something else to say. Suddenly, he leaned down and planted a swift kiss on Karrie's mouth, then bounded away without looking back.

Karrie stared after him, shocked. She touched her lips with her fingers, then furiously wiped them with the back of her hand. Bubbabill was a good-looking boy, and had even played the hero for her, but what business did he have giving her her first kiss?

"I'm not going to count it," she declared out loud. "Abner, why didn't you bite him?"

But Abner merely wagged.

7.

"What is it you're not going to count?"

Karrie started and jumped up. "Miss Jane, where did you come from?"

Miss Jane laughed at Karrie's confusion. "The Chevy overheated on the highway, and I hiked over to fetch some water for it. Who's that walking off in such a hurry—who did you want Abner to bite?"

Karrie's face colored. "Bubbabill Morris—Well, *Bill* Morris now. He's graduated into a real name."

"About time. Yes, I heard he was in town for a couple of days. I guess he'll be shipping out. What's the matter? Did it upset you to see him again?"

"No-o. It wasn't that."

Miss Jane sat down beside her. "Well, come on, what was it? Something he said?"

"No. Something he *did*." Karrie tossed a stone into the stream.

Miss Jane smiled. "Did he try to kiss you?"

Karrie laughed ruefully. "He *did* kiss me—before I knew what was happening. I—why did he have to do that?"

"Uh oh. First kiss. I take it there were no crashing waves, violins and shooting stars, as advertised?"

"No *nothing*! Zero! Zilch! And *Bubbabill*?"

Miss Jane looked sympathetic. "That's too bad, Karrie, but I'm afraid it often happens like that."

"Was it that way for you?"

This time it was Miss Jane's turn to blush, and she laughed to cover it up. "Me? Oh—not really. Well—to tell you the truth, it was violins and shooting stars."

"Hmm! My Uncle Martin, right?"

"Martin? Heavens no!"

"No? I thought—"

"Oh, mercy, my eternal torch for Martin Webster! There's a legend like that for every old maid in town. 'Poor thing, she never married because of—' somebody or other!"

"But weren't you engaged to him?"

"Karrie, I was only about your age when he went away—and not half as mature. My parents would have locked me in my room and thrown away the key."

"But you were dating him?"

"Oh, sure, more or less. He took me to dances and picnics and things like that. Put a lot of noses out of joint. Martin was the biggest heartthrob in the county."

"Sometimes I think I wouldn't have liked him much."

Miss Jane scooped up a handful of pebbles and idly began to flick them, one by one, into the stream. "Um-m. That's because they've elevated him to sainthood at Windy Crest. No, you would have liked him. Martin was a wonderful guy. I must have been the only girl in town who didn't have a crush on him."

Karrie was silent for a minute, then she asked, boldly, "So who provided the violins and shooting stars?"

Miss Jane hesitated, shot a pebble into the stream, then glanced at Karrie. "His little brother."

"*Dad?*"

"Oh, dear, you're shocked, aren't you?"

"No, of course not! Just surprised! I never heard anything about you and Dad. But then—nobody talks about him much."

"We were best buddies from the time we were toddlers. We used to play house out here with these same funny little dishes."

"Really?" Karrie picked up a tea cup and examined it as though she were seeing it for the first time.

"They looked pretty old, even then."

"How come you never told me that?"

"I guess I was afraid it might upset you."

"But I love to hear about Dad when he was a kid. So why did you go to dances with Uncle Martin?"

"I don't know. Richard never wanted to do those things. Maybe I was trying to make him jealous. It hurt him more than I'd expected. Richard grew up in Martin's shadow, you know. And there I was, his special friend, stepping out with his brother. It made him feel second-best again, and I felt—awful. It wasn't until Martin left that I got up the nerve to explain it to him."

"Did he understand?"

"Richard—always understood. We were standing right here in front of this cave that evening."

"Violins and shooting stars?"

Miss Jane colored slightly and smiled. "Absolutely."

"Why did you break up?"

"We didn't, exactly. Martin was killed in action that summer and Richard was devastated. He went off to the university a few months later. He wrote now and then but he practically never came home. Windy Crest was pretty grim in those days, and then the whole town started treating me as though I were Martin's widow or something. And I was all of sixteen!"

"Well—was *Dad* the reason you never married?"

Miss Jane laughed. "Oh, Karrie, you've been in Benbenitas too long! I never married because—it didn't happen. *My* dream was to travel and study art and live a crazy bohemian life in a garret in Greenwich Village! But—with one thing and another—that never happened either. Anyway! I've enjoyed being a teacher. And I like being an old maid. I like living alone and puttering with my old car and I don't even mind being one of the local 'Poor dear' legends. Now, you know all my deep dark secrets. But Karrie—"

"Uh-huh?"

"Just wait. One of these days—you'll see—it *will* be violins and shooting stars."

Chapter 13
Changes

1.

In Benbenitas, 1945 began with the news that Bucko Riddle had been killed in action during the Battle of the Bulge.

Karrie learned it first from the janitor after school.

"Thought that boy was too mean to die," Rollie Johnson said.

On the bike ride home with January that afternoon, Karrie had little to say, and when they pulled up at the Windy Crest driveway, January asked,

"What's bugging you, anyway?"

"I—I—hated Bucko Riddle," Karrie said.

January shrugged. "Everybody hated him—so what? Look, I'm not glad he's dead, but I'm not going to be a hypocrite. Just wait! Benbenitas will turn him into some sort of saint!"

Karrie smiled, but somehow she felt miserable. Like Mr. Johnson, she'd thought Bucko was too mean to die. Other boys—good boys like Uncle Martin, Jimmy, and Doug Schulman—got killed in wars. Was Bucko's death less tragic?

The mood hung over her all through the week. "Forget it," January advised, but that was impossible in any case, as it was the only topic of conversation in school and around town. As January had predicted, the general attitude about Bucko had softened considerably.

"Once he climbed up the water tower and rescued my kitty," Joycie Wallace recalled.

"Uh huh," agreed Sister Bee, "only, he'd put her up there in the first place. Miss Jane made him get her down."

"Well, he coulda just walked away."

That was about as kindly as recollections of Bucko got, try though folks would to find something good to say about him. The *scuttlebutt* (a word Benbenitas had recently adopted and was putting to excessive use) was that he was going to be awarded a posthumous medal.

"At least his poor mamma's got the comfort of knowing her lad died a hero," Karrie heard Mr. Appleby remark to Sam Wirtz, when she stopped by the barber shop. "Guess the boy got straightened out in the Army."

"Be that as it may, Ben," said Mr. Wirtz, "Lydie Bateson married one bum and raised another, but she needs all the comfort she can get, and God knows I wouldn't deny her any."

Neither would she, Karrie reflected. She truly pitied Mrs. Riddle, a foolish, unpopular woman, who'd had nothing in her life but her big bully of a son. Now he was gone, along with any motherly hopes she'd probably cherished in spite of everything.

One Sunday morning, when Karrie was helping in the kitchen before leaving for Grannie Opal's, Martha noticed that she was unusually quiet, and asked, "What is it troubling you, baby?"

"Nothing, I guess," replied Karrie somberly.

"Bucko Riddle?"

Karrie nodded. "You know, Martha, it's because of me he enlisted in the first place."

Martha put down her paring knife and looked Karrie square in the face. "Now you listen to me. Bucko Riddle was past due for the Army. The other fellers his age was already called up. Only reason he got to stay out so long was the sheriff whining to the draft board. Poor mamma needs him, he say. Let him finish school, he say."

"Yes, but—"

"You got some notion if you hadn't made a fuss Bucko wouldn'ta gone to the Army and got hisself killed. Baby, blaming yourself for Bucko dying would be like Israel and me blaming Bucko for Jimmy dying."

"I *do* blame him for that—"

"But that ain't right. Bucko pestered Jimmy till he run off to the Navy, but Bucko didn't bomb Pearl Harbor. Japanese done that."

"Okay. You're saying I didn't fire the gun or throw the grenade or whatever it was that killed Bucko. But, Martha—I set it in motion."

Martha sighed. "No," she said firmly. "Hitler set it in motion. You didn't do nothing, except live the best you knew and try not to hurt nobody. If Bucko'd lived that way, most likely he'd still be dead in the war but he wouldn't be leaving all this ugliness behind him to trouble people's minds."

Karrie frowned as she silently applied herself to potato peeling.

"What I'm saying, baby," continued Martha gently, "is it weren't in your hands. A whole lot of people got killed in this war, and a whole lot more gonna die yet, and it's the biggest sorrow this world's ever known."

"They say he died a hero."

Martha shrugged. "I ain't saying he didn't. Maybe there's a little hero in just about anybody. But that don't change the meanness he done. If somebody'd said to you, that boy gonna die in the war, you wouldn'ta said, oh well, then, let him go ahead and hang Abner, let him tie Jimmy to that ole horse, let him run Charlotte down in the street, let him do whatever he had in mind in that cave—"

Karrie felt a little shiver go through her. "Martha, I'm a silly jerk. Why do you put up with all my agonizing?"

"Oh, well," said Martha, settling down to work again. "Gives me something to do while I'm peeling these ole potatoes."

As soon as the news of Bucko's death ceased being fresh, the obligation to speak his name with reverence ceased as well, and when it turned out that no posthumous medal was to be awarded, most folks said they weren't surprised.

Conflicting rumors, some bearing out the hero story, others of quite a different nature, drifted back from overseas from hometown boys who knew somebody who'd been at the Bulge.

Benbenitas was never to learn the truth about the matter, but for several months the main scuttlebutt around town was: Bucko Riddle might have been shot by one of his own men.

2.

One rainy evening in early April, Karrie talked her grandfather into letting her have the car to go downtown with January to see a movie. Afterwards, when she drove her friend home, she waited, as she usually did, until she was sure that January hadn't been locked out of the house. This time the door opened easily, January waved, and Karrie drove off.

She arrived at Windy Crest just in time to answer the ringing telephone. It was January.

"Karrie, listen. It's your grandfather I have to talk to."

Karrie hastily summoned the mayor. Her heart thumping in her throat, she stood at her grandfather's elbow as he talked.

"Yes, January. What? I see. You *have* called April then. Good. Do you have the license number? All right, I'll take care of things from here. Stay by the phone. I'll be right over."

The mayor hung up, then immediately rang up the switchboard operator, halting Karrie's anxious inquiries with a shake of his head. "Mabel? This is the mayor. Connect me with the State Highway Patrol."

Steadily, he fed information into the telephone: the license number of Ned Welles's pick-up truck, its probable destination. Then he hung up and turned to Karrie.

"You'll have to drive me over to January's," he told her.

Miss Prune and Miss Ginger were on the scene now. "Henry, whatever—"

"No time to explain," he said brusquely. "Ned Welles is

248

missing, and January's over there alone, expecting the worse. Stay by the phone, and if you hear anything, have Mabel ring the Welles house."

On the brief, tense ride to the lumber mill, the mayor filled in the details for Karrie.

"When she got home, she found a scrawled note, something about bringing Danny home. He hasn't seen that child since the day he was born. January didn't say so, but I'm sure the man had been drinking."

"Oh, no!" cried Karrie.

"January had the presence of mind to call her aunt in San Antonio and April in Austin. April's on her way here. I hope she drives carefully, in this weather. The aunt alerted the highway patrol down that way—"

"Maybe he'll just show up," said Karrie, trembling. "I mean, maybe he'll make it to San Antonio."

The rain had picked up and was lashing so hard against the windshield that Karrie could scarcely see the road. They pulled up in the driveway of the small Welles house, now brightly lit.

A pale but composed January met them at the door. For the first and only time in her life, Karrie entered the house that had always been off limits for her.

It was a plain little house, sparsely furnished, but Karrie saw at a glance the attempts of April and January to give it some semblance of a home—the bright gingham curtains at the windows, and matching sofa cushions, which, just now, were strewn about the floor. On the kitchen table was a vase of wild flowers, the only item in the room that stood undisturbed.

Chairs were overturned, empty bottles were everywhere, and the panes of one window had been shattered. The broken glass had been swept into a pile, the broom and dustpan propped against the wall. January had been trying to straighten up.

She let them in, then motioned at the room, helplessly.

"I'm really scared, Mr. Mayor," she said. "Are they going to find him?"

"I'm certain they will, January," said the mayor gravely.

Has—this happened before?"

"No—never. Not like this. He gets depressed, but then he usually goes to sleep and sleeps really hard. He's never torn the place up before, and he never drives when—when—"

"All right, January. Hang on. We'll hear something soon."

"If only I'd been here to stop him! If only I hadn't gone to the picture show—"

"January," said the mayor firmly, "you are in no way responsible for this. In no way. Now, Karen and I are going to help you put things to rights. I'll see about that broken glass, and Karen, why don't you wash those dishes while January—picks up?"

The three of them went quietly about their work. Karrie, filling the dishpan with hot suds and glancing over at the mayor absorbed in the humble task of cleaning up after a drunken man's rampage, felt a new respect and affection for her grandfather.

By the time they heard April's car in the driveway, the clean-up was nearly completed. Karrie had never seen January's sister before. She was a plumply pretty girl, with a round sweet face too young for the mature expression it wore.

The sisters grasped each other's hands.

"Any word?" asked April.

January shook her head, then introduced her sister to the mayor and Karrie.

"So we wait," said April with a sigh. Her eyes took in the recent attempt to set the room aright. "Was it bad?"

January nodded, her lips trembling. "I think he went crazy."

"Sh-h-h," said April. She hugged the girl briefly, then disappeared into one of the bedrooms. She called out, "Let's get these sheets changed, okay?"

January went to help her. Karrie looked at her grandfather. "Why are they doing that?"

He shook his head. "They don't know who'll be staying here tonight. Go help them. I'll put on some coffee."

When they'd finished in the bedrooms, the girls came back and sat down at the kitchen table to drink the coffee, which, reflected Karrie, was probably the first her grandfather had ever made.

Finally the phone rang. The mayor answered it, listened, shook his head as he met April's eyes, then gravely handed the receiver over to her. She also listened, said yes, listened some more, finally said "thank you" and hung up.

January waited, saying nothing. April looked at her.

"He almost made it to San Antonio. He went off the road just outside the city limits. He hit a telephone pole. They think he died instantly, baby."

January's hands flew to her face. Her sister's arms were around her immediately. Murmuring soothingly, April guided the younger girl into one of the bedrooms and closed the door.

Karrie stared helplessly at her grandfather. She was January's best friend, surely closer to her than April was, but she felt utterly out of place, superfluous.

"What can we do, Grandfather?"

"Very little," responded the mayor. "Allow them to grieve in privacy. Sit and wait. The San Antonio aunt is on her way. When she arrives, we'll get out of here, and let the family be together."

"Family? But Grandfather, Jano doesn't really know her aunt!"

"She's family, nevertheless."

Karrie washed up the coffee cups while the mayor dried, in silence. Presently April came out of the bedroom. Her eyes were red but she was calm and gracious.

"There's no need for y'all to stay any longer," she told them. "I sure do thank you for being here with Jano. I'll call in the morning and let you know what arrangements we've made."

Having been dismissed, Karrie and the mayor climbed back into the Packard for the short drive home.

"It's so unreal," said Karrie.

"No, it's quite real," said her grandfather.

"Grandfather, what will happen to January? Could she— could she come to live at Windy Crest?"

The mayor nodded. "I intend to propose that. But that's up to her family."

"They won't want her. They never have."

"Well—we'll see."

Ned Welles was buried beside his wife and his parents in the Methodist Cemetery. January and April stood apart with people who were strangers to Karrie, and, Karrie knew, to January as well. There was Aunt Fay, in a black dress and veiled hat, and her tall husband in a dark, well-tailored suit. Between them stood a solemn, handsome boy with his blond hair slicked down— twelve-year-old Danny, the little brother January hardly knew.

After the brief graveside service, there were introductions, handshakes, condolences and murmured responses. Karrie had only a moment to speak to January.

"Jano, we wanted you to live with us."

"I know. That was nice. But Aunt Fay says I have to live in San Antonio with them."

"Wouldn't you rather go back to Austin with April?"

January shrugged. "I can't. April lives with her mother-in-law. Will you write to me?"

"Every day! Maybe you can come see me this summer and we can rebuild our raft—"

"Uh huh. Maybe. Remember that first day by the cave when we talked about *changes*? I guess they never stop coming."

"Say goodbye now, dear," called the veiled Aunt Fay.

And that was all. It was over.

3.

"I feel almost as empty as I did when you went away," Karrie wrote to Marty. "Nothing's any fun any more, with Jano gone. I'll be glad when a little time passes."

But before Karrie had a chance to get over her sadness, something occurred which only deepened it.

On the twelfth of April an unfamiliar mood settled over Benbenitas. The ordinary things that people were used to seeing, the sidewalks, the storefronts, the churches and farmyards, suddenly appeared old, worn-out, belonging to some past time. Yet life went on as always. Mr. Wilkins stayed at his post at the Mercantile, but mainly just to say, "I swan—I can't hardly believe it," to the few people who drifted in, who were also shaking their heads in disbelief. It was much the same at the other businesses in town. Life went on, yes, but it would never be the same again.

Only Mrs. Schulman closed her shop, with a black ribbon of mourning on the door.

The President was dead.

Karrie was stricken anew. She had been born at the very end of Coolidge's term in office; Hoover was President during the first four years of her life; but the only president she had any memory of was Franklin Roosevelt. His face, his grin, and his voice had reassured her throughout her childhood. When disaster was imminent, he had promised that no matter what, whatever sacrifices lay ahead, good would prevail in the end. Karrie, sitting small and safe between her mother and father, later, between Marty and her father, and more recently, in the parlor with her grandfather and great-aunts, had listened to the president's fireside chats on the radio, and always believed him.

While the town mourned, her own grief was greater than sorrow for a public figure. Somehow it became mixed up with all the fears and doubts she had struggled with for nearly five years. Deep inside she knew now that her father was never coming home, that Richard Webster was dead, too.

Yet in the field beyond Beals' farm, a sea of bluebonnets reflected the bright, untroubled sky over the hill country, and the valley was glorious with black-eyed Susans and Indian paint-brushes.

It was an April like no other.

4.

Rumors and false alarms were rife that spring, but on May 8, 1945, the war in Europe ended at last, and on a perfect day in June, Howie Schulman came home to Benbenitas.

"Don't be put off if he sticks close to the house for a while," his family had cautioned everyone before his arrival. "Boy's got adjusting to do, him being a prisoner so long."

But an hour after he got off the afternoon train from Austin, Howie was ambling around the town square, greeting people and shaking hands. Mrs. Schulman took the closed sign off her shop door, and Howie stationed himself on the long wooden bench outside and held court. Just about everybody in town came around to say, *Howdy! Welcome back! We're right proud of you!*

The Windy Crest contingent was no exception. The long black Packard pulled up in front of the town hall and the mayor's family, along with Martha and Israel and even Abner, made their way across the street to Schulman's Bread and Cakes.

Karrie was curious and excited to see Howie Schulman at last. He looked a lot like his brother, people always said. Seeing Howie was almost like seeing Doug.

What she saw, over the shoulders of the people crowded around that bench, was a long-legged, thin young man in Air Corps uniform, with short-cropped hair so blonde it was almost white; a grin so youthful it made the lines of strain that surrounded it appear to be some sort of mistake; and, squinting in the Texas sun, the bluest eyes Karrie had ever seen.

The people who had gathered around him seemed to be doing most of the talking. About all he had a chance to say was, "Why, hello there! Glad to see you! Fine—fine—I'm fine, thanks!"

The Windy Crest group paid respects and then returned to the Packard.

"I expect he decided to get it over with," remarked the mayor. "Now maybe they'll let him be."

"I just can't imagine Howie without Doug," said Miss Prune, wiping her eyes and sniffling. "It must be so hard on him."

"Doug's been dead for three years," said Miss Ginger.

"Howie's used to it by now."

"Oh, but Ginger," said Miss Prune, "this is his first time home since it happened!"

"May not stay," said Martha. "Howie always say he was going to see the world, live in New York or Chicago or some place like that."

"Why, Martha," said Miss Prune, "whenever did Howie tell you that?"

"Oh, well," said Martha, "him and Doug and Bubbabill used to come begging around my kitchen, after they'd been over poking around them caves. They knowed I always had some cookies or gingerbread. They was good boys, just full of mischief."

"Well, I certainly never knew that," declared Miss Ginger, a trifle indignant, many years after the fact.

It was a few days later that a surprise visitor appeared at the kitchen door of Windy Crest. It was Howie Schulman, bearing a box of his grandmother's doughnuts and wearing a wide grin.

"Thought I'd pay you back a little for all the treats I mooched," he told the delighted Martha.

She invited him to come in and sit at his old place at the kitchen table and immediately put on the coffee pot.

"Not quite like old times, is it, Martha?" said Howie with a smile, as he sipped a cup of the fresh-brewed coffee.

Martha patted his arm. "No, honey, never be old times again. By-and-by, you gonna get started on making a new life for yourself."

"Well," said Howie, "I've sure had a lot of time to think about that, but now—Well, now that it's all over I can't quite figure things out."

"You will, baby. Don't you push it, hear? It'll come to you. Got to make peace with the past before you get on with the future."

Howie smiled and squeezed her hand. "That's what I figure. Thought I'd stroll over to Dead Man's Caverns and have a look around. Sure sorry I missed the bluebonnets. That's what I kept telling them after I was liberated—'Hey, guys, if you send me home now I'll just catch the tail end of the bluebonnets!' They wouldn't listen. Took me to the hospital instead. They said they had to put some meat on my bones so I wouldn't scare my mother."

Howie stood up. "I'd better get going, Martha, if I'm going to beat the noonday sun to Dead Man's Caverns."

"That's a pretty long stroll you going on," remarked Martha. "Sure you're up to that, puny-looking as you is?"

Howie shrugged. "I'm not *that* puny. They pumped me full of vitamins at the hospital. In the old days Doug and I could cover those two miles in fifteen minutes. I swear we could smell your gingerbread all the way from Squaw Mountain!"

Karrie was sitting in the shade under the overhanging rock outside the little cave, musing over Doug's book of poetry, which she'd been picking up more often than usual lately.

When she glanced up and saw the tall young man walking up the hill toward her, she knew it was Howie before he was close enough to be recognized. Her pulse quickened and the blood climbed to her face, but by the time he approached, she had composed herself.

"Hi," he greeted her, smiling, and shading his blue eyes with one hand to look at her. "You're the mayor's granddaughter, aren't you? Carol?"

"Karen. Karrie. Spelled with a K."

"With a K, huh?" Howie sat down beside her and offered her his lean right hand to shake. "Glad to meet you, Karrie."

"We already met outside your grandmother's," said Karrie shyly, shaking hands with him.

"I know, but the whole town was there. Grandma's told me all about you and your brother. He's in the Pacific, right? Heard from him lately?"

Karrie shook her head. "It's been more than three weeks. He writes to Jolene Ross in Austin, too, and she hasn't had a letter either."

"Sounds like the usual mail snafu. You'll get a bag full one of these days. Another year, it should all be over. Russia will probably come in now and help us lick Japan."

Howie picked up one of the china tea cups and laughed softly.

"These things still here? Doug and I used to play with them when we were little. Never knew who they belonged to."

"They've been here forever. Miss Jane and my dad used to play with them, too. Even Grannie Opal did—I think!"

"Grannie Opal? Really? I guess they *have* been here forever." He examined the little cup with a bemused expression on his face, then scooped up some spring water in it and drank. "Just the way I remember it. The best tasting water in the world. What's that poem about the brook? *...for men may come and men may go...*"

"*...but I go on forever,*" Karrie finished for him. She saw that Howie's eyes were on the book in her hands. "It's Doug's," she volunteered. "Your grandmother gave it to me when I first came to Benbenitas."

She handed the book to Howie and he leafed through it briefly, then glanced up and smiled at her.

"Doug bought this in San Antonio when he was about twelve. Dad had taken us over to see the zoo, then he took us downtown and gave us each a dollar to spend any way we liked. I bought out the dime store, but Doug held on to his money till we started prowling through a little secondhand bookstore. He picked up this book and read the first poem—"

"*A wet sheet and a flowing sea; a wind that follows fast,*" quoted Karrie, "*And fills the white and rustling sail—*"

"*And bends the gallant mast,*" Howie responded. "That was the one. I guess Doug thought he'd discovered the key to his soul. He forked over his dollar, and I stood there with my bag of dime store junk, fussing at him. I couldn't believe he'd blown a perfectly good dollar on a dumb book of poems."

Howie rubbed his hand over the leather binding, then

brusquely handed the book back to Karrie.

"I can see it ended up in good hands," he said, rising.

Karrie stood up, too, flustered and uncertain. Should she give up this book she cherished to Doug's brother?

"Oh, say," said Howie, as he was turning to go, "I'm told there's a dance in the opera house every Friday. Going to be there tonight?"

"Well, I—I don't usually—"

"I used to do a mean jitterbug. See you there, okay?"

"I don't think—"

But Howie's long strides had already taken him halfway down the hill.

5.

All the way into town Karrie seriously considered turning around, but—well, suddenly there she was. She sighed and parked across the street from the opera house, to facilitate a quick escape. No use. There were the Wallace twins waving to her, waiting for her at the door.

Karrie glanced quickly in the rear view mirror, regretting her too-curly hair and wishing she owned a lipstick. The other girls used lipstick, but she never had, mostly because she could imagine her grandfather's look of derision.

"Come on, get the lead out!" called Sister Bee.

"What made you decide to honor us with your presence tonight?" asked Joycie when Karrie caught up with them.

"Oh, I was bored," mumbled Karrie. "Thought I'd try it."

"I hope there are some fellers here tonight," said Sister Bee. "I *hate* having to dance with girls all the time."

"There were some soldiers walking around town today," said Joycie hopefully. "Maybe they'll be here."

Karrie, standing in the doorway of the dimly lighted noisy hall, looked around her with a sinking feeling of disappointment. There were a few soldiers, but mostly it was girls dancing with other girls. Mrs. Tulla Swenson was presiding over the record player, Miss Jane and Mr. Wirtz were circulating and pouring soft drinks, and there was absolutely no sign of Howie Schulman.

"Oh, well," sighed Joycie. "The soldier boys are taken for now. Not enough to go around. Guess they're all over in Hospitality tonight. Well, come on, Karrie, let's jitterbug. Maybe one of them will cut in."

"I don't know how to jitterbug," said Karrie. "You go ahead and dance with Sister Bee. I'll just stand over here and watch."

"Dadgum it, I get sick of dancing with Sister Bee," grumbled Joycie, but the two had soon swung out onto the dance floor and were executing some tricky steps with precision and joy.

Karrie let a slight sigh escape, as she watched the young people swinging to the music. She was startled by a touch on her elbow. She turned and there was Howie Schulman, looking— *very beautiful*. She blushed deeply at the obtrusive thought and was grateful for the dim lighting.

"Care to cut a rug, Miss Webster?" Howie said, smiling, his arms inviting her.

Mrs. Tulla Swenson had just put on another record. This time it was a slower tune—"I'll Be Seeing You." Karrie felt awkward stepping into Howie's arms, but his hand on her back guided her firmly and easily. She quickly relaxed and flowed with the music, realizing all at once that she loved to dance—she loved to dance with Howie Schulman.

It was not to last long. In a hall where young men were in short supply, the girls cut in on each other mercilessly. Howie was soon swept away by Bev, Joycie, and others, but Norma Swenson, an older girl home from college, hardly allowed anyone to dance two steps with him before cutting in again.

Karrie stood forlornly alone, with no more than one lovely moment to remember. She almost hated Norma Swenson!

"What's the matter with me?" she asked herself angrily. "I'm acting like—like Jolene Ross, mooning over Marty!"

At that thought, she waved goodbye across the room to Miss Jane—who lifted her eyebrows quizzically—and left the hall.

She was already in the car when she saw Howie Schulman running across the street after her.

"Wait up!" he called. "We didn't have our dance out. And it's not even nine o'clock."

Karrie smiled and shook her head. "I can't compete with all those desperate women," she told him lightly. "I really only came to bring you something."

She handed him Doug's book through the car window. Howie took it and quickly looked into her eyes.

"Are you sure? I know you love this book."

"I do. It meant a lot to me when I was very lonely, and I feel as though I really got to know Doug."

"Yeah." Howie gently rubbed the book's cover. "He used to write things in the margins, and mark the poems he liked."

"I'm afraid I did, too. Maybe you could erase—"

"No. Good. That way I'll really get to know you, too." A moment passed. "Hey, want to take a walk? Twice around the square before you call it an evening?"

They went twice around the square, then strolled down Tolliver Street. It was Karrie's favorite street in town because it was a *green* street in a place where green was hard to come by, and because it looked like an illustration in a turn-of-the-century novel. The cracked old sidewalks led past Victorian houses, delicious with mystery behind deep porches, high shrubbery, and thick-trunked trees that had been planted in another century, but warm with light behind the drawn shades. Here lived the more prosperous citizens, such as Dr. Ross and Mr. Miller, and here, long ago, the Irishman Tolliver had built the first rough-hewn cabin and put up a sign that said *Bienvenidos!*

Tolliver Street ended at the river, and Howie and Karrie continued along the river bank, following the well-worn dirt path through the brambles. It was a warm evening and the rising moon was visible through the tangle of vines that had made their way to the tops of the riverbank trees. Away from the dust of the road, elusive scents stole through the air and disappeared, only to steal back again a moment later.

Howie talked—casually, at first—of the dance, the town, growing up around there, then, with Karrie attentive and quiet at his side, he began to speak of Doug.

"I couldn't stop writing him letters, even after I knew he was dead," he said. "You see, Doug and I—well, he was two years older, but we were just like twins. I could tell Doug *anything*. Didn't need to, half the time. He always knew what I was thinking, what I was feeling. Even when we were far apart, he was *there*—and then, all at once he wasn't. And I just couldn't stop writing letters to him."

Howie was quiet for a minute. Karrie felt no compulsion to fill the silence. Presently Howie said,

"Those letters are in my foot locker. I ought to chuck them. I doubt if I'll ever be able to read over them again. Funny, the way people deal with things. My mother—she painted his room and packed all his things away."

"When my Uncle Martin was killed in World War I, my grandfather closed the door to his room and wouldn't let anyone change anything," Karrie volunteered quietly.

"I wish Mamma had left things alone. Just till I got back. Coming home and finding nothing left of Doug but a photo on the mantle—But, that was her way of getting through it, I guess."

Howie was silent again. After a while he resumed talking. His thoughts had drifted back to the war.

"I wanted to be a fighter pilot. Sounded glamorous, I guess—but they taught me to fly a bomber instead. Either way you're killing people, but a bomber—" He shook his head. "We weren't supposed to think about what was happening below. You had your target, you delivered. It didn't really get to me till we lost the plane. We bailed out over Germany and got captured. They herded us into a truck with a bunch of other guys. We were so packed in we couldn't sit down. It was pretty foul. Some of the guys passed out but were still standing up because there was no place to fall. I was lucky because I was jammed up against the side. The sides of the truck were slatted but it was covered with a heavy canvas so we weren't supposed to see out—or breathe, I guess. But there was a hole worn right in front of my nose, so I managed to get some decent air into me and I got glimpses of the countryside we were passing through.

"The country was beautiful—that was the weirdest thing of all. I hated everything about Germany, even though my ancestors came from there, and I wasn't prepared to see anything beautiful, not even the landscape. On the second day when I woke up from dozing and peered out I saw we were going through a city. What city, I still haven't figured out, but I got a ground's eye view of what our bombers had done.

"Unbelievable destruction. Buildings leveled, people picking around the debris. I'd seen it before—in England. But peering through that hole in the canvas I kept thinking, maybe we did that. Maybe I flew over this target and old Sam, our bombardier, let 'em have it, and kids and women and old folks—"

After a minute, Karrie said quietly, "Martha would say it wasn't your fault, it was Hitler's. Martha would say you did what you had to do, but you did it with sorrow because you're a good person."

"That's—just what Martha would say. That's what I said to myself. I had a lot of time to think in prison camp. I came to terms with a lot of things. At least I thought I did. Coming home is another ball game."

"I know. Lots of changes. But people can get used to almost anything."

"Well—I guess we should start back, before they send out a posse."

They started walking in silence, but presently Howie reached over and briefly squeezed Karrie's hand.

"You know all about that, don't you? Getting used to almost anything? My grandmother's told me a lot about you. You're a pretty tough little kid. Thanks for listening. That's the first time I've been able to talk about it."

Howie walked her back to her car. Karrie got in and he closed the door after her.

"Thanks for giving me Doug's book."

"It was never really mine. Goodnight."

Howie leaned through the window, took her face in his two

hands and kissed her lightly on the forehead. "Stay as sweet as you are, Karrie Webster," he said softly. "Goodnight, little girl."

Karrie drove home in a bittersweet cloud, thinking how awful it was being just sixteen when Howie was twenty-two. In a few years, those six years would mean nothing, but now they meant everything. As soon as she'd driven away Howie had probably walked back into the opera house, and was even now whirling around the dance floor with somebody. Somebody a little older, like Norma Swenson. Somebody who was not a little girl.

6.

Israel looked sympathetic when Karrie handed him a letter to Marty to mail in town. "I know it's hard, honey, to keep writing these letters and not get no answers," he said.

That nightly letter was as much a habit as eating supper. She tried not to think of Howie writing to Doug long after he'd known Doug was gone. Marty was not gone. If anything had happened to him, she would have been notified. It was just some FPO mix-up.

"I assume the mail is catching up with you somewhere, but it's been four weeks now since we've heard from you. Jolene calls from Austin every evening—I'd hate to pay her phone bill! She's in summer school again this year. At the rate she's going, she'll be in medical school before you ever get to college.

"I'm working at the hospital six days a week now. They're so short-handed, and I don't mind keeping busy since I don't have Jano to hang around with any more. She writes one letter to my six. She's very unhappy. Her little brother resents her and she hates San Antonio even more than she did Bienvenidos. She was talking about dropping out of school and running away, but April did that, you know, and she threw a fit when Jano told her what she had in mind.

"So instead she's going to summer school and taking some special courses at a junior college. She's determined to graduate as soon as possible and then, she says, she can do as she pleases.

Aunt Prune and Aunt Ginger worry about her, but Grandfather says January will always be okay because she's straight as an arrow and tough as nails!

"What else can I tell you? Everything is about the same. Quite a few guys who were in Europe have come home, and they're hoping to be mustered out in time to get into school in the fall. Grandfather says it's amazing how many boys from around here have decided to go to college on the G.I. Bill. Howie Schulman's already in Austin, enrolled in summer school. Before he left he stopped by and gave me back Doug's book. He said he thought Doug would like me to have it.

"Jolene's been very helpful to Howie, showing him around Austin and all. But you don't have to worry. She's true-blue. Besides, the scuttlebutt is—Howie is sweet on Norma Swenson."

There were some feelings Karrie couldn't share, even with her brother. Especially with her brother.

7.

"Karrie, come *on!*"

Marty's voice was insistent. Karrie was sitting on the flat rock outside the Windy Crest gate. She rose to run after her brother, but he was moving away so fast—down the highway, past the lumber yard, the cedar woods.

But wait, there he was, in his short wool jacket and knitted cap, weaving through the crowd of skaters. "Karrie, come *on!*" he cried. The skyline of the city glistened against the sparkling winter sky. "Karrie, come *on!*" The blades of her skates were sluggish and wouldn't glide. She was moving inch by agonizing inch, and Marty was skating away fast, through the crowd, to the other side of the pond. She was alone and almost motionless in the middle of a dizzying whirl of skaters. It's all right, she thought, I can find my way home. Then she remembered. They'd moved out of the apartment. There was no home any more.

Karrie sat up suddenly in bed, her heart thumping in her throat. She looked around her. *This is my room at Windy Crest,* she told herself. She slipped out of bed and went to sit in the window seat. It was first light. She looked out on the valley, the windmill, the distant pond. It was familiar, it was even—home. But she felt shaky and disconnected, as though she didn't belong anywhere in the world.

She slipped into her robe and tiptoed down the stairs. She heard a murmur of voices in the kitchen, and when she entered, she found Miss Ginger and Miss Prune sitting at the table near the window, drinking coffee by the faint morning light.

"Why, Karen, what are you doing up so early?" cried Miss Prune. "Ginger and I were just sitting here enjoying the sunrise. Get yourself some juice, honey. I just squeezed a whole bunch of oranges."

Karrie poured herself a glass of orange juice from the pitcher, and joined her aunts at the kitchen table.

"Aunt Prune, do you really believe in dreams?" she asked casually. Her aunts glanced at each other.

"Oh, she just goes on about that stuff," said Miss Ginger briskly. "She knows there's nothing to it."

Karrie was silent, staring into her glass.

"Why don't you just tell us what you dreamed, honey?" suggested Miss Prune gently.

Karrie laughed shakily. "Ah, but you said if people told their dreams before breakfast, they'd come true!"

"Well, now, you know that's rubbish," declared Miss Ginger. "But we'll play Prune's little game, anyway. Drink up your juice and we'll say you had breakfast."

Both women listened quietly as Karrie recounted the dream, their expressions interested but unreadable. Then Miss Prune patted her hand.

"Doesn't mean a thing, honey, except that you haven't had a letter from Martin and it's on your mind. I read somewhere that we dream all night and only remember the ones we have right before we wake up. I once dreamt I was at church, with my best hat on, and I looked down and I was wearing my old nightie and you could see right through it! Well, there was nothing to do but hold my head up and hope nobody else would notice. Oh, my, I was relieved when I woke up!"

"Good grief, Prune, I'm glad you didn't tell *that* one before breakfast!"

Karrie laughed. "Aunt Prune, that's almost as good as Lollie Beal eloping with Clark Gable." She rose. "I think I'll get dressed and take Abner for a walk before it gets too hot. He's getting awfully fat and lazy, hanging around Grandfather's study."

Karrie left her aunts sitting at the table in the ever-lightening kitchen. They were silent for a moment. Then Miss Prune said in an anguished voice, "Oh God, Ginger!"

"Hush now, don't think of it," admonished Miss Ginger.

"I've thought of it every day for twenty-seven years," said Miss Prune. "That night I dreamed about *our* Martin. 'Come on, Aunt Prune!' he was calling, and I was trying to keep up, trying to find him, but he just kept slipping away from me, fading into the distance. And that very night he was dying, four thousand miles away, across the ocean."

Chapter 14
Richard's Story

1.

The afternoon train from Austin was right on time. Mr. Peevy forsook his bench and the shade of the station house eaves to greet the mailman ("Howdy, Ken! Hot enough for ya?") as they exchanged mailbags. Benbenitas always received two bags now— lots of mail from lots of boys gone from home.

It seemed a usual kind of day until the conductor set down a tattered old suitcase on the platform, and the train tarried a bit to allow two arriving passengers to get off. First, a tall, thin man in a worn brown suit climbed down—a man no longer young, and yet not old. He turned to assist the slow descent of a small elderly man, similarly dressed. As the train went clanging off again, the younger man stood supporting the older one, who appeared to be struggling for breath. Finally, arm in arm, they approached the startled station master.

"Oh by Jupiter," whispered Mr. Peevy. "By the great god Jupiter!"

2.

The distinctive noises of Ole Ben Clinton's taxi in the driveway disturbed the tranquility of siesta time at Windy Crest. Miss Ginger and Miss Prune hurried to their bedroom windows to see what was going on, and Karrie, who was curled up on her front window seat, looked up from the book she was reading. Israel, with the mayor following behind him, headed toward the door, and before the knocker could sound, had it open.

And there on the porch stood two men—one small and old, one tall and not old, not young—both looking tired and shabby.

There was no time for Israel or the mayor to react. Before a word was uttered Karrie came flying down the stairs, and whether she simply ran past her great-aunts, who were also on their way down, or actually sailed over their heads, it was hard to say. She hurled herself at the tall man, who swept her up and stood swaying with her in his arms, while the others, momentarily stunned, each began to respond to the amazing turn the afternoon had taken.

Miss Prune and Miss Ginger burst into tears at the exact same second and crowded near to be embraced. Israel kept patting the tall man on the back and murmuring, "Miracle! Miracle!" and Martha, appearing at the kitchen door, looked hard on the scene for an instant, then screamed before rushing forth to join in the hugging and the crying.

Only the mayor stood back, wordless and staring.

Then the tall man, when he could speak over the confusion, said to Karrie: "Can you guess who this is with me?"

The girl looked at the other newcomer for the first time. Pitiably thin and unsteady, his face creased and drawn, he gazed back at her through streaming eyes.

Karrie slowly shook her head, then suddenly she cried, "*Opi!* Oh, God, is it *Opi?*" She threw her arms around the old man, who held her tenderly, while he stroked her hair with trembling hands and sobbed into her shoulder.

The tall man and the mayor had not yet spoken to each other. Now for the first time their eyes met over the heads of the others, and the mayor's eyes were fierce and shiny with tears.

The tall man smiled.

"Richard," said the mayor gruffly. "Just where the hell have you been?"

3.

In the midst of all the confusion, Martha somehow came up with lemonade, sandwiches, and ginger cookies, and soon managed to have everyone seated around the breakfast room table. Karrie's Opi, sitting beside her, quietly began to eat, but Richard could scarcely take a bite between asking questions and answering them.

"Tell me about Marty," he said.

"He's overseas," Karrie explained.

"I know," said Richard. "I got in touch with John Cory at the bank as soon as the war in Europe ended."

"Back in *May*? Then why—?" began the mayor indignantly.

"First—give me the news of Marty."

There was a brief silence. Then Miss Ginger said, "No news, Richard. No letters in weeks."

"But that's happened before," said Miss Prune hastily. "The overseas mail gets hung up somewhere."

"Never this long before," said Miss Ginger. "We just keep writing, of course—"

The mayor cleared his throat. "Richard," he said. "I believe you owe us some explanations. No word in all these years!"

Richard sighed. "I know. It's a long story. Cory was amazed to find out I was alive. He told me that Marty was overseas and Karrie was here. I asked him to keep quiet about my call for a while. I—well, I thought it would be better—you know—face to face—"

The mayor looked stoic as he remembered Marty's words from three years earlier: "I brought her here so we could deal with you face to face—"

"You see," continued Richard, "since I was assumed to be dead, I decided it would be less traumatic for everyone if I didn't make contact until I had a chance to concentrate on what I'd set out to do five years ago—finding Herman. That wasn't easy, but one day there it was—his name on a list—"

At that moment Herman reached over and patted Karrie's hand and whispered to her in German.

"What did he say?" Karrie asked her father.

"He said—you're the image of your mother," Richard told her gently.

Karrie's eyes instantly filled with tears, and she lifted Herman's hand and rubbed it against her cheek.

"Why, Ginger, we'll have to brush up on our German," murmured Miss Prune.

"He wants to learn English," said Richard. "He wants to be an American. He says he has no country any more."

"He was in a concentration camp?" asked the mayor quietly.

"For five years. I found him in a hospital in Holland. He looked—you wouldn't believe how he looked! But he was—so happy to see me. He—hadn't known that Inge died, of course."

The room was silent for a moment. Herman slowly continued to eat. Israel, holding the pitcher of lemonade with an unsteady hand, refilled the old man's glass. Herman looked up at him and nodded his thanks.

"Richard," said the mayor, "start at the beginning."

4.

"The beginning!" Richard shook his head. "That was a lifetime ago!"

"You said you'd set out to look for Herman," prompted the mayor. "Karen said her mother's letters to him came back stamped *Address Unknown*—"

"That's right. Inge was frantic. She was very ill by then, but she made me promise I'd find her father. After she died, I tried to keep that promise. I left my poor sad children with a housekeeper and traveled to Germany—to Stilldorf, where Herman had lived. It's a little village in the Black Forest.

"It was the first time I'd seen it since '33, when we'd taken the kids over to meet their grandfather. In '33 it had still looked like a picture out of a fairy tale, but there was something poisonous in the air."

"Hitler was appointed chancellor of Germany in '33," remarked the mayor.

270

"That's right. Inge and I were very worried. We tried to persuade Herman and his brothers to emigrate to America. They thought we were being alarmists. Germany was a civilized country, they said, what could happen?

"But—in '39, when I went looking for them, they simply weren't there any more. I found Herman's shop boarded up, and anti-Jewish slogans were scrawled all over it. I stopped people in the street to ask what had happened to him, but they shook me off and hurried away. I knocked on doors and had them slammed in my face. I wasn't there more than an hour before the local policeman picked me up. There was a Gestapo agent waiting in his office. I was grilled for hours about stupid, made-up offenses. Then I was driven to the border and literally thrown out of Germany, with the warning that if I ever tried to return I would be arrested immediately.

"I'd intended to go on to Munich to look for Herman's other brothers, but now that was impossible. I was worried sick about the kids, so I decided to go home. First, I asked some of my friends in Switzerland to find out what they could.

"In the next few months I made one or two business trips to Europe, but couldn't come up with any leads about Herman's whereabouts. All I learned was that in Germany Jews were being rounded up and sent to forced labor camps, and things were very, very grim. Then in September Hitler invaded Poland, and Britain and France declared war on Germany.

"That final journey I undertook was a last ditch effort to find Herman before the whole world was swallowed up by war. That was late spring, 1940, remember. Denmark and Holland had both fallen, Belgium had surrendered, the British had just evacuated Dunkirk and everything was coming apart.

"The kids were pretty self-sufficient by then, and I figured they'd be all right for a few weeks. I let them think I was going abroad on business, but actually, I took what I thought would be a short leave of absence from my company. I went to Switzerland first, and met with one of my contacts. He showed me on the map where he knew forced labor was being used. He'd heard that guards could be bribed. But there were many of these camps, some deep inside Germany. The situation seemed hopeless, but I couldn't go home without trying one more time. I owed it to Inge.

"That's when I wrote the kids I'd be delayed. I'd left instructions in case anything happened to me. I knew you'd take care of them. I never doubted that for a minute, Papa."

"Hr-rumph," said the mayor.

"What I hadn't figured on was my independent son making up his mind to wait two years so he could finish high school before coming to you!"

"We were fine, Dad," said Karrie.

Richard grinned. "I'm sure you were. I'm just glad I didn't know about it at the time. Well, anyway, the only thing I knew to do was to return to Stilldorf and bribe someone to talk to me. Of course I could no longer enter Germany legally, so—"

"You had to sneak in?" Karrie asked.

"Right. I let my whiskers grow for a couple of days, then I left my passport in a safety deposit box in Basle, and disguised myself as a peasant. I figured my German would pass if I didn't say too much. I hid a bunch of Swiss and German bills in my clothes and set out in the middle of the night.

"It went like a breeze. I got over the border and reached Stilldorf by early morning. I remember that it was a beautiful spring morning. There were flowers blooming in the town park and birds were singing. Stilldorf looked as quaint and pretty as it had the first time I'd seen it, when Inge and I were newlyweds.

"I walked by Herman's shop. It was exactly as I'd found it the year before, boarded up. From there I wandered by Meyer's house. It was a beautiful old house. Meyer's office had been on the first floor—"

"There was a garden!" cried Karrie. "And a veranda!"

"Yes, there was a garden and a veranda. German soldiers were sitting around on it, reading and drinking beer. Obviously they were billeted at the place. That hit me like a hard blow to the stomach. I had to get away from there."

Richard went on to relate how, sick at heart, he had made his way back to the little park, found a bench out of sight from the street and sat down to think about his next move. Presently, an unshaven old man in a threadbare suit had come and sat down beside him. Conscious of being looked over, Richard had glanced away.

"Stranger," said the man.

"Yes," said Richard. "Passing through."

The old man shook his head. "Don't stay too long."

"Where are all the Jews?" Richard asked boldly.

The old man looked at him sharply. "There are no Jews here. I am not a Jew!"

"Were they taken away?"

"Who knows? Who asks?"

"I'm looking for my father-in-law—the tailor—"

The old man grunted. "Gone. And his brother, the doctor, he's gone, too. We have no doctor now."

"But where?"

The old man shifted uncomfortably and glanced around before whispering, "North. The Saar perhaps."

"Labor camps? What about the women and children?"

The old man shrugged. "Gone. Signed over the property, you know. Everything legal! There's a law. Any Jew owing money can be sent to labor camps."

"They never owed money—my father-in-law or his brother!"

"They are gone, all the same." He looked at Richard with sad eyes. "Soldiers all over town. They push me off the sidewalk. I was a decorated soldier, fighting for the Fatherland when they were puling infants!" He spat over his shoulder, then leaned toward Richard, with a confidential air. "We have no doctor now, did I tell you that?"

Richard knew it was dangerous to remain longer in Germany. If he were picked up, he could be held as a spy. Staying out of sight as much as possible, he headed back toward the Swiss border and was there by nightfall.

Safely back in Switzerland, he decided that his best chance of getting into the Saar region was to travel north through France, then attempt to cross back into Germany. France was on the verge of collapse and German troops were everywhere, but he hoped he could pass unnoticed in all the confusion. He set out immediately for the French border, still dressed in peasant garb.

All of France seemed to be heading south. The roads and lanes were choked with automobiles, bicycles, wagons and carts. Richard pushed on against the tide, becoming more and more convinced that his mission was doomed, for the war was moving much too fast.

After a while there were no more civilian vehicles on the road, only German trucks and troops. Richard kept to the woods and fields, and towards dawn he sat down to rest behind a clump of trees. Exhausted, he fell into a heavy sleep, and when he awakened abruptly, he was startled to see a man standing over him, holding a wad of money. Richard leaped to his feet, swearing in English. The man laughed.

"We always curse in our native tongue," he said in French. "You are a rich Englishman, huh? So what are you doing here, dressed like one of us?"

"Looking for someone," Richard replied, also in French. "And I'm not English."

"No? You speak like a Frenchman, but I don't think you're French. What then? *German?*" and the man suddenly grabbed Richard by the collar and held a knife to his throat. Seeing that he had nothing to lose, Richard told him the truth. The man put away the knife and offered him a cigarette.

"A bold man, but on a fool's errand," he said, shaking his head. "You speak German as well as French? And what else?"

Richard admitted to knowing several other languages. The Frenchman seemed impressed. He still held Richard's money.

"A great deal of money. It won't buy your father-in-law's freedom, but it could be useful."

"Well, you have it," said Richard. "And you have the knife. There's not much I can do about that."

"So many languages! Also useful. So what are you? Professor?

No? Businessman?"

"Yes—well, I'm an engineer."

"Ah! What kind of engineer?"

"Structural."

"That means what? Buildings? Bridges? You know all about bridges, how they are put together? How they come apart? My friend, you were sent by angels!"

"What I don't know is, who *you* are, and who you're with!"

"My name is Jacques, and I am a farmer. I'm with myself— and a few others. Perhaps you don't know. Yesterday Petain asked for an armistice. France has surrendered. They say Hitler himself is in Paris, strutting around our sacred places."

"Oh, God! It's hopeless! I must get to the border—"

"The border! You are insane. The borders are closed. You have no passport. How will you explain that to the *Boches*? No, no, my friend, your best chance is to work your way south—to the unoccupied zone. I will help you. But first, you must help me. Can you fix a radio?"

"All right. Yes. But I must get home. I have children."

The man shrugged. "We all have children. Yours are safe in America."

Richard followed the farmer to a small, thatch-roofed house, was given bread to eat, then taken up a ladder to a rough attic, where three men and a teen-aged farm boy were tinkering with a short-wave radio.

It took Richard most of the afternoon to get the radio working, but his efforts were rewarded when he was finally able to pick up a BBC broadcast, and the little group in the attic heard the stirring words of General de Gaulle from London:

...Is the last word said? Has all hope gone? Is the defeat definitive? No...Whatever happens, the flame of French resistance must not die and will not die.

It must have been apparent to Jacques that his American guest was as moved as any of them by De Gaulle's speech, for he decided to take a gamble. He took Richard out to the barn, and showed him where they had concealed a cache of weapons and a small amount of dynamite.

"We don't know how to use it," explained Jacques, "and we cannot afford to squander it. If we knew just where to place an explosive to disable a bridge—" He grinned at Richard. "We are two farmers, two merchants, and one brave boy. What we require is—a structural engineer."

5.

"I suppose I should have wished them luck and headed south," Richard said, as Martha poured him another cup of coffee, "but I liked that plucky bunch, and I was quite inspired by De Gaulle's speech. I figured the kids would be okay for a little longer, and I decided I'd do what I could to help this group get started.

"We pulled off a couple of acts of minor sabotage—nothing very effective, but it seemed to lift morale. Meanwhile, some other group in the area was circulating mimeographed flyers urging resistance to the occupation. Jacques didn't know who was responsible, but he was anxious to make contact, and I offered to make some discreet inquiries. Unfortunately, I inquired of the wrong party and got picked up by the French police. They kept me for several days, but when they got nowhere questioning me, the Germans stepped in. They proved to be a different breed of inquisitors.

"I don't think I've ever been so terrified in my life. I had never known much physical pain, and I wasn't sure how I would hold up under torture. I only knew that I must not betray two farmers, two merchants, and one brave boy.

"I stood it pretty well for two or three days, but the longer it went on, the more afraid I was I'd break."

"Oh, Richard, you poor boy!" cried Miss Prune. "Were you badly hurt?"

"Did you—hold out?" asked the mayor stiffly.

Richard smiled. "Yes, yes, Papa, I held out. I hit upon a

device to focus my mind. I started conjugating Latin verbs, declining Latin nouns, thinking in Latin, filling every corner of my mind with Latin. Didn't allow myself another thought."

"Oh, Dad!" said Karrie. "Miss Pringle would be so proud!"

"Is Miss Pringle still around? Bless her! You remember, Papa, when we were in high school, Martin and Ned Welles and I used Latin as a code? It drove the other boys crazy. Well, it drove the Gestapo crazy, too. They couldn't even determine my nationality. When I was questioned, I answered in Latin. They would keep me from sleeping, get me to the point of utter, total physical and mental exhaustion, and the only words that would escape my lips would be Latin. I must have recited the whole *Aeneid* to them a thousand times.

"I have no idea how long this went on. Then—luckily, as it turned out—they went too far. They nearly killed me, and I was sent to a hospital. *I* didn't even know who I was by then, but I was still mumbling in Latin when Jacques rescued me.

"How he found out where I was, I never knew. He must have had a pal on the hospital staff, because somehow he managed to have me smuggled out of there, and when I eventually became sensible again, I was in a farmhouse, being nursed by two old women I'd never seen before.

"When I learned it had been months since the police had first picked me up, I went into a panic. I remember grabbing Jacques by the collar and saying, 'My children! My children!' 'We'll get you home,' he promised. 'You kept faith with us—we will keep faith with you. But first, you must get well.'

"And then, I think I must have slept the next few weeks away. When I was finally well enough to walk a bit on my own, my friends started planning my escape."

"This was—when? Early in '41?" asked the mayor.

"It was summer by that time. I'd been pretty sick, Papa. Anyway, the idea was to get me south into the unoccupied zone. The government of France had moved to Vichy and there was an American embassy there.

"I was still weak, but my condition worked as a good cover.

277

I was given the identity papers of a man who'd recently died—a war veteran from Lyon who had joined the Resistance. If I were stopped and questioned, I was to say I was traveling home to see my mother.

"I did stop in Lyon. I had another mission there—one last thing I could do for the people who had saved my life. Jacques's group had become allied with a larger Resistance movement during the months when I was a prisoner, and they had established contacts and safe houses in several sections of France. Their most urgent problem was raising money and arms. They knew of a prominent business man in Lyon who might be willing to help with funding, but he'd balked when he was approached.

"It happened that I used to have business dealings with that man, so I offered to contact him. Well, it turned out he was eager to be part of the Resistance but he'd been afraid to trust anyone. He gave me a sizeable amount of cash, which I passed on to one of Jacques's agents in Lyon. I figured in this way I was atoning for my clumsiness in getting myself arrested and putting everybody's life in jeopardy."

"What about the embassy in Vichy?" asked the mayor.

"Oh, I got there all right, fully expecting to be sent home, though not without some regrets. I'd formed strong friendships with Jacques and the others, and if it hadn't been for my kids, I would have gladly stayed."

"But—you *did* stay!"

"Yes, it turned out I did. The way it was put to me I had very little choice. At the embassy they seemed to know who I was. They knew I'd disappeared into Europe over a year before and they were curious about me. And very interested in what I'd been doing.

"I told them how anxious I was about my children, told them about the letter I'd left in my desk and everything. They offered to make immediate inquiries. In a short time, they came back and told me that my children were safe in Texas and that I had been given up for dead."

"But—Wait! They were still in New York at that time! They

didn't show up here till the following summer!"

"Papa, I know that now. They told me what I wanted to hear, and what suited their purposes. They treated me with great kindness—brought me coffee and sandwiches, newspapers to read, American cigarettes. After a while two men in business suits came in and were introduced as Mr. Jones and Mr. Brown."

"American Intelligence?" guessed the mayor.

"Right. OSS, they were called later. They had plans for me. They wanted me to 'stay dead' and serve as kind of an unofficial liaison between them and my friends in the underground. They had money to contribute—they handed me a battered old suitcase full of it, and they promised weapons, eventually. Though America still wasn't at war with Germany, they were thinking ahead to the time when the Allies would invade Europe and it would be vital to coordinate the actions of the Resistance with the invasion."

"Then you were an American spy, Dad?" asked Karrie.

"More like a go-between. They put it to me as my patriotic duty, but I told them I would agree only if they understood that my first loyalty had to be to my friends in the Resistance. I had no intention of revealing their names or whereabouts to anyone, not even to my own countrymen. Jones and Brown—or whoever they were—said this was acceptable to them, and they assured me that my children in Texas would be told I was all right but had to remain incommunicado."

"Indeed!" said the mayor with a snort. "There was no word ever—no word from anyone."

Richard smiled. "Over the next four years, every time I made contact with them, they said they were keeping tabs on my kids. Around the time Marty turned eighteen, I asked if he was in the service, and they told me he was in the Army!"

"Outrageous!" fumed the mayor. "Why would they lie to you like that?"

"I guess it was the easiest way to keep me cooperating. I *needed* to believe them, especially that first day at the embassy. I was still weak and sick then, but I couldn't wait to get back to

Jacques with that suitcase of money and start working in earnest for the Resistance.

"But first, I stopped off in Lyon again and went to see the mother of the dead man whose identity papers I was carrying. I told her that her son had been a member of the Resistance, had died of his old war wounds, and that I was carrying his papers as a cover. I asked her not to betray me."

"You took a great risk," remarked the mayor.

"Yes. But I hated to think of her enduring—all that uncertainty."

"As *we* did," said the mayor gruffly.

"I know. About a month ago, while I was waiting for Herman to be released from the hospital, I made a short trip back to Lyon. Madame told me she had lived with her lonely secret all those years and it was not until the war ended that she revealed to the rest of her family and friends that her son had died."

"That must have been so hard for her," said Miss Prune, wiping a tear.

"They were—hard years, Aunt Prune."

6.

"Richard, you are thin as a wraith!" declared Miss Ginger.

"I know, Aunt Ginger, but I'm fine, really. Looking like a wraith was an advantage back there. They gave me a name in the underground—*Le Spectre*—the shadow. Because I looked sickly and harmless, I could slip in and out of towns that were crawling with Gestapo without attracting notice."

"What was it you did—blow up bridges and things like that?" asked Israel.

"Sometimes. Sometimes we smuggled downed Allied airmen safely across the channel—or Jews who'd escaped internment camps in France. There were a few who'd even made it out of Poland or Austria or Germany. I was especially grateful to be able to help *them*—always hoping that someone, somewhere, was helping Herman. But—that wasn't the case, of course.

"After D-Day, all I did was serve as a liaison between the

Allies and the Resistance. When France was finally liberated, the OSS asked me to go to Belgium and make contact with the Belgian underground. I was there during the Battle of the Bulge. It was a mess. The Germans had parachuted troops in American uniforms behind the lines and it was hard to tell who was what. It was a crazy, confusing time.

"But, then, finally it was all over. I made that call to Cory in New York—then started looking for Herman again."

It was early evening in the kitchen at Windy Crest, but no one had any thought of supper. Martha and Israel were sitting around the table with the others, and as Richard answered questions and related specific incidents, occasionally, if he was recounting some deed of violence, his hand would reach out to grasp Martha's, as if he was silently asking forgiveness of that gentle soul.

"If all of this is hard for you to accept, I can only say that I was operating from a different perspective then. I was living among desperate people, and I became a desperate man. All we wanted to do was stop them, *beat* them—"

"And we finally have," said the mayor quietly.

"Yes," said Richard. "Yes, finally, we have. But too late for too many." He glanced at Herman, an incongruous figure sitting passively in the evening light at a breakfast table in a little town in Texas. "He had four brothers—Meyer, Nathan, Julian, and Frederic; three sisters-in-law, twelve nieces and nephews, their husbands and wives, nineteen grand-nieces and -nephews. All dead."

"Oh, God," whispered Karrie. "All those people! The little girl I played with once—on that veranda—where you saw the soldiers—in that garden—her name was Frieda—"

"Yes. Meyer's granddaughter. She was just your age. Frieda was the last of the family to die—in Bergen-Belsen, a week before it was liberated. Her brother Paul never made it to a death camp. When the Nazis came for the family, they shot him because he tried to protect his mother—shot him right in front of her eyes."

A stunned silence fell over the group around the breakfast

table. Herman looked up, quizzically. Karrie buried her face in her hands and began to cry, softly. Herman had not understood the conversation, but he understood grief very well. The tears welled up in his own eyes as he patted his granddaughter's shuddering shoulders with his thin, uncertain hand.

Karrie stared bleakly at her father through her streaming eyes. "It would have been Mom, too, if she hadn't married you and left Germany. But—but—she died anyway!"

Richard reached over and stroked his daughter's dark hair. "Not—like that! Karrie, Karrie. She was so happy in America— and she had you and Marty. You are her posterity, and Opi's. The only family left. He needs all our strength."

Karrie stifled her sobs and scrubbed at her eyes with the back of her arm. The mayor wordlessly passed a handkerchief to her across the table, and she took it gratefully and blew her nose. Then she smiled at Opi and took his hand in hers.

Richard continued to caress her hair. "A good many of my friends in the underground were killed, too," he told her, "but those who survived are like brothers and sisters to me. Someday, maybe in the not too distant future, I want to take you and Marty back there, to meet them."

"That's a journey I would also like to make," said the mayor gruffly.

Richard grinned at his father, and for a fleeting instant, Karrie saw Marty's teasing expression on his tired face.

"Papa," he said, "you're invited."

Chapter 15
Victory

"**If** you're getting your mail," Karrie wrote to Marty, "you will have had Dad's letter by the time you get this. I can just imagine the look on your face when you saw his handwriting on the envelope. I'll bet your whoops were heard all over the Pacific!

"It's like a miracle to have him back, and to see Opi here! Dad is much older-looking, and awfully thin, but seems well. Opi grows a little better every day, and no wonder, with Martha plying him with food and the aunts clucking over him like a pair of mother hens!

"The town is beside itself with excitement—the party line never stops humming! They've rolled out the red carpet for Dad and Opi. It's amazing! Dad is everybody's hero. His twenty-three years of being *persona non grata* and those Nazi spy rumors never happened! As for Opi—well, Shirleen Haus said it best: 'Maybe Hospitality had four English refugee kids, but they sure never had anybody from a concentration camp!' What can I tell you? Bienvenidos is *proud*!

"Dad's old company in New York says he has his job back whenever he's ready, but he feels that, for now, it's best for Opi to be here where everybody's taking such good care of him. I think another reason Dad's not in any hurry to leave is because (are you ready for this?!) he's stepping out with Miss Jane!

They are so sweet together! Like a couple of kids, which is what they were when they saw each other last. I don't get much time at my little cave any more—they've taken it over! Oh, well, I guess it was their place first! It will be interesting to see what develops—I'll keep you posted.

"Opi is able to take short walks around the property. I remember how ugly I thought the land was when I first saw it, but Opi told Grandfather he finds it beautiful. Grandfather understands German, you know, as it was spoken a lot in town when he was growing up, and he's trying to help Opi learn English. We all are. It's pretty slow work!

"How strange it is to see them together—those two old men from such different worlds, on opposite sides in the first World War, their sons killed on the same battlefield. I look at Grandfather and wonder what's in his mind—the regrets he must have that he never knew our wonderful mother and never heard her beautiful voice. He is so kind to Opi. He treats him like a brother. Maybe it's his way of trying to atone to Mom.

"When we were all sitting around the parlor after supper last evening, Dad asked me to sing something for Opi. I was caught off guard, and for a minute I couldn't think of anything but "The Old Rugged Cross" or "The Boogie-Woogie Bugle Boy"—neither of which would have been real appropriate! Then Dad asked if I could remember any of the Schubert *lieder* Mom used to sing.

"So—rather bravely, I must say—I tried to sing something Dad later told me is called *Ständchen*. I not only didn't know the title of what I was singing, I hadn't any idea what the words meant! I learned it by singing along with Mom.

"It was amazing how it all came back to me. I had to sing a capella, of course, and probably made lots of mistakes, but Opi and Dad both had tears in their eyes, and Grandfather cleared his throat the way he does—hrumph!—and told the aunts rather crossly it was high time there was a piano in that parlor. As if it were all their fault there wasn't one!

"Marty, is it possible for you to send a cable or something?

We are so desperate to hear from you..."

Karrie got on her bike and took the letter downtown herself. She was warmly hailed at the Post Office by Mr. Miller, Mr. Appleby and Woody Beal. Ever since her father's return she had found herself—for the first time—to be completely accepted as a citizen of Benbenitas.

After she'd responded to the usual inquiries about Richard and Herman, the men resumed the discussion they'd been having about the war in the Pacific. Mr. Miller was of the opinion that it was a only matter of days before troops would be storming the Japanese mainland, and Mr. Appleby said he'd heard the Allies might suffer a million casualties in the invasion. Woody Beal shook his head and declared that it would take another year to mop the whole thing up.

Karrie listened for a moment, then mumbled her goodbyes and hurried out of the Post Office.

2.

The train from Austin left off two mail bags and a stack of newspapers, then rattled off down the tracks. Mr. Peevy helped himself to a paper, stared at it for a second or two, then exclaimed:

"Why, lookee here, Ole Ben. By Jupiter, that's a big headline!"

Ole Ben Clinton took the newspaper, held it at arm's length and squinted at it through his shrewd little eyes.

"Now what in Sam Hill is an 'Atom Bomb'?" he mused.

The two old relics of a waning era stood on that sun-baked platform on an afternoon in early August and pondered the news of the day, unaware that they were witnesses to the dawning of a new age.

They had no inkling of the future being launched on that day; wouldn't have believed any of it in a million years—the Cold War, jet planes, men walking on the moon; shopping malls, supermarkets, superhighways; television, computers, rock 'n' roll!

Well, if truth be told, Mr. Peevy and Ole Ben Clinton seldom thought much about the future at all, beyond whether or not it was going to rain tomorrow. But they had a pretty good idea of what that newspaper headline was saying about the present.

World War II was over.

3.

Many years later the people of Benbenitas were still bragging that it was the best parade the town ever had.

And it was led off by the best derned cheerleader the town had ever had—none other than Jolene Ross, University of Texas sophomore and premed student, who tossed her golden hair, flashed her Pepsodent smile, and pranced like a colt in her tasseled boots. She was followed by a large battalion of baton-twirlers—notable among them, Baby Dodds, Bev, and the Wallace twins—and oh, how they twirled! How they hurled those batons high into the air and caught them every time! Or almost.

Next came the half-dozen boys and girls of the high school band, looking magnificent in their hand-me-down uniforms, with the August sun dancing on their ancient instruments. And for once, they all played in tune, or so everyone was willing to believe. In any case, they played with an exuberance they'd never exhibited at football games, and went through their entire repertoire two or three times—"Welcome to Bienvenidos," "It's a Grand Old Flag," "Texas, Our Texas," "Yankee Doodle," and "Don't Sit Under the Apple Tree."

Then there were the Benbenitas boys who had already come home from the war—Howie Schulman, Henry Swenson, and a few others—one fellow limping, one being pushed in a wheelchair, all of them proudly wearing the uniforms they would soon be packing away. And behind them, smelling of mothballs and straining the buttonholes on their khaki jackets, marched the Doughboys, survivors of the original War To End All Wars.

Right on their heels came the starched and coiffured troops of the Ladies Auxiliary. Sheriff Clyde (Hoss) Bateson was right behind them in the police car, waving benevolently but a little miffed that he'd been asked not to drown out the band with his beloved siren. He was followed by the fire engine with all the volunteer firemen on board; the seat of honor next to Bill Pruitt, the fire chief, going to Grannie Opal, born when Texas was a Republic. She was accompanied, of course, by a smiling Maybelle with a brand new permanent wave.

Ole Ben Clinton's taxi was next, with Miss Ginger, Miss Prune and Martha in the passenger seat, and then the '38 Packard, polished to a sheen and driven by Israel. Beside him sat the mayor, unbending occasionally to wave a hand at his joyful constituents. Richard, in the back seat with Herman, also waved, in response to the shouts and the kisses that were blown his way.

It was Karrie who brought up the rear, on Jimmy's bike, with fresh feathers of red and blue fluttering from the straw basket on the handlebars.

The parade circled the square twice before disbanding at the steps of Town Hall, where card tables laden with refreshments awaited the celebrants. The ladies of the town, gloriously spendthrift with the last of their rationed sugar, had prepared lemonade, iced tea, pies, cakes and cookies.

The mayor was obliged to make a speech, which, according to his custom, was blessedly short—this time even shorter than usual. All he said was, "Thank God it's over!" He may have meant the parade, but he most certainly meant the war, too, and a great deal of cheering, shouting and flag-waving ensued. Then the sheriff felt that he, too, should make a speech, although no one could recall suggesting it. As he showed signs of becoming long-winded, he was good-naturedly cut short with shouts of "Sit down, Hoss!" "Stuff that man's mouth with pie, Mabel!"

Some who remember that day say the celebration continued far into the evening, and that Woody Beal came up with a bunch of old firecrackers left over from before the war. They wouldn't go off, but that seemed appropriate, on the whole, and added to the crowd's hilarity.

But by that time the mayor and his family had long since left the scene. With a cloud of uncertainty still hanging over them, they found it hard to enter wholeheartedly into the spirit of the occasion, and decided to wave their goodbyes early.

It was Karrie who slipped away first. Right after the mayor's speech, she headed back up the highway on Jimmy's bike and arrived home well before the others. It was she who found the telegram in the mailbox, and stood staring at it in dread before finally tearing it open with trembling hands.

And when the mayor's car and Ole Ben Clinton's taxi approached Windy Crest, it was Karrie who waited at the end of the driveway, waving that yellow piece of paper and trumpeting in a voice that was surely heard throughout the valley:

"It's from Marty! He's coming home!"

Afterwards:

At the end of their novels, my favorite authors of the previous century often obliged the reader with a glimpse into their characters' later lives. Even authors, of course, don't know *everything* about their characters, but, for anyone who has stayed with me up to now, I'll make a few guesses about what became of some of the people you've met in Benbenitas.

We won't talk too much about Karrie and January, just in case they decide to show up on other pages someday, but this much we can surely say about them: They will remain best friends and kindred spirits for the rest of their lives.

Richard Webster married Miss Jane Llewellyn (was there ever any doubt?) and lived happily ever after. They made their home in New York City, traveled all over the world and visited more museums than Miss Jane ever dreamed existed.

And did Howie Schulman marry Norma Swenson? Heavens no! It was only a fling. In fact, I'll bet Howie surprised Karrie one day by looking her up in New York.

That brings us to Jolene's romance-by-mail with Marty. We know they were both dedicated to becoming doctors, but do you suppose they ever got married? (I told you authors don't know everything!)

Most of the young people we met in Benbenitas moved on and prospered after the war. Baby Dodds and Bev went to business school in Austin and landed good jobs. Baby Dodds fell in love with a returning GI, married him, supported him while he went to law school, then let him support her while she raised five red-headed children. Bev married her boss and became a mover and shaker in the Junior League.

Bubbabill forged a pretty good career for himself as an engineer, moved around a lot, and married a Denver girl. Sister Bee and Joycie married brothers and settled in Corpus Christi. Bettie Rae's husband went to work for an oil company, and she and her children got used to packing up and following him to far-flung places. Shirleen Haus eventually bought Mr. Webber's drugstore, and people from all over the hill country still regularly go out of their way to stop in for "Shirleen's Old Fashion Ice Cream Sodas," because the truth is, nobody anywhere ever made them better.

Mr. Eagleton didn't stay in Benbenitas for too long after the war ended. He got a bit impatient, asked a little too much of his congregation (who figured they were pretty dadgummed good the way they were), and got fired again. He became pastor of a church in his native East Texas, got fired from there in about two weeks, and decided it was time to retire. But in the 1960's, old and ailing, he joined the sit-ins and Freedom Riders in the South, and a photo of him being arrested along with Martin Luther King, Jr. was featured on the front page of the *Bienvenidos Bugle*. "Used to be our preacher," the Methodists boasted, quite forgetting they had fired him twice. "Regular firebrand!"

Grannie Opal, who was older than anybody else in 1945, was older yet in 1955. When she finally died peacefully in her sleep with that slight smile still on her face, she made the national news and the Governor of Texas came to her funeral. Afterwards, Maybelle moved into town, where she could walk to Sunday school and the beauty parlor.

Herman, Karrie's Opi, stayed on in Benbenitas. When the burned-out section of the downtown square was finally rebuilt, he opened a small tailor shop there, right next to Wirtz's Barber Shop & Opera House.

Mr. Wirtz rented him a room in his own apartment above the barber shop, thus assuring himself of a checker game almost every evening. But Herman spent weekends at Windy Crest, enjoying the pampering of Miss Ginger and Miss Prune, who at last had a "brother" who would allow them to fuss over him. He liked to take long walks with the mayor, putter around the garden with Israel, and help Martha with the canning.

He had a good ear and picked up English quickly, but as his chief linguistic influences were the mayor and Mr. Wirtz, he spoke it in a one-of-a-kind dialect. "Dis nincompoop feller does not pay no dadburned bill," he sometimes complained about Sheriff Hoss Bateson. "Vat y'all advise I should do?"

Every June, to escape the Texas heat, Herman accompanied Martha, Israel, the mayor and his sisters, to Richard and Miss Jane's summer place on Cape Cod in Massachusetts. Miss Ginger and Miss Prune never tired of gazing at Grannie Prudence's sea, or of visiting their ancestral home, now an elegant bed-and-breakfast in a neighboring village. But at summer's end, they were all glad enough to return to the hill country, the land that Herman loved as deeply as any of them, because it reminded him of no other land.

A few years after the war ended, the old depot where we began this story was abandoned, having been made obsolete by new super highways and the soaring popularity of the automobile, and the railroad tracks became overgrown with weeds. Did Mr. Peevy grieve? No, by Jupiter, he pretty much enjoyed sitting in a rocking chair on his front porch, jaw-boning with Ole Ben Clinton over a tall glass of lemonade. Did those two old codgers philosophize much about the good old days? We-ell, mainly they kind of fell to discussing things like Ben Appleby's son keeping company with that divorced woman over in Bastrop and how Shirleen Haus didn't have the legs for them short skirts she was wearing.

Benbenitas doesn't appear all that different, even today, if you stick to the middle of it. In fact, its old-timey downtown was used for location shots for a movie recently. You can imagine the excitement, with local people getting hired as extras and all. Of course, it was a nuisance, too, having to park all those cars where they couldn't be seen from the square, but Gladhand could have been picked (if it wasn't for that new bank building), so nobody was complaining.

Appearances aside, there've been plenty of changes here. For one, people have had private telephones for so many years now, they no longer recall how listening in on the party line used to liven up a dull morning. For another, the "colored" school has disappeared, and nobody seems to remember that it ever existed. When Rollie Johnson's grandson bought Mr. Miller's Feed Store there was a little to-do, but that soon blew over, was totally forgotten, and business went on, same as before. Anybody can go to the Bijou any night of the week now and nobody has to sit in the balcony, unless, of course, they've a mind to do some necking.

So has Martha's dream of everyone living here like good neighbors come true? Not yet, but perhaps that day will come. One thing's for sure: When it does, folks are bound to swear that nothing's changed at all. They'll claim that Benbenitas was *always* a tolerant, live-and-let-live sort of town, and anybody who tells you different is just making up stories.

ADDITIONAL ACKNOWLEDGEMENTS

Lines from these poems are quoted on the following pages:

74:        "On His Blindness" by John Milton
78-79:   "A Psalm of Life" by Henry Wadsworth Longfellow
80:        "Rules For the Road" by Edwin Markham
191:      "Drifting" by Thomas Buchanan Read
232:      "Requiem" by Robert Louis Stevenson
232:      "Long, Long Ago" by Thomas Haynes Bayly
257:      "The Brook" by Alfred, Lord Tennyson
257:      "A Sea Song" by Allan Cunningham

The reminescences of Israel, Miss Prune, and Miss Ginger about their childhood Christmases in the Hill Country were adapted from the writings of the author's late grandmother, Juliet Johnson Christian.

Many thanks are owed to those kind friends who read this book as a work-in-progress and offered suggestions and encouragement; special thanks to Liz Abrams-Morley, to Ginnie Newlin and her Monday Morning writers, and to the book's first Young Adult reader, Erica Abrams-Morley.